Praise for No Greater Love

No Greater Love captured my attention from the first page! Gina Holder has crafted a novel of love and intrigue that will leave the reader wanting more.

- **Patricia Bradley**, author of Justice Delivered

No Greater Love is a wonderful dive into tense family history that doesn't want to be unearthed. With a refreshingly imperfect heroine and a close-knit town hiding its secrets, Holder pits her characters against their worst fears and unseen dangers for a climactic redemption story. Readers needing a glimpse of our Savior's love, the hope He offers sinful people, will find it in the pages of this novel.

- **Joanna Davidson Politano**, author of Lady Jayne Disappears

No Greater Love will take you on a joyride you won't soon forget with its relatable characters, vivid storytelling, and pulse-pounding suspense.

- **Tabitha Bouldin**, author of Trial By Courage

I got hooked on Paige and Hamilton's story in the first five pages and as I read the last page less than 24 hours later, my heart wildly thumping, I didn't want it to stop! Gina has beautifully crafted a romantically suspenseful story that kept my imagination churning with clues and tying together loose threads. There's never a dull moment with plenty of intriguing twists and turns, and the bad guys get exactly what they deserve! The characters are complex yet down-to-earth. You feel their pain, want to heal their wounds, and seek answers to their impossible-to-answer questions. "No Greater Love" drives home the undisputable reality that heroes are fragile, human, and fears of tragic "what ifs" always hover over them and their loved ones.

- **Janell Butler Wojtowicz**, author of Embracing Hope

No Greater Love

Books by Gina Holder

Historical Romance

Whither Shall I Go? (Standalone)

Contemporary Romantic Suspense

Shadows Over Whitman

No Greater Love
Forgiven Again

Shadows Over Whitman · 1

No Greater Love

GINA HOLDER

No Greater Love
Shadows Over Whitman · 1
Contemporary Romantic Suspense

ISBN-13: 978-1-79-795958-0
Also available as an eBook

Scripture quotations are from the King James Version of the Bible.

Cover design by Daniel Holder

In memory of William J. Donnelly IV
First Lieutenant, United States Marine Corps:

Killed in action November 25th, 2010 at the Battle of Thanksgiving, Sangin, Afghanistan.
He died a hero.

To all our first responders and military (including their families):

Thank you for your sacrifices.

Greater love hath no man than this,
that a man lay down his life for his friends.

John 15:13

For scarcely for a righteous man will one die:
yet peradventure for a good man
some would even dare to die.
But God commendeth his love toward us,
in that while we were yet sinners, Christ died for us.

Romans 5:7-8

1

T*here isn't another smell like this in the entire world.* The musty scent of vintage paper enveloped her like the familiarity of a security blanket, drawing her into her happy place. The smell of various perfumes and lavender vacuum powder lingered in the air. Several dimly lit, antique lamps sat atop the stand-alone marble-topped bookcases in the middle of the room. A terracotta rug and leather chairs gave the room the appearance of a cozy den. Paige McDonald closed her eyes and jostled her hand along the fraying spines where their roughness tickled the pads of her fingertips. She imagined the lives they'd lived, the places they'd been, and the stories they could tell beyond the ones written on their thinning, yellowed pages.

A shrill noise echoed in the distance, breaking into Paige's daydreams. She lowered her hand and sighed, moving to open the interior door of the Rare Book Room. She stepped through the doorway into the Pearl Room on the third floor of the largest bookstore in the world. Florescent lights momentarily blinded her. She clicked the door shut behind her, protecting the rare literary volumes against the ultraviolet rays.

"Paige! Paige McDonald!"

Customers lifted their heads as the intrusive sound interrupted their browsing. The source of the offensive voice topped the stairs leading from the color-coded Red and Purple Rooms below. "I've been searching everywhere for you."

"Yes, Mrs. Bastille. What can I do for you?" Paige clasped her hands behind her back and waited for instructions as the swanky assistant manager stalked her direction. Cat Bastille's red hair complemented her fiery personality. She wore an outdated navy pantsuit and a gold scarf around her neck. Paige detested the woman, but she was all that stood between herself and the unemployment office.

The manager invaded Paige's personal bubble and blew coffee breath in her face. Paige scrunched her nose against the odor. "The toilet is overflowing. Get in there and put a stop to it. Then, clean out the fridge in back. Some of the employees' lunches are growing mold." Cat tossed her hair over her shoulder with a show of dramatics. The woman should have been an actress…or a troll.

"Of course, Mrs. Bastille. I'll take care of it." Paige kept her voice sweet and submissive, when all she really wanted to do was grab the woman by her oversized hooped earrings and shake her. Cat repeatedly assigned her to the lowest and most demeaning tasks in the store. However, working at Powell's City of Books in downtown Portland was the closest thing to her dream, and if it required groveling at the feet of Cat Bastille, then so be it. Without another word, she ducked under her boss's outstretched arm, heading for the janitor's closet on the second floor.

As her lunch break ended, Paige finished her turkey sandwich, then dropped the trash into the can. She swallowed one last swig from her water bottle, tossed it into the recycling, then returned her lunch bag to her locker.

"I have another job for you."

She spun around at the sound of her manager's voice, slamming the locker door a little louder than she intended. Okay, a lot louder. She flinched as Cat's eyes narrowed. In the manager's pinched fingers, she held aloft a small key. Paige could only imagine what lock it might open. "What's that?" She mentally face-palmed herself for asking such a dumb question.

"A key."

Ask a stupid question, you deserve a stupid answer. "What does it go to?" *That's what I should have said the first time.*

The red-haired woman heaved an audible sigh. "A container from the warehouse." Her whiny voice grated on Paige's eardrums. "Management wants to have a sidewalk sale tomorrow and Sunday. Go unload the books and arrange them on carts. Get one or two of the other employees to help." Cat shoved the key toward Paige's chest.

Paige wrapped her fingers around the metal as she attempted to compute her manager's request. "That only gives me a few hours before my shift ends." She already had plans for the evening with her aunt. *So what if it consists eating dinner and watching TV?*

"I guess you'd better hurry."

Paige gathered her thoughts. She'd simply have to channel her uber-organizing skills and accomplish the task before leaving. "Where's the container?"

"In the storeroom. Duh." Cat Bastille drew out the one-syllable word like an adolescent teenager.

Paige squared her shoulders and lifted her chin. She could handle anything her superior could throw at her. "Yes, ma'am." She headed out the doorway. *Besides, there might be some books for my collection. Gotta love that employee discount.*

Cat spoke again from behind her. "I need you to work Sunday, and you can't use your employee discount on any of the books until after the sale ends." *Can that woman read my mind?* A shiver swept over Paige. That was a scary thought.

With the help of two other employees, Paige managed to unload the books and set them upon carts to be rolled out come the morning. With a satisfied grin, she stepped back and admired her work. They'd sorted each cart by genre and alphabetically by author. She had already spied a handful of books that she hoped would last until the end of the sale. Few people researched antiquarian literature quite like her and fewer would be searching for these particular volumes. She slipped one from the metal shelf and caressed the embossed title. An excited tingle ran up her arms. *I need to check eBay again tonight.* She was bidding on a couple of items and the current bid for one in particular was far less than its worth. If she could get her hands on it, she hoped to sell it to a rare book dealer for a tidy profit.

"Call 911! Call 911!"

Years of training kicked in. Paige dropped the book in her hands like a hot coal and bolted into the Green Room. A small child jerked on the floor, coughing and sputtering, while an overwrought gentleman knelt beside her.

Paige dropped to her knees and grabbed his arm. "What happened?"

He raked his hands through his hair, then clenched his fists. His words came out shaky and broken. "I don't know. Please, help my daughter."

The child stopped coughing. Her lips tinted blue. *Not good.* "I have first aid training. With your permission, I'll do CPR." The anxious father nodded. Paige tucked strands of her hair behind her ears. Ignoring the gathering crowd, she bent over the small child and opened the little girl's mouth, checking her airways. Something white was visible at the back of her throat. Paige eased her hand in and felt a stick. She tugged. A lollipop came loose. She sat back on her haunches and handed the candy to the father. His face blanched. "I—I thought…"

She's still not breathing. Paige focused on blowing into the girl's lips. After what seemed like an eternity, the child gasped for air and began coughing again. Paige rolled her onto her side, then stroked her hair and patted her back, whispering soothing words. "It's OK. That's good. Just breathe."

Moments later, the crowd parted as the EMTs came through the front door with their equipment. Paige stepped back while the father explained what had happened. She wasn't needed here any longer, so she slipped away. Just before she reached the stairs, a cold hand grabbed her wrist. Cat Bastille's face was ghostly pale. "How did you know what to do?"

"My grandpa required me to take the first aid class for babysitters at the Red Cross when I was twelve. I've renewed my certification ever since."

Without waiting for a reply, she climbed the stairs to the third floor and entered the employee lounge. She crossed to the lockers and leaned her head on the cool metal, shaking as the adrenaline wore off. A warm feeling spiraled like waves over her heart. "You would be so proud, Grandpa. I saved someone today." She wiped at the tears on her cheeks, sniffled, and unlocked her locker. She checked the time on her cell phone. It was already a quarter after five. Her aunt would worry when she wasn't home at the usual time. *I'll call her on my way to the bus stop.* Aunt Hattie, her grandfather's sister, had been her caregiver ever since his passing. At twenty-five years of age, Paige hardly needed watching over, but she couldn't bring herself to get her own place.

Once downstairs, she pushed through the revolving door. Portland's Pearl District bustled with boutiques, restaurants, and art galleries. People rushed here and there, never taking their eyes off their cell phones.

"Hi, cutie." A paramedic stood outside, waiting for the others. She tried to ignore him. She swung her backpack over her shoulder and moved down the sidewalk toward the crosswalk. He followed at her heels. "You're the one that saved that little girl."

She pretended that a plastic bag rolling down the street distracted her. *Almost to the crosswalk. Just a few more steps. Please don't ask me out.*

"I'm Alex Fletcher. Do you want to catch a movie sometime? Maybe go out to dinner?"

Paige stopped walking and shifted her backpack strap to the other shoulder. She turned to face the medic, shielding her eyes from the setting sun behind him. "I don't date first responders."

"Really? You don't know what you're missing." Paige walked backward, shaking her head. "Come on, what's not to like about us hero types?" The paramedic puffed out his chest.

What's not to like? "The hero part."

His mouth fell open as she turned to face the crosswalk. The little man appeared in the walk/don't walk box and she crossed the street without looking back.

"Hey Alex. Let's roll." The EMTs called to their partner. The ambulance engine rumbled and they drove off without a siren. *Good. The child didn't need the hospital.*

When she reached the bus stop, Paige sat between an elderly woman carrying grocery bags and a Mario look-alike from the Nintendo game, complete with red jumpsuit and thick mustache.

Holding back tears of frustration, she leaned forward and pressed her face into her hands. *Thirteen years.* Thirteen years had passed since she'd vowed never to get involved with a civil servant—*a hero.* She had no argument against helping people—a little kindness went a long way in this messed up world, but she didn't understand someone who was willing to risk or to give their life for someone they didn't even know. She'd lost her grandfather to hero work. She wasn't about to risk her heart to someone who would put the welfare of strangers before those they loved and who loved them.

Right on schedule, the city bus came to a squealing stop and the folding door opened. Paige brushed her hair into place, then picked up her backpack, slung it over her shoulder, and followed the other passengers onto the bus.

Through the windshield of his BMW, he watched Brooklyn McDonald board the city bus. She was late today—something must have held her up. She'd had a quick, strained conversation with the paramedic out front of the bookstore, then went to wait at her usual bus stop. He took a drink from the paper coffee cup in his hand. It had grown cold while he waited. He gagged, and then dumped the liquid on the ground outside the open window. The bus rolled away from the shelter. He tossed the empty cup into the back seat, then put the car in gear. He flipped on the left blinker and pulled into traffic.

At her stop in the Hawthorne District of Southeast Portland, Paige unlocked her bicycle from the bike rack. When the traffic cleared, she walked her bike across the busy road and then pedaled home to the Foursquare on Southeast Madison Street. After locking her bike in the garage, she jogged up the steps and opened the back door.

Grandpa McDonald had bought the house before Paige was born and long before the local housing market had exploded. The paint was chipping, and the gardens were in need of tending. A few shingles were missing from the roof, and one of the windows had a growing crack, but it was home. Paige closed the door and locked it—the only way it stayed closed. "I'm home, Aunt Hattie."

At the sound of her voice, Aunt Hattie's animals clamored to greet her: two Dalmatians, a long-haired Persian cat, and a forty-year-old African Grey parrot who was sitting on the back of the couch. "Paige home," he squawked. "Paige home." Paige's lips tilted with a smile. He sounded just like her boss. She squatted and was nearly knocked off her feet by the overwhelming love. They licked her face and stroked their heads against her jeans and turtleneck.

She pushed the pets away and stood to her feet as Aunt Hattie appeared from the kitchen. Her aunt wore a flour-covered apron over her ample bodice and skirt. Her white curls bobbed up and down as she jiggled her way across the linoleum flooring. "Paigey. You made it. I was worried."

Aunt Hattie buried her in a warm embrace. Her chapped lips planted kisses on Paige's cheek. "Yes, Aunt Hattie. I made it. Sorry I'm late." Her aunt greeted everyone as if she hadn't seen them in years, even if it had only been since breakfast.

Paige walked to the closet, tripping over the excited animals. She set her backpack inside and hung her house keys on the hook nearby. "What's for dinner?"

Aunt Hattie beamed. "I'm trying one of Ina Garten's recipes." Paige held back a chortle. Her aunt said the name like *in a garden*. "Chicken pot pie. She fixed it on her TV show this morning."

She followed Aunt Hattie into the kitchen where white flour coated every surface. "What happened in here? There's more flour on the counters than in a pie crust."

Aunt Hattie threw her hands in the air. "Don't I know it? Ina says, 'how easy is that?' But it's not that easy."

Paige kissed her aunt on her flour-streaked forehead. "Let me change into some sweats and I'll help you clean up in here."

She patted the dogs' heads as she passed, then climbed the steep staircase to her bedroom. Inside the room, every wall was lined with bookcases, and every bookcase was stacked with books. Every stack was organized according to genre, author, and publication date. A pair of gray sweats waited in a laundry basket on her bed. Aunt Hattie washed, dried, and folded the laundry, but Paige insisted that she put it away herself. She changed her clothes and returned to the kitchen. After they cleaned, Paige and her aunt sat down to dinner at the wobbly dining table. Aunt Hattie had covered the water stains and scratches with a lace tablecloth. A fresh bouquet of spring flowers from the flower beds filled the vase in the center. Paige tucked her napkin on her lap and scooted her chair close. "Smells good, Aunt Hattie." She stuck her fork into the individual ramekin. *Only Aunt Hattie could make the crust raw and burnt at the same time.* It soon became clear that the crust wasn't the only thing wrong with Aunt Hattie's chicken pot pie. The chicken was overcooked, the vegetables were still rock hard, and the gravy was much too salty.

Aunt Hattie stuck out her tongue. "Oh, this is terrible."

"I'm glad you think so, too." Paige took a long drink of water to wash the foul taste from her mouth.

They dumped the pot pie into the garbage and ordered pizza from Rovente Pizzeria and ate it in the living room while watching an episode of *Downton Abbey*. Paige tucked her legs under her on the sofa and took a swig of root beer. Aunt Hattie wiped Ranch dressing from her lips where she sat on a floral chair catty-corner to the couch. "How was work today, Paigey? You haven't said much about it."

Paige set her glass bottle on a crocheted coaster on the coffee table. "It was all right, I guess."

"What's wrong?"

"It's my boss, Cat Bastille. She treats me like a servant."

Aunt Hattie took a drink of a vanilla creme pop poured into a glass. "What is your job title again, dear?"

Paige cringed. "Inventory Specialist One."

"I thought you were the janitor." Aunt Hattie's eyes twinkled.

Paige shifted on the couch as the long-haired cat, Delilah, jumped into her lap and began to purr. Aunt Hattie tossed the pizza crusts to the dogs. "Some days I feel like the janitor, but I want to do so much more than clean toilets, change light bulbs, and sort books. How will I ever learn how to run my own bookstore? That's why I wanted the job. I was hoping to learn how to be a successful entrepreneur, not just a glorified housekeeper. I don't know…" She hugged her knees as the credits began rolling on the flat screen. It was her dream to open a hole-in-the-wall bookstore in small-town America—a book nook where every patron was well-known and well-loved. It would be the heartbeat of the community, where people met daily to socialize and enjoy fresh brewed coffee and homemade treats. "I saved a little girl today. She was choking on a lollipop."

"Good girl. Your grandfather would be so proud of you." Aunt Hattie leaned forward and picked up the remote from off the coffee table. "Do you want to watch something else? It's still early."

"Sure. What's on next?"

Aunt Hattie waved the remote in Paige's direction. "I don't know. You'll have to check. I don't have any idea how to find that listy thing."

Paige pushed the cat off her lap and moved to take the remote from her aunt's outstretched hand. She grabbed it, then flopped back on the center couch cushion. "It's called the guide, Aunt Hattie. And there's a red button that's marked 'Guide.' You just press it."

Aunt Hattie waved her arms. "Of course there is." Aunt Hattie's theatrics brought a smile to Paige's face.

"What do you want to watch?"

"Pick something from my generation. These new-fangled shows are too much for this old heart."

The colored stripe flashed down the screen. "*Little House on the Prairie* is playing at eight thirty." Her eyes scrolled the listings. "Wait. This movie looks interesting."

"What's it about?" Aunt Hattie raised her glass to her lips.

"It's on the Hallmark Channel. A man and his wife adopt an orphan girl. Twenty years later, she goes in search of her birth mother—Aunt Hattie, are you OK?" She jumped from her seat and removed the sloshing glass from her aunt's shaking hand. Aunt Hattie bent over and coughed. Paige slapped her back until the piece of ice dislodged from her aunt's throat and she spit it into her hand. "Thank you, Paigey. I should be more careful. Piece of ice slid right into my mouth."

Paige eased back onto the edge of the wooden coffee table, her eyebrows drawn and filled with concern for the old woman. Aunt Hattie's face was flushed while she continued coughing and clearing her throat. "Can I get you some water?"

"Yes, please."

When Paige returned with the glass, Aunt Hattie took it with a grateful smile. "Thank you." She sipped on the cold water. "Oh, that feels good. Did you say *Little House on the Prairie* was on?"

"At eight thirty."

Aunt Hattie set the glass of water on the table. But not on a coaster. *Something is wrong. She always uses a coaster.* "How about we walk down to that ice cream place on Hawthorne, Ken and Harry's or whatever it's called?"

Paige chuckled. "Ben and Jerry's, Aunt Hattie. Sure, I could use some fresh air too."

After donning their jackets, the two women stepped out into the nippy spring air and walked down the well-lit street. The signal light turned red and the little man signaled that it was safe to cross. At Ben and Jerry's, Paige and Aunt Hattie shared a Mini-Vermonster and then returned to the house and curled up on the couch for a rerun episode of *Little House on the Prairie.*

At 9:30, when the credits rolled, Aunt Hattie said goodnight and climbed the stairs to her room followed by her pets, including the parrot, who put himself to bed in his cage in the hallway. "Goodnight Paige. Goodnight Hattie," he squawked.

"Goodnight, Gerald," Paige called up the stairs. The parrot would not go to sleep until she said goodnight. She dug another pop from the fridge and turned on an episode of *American Pickers*. She tossed a blanket over her legs and snuggled into the couch.

2

On Sunday morning, Paige drove to work in Aunt Hattie's fifteen-year-old beige station wagon, so she'd be able to transport her purchases home from the sidewalk sale. In between her other duties, she paused often to browse the remaining selections.

At the end of the workday, Paige and the others broke down the display. The sale had gone well, of course, but there were still two full metal racks of books available for purchase. With her employee discount, Paige filled a cardboard box with books and then headed home. She parked in the driveway, and carried the box inside, dodging the dogs as she went. The screen door slammed behind her. Aunt Hattie's voice carried from the kitchen, "Is that you, Paigey?"

She cocked a mischievous grin. "No, it's a burglar. Of course, it's me. I'm going to take some stuff upstairs."

"Okay, dear. Dinner will be ready soon."

Paige carried the box up the stairs and froze. Her bedroom was filled to capacity—every square inch. She barely squeezed in a bed, dresser, and walking space. She turned her neck to take in the second story and spotted the attic doorway. She would have to store her new books there for the time being. She turned on the light, then carried the box up the creaky staircase, leaving the door open behind her. She set the box on top of a piece of cloth-draped furniture. A cloud of dust puffed into her face, causing her to cough and swing her hand as if swatting flies.

As she twisted around, her eyes wandered over the attic space jam-packed with boxes of photo albums and baby clothes; pieces of furniture covered with white drop cloths; hat boxes; grandpa's trunk; and plastic totes filled with keepsakes, school report cards, and Christmas decorations. She opened one of the dusty boxes, uncovering stuff she hadn't seen in years. She lifted out her old Cabbage Patch doll and held it to her chest, rocking back and forth while stroking the doll's yellow yarn hair. She'd spent many hours playing with her—a present from her grandfather for her fifth birthday. She put the doll aside and rummaged deeper into the box, removing two brightly-colored My Little Ponies, a Dalmatian Pound Puppy, and a dried-out container of Play-Doh. She dropped the toys back in the box, then turned and knelt in front of her grandpa's trunk. She wiped the dust away with the end of her shirt and ran her fingers over the etched letters on the gold plate: B. McDonald. She grunted as she raised the heavy lid. Inside, neatly folded, lay Grandpa's Class A dress uniform. A knot formed in her throat. A familiar feeling squeezed her heart as her thoughts drifted back to her childhood.

In the early morning hours, long before dawn, he'd slip into her bedroom before his shift and kiss her on the forehead, and then the following morning he'd kiss her again when he returned. Her babysitter had slept in the spare bedroom across the hall from her room. 24 hours on/48 hours off. It had been his schedule for as long as she could remember. He was considered a brave and noble man, risking his life day after day for strangers. After he'd leave for his shift, she'd lie alone in the dark, frightened by the possibility that he may never come back. Then one night, he didn't. She never saw him again.

The next couple of months after his death, Paige didn't sleep. She'd sob quietly into her pillow until the loneliness became too much to bear. Then, she'd slip out and climb into bed with Aunt Hattie until morning. Her aunt never scolded her or sent her back to own room. She'd simply lift the covers and Paige would crawl under the blankets, curling against Aunt Hattie's warm body.

Coaxing her thoughts back to the present, Paige wiped the tears from her eyes and closed the trunk lid. Dinner was waiting. She stood to her feet and wiped the dust from her slacks, then turned to leave the attic.

She heard them before she saw them. Like the sound of a massive rock slide, Aunt Hattie's animals charged up the attic stairs. A streak of cat fur whipped past her. The Dalmatians were close behind, their larger bodies not nearly as sleek or agile. 'Round the attic they ran. The stacks of boxes toppled over. "Watch out!" She waved her arms, trying to stop them. The three renegades plowed into her legs, knocking her off balance. She scrambled for something to grab hold of, and her fingers clutched a sheet at the last second as she tumbled backward. Cardboard boxes and Christmas decorations crashed around her. "Thanks, guys." She called after the pets as they clambered down the stairs and disappeared out of sight.

Maneuvering out from under the fallen boxes, she stood to her feet, brushing the dust and cobwebs from her clothes. *What a mess!* She restacked everything into neat piles, making her way toward the antique washstand she'd uncovered while trying to maintain her balance. She picked up the fabric cloth and shook it out. As she turned to recover the washstand, a wooden apple crate on top grabbed her attention. She set the sheet aside and took a closer look. Inside the crate lay a leather-bound book with gold letters forming the words: *Holy Bible. A Bible? That's odd. Grandpa wasn't a religious man. We never went to church. Maybe it belongs to Aunt Hattie.* She lifted the leather book from the crate and flipped through the gold-fringed pages. She withdrew a laminated bookmark with the words, Wallowa Mountains Baptist Church, Whitman, Oregon, Pastor Michael C. Whitestone. Est. 1934.

Whitman? Where's that? She tried to remember if she'd ever heard Aunt Hattie mention a town called Whitman. *No, I don't think so.*

She flipped back to the title page of the Bible where a handwritten note drew her focus. A total of ten words, but their message brought butterflies to her stomach. *To my baby girl. I love you. I'm sorry. Annie.*

Her heart pounded against her ribcage, fueled by her curiosity. *Who's Annie? Who's the baby girl? Aunt Hattie?*

Before Paige could wonder further, a voice called from downstairs. "Dinner's ready, Paigey."

"Coming." Paige tucked the Bible under her arm, then closed the attic door behind her.

Downstairs, she set the Bible on the hutch and went to the bathroom to wash her hands. Aunt Hattie's voice carried from the kitchen as she chattered to no one in particular. "Today, Rachael Ray fixed the yummiest-looking dish I've ever seen. Spinach and Mushroom Lasagna roll-ups with Gorgonzola cream sauce. I wanted to make it for us, but I don't have any idea what Gorgonzola is. Do you know what Gorgonzola is, Paigey?"

"It's a type of cheese," Paige said as she entered the dining room.

"Oh. Well…" Aunt Hattie set a heavy ceramic soup tureen on the table with a *thump.*

Paige raised her eyebrows. Her voice acquired a nervous tone. "What is for dinner?" She crossed her fingers behind her back. *Oh please, let it be normal.*

"Grilled cheese and tomato soup."

Her shoulders lowered as she released a sigh of relief. *Oh, good. Not too bad.* "I thought we were having salad." She sat on the ruffled floral cushion and tucked her legs underneath the table. Aunt Hattie walked back into the kitchen and returned with a plate of about eight charcoaled grilled cheese sandwiches.

"We were. I burnt it."

Huh? Paige's eyes grew wide. "How did you burn… Oh, never mind." Her aunt served up the plates and bowls and Paige ate the burnt sandwiches and the watery soup without complaint. Reddish liquid dribbled down her chin. As she wiped her face with a paper napkin, her eyes fell on the book resting on the hutch. It called to her—taunted her… "Who's Annie?" She blurted it out before she could stop herself.

Aunt Hattie's face paled. Her hands began to tremble as she scooped another serving of soup into her bowl. Several droplets splattered onto the white tablecloth. "Oh, me. Look what I've done. Remind me to put some stain stick on that before I go to bed."

The delay only heightened her curiosity. *Aunt Hattie's avoiding my question. Is it that much of a secret?* "Aunt Hattie?" Paige whispered. Her mind whirled. Her stomach fluttered. "Who's Annie?" Her chest tightened. What was Aunt Hattie hiding from her?

The poor woman suddenly looked older than her seventy years. Pink lips and blue vein lines stood out against pale cheeks. She was still dabbing at the stains on the tablecloth with her napkin. Paige leaned forward to hear her aunt's whispered answer. "Your mother."

Time stopped. Dizziness washed over her like an ocean current dragging her down into the depths. Paige struggled to draw a breath as anxiety constricted her lungs. Her pulse raced like the Amtrak train. All other sounds faded. Aunt Hattie's lips moved, but she heard nothing. *My mother?*

She compelled her voice to speak, disbelief dripping from every enunciated word. "That—that's not possible. My mother's name was Maggie. Grandpa told me what happened. Mom and Dad died in a car accident right after I was born." *Had Grandpa lied?*

"I'll tell you the whole story if you let me."

Paige pursed her lips together in a feeble attempt to hold back the flood of questions threatening to breach the dam of her razzmatazz lip gloss.

"One summer's night in 1992, Benjamin McDonald was on duty at station number nine. The other firefighters were asleep, but he couldn't get comfortable. He stepped outside for some fresh air and there on the concrete steps, bundled in an apple crate, lay a beautiful newborn baby girl. Ben's wife had only recently passed, and as he looked into your big blue eyes, he fell in love. He made up your parents' accident and had you call him your grandpa."

A sudden pang in her head confused Paige's thoughts. *What about Maggie? And Benny, my father? Did Grandpa make them up?* She pressed her hands to her temples. "Are—are Benny and Maggie even real?"

Aunt Hattie gave her a weak smile. "Benny was Ben's son, my nephew. He was a soldier and died in the Gulf War more than a year before you were born. As far as I know, Maggie never existed."

Paige leaned back in her chair in a daze. "If Benjamin McDonald isn't my grandfather, then you're not really my great aunt either?"

Aunt Hattie's countenance turned downcast and her shoulders slumped forward. She stared at the tablecloth and played with her spoon. "No, dear. I'm not."

Paige pushed her chair back from the table. She swallowed gulps of air. "Everything I've known is a lie." The ocean wave dragged her down again. The pressure in her temples swelled. Aunt Hattie wouldn't make eye contact, but her head bobbed up and down. "Who am I? Who are my parents? Where did I come from?"

Aunt Hattie swallowed a sob. Large tears brimmed beneath her eyelashes. "I don't know, Paigey. I'm—I'm so, so sorry. Ben always meant to tell you. Someday. When you were old enough. But then…you know…"

"If you knew all this time, why didn't you tell me?"

"I…" Sniff. "I was afraid…" Sniff. Sniff. "I was afraid you'd leave me." Tears spilled full throttle now.

Paige made a shushing sound. "Please, don't cry. It's OK. It's OK." But it wasn't okay. How could anything be okay ever again? *Everything I know about myself is a complete and total sham. My heritage…my parentage…my…* She swallowed. *My name? Is any of it real?* She had to ask. "Is my name actually Brooklyn Paige McDonald?"

"Of course!" Aunt Hattie cried out. Her cheeks flushed and she lowered her voice. "You were turned over to Child Protective Services. Then, when he legally adopted you, Ben gave you that name. You are Brooklyn Paige McDonald."

Paige stared into her bowl of cold, watery soup. Her reflection stared back. *What do I do now? My whole life's been turned upside down. I need answers. Annie…*

Annie had the answers. *Except…* Annie had given her away. The terrible truth hit hard. Her own mother had abandoned her at the front door of a fire department. *Why would she do that? Why would my mother just leave me? Who does something like that?*

3

"Thank you for coming."

Mayor Kathleen Phillips had already said those words a few hundred times that morning and after one glance at the line of people entering the Whitman Funeral Home, it was a phrase she would say at least a few hundred more before the day was over. She gave the stranger in front of her a solemn smile. More than half of the attendees were strangers—to be expected when the deceased was once governor of Oregon. The parking lot was packed, and the street lined with cars. In the distance, the snow-peaked "Little Alps" created a picturesque backdrop. The strength and grandeur of the Wallowa Mountains reminded her of her father. Mayor, governor, state attorney general—nothing could bring him to his knees. He had once stood face to face with a mafia boss and didn't back down. Death threats were as regular as the daily mail delivery. What finally took him out? Microscopic cancer cells. A teeny, tiny, convoluted cell put an end to the most feared man in the state.

Kathleen turned her attention indoors. The funeral

director, Billy Myers, moved restlessly around the open silver coffin lined with white satin, quietly arranging the flowers: bouquets of lilies, carnations, and Gerber daisies, special ordered from Portland. The elderly organist pumped out the old gospel hymns. A wooden podium stood to the side of the chapel and beside it, an easel bearing a portrait of her father during his governor years. The man in the portrait had a fire in his eyes—a fire that had slowly extinguished until he couldn't walk, couldn't eat, and finally couldn't form a coherent sentence. He'd lost two-hundred pounds over the course of his sickness. And she'd been there at his side. Just as he'd been there for her all those years ago.

"Hey, sis."

"Erik!" She turned into the waiting arms of her younger brother. "Thank you for not making me do this alone." They embraced, then she held him at arm's length and took a good look. He was the spitting image of their father: raven mustache, tanned skin, suave in appearance and step, but that's where the resemblance ended.

Erik wore an Armani suit and at forty years old, his hair had yet to turn gray. In fact, if she didn't know better, she would have guessed him to be no older than thirty-five. He'd never married, but not because he couldn't find a willing partner. Erik loved the single life. No commitments. No responsibilities. The exact opposite of his sister. "I'm not here for him."

Kathleen frowned. Her eyebrows tipped toward each other. "Dad loved you."

"Maybe. He loved you more."

She punched his arm. "Don't say things like that."

"You're the son he never had."

"Erik." His name left her throat as a groan, but in her heart, she knew he spoke the truth. Her father and brother had never had the best of relationships.

"Come on. You know he was disappointed when I didn't go into politics like the two of you. I've always been more like

Mom."

Out of the corner of her eye, Kathleen saw Billy move into his place behind the wooden podium. "If you c-could all take your s-seats. We will b-begin the s-service." Billy's stutter was still as prominent as it had been when she'd babysat him thirty years ago.

Kathleen found her seat at the front marked with a Reserved for Family sign. She smoothed the back of her black Calvin Klein pencil skirt, then perched onto the hardback pew. She straightened her suit jacket as Erik took a seat beside her.

Her daughter, Kylie, slid onto the pew at the last second. "Uncle Erik." Kylie was pleased to see him.

"Hey, kid." He squeezed his niece's arm.

Billy shuffled through his notes and began to speak. "F-Friends. F-Family. Thank you for c-coming today to support the Phillips and S-Staten families as they g-grieve the loss of a great man, former G-Governor Richard M. Staten. M-Mr. Staten is survived by his ex-wife, Oscar-winning actress D-Dawn Winters, his daughter, M-Mayor Kathleen Phillips, his son, Erik S-Staten, and his granddaughter, K-Kylie Phillips. Before I g-give the eulogy, M-Miss Phillips would l-like to sing a s-song in honor of her grandfather."

Kylie moved to the front of the chapel. The soundtrack played over the speakers, and she sang the sweet words to her grandfather's favorite hymn, 'What a Day That Will Be.' When the song finished, Billy gave the eulogy, beginning with a glowing list of her father's achievements. Mayor of Whitman for fifteen years, two terms as governor of the State of Oregon, and state attorney general for twelve years. All things she'd heard before. Lived before.

"M-Mr. Staten was a f-force to be reckoned with. A f-fact well-known in b-both the political and criminal arena. H-he was a role-model f-for old and young. A living testament t-to the power of God and the ch-changing grace of Salvation. Only God could make that much d-difference in a p-person's life."

Kathleen allowed her mind to drift to the past—a place she rarely ventured. It was a waste of time to dig up old memories, but she couldn't help herself—not today. In her opinion, funerals had a way of codling nostalgia. Even her own.

Every Sunday morning for ten years, the Wallowa Mountains Baptist Church van had arrived to give Kathleen and Erik a ride to worship service, and every Sunday morning, she'd beg her father to attend with them. But his answer was always the same. He had more important things to do. He didn't need a crutch. Religion was for weaklings.

Eventually, Kathleen left home for college, married her husband, Formula One driver Lionel Phillips, gave birth to Kylie, miscarried three other babies, and finally lost her husband in a freak accident on the race track—not that she was sorry to see him go.

The week after her husband's funeral, her father telephoned. They hadn't spoken in twenty years. His voice crackled, weak and defeated. The man on the other end of the line sounded nothing like the father of her youth. "It's cancer."

"Oh, Daddy."

"I need you, baby," he said. And that was all it took. The years of silence melted away, and that same night, she'd contacted a real estate broker to put her house in Indiana on the market. Within a week, she'd given her notice at her lucrative job with Samuels, Trainer, and Wade, attorneys-at-law, pulled her daughter out of a prestigious private school, and returned to the town of her childhood, exactly in the middle of nowhere.

Not long after, her father began attending church and during his final five years on earth, he'd been a completely different man. She was grateful for the change in her father, but she had very little use for God in her life. She didn't need God, especially not one who allowed men like Lionel Phillips to exist. Not one who'd snatched her three babies to Heaven even while she'd begged Him to let them live. She didn't believe in that God of love that Pastor Whitestone had spouted on about all those years ago. A God of love would never have allowed those things to happen to her. Others could believe what they wanted, but she didn't buy into the fairytale. Not anymore.

"Is he talking about when Dad got religion?" Erik whispered in her ear.

She scrunched her eyebrows. "He didn't just get religion, Erik. He found true peace." *Something I long for.*

"You used to believe in that religion, too."

Exactly. Used to.

"I just went to church to have something to do on Sundays rather than listen to another one of Dad's lectures."

"Maybe if you weren't getting into all kinds of trouble, Dad wouldn't have had to lecture—"

"Shush." Erik pointed at the podium. Billy was wrapping up the service. Short and to the point. Just like Dad wanted.

"B-before we begin the p-procession to the cemetery, I've asked Pastor Whitestone to say a p-prayer."

Kathleen sucked in a breath as a tall, clean-cut gentleman stepped behind the podium. *Where did he come from?* This was not the gray-haired man of her childhood. This was a ghost from the past. One she'd truly hoped would always remain there.

Kathleen stood at the back of the chapel alone. The guests gathered outside, loading into their vehicles to proceed to the cemetery for the internment. Kylie had disappeared, and Erik stood near the front with the other pallbearers, preparing to carry the coffin outside to the waiting hearse.

Senator Chatham approached from the far side of the room. He was pushing seventy, however, he had the strength and stamina of a much younger man. The senator stopped in front of Kathleen and grasped her extended hand firmly between both of his. "Mayor Phillips, please allow me to express my condolences on your father's passing."

"Thank you, senator. It's been coming for a while, but it's still a shock just the same."

"Most definitely, Kathleen. You will let me know if there is anything I can do for you, won't you?"

Kathleen nodded. Of course, she would. As likely as she was to give a fox the key to the hen house.

"And best of luck in the primaries. Following in your father's footsteps—those are some mighty impressive shoes to fill."

"Yes sir, but I think I'm up to the challenge."

As the senator moved on, her father's estate attorney, Don Wall, appeared at her side. Kathleen turned to greet him, and he squeezed her outstretched hand. "Please accept my condolences, Mayor Phillips."

"Thank you, counselor."

"Forgive me. I'm unable to attend the graveside. I must return to Portland tonight." Don cleared his throat. "You'll receive a copy in the mail in a few weeks, but I thought I should let you know… Your father filed a new will with my office about six months ago."

Kathleen frowned. She had no knowledge of a new will. *Why would he do that and not tell me about it?* She couldn't keep the concern and curiosity from her voice. "Did he change the will?" She didn't remember the exact amount of her father's worth, but it was upward of fifty million, most of it tied up in stocks, bonds, and other investments.

"I'm sorry. I'm not at liberty to discuss this further, but I do have one question before I leave."

Don paused to stroke the five o'clock shadow along his jaw. "Mr. Staten seemed to be under the impression that there was another grandchild born years before Kylie. Is this true, Mayor Phillips? Do you have any other children?"

The room grew warm. She shed her jacket and tossed it

over the back of a pew. The attorney stared straight at her, his eyes never leaving her face. She squirmed under the scrutiny. "No. The cancer messed with his mind. Kylie is my only child." If her secret reached the media, her chances of being elected governor would vanish. She was the only person in the room who knew she was lying, and she would do whatever was necessary to keep it that way.

Kenneth Chatham marched out the door of the Whitman Funeral Home. His heavy steps clomped down the stairs as irate frustration permeated his Armani. That woman got under his skin faster than a cactus needle in a flipflop. "Kathleen Staten cannot be allowed to run for governor." He paused beside the black Hummer parallel parked along the street.

His assistant opened the car door and pushed the end call button on his phone. "But sir, what's the harm in letting her run?"

He growled at the stupidity. "She's Richard Staten's daughter." That alone should answer his question. "Get in the car."

"Yes sir." The Hummer door slammed shut, and a second later, the opposite side door opened, and the younger man lunged onto the seat just as the SUV pulled away from the curb. The assistant shifted on the seat and straightened his tie. "You were saying, sir?"

"We have to do more than make her drop out of the race. I want you to destroy her. Make sure no Staten ever runs for political office again."

4

A shrill *beep* woke Paige from her dreams. She flailed her arms and legs, startled by the abrupt noise. She pitched sideways, rolling off her mattress with a loud thump and bumping against the nearest bookcase. Books crashed to the floor, whacking her head and limbs. *Ouch.* She rubbed the sore spots and worked to untangle herself from her blankets. The bedroom door flew open, and Aunt Hattie filled the doorway, donned in curlers and a bathrobe. The dogs scurried across the floor and licked Paige's wounds. "I heard a commotion. Are you all right in here?"

Paige shoved the dogs out of the way and rose to her feet. "I think so. My alarm startled me." She stretched and tried to cover a yawn before Aunt Hattie saw. It didn't work.

"What time did you go to bed last night?" Aunt Hattie gave Paige a knowing grin as she turned off the alarm. She flipped on the light switch.

Paige blinked at the sudden bright light. "The last time I checked, it was midnight." She picked up her blankets off the floor and dropped them back on the bed, then she covered another yawn.

"Come on downstairs. I've got some coffee brewing. After you have a cup, you can shower and dress for work."

If only coffee and a hot shower could wash away yesterday. She couldn't sleep last night. Aunt Hattie's revelation possessed her every thought.

Twenty minutes later, Aunt Hattie poured a bowl of granola and milk and sat it in front of her at the table. "What do you want for dinner tonight?"

Paige spooned some granola into her mouth. Droplets of milk dribbled down her chin, so she grabbed a napkin from the holder and wiped her face. She swallowed before answering. "We could just order pizza again."

Aunt Hattie's bottom lip stuck out in a pooch. Paige sighed. *Why does she insist on cooking? She could be on that television show about the worst cooks.* "How about spaghetti?"

Her aunt's eyes lit up like fireworks. "I can do that. I'll walk down to Freddie's later this morning." The Fred Meyers grocery store was only a couple blocks away from their house.

"Sounds like a plan." Paige hit the home button on her phone, and the screen lit up. She bit her lower lip. "I'm late. I'll never make the bus." She scrambled out of her chair, tripping over the dogs sprawled out on the linoleum floor.

"Love you, Paigey. Have a lovely day." Aunt Hattie waved and then busied herself by washing the breakfast dishes.

Paige grabbed her backpack and jacket as she dashed out the back door. She retrieved her bike from the garage, then pedaled as fast as she could to the bus stop. Sure enough, she had just missed her bus. She locked her bicycle in place on the bike rack, then took a seat on the bench to wait for the next available bus.

A while later, Paige exited the bus at her stop in the Pearl District. She jogged across the street, slowing as she approached the building. Outside of Powell's Books, she stopped beside the concrete column shaped like a stack of books and ran her fingers over the rough stones. If only she could harness the brilliance of these ancient writers to help her make the right decision. Should she try to find her birth mother or not?

She entered the Green Room at the Burnside Street entrance, then skipped up the stairs to the Red Room on the second floor. She took a few minutes to scan the shelves of travel guides. Late into the night, she'd researched Whitman, the town on the bookmark she'd found in the Bible. Whitman had a courthouse, a library, a hospital, and only three-thousand people. Rolling farmland and the Wallowa Mountains sur-rounded the town. It was only four hours away, but it might as well have been on the other side of the world.

She was determined to travel to Whitman and… That was the extent of her plan. She hadn't the slightest idea what to do once she got there. How did a person go about finding his or her birth parents? How long did it take? Did she need a couple of days or a couple of months? Unfortunately, she'd already used up most of her vacation time for the year, and it was only the twenty-first of May.

She left the Red Room, winding her way through the crowds of customers and the aisles of books. Cat Bastille, her supervisor, could be anywhere in the store. She didn't have to search long.

"Paige!" Cat's voice screeched from somewhere in the building.

Paige hurried to the Orange Room on the first floor where the manager impatiently tapped her foot. Her nose was wrinkled with distaste as she spoke. "What is this?" She gestured at a bookcase beside her.

"What is what?" Paige stared at the bookshelves. Everything appeared to be in order.

"Don't you see it?" Cat waved her arms. "How could you

miss it?"

Again, Paige scanned the shelves. Nothing looked amiss. Cat must be losing her mind.

"Ugh." Cat pointed at the middle shelf. "Some customer shelved these books themselves. They're out of order."

Paige swallowed against the smart aleck reply that rose in her throat. Instead, she quickly shifted the books into place. "There. All fixed."

Cat turned to walk away. *It's now or never.* Paige leapt forward and grabbed the manager's elbow. Cat's laser-like gaze looked ready to melt Paige's skin off her fingers. She jerked her hand back. "Sorry," she muttered.

"Do you want something?" Cat's voice was sharp with annoyance.

"I'm going on a trip, and I'd like to take some time off."

Cat folded her arms across the front of her peasant blouse. "How much time off are we talking about here?"

Paige swallowed. This woman scared her right down to her toes. "I'd like an extended leave."

"For how long?" Cat raised an eyebrow, causing Paige to wither under her stare. "You're not pregnant, are you?"

Paige's eyes widened with shock. "No, no. Most certainly not." She waved her hands in the air. "I just don't know how long I'll be gone."

"Then tell me what you need the leave for?"

Her heart thudded against her ribcage. How could she tell this woman her secret shame? "I don't want to talk about it."

Cat obviously wasn't convinced. "Boyfriend trouble?"

"Mrs. Bastille, please. I just need to go out of town for a while."

"No."

"Why not?"

"I can't just give people extended leave without a valid reason. I don't give special treatment."

I noticed. "I have a reason. It's just… It's personal."

"Sorry. You can use whatever vacation time you have, but I can't give you more than that."

Three days. She had three days left. It wasn't enough. She took a deep breath. *What am I going to do?*

Paige chained her bike outside the Cup and Saucer and went inside. The earthy aromas engulfed her in their familiarity. At the counter, she ordered her favorite: a caramel chocolate chip frappe with extra foam. The barista whipped up the order then called her name. Paige grabbed her coffee and went to sit at a window table facing the street. She watched the neighborhood through the glass. The Baghdad Theater, just down the street, was where her grandpa—no, she reminded herself—where Benjamin McDonald had taken her as a child to watch the movie, *102 Dalmatians.*

Afterward, he'd brought her into this very shop for her first cup of coffee. Of course, it had been more cream than caffeine, but she'd instantly fallen in love with the drink.

Farther down the street was the Hawthorne branch of Powell's Books where she'd developed her love for all things literature. It was where she'd determined to own her own bookstore someday. The first step in that direction, after attending business school, had been securing a position at Powell's City of Books downtown. All of that was gone in a single sentence: "I quit." What possessed her to quit her job? She glanced down into her cup. The foam had dissolved into the brown liquid. Like her entire life had dissolved when she'd learned the truth. She was adopted. And now, unemployed. *You've got time to search for your birth mother now.* But without a paycheck, how would she finance her trip? *What about the books you bought last month?* She could sell them to the right buyer for twice what she'd paid. But, that took time, time she didn't want to waste. Paige swallowed the last of her coffee and dropped the cup in the trash. It was time to go home and tell Aunt Hattie what she'd done.

The screen slammed as she entered through the back door. The dogs greeted her, jumping up on their hind legs and licking her face. "Paige home. Paige home," Gerald squawked.

Aunt Hattie jerked from her place on the sofa where she was watching the morning news. "What are you doing home?" She pushed herself out of the deep cushion with a little groan, then grabbed Paige's face and kissed her on the cheek.

"Hi Aunt Hattie. What's for lunch?"

"Tuna sandwiches, but why are you home so early? I may lose track of time, but I know it's not five forty-five."

"I'll help you." Paige went into the kitchen. She found the tuna fish cans in the cabinets hidden behind the box of spaghetti noodles and the jar of tomato sauce for dinner. She opened the tuna with the can opener, scraped it into a bowl, then set the empty can on the floor. Delilah came out from behind the curtains and started licking the can clean. It made a rattling sound as she licked up the remnants with her tongue. Paige removed the mayo from the fridge, mixed a scoop with the fish, then added salt and pepper. When she reached for the bread box, her aunt's blue-veined hand stilled her arm, then she pulled her from the counter and clasped both of Paige's hands in her own. Paige closed her eyes and tilted her chin toward the floor. *Why is this so hard?*

"Paigey, what happened today?" Aunt Hattie's voice was soft and gentle as she rubbed her thumb over Paige's knuckles.

Tears squeezed out from under Paige's eyelids. "I quit."

A gasp came from the sweet, elderly woman. "Why did you quit?"

Paige turned her eyes toward the ceiling. Her grandpa had always claimed that he'd used one of her diapers to mold the ruffled spackle. A water stain marked the place where the toilet had leaked a couple of summers ago. "I tried to get an extended leave to go to Whitman, and Cat wouldn't give it to me." She sat back on the edge of the marble counter next to the fridge and folded her arms across her chest. "I don't know what to do now."

"We'll figure it out together. I'll help you."

Two days later, her duffel bag lay open on her bed. Paige folded a blue T-shirt and tucked it into the corner. Aunt Hattie sat cross-legged at the headboard. Her eyes crinkled with crow's feet and unshed tears. "We'll miss you, Paigey."

Aunt Hattie had always been there for her. How could she leave the woman who had taken such good care of her over the years? The one who'd hugged her through the nightmares and had visited her faithfully every week while she was at… She shook her head. At least one person in this crazy world loved her. She ran her bare big toe along the crack between the floorboards. "Aunt Hattie? How would you like to come with me?"

"Really, Paigey?" Her aunt's face lit up. "You'd take me with you? But what about the house? We'd have to sell the house. And what about all your books? What will you do with your books? And all my stuff? What are we going to do with all this stuff?"

"Don't go selling the house just yet, Aunt Hattie. I'll find us a place to rent, and then you can join me. I don't know how long we'll be in Whitman. My mother might not even live there. This might all be for nothing." She zipped her duffel bag shut and dropped it in the hallway with a thump. The two dogs sniffed at it, and Delilah climbed on top, curling up to take a nap. Gerald swung in his cage, repeating, "Paige go. Paige go."

Paige tucked her hair behind her ears, then sat cross-legged on the floral comforter. Aunt Hattie frowned, all her wrinkles pulling toward the center of her face. "I do hope you find her."

"Me too." Although she said so aloud, in her heart she wasn't sure she believed it. Did she really want to find her birth mother? Would she be able to handle the truth?

Paige shifted, letting her legs hang over the edge of the bed. Delilah left her perch on the duffel, pounced up on the bed, and climbed into Paige's lap. Paige stroked the soft fur. Delilah purred and ran her head against Paige's arms. Paige shook her fingers, dislodging the fluffy hair that had stuck to them. The cat began licking her paws, then moved on to Paige's legs. Delilah's rough tongue tickled her skin. "Maybe this is a terrible idea. I could be walking into a hornet's nest messing with people's lives like this. Besides, I have absolutely nothing to work with."

She'd already tried contacting the Department of Human Services, but as a "safe haven" baby, they had no information about her, except for the date she'd been found and the date she had been legally adopted by Benjamin McDonald, information Aunt Hattie had already given her.

Paige left her bedroom and walked downstairs. Aunt Hattie and the animals followed. Paige ran her tongue over her dry lips. She retrieved two bottles of water from the fridge, handing one of them to Aunt Hattie. She opened the other and drank a long swig, then wiped her mouth on the back of her hand. "Besides, I can't afford a trip right now. I should just forget the whole thing."

Aunt Hattie stood still for a moment as Delilah brushed against her legs. She lifted the cat in her arms and distractedly stroked the purring ball of fur, then she nodded as if answering a question. To Delilah's surprise, Aunt Hattie dropped her to the floor, then crossed the living room to the antique desk. The lid arched back as Aunt Hattie raised the handle. The surface was cluttered with papers and sticky notes. She dug through the chaos, obviously searching for something in particular.

Paige took another swig of water, then set her bottle

down on the counter. *What is she looking for?* She crossed the carpeted floor and leaned over Aunt Hattie's back.

"Aha." Aunt Hattie yanked out an envelope with a flourish, whacking Paige in the mouth. *Ouch.* Paige licked her stinging lips and tasted blood. "Sorry, Paigey. I didn't know you were so close."

Paige wet a paper towel and dabbed at the split on her inner lip. "Never mind. What's in the envelope?"

"Are you sure you're okay?" Paige nodded. Her aunt held out the envelope. "This is a little something I saved for a rainy day."

"We live in Portland. Every day is a rainy day."

Aunt Hattie's lips tilted in a playful smile. "Open it."

Paige opened the flap on the unsealed envelope. Her eyes widened at the stack of greenbacks. "What is this?"

"Some of the profit I made when I sold my house in Seattle."

"How much is it?"

Aunt Hattie shrugged her shoulders. "Should be about fifty thousand dollars."

"Wait! This has been in our home? We could have been robbed! Why isn't this in the bank?"

"I was going to deposit it, but the banker man was rude to me. I decided not to give him my money."

Paige shook her head. "I'm not taking this money. It's yours."

Aunt Hattie's lips pooched out, and her eyes watered. The poor old woman was just being kind. It was wrong of Paige to reject her gift. She caved and kissed her sweet aunt on the cheek. "Thank you. But I can't carry this much cash with me. I'll have to deposit it first."

"Oh, dear. Don't go to that mean man."

"I won't, Aunt Hattie." It was far more than she needed, but she wouldn't hurt her aunt's feelings. She would pay back every cent, whether her aunt wanted her to or not.

Late that night, Paige sat curled up on the couch alone, stroking Delilah's silky fur. The only light was an antique lamp on the side table. She raised her cup of hot coffee to her lips and blew on the steam. The Persian cat purred and rolled over, exposing her belly. "Delilah, do you have any idea what it's like to discover your whole life is a lie? To learn that the family you thought you had wasn't your family at all, but the family you should have had might not want you?" Paige sighed and leaned forward to set her mug on the coffee table. "Of course not, you're a cat. You don't even know who your parents are." The corner of her mouth turned up. "You don't care, either. What am I going to do? How can I learn the truth? How will I ever find out who I really am?"

"The only way to find the end is to start at the beginning."

Paige's eyes grew large. "Delilah?" She was seriously losing her mind.

A chuckle came from behind the sofa. Paige turned sharply, causing the cat to jump to the floor. "Aunt Hattie, you startled me. I didn't hear you come down."

"I heard you—talking to that cat as if she understood you."

Paige's neck grew warm. "She's a pretty good listener."

"Yes, she is." Aunt Hattie came around the furniture and eased down onto the sofa. She held Paige's hand in her wrinkly one. "I'm so sorry. I should have told you about your adoption years ago."

"It's OK. What's done is done." Paige shifted, tucking her legs underneath her. She yanked a throw from the back of the couch and draped it over hers and her aunt's laps. She snuggled into her aunt's warm side and laid her head on the old woman's shoulder. "I'm scared, Aunt Hattie." Her fear was much easier to admit in the dead of night. Her stomach knotted in an uneasy way as anxiousness crackled through her like a lightning bolt. "Annie gave me away for a reason. What if she still doesn't want me in her life? What do I do then? Forget her? Move on as if she never existed? Are my children to grow up never knowing their real grandparents?"

"Children? You are getting so far ahead of yourself. Just take it one moment at a time. One decision at a time. Don't borrow trouble. Charles—what's his name, you know, the Snoopy guy, said, 'Don't worry about the world coming to an end today. It is already tomorrow in Australia.'"

Aunt Hattie always could bring a smile to her face and relieve her troubles with just a few simple words. "OK, Aunt Hattie, I'll remember the words of the Snoopy guy."

"Everything is going to work out, Paigey. You'll see." *New adventures are waiting over the horizon. If only there was a way of knowing whether the consequences would be good or bad.* Aunt Hattie ran her knobby fingers through Paige's hair. "Go to Whitman. Go find your mother."

5

Patrol Officer Hamilton Bryant stood outside the Wallowa Mountains Baptist Church, staring at a pool of blood in the parking lot. He'd gotten off-duty at six o'clock and had run home, showered, and changed clothes before Wednesday night prayer meeting started. The service had just ended when they'd heard three gunshots. Like lightening, he'd bolted out the door on high alert to find a young man, in his late teens, crumpled on the blacktop. He'd immediately dialed 911, then applied pressure to the bullet wounds.

Whitman Memorial Hospital was only a few blocks away, and it hadn't taken long for transport to arrive. The paramedics had stabilized the young man before taking him to the hospital. Hamilton hadn't managed to get the victim's name before the ambulance left. Officers Hurston and Martin were on duty. They'd already arrived and were gathering preliminary testimonies from the witnesses.

"What do ya got?" Chief Mark House slammed the patrol unit door and crossed the grassy right-of-way between the street and the parking lot.

"Possible attempted homicide. Teen shot twice. I didn't

get his name. Witnesses say they saw a man wearing a matching red shirt and hat fleeing the scene."

The chief's forehead wrinkled. "Aren't you off-duty?"

Hamilton pointed to the building behind him. "Church. We just finished services half an hour ago."

Chief House pulled a regulation notepad from his duty belt. "Is the kid a member?"

"I don't think so. At least, I've never seen him here before. Doesn't mean he's not part of the youth program though."

"Will he make it?"

"Medics seemed to think so. They've got him bandaged up and are transporting him to the hospital now."

"How many witnesses?"

Hamilton nodded toward the small crowd milling near the double-door entrance of the church. Several elderly ladies had their arms wrapped around them as if they were cold, but he suspected it was more from shock than a chill. "Officer Hurston has finished the interviews. She's just waiting for your permission to send these poor people home."

"Sure. I'll check with the others and see what info they've gathered." The chief moved toward Officer Martin who was picking something up off the ground with a pair of tweezers.

Hamilton shook his head. Bagging and tagging hair fibers, chewing gum, and cigarette butts was not his cup of tea. He preferred the human element—interviews, interrogations, profiling—his private fascination and late-night hobby. He signaled to Officer Lillian Hurston to release the witnesses—the members of his own church family. It was hard to watch them like this. He was used to scenes like the one tonight—hardened was more like it. His sister accused him of becoming an emotionless robot. It wasn't intentional. It was a subconscious method of survival. His was a tough job, one that required a certain level of emotional detachment.

As they walked to their cars, the congregation tried to avert their eyes from the dark stain on the asphalt, but no matter how hard they tried, it was impossible for them to turn away. Officer Hurston approached him. She reached up and straightened his clip-on tie. "You're quite handsome in your civvies, you know that?"

Hamilton ran his sweaty palms through his thick brown hair and rubbed the back of his neck. He read the interest in Lillian's eyes. Both residents of Whitman, they'd grown up together and had even dated a few times. Lillian was pretty, sweet, generous, and as loyal as a golden retriever. He always knew she had his back and he had hers. If he was looking for a life partner, she had all the important qualities, but marriage was out of the question. To Lillian. To anyone.

"I've got to get back and start typing up these notes while they're still fresh in my mind."

He nodded. "I'll come with. Pretty sure my night's ruined. I don't think I could sleep now."

"Do you wanna grab some coffee on the way?"

Coffee was a given. "Need a ride?"

"Please. Officer Martin left to canvass the neighborhood."

They walked toward an Odyssey minivan. When Hamilton held open the passenger door for her, Lillian eyed the sticky cup holders, stained seats, and gobs of McDonald's cheeseburger wrappers. "What's with the soccer mom vehicle?" She climbed inside the van.

"It's my sister's minivan," Hamilton answered, then ran around to the driver's side. He hopped in and put the key in the ignition.

"Where's your truck?"

"At the shop."

Lillian rolled her eyes and locked her seatbelt into place. "Again? Why don't you get a new vehicle?"

Hamilton scoffed in mock annoyance. "That truck's a classic!" His 1962 Chevy spent more time in the shop than it did on the road, but he couldn't bring himself to part with it.

"*Classic* is just another word for piece of junk."

He turned the key, and the engine rumbled. He checked the left mirror, then pulled out onto the quiet street. "It was once my grandpa's car. Call me sentimental."

"Definitely mental." Lillian whispered under her breath. In a normal voice she said, "Sentimental over a piece of metal."

"Wow. That was almost poetic."

"Poetic justice every time it breaks down on you. I know how much you make. You can afford a new car."

He flipped the left blinker and slid into the center turn lane. When the traffic cleared, he pulled into a space in front of their favorite coffee stop, Rustic Cup. He left the truck idling, ran inside, and at the counter he ordered two coffees, one with cream and sugar, one black—both regular. They might need the caffeine. He knew he would. It had already been a long day, and it was about to get even longer.

The rest of the way to the station, the two sipped their hot coffee in silence. Hamilton parked in the vacant lot. The station was lit like a Christmas tree as florescent lights beamed through bullet-proof windows. He opened the front door for Lillian and then followed her into the lobby. A large glass window partitioned off a reception counter and empty swivel chair. The cold-natured receptionist, Joy Knoll, had long since gone home for the evening, but her white sweater still hung over the back of her chair.

The officers crossed the tile floor. Hamilton swiped his badge to gain access to the restricted area. They stashed their personal effects in their desks before heading into the room designated for writing reports. They spent the next two hours typing up the witness interviews and comparing notes about the case.

"Anything useful?"

Lillian shook her head. "The person of interest was a white male with matching shirt and hat, and he left the scene on foot. Unless he never does laundry, I doubt we'll spot him wearing the same combination. Any bullet casings?"

Hamilton glanced over his notes. "Martin recovered the brass from twenty-two caliber bullets. Either the shooter wasn't very close, or he wasn't aiming to kill. We still have to identify the victim and alert next of kin. Nobody at the church recognized him."

Lillian leaned back in her chair and rubbed her tired eyes. "Poor kid."

"Maybe. We still don't know why he was shot. He might not be as innocent as you think."

"Of course." She sighed. "How did the Night Out go?"

Once a year, the Whitman Police Department held a community barbecue. It helped strengthen the bond between law officers and civilians—a much needed boost in these present times. "It went great. The kids love sitting in the cars, and McGruff was there."

"I wish I could have been there, but my sister would have never forgiven me if I'd skipped out on her wedding."

Hamilton laughed and Lillian's eyes twinkled. He slapped his hands on his thighs and turned to read the clock on the wall. "It's getting late. Do you need a ride home?"

"Not yet. I still have some other business to take care of."

He raised his eyebrow. "Anything I can help with?"

"No, not really. It's personal." Her eyes shifted away from him. She was hiding something. Secrets garnered distrust, and it wasn't safe to distrust the one who held your life in their hands. He considered pushing her for an answer, but the burdened expression on her face convinced him to let it go—for now. He changed the subject. "Did Chief House mention that thing on Saturday?"

Lillian took a sip of her coffee and stuck out her tongue. "Yuck. It's cold." Her wrinkled nose made Hamilton smile. "Yeah, he mentioned it. What time are you getting there?"

"Probably zero nine thirty to start setting up."

"Sounds good. I'll meet you there."

Hamilton returned to his desk and retrieved his wallet, keys, and weapon from the drawer. He dropped the gun back in the holster on his hip and went outside. Leaving the minivan at the station, he started the engine of Patrol Unit Two and drove home to his apartment, pretty sure there was still leftover pizza in the fridge.

The next morning, Hamilton's cell phone rang while he was in the shower. He turned off the stream of water then stepped into the steamy bathroom where he grabbed a towel and wrapped it around his waist. His phone vibrated on the ceramic counter top. He smiled at the name on the caller ID, then tapped the button for speaker phone. "Morning, Becky." He spread shaving cream on his face, then shaved as he talked.

"Morning, Hambone." He was thirty-two-years-old, a police officer, and still his big sister couldn't come up with a more dignified nickname. "Whatcha doing during your lunch break?"

"Eating."

"Ha ha." Becky mocked. In a normal voice she added, "I'm going to The Bookshelf later. Can you join me?"

He washed the shaving cream off his face before answering. "What's up?"

"Nothing. I just want to catch up with my baby brother."

Right. Sure, she did. "I can be there about twelve-thirty."

"Works for me. See you then."

No way his sister just wanted to visit. She was always up to something, and that something usually involved his love life or lack thereof. Hamilton combed his hair to the side, dressed in his uniform, put on his peaked cover, and buckled his duty belt around his waist. He glanced in the mirror and straightened his clip-on tie. The transformation was complete. In the kitchen, he ate a bowl of cornflakes while standing up, then stacked his bowl and spoon in the sink along with the other dishes. He scrunched his nose at the pile of unwashed enamelware. He'd get to them—eventually. Officer Bryant dotted his i's and crossed his t's. Hamilton left dishes in the sink until they grew mold.

He left the apartment, jogged down the exterior stairs, scanned the area for anything abnormal, then knelt on the sidewalk, his right elbow propped on the hood of his patrol car. He bowed himself before the throne of God, humble and vulnerable. His daily prayer was simple, but sincere. *Dear God. Protect the community I serve. Use me to minister grace to those who need it and justice to those who deserve it. If my time comes due, that's fine, but I'd rather it not be today.*

He pushed from the ground, then sat in the patrol car and put the key in the ignition. He turned over the engine, then keyed in the microphone and signed in with dispatch. "This is Officer Bryant. Patrol Unit Two. Ten-eight. Ready for service."

He drove across town, stopping once to alert a civilian of a burnt-out brake light. Several minutes later, he pulled into his marked parking space at the station and went inside. The secretary, Joy, sat in her place, phone to her ear and typing on her keyboard at the same time. Hamilton waved as he passed. She stopped typing long enough to return the gesture.

He swiped his key card and went through the secure door into the bullpen. Officer Cody Stone and the rookie occupied their seats at their desks. He spotted Lillian through the window of the chief's office. Her hands waved wildly, and the chief had his "no argument" look on his face. The office door flew open and slammed against the wall. Hamilton picked up his desk phone receiver. "Yes, sir. I can take care of that right away."

Lillian thundered toward her desk, jerked out her chair, and flopped down. "You can quit pretending, Hamilton."

He laid the receiver back in its cradle. "How'd you know?"

"I know you." She fingered through a pile of folders on her desk, her eyebrows pinched together. She scowled as she moved the computer mouse and her screen lit up. Her eyes flittered back and forth like she was reading something, then she slammed her hand against the edge of the desk. The metal clanged when the two desks bumped each other.

"Lillian? Officer Hurston—"

She cut him off with a glare that could melt asphalt. "It's not for you to worry about. It's personal."

"But Lillian—"

"It's nothing Leave it alone." Officer Hurston pushed back from her desk and crossed the room to the water cooler. The other officers ducked their heads as she passed. *What's bothering her so much? And why won't she talk to me about it? We've always talked things over before.* How could he trust her if she was keeping things from him?

"Officer Bryant." The chief signaled from his office doorway.

When Hamilton entered the office, Chief House closed the door behind him. "Sit down. I want to talk to you."

Hamilton took a seat. The chief leaned against the wall, his back to the interior windows. Behind him, Lillian paced the room, throwing her hands in the air. The rookie doubled over his desk as she came close, and Officer Stone pretended to ignore her. She wasn't acting like her normal self at all. Chief House followed Hamilton's eyes and saw the rampaging officer. He closed the blinds and sat in his chair. "I'm putting Officer Hurston behind a desk for the foreseeable future."

Hamilton started to protest. Chief House held out his hand like a stop sign. "No. No. I'm sticking with my decision."

"What's going on?"

"I'm not at liberty to discuss her personal business with you. Let's just say—"

"It's personal." They spoke at the same time.

Chief House leaned back in his chair. "I'm giving you two options. You can work alone if you'd like. Whitman is a small town and not much happens around here. Or, I can pair you with the rookie."

"No. I'd rather work alone."

The chief smiled. "Yeah, I thought you might."

"It's not that I have anything against—"

Chief House cut him off. "I get it. I really do. Rookies are not the easiest to work with sometimes, but remember you were new once."

Fresh out of the Academy, he was partnered with Mark House, a Field Training Officer at the time. He'd had his share of mistakes. "Why'd you put up with me anyway?"

"I guess I remembered back when I was young myself—you know, back in the Stone Age."

Hamilton returned his grin. "I should get back to work. We're still trying to identify that kid that got shot last night. Any missing persons reports this morning?"

"No. Just Mrs. Perkins calling about her missing cat."

"Doesn't that cat come back every morning?"

"Yeah, she lets him out at night, and then calls us when he doesn't come back by zero eight hundred hours. By zero nine hundred hours he's sitting on the front stoop."

Hamilton returned to his desk. Lillian was sitting in her chair, typing on her keyboard. "Lillian?"

She wouldn't even look his direction.

At noon, he swung by Rooster Café and grabbed a cheeseburger and fries, then drove across town to the bookstore where his sister, Becky, planned to meet him. Lillian's behavior this morning bothered him, but he put it out of his mind while he went to see who his sister was setting him up with now. He parked the patrol car and went inside. The Bookshelf smelled like Clorox and musty books. His sister rifled through boxes near the back of the store. He snuck up behind her and grabbed her around the waist. Becky shrieked and jumped off the ground. "Don't do that!"

"Good to see you too, sis."

"When can I have my minivan back?"

"Hopefully, by the end of the week."

"Tomorrow?"

"No, the end of next week."

She groaned. "Hamilton!"

"I know. I know. Sorry."

His sister turned back to the boxes and continued sorting through them. "Here, hold these." She piled a stack of books onto his outstretched arms. "Have you heard anything more about that kid from last night?"

"Only that he's going to make it. Did you recognize him?"

"Yeah. He was a student at the school a couple of years back, expelled for drug usage. I guess he fell in with a bad lot. I'm sorry I don't remember his name though." His sister had always been terrible with names—and faces. She laid a few more books on the growing stack. "Thanks for taking the boys to that movie at the park last Thursday. They had fun, and Dave and I enjoyed the time alone."

Hamilton shifted the weight to his other arm. "No sweat. I had fun, too. There's another one in a couple of weeks, if they want to go. They're good kids."

"Speaking of kids…" *I knew she was up to something. Here it comes.*

"I talked to Lisa McKinney at Tyler's taekwondo class. Her divorce finalized a month ago. Her son is just starting kindergarten this year. I thought—"

"Becky." He cocked his eyebrow, warning her to change the subject.

"What?" She feigned ignorance.

"Stop trying to hook me up."

"But Hamilton, she's a nice lady. I just think if you give her a chance…" His sister's voice had taken on a pleading tone.

"I'm sure she is, but you know how I feel."

"I'm just looking out for my baby brother. I want you to find someone and settle down."

"Can't do that, Becky." Hamilton set the heavy pile of books on an empty shelf. He pulled at his collared shirt and clip-on tie. The bookstore grew warmer by the minute.

"Because of the shootings," his sister whispered, "You can't let fear stop you from living your life."

"I'm not. I just don't want to ruin someone else's." Law Enforcement Officers were being killed all over the country. What kind of future could he give a woman? His career choice had always been a risky one. Now more than ever before. It seemed so wrong to involve a wife in that kind of uncertainty. It wouldn't be fair to her. He was prepared to spend his life as a bachelor. "Do you want all of these? This stack's getting heavy." He lifted the pile of books from the shelf.

"Don't change the subject."

"I'm not."

"Yeah, I want them."

He followed his sister to the front of the store where the elderly owner, Jessie Faye, waited. He set the pile next to the ones Becky carried. She dug in her purse and pulled out her wallet, while the shopkeeper used a handwritten receipt pad to record the purchases. "How are you today, Jessie?" Becky asked.

"I'm doing all right. The old ticker's not what it used to be." *Does she mean the adding machine or her heart?* The community grandmother, Mrs. Jessie Faye, was older than dirt, or at least that's what she claimed. The adding machine made a gentle *tick tick* as she added the purchases.

"I'm sorry to hear that. If there is anything that Dave or I can do…"

The women chatted; however, Hamilton stopped listening. He had been changing the subject, and his sister knew the truth. It just wasn't something he wanted to discuss right now, at least not in a public store. Marriage was too risky in his line of work. He couldn't do that to a woman. He wouldn't do that to a woman.

Jessie finished totaling up the purchases, and Becky paid, then he and his sister carried them out to his brother-in-law's truck. They stacked the books on the floorboard of the cab. Becky closed the door and paused on her way around to the driver's seat. "So, when can I have my minivan back?"

Hamilton opened the driver's side door. She climbed up onto the running board and took a seat on the bench.

"Jeff said it should be ready by next Thursday or Friday."

"Why can't you just use the patrol car?"

She rolled down the window. He shut the door and then leaned his arms on the ledge. "I can't drive a government vehicle for personal use. It's against policy."

"Fine. The things I do for you, little brother." She put the key in the ignition and turned the truck on. It roared and vibrated. "When are you off-duty next?"

"Sunday."

Becky stuck out her lower lip.

"Sorry." Hamilton shrugged.

"Mark House works you too hard. Stop by for dinner sometime?"

"Sure, sis. See you later."

She put the truck in reverse, watched over her shoulder, and backed out of the space. Hamilton jumped into the police cruiser and keyed into dispatch, ready for another call.

6

With a swipe of her finger, Paige cranked up the music on her MP3 player. She wore jeans, a mustard-colored sweater, and a green and yellow scarf. She had silver dangly earrings and a yellow 1990s scrunchie on her short ponytail. She craned her neck to take in the view as the public transit from La Grande passed a road sign that read, Welcome to Whitman. Population. 3,303. The rosy hue from the sunset cast a sense of hope and expectancy all the way from the snow-peaked mountains to the rolling farmland below them. Businesses dotted the countryside like the spots on Aunt Hattie's Dalmatians.

Several minutes later, the bus screeched to a halt at the bus stop on the east side of town. The driver cranked open the hinged door and exited the bus to retrieve her luggage from the cargo hold. Paige gathered her purse and backpack, then stepped down the stairs. She paused on the concrete sidewalk and filled her lungs with crisp air bursting with possibilities and the smell of freshly plowed dirt. Her rear end was sore from sitting on the bus seat all day, and her knees quivered at the unknown journey ahead. Her bright yellow duffel bag and black bike bag waited on the curb. The driver waved then returned to the bus. Another screech echoed over the valley as the bus pulled away from the curb, then stopped again several feet away. The folding door opened, and the driver appeared at the top of the stairs. "Miss. Is this your phone?"

Paige's hands flew to her pants pockets. Her cheeks flushed with embarrassment. "Oops. Yes, that's mine." She recognized the purple Eeyore cover. She muttered to herself as she retrieved her forgotten electronic. "It's just my tail, but I'm kind of attached to it." She'd leave her head if it wasn't already attached. The bus driver closed the door and drove away.

A sudden urge to give chase overwhelmed Paige. She sank down on the curb facing a two-lane road and dropped her purse to the ground. *Might as well get on with it. Sitting here won't accomplish anything.* She jumped to her feet, brushed the dirt and bits of gravel off her jeans, and then reassembled her bike. Whitman was a small town. If she could use a bicycle to traverse the streets of Portland, it would certainly be sufficient here.

Paige mapped a route on her phone to a brand-name hotel, then pedaled into town. At the hotel, she locked her bike with a padlock on the rack, then entered the lobby and booked a room at the registration desk. She carried her duffel bag and backpack to the assigned room, then slid the key card into the automatic lock and turned the handle. She found a light switch next to the bathroom door and another on the small desk. She dropped her duffel bag to the floor, then flopped back on the striped duvet, kicking off her tennis shoes and sighing with relief. She was one step closer to finding Annie. She hoped.

She rocked forward and jumped to her socked feet, then crossed to the window and yanked back the heavy curtains. The hotel room had a sweeping view all the way to the Wallowa mountains. A gasp of delight slipped from her lips.

Had she ever seen anything so incredible? What would it have been like to grow up here in a town with a population of three thousand rather than a city of six hundred thousand? Everything about her life would have been different.

Her stomach grumbled, alerting Paige that she'd had nothing to eat since she switched buses in La Grande. She checked the time on her phone. It was getting late. On the way to the hotel, she'd ridden past a pizza restaurant. Hopefully, they were still open. These small towns were known to roll up their sidewalks at five o'clock. Paige put her tennis shoes back on and left the hotel in search of a big slice of cheesy pizza.

The next morning, after a continental breakfast, Paige pedaled her bicycle along the street, enjoying the first warm rays as the morning sun glowed like an ember at the edge of the horizon. A few lazy clouds floated overhead, and bird calls trilled with the welcoming of a new day. As she headed toward the northeast side of town, residential homes and commercial buildings grew farther and further between. Along the way, the road changed from blacktop to gravel. A massive brick antebellum home seemed to appear as if rising from the hillside.

She stopped pedaling and skidded to a stop, then dropped her feet and balanced on her tiptoes. White columns on the front porch led to a circular balcony on the second story. Windows covered the front side and white shutters bookended each one. A massive chandelier hung visible in an arched window behind the upstairs balcony. A brick wall surrounded the property, and a winding paved driveway traveled from the street to the top of the hill. An American flag snapped with the wind from its place in a manicured flowerbed. *Who lives here? They must be wealthy to afford a place like this.* The home was statelier than any she'd laid eyes on before. Someone certainly had wanted to stand out. It was oddly out of place and didn't fit with the rest of the town.

A vehicle crunched the gravel behind her. Paige turned. A marked police cruiser slowed, then came to a stop. Her pulse quickened. *Am I in trouble for loitering? I haven't been sitting here that long.* Had someone called the police already? She swallowed hard, fighting the urge to flee, as the police officer stepped out of his car. No one here knew who she was. What she was.

He touched the brim of his regulation cover as he approached. "Good morning, ma'am." The name plate on his uniform read Bryant.

She pried open her nervous lips. "Good morning, officer." *Stay calm and see what he wants.*

"Sorry to bother you, but have you seen a goat running around anywhere?"

Paige's eyes widened. Her mouth fell open. *What?* "Excuse me?" *A goat? Is this some kind of joke?* Officer Bryant looked official, right down to the Glock 22 in the holster clipped on his duty belt.

"We received a call about a loose goat wandering through some properties. Have you seen it?"

Paige held back a chuckle; this was just too funny. What kind of hick town had she found herself in? "No, sir. I haven't."

"Just out for a bike ride?"

Her defenses surged into place. "Yes, sir." She nervously licked her lips. He wasn't going to get too personal, was he?

A smile spread across the officer's face. "It's nice weather for it. Have a good day, miss. Welcome to Whitman." He touched the brim of his hat again and turned toward his parked car.

Paige blew out a breath. At least he didn't ask what she was doing in town. Although, he could be a reliable source to ask about rental properties. She groaned, then called after the officer. "Hey, um, I'm searching for a place to rent." *Great. Let's continue the conversation with the cop. That sounds like a good plan.*

He walked back in her direction. "Temporary or permanent?"

Paige cocked her head to the side and scrunched her nose. "Temporarily permanent?"

"I'll see what I can do. Can I get a number?"

She rattled off the ten digits, then chuckled. "I've never willingly given my number to a cop before." *That was a stupid thing to say.*

Officer Bryant raised an eyebrow as he typed her number into his cell phone. "Have you ever unwillingly?"

She held up her hand like swearing an oath. "I plead the fifth." *Yeah, because that won't make him suspicious at all.*

"Can I have a name to attach to that number?"

"Oh, um, Paige."

He typed on the screen, then put the phone back in his pocket. "I'll give you a call if I think of something, Paige. Later today or tomorrow. Right now, I've got to find that goat."

That's right. The goat. She'd forgotten what had started their conversation in the first place. "Good luck."

The officer returned to his unit. The engine turned over. He drove a short way down the road, then did a U-turn and passed her. She raised her hand as he waved, immediately scolding herself. She turned her bike and pedaled back toward town. She did not need the attention of the police. She still hadn't figured out the best way to find her birth mother.

Should she just walk up to people and ask if they knew a woman named Annie? That's what they'd do in a movie, right? But this wasn't a movie. This was real life and things didn't always work out so smoothly. She longed to have the mother she never knew wrap her in an embrace and tell her how sorry she was for letting her go—that it was the biggest mistake she'd ever made—but that might not actually be the case. What if she had been the product of rape or worse?

What if her presence stirred up bad memories for Annie? What if her birth mother was married with kids and had never told her family about her other daughter?

She should go back to Portland and pretend this never happened. Pretend she'd never found Annie's Bible in her attic. Pretend she'd never been given up for adoption. Pretend that a car crash had killed her parents just like she'd always believed. That Grandpa was Grandpa and Aunt Hattie was Aunt Hattie and none of this mess had ever taken place…

Buildings flew passed. Paige squeezed the brakes on her handlebars and slowed her pace. Coffee. She needed coffee. A nice cup of iced coffee always made things better.

A bell jingled as Paige entered the Rustic Cup. Two elderly men played a card game of some kind at a corner booth, but the rest of the place was deserted. Paintings, all for sale, lined the brick interior walls. She squinted and leaned in to catch the name of the artist. Someone named Lawrence Faye signed the bottom left corner of each painting. A young woman, wearing a hot pink hoodie and ear buds in her ears, balanced on a stool behind the counter and stared at the cell phone in her hands. A half-erased chalkboard advertised the café's various coffee drinks. By the remaining letters, Paige made out mocha, latte, cappuccino, decaf, and the word pastry, but it looked more like paste. Hopefully, the pastries didn't taste like paste. "Hello." Paige waved her hands. "I'd like to order."

The girl's head popped up. "Oh." She jerked the ear buds from her ears. "What can I get you?" She asked as she hopped from the stool. "We have fresh coffee, hot muffins, and delicious breakfast sandwiches. I know they're delicious 'cause I already tried one. Miss Jenn makes them fresh every morning. She has to get up at like four o'clock in the morning to make them."

"Wow, OK. May I have a caramel chocolate chip frappe?"

The girl stared blankly at Paige. "A what?"

She obviously doesn't know what a frappe is. Let's try something else. "How about an iced blended Grasshopper mocha?"

The girl's eyes grew wider than the cinnamon rolls in the pastry window. "You want grasshoppers in your coffee?"

Paige racked her fingers through her hair. Forget hick town, what planet had she landed on? "May I have a hot coffee with French vanilla creamer?"

The young barista smiled. "Sure. Regular or decaf? I'm more of a decaf girl. Mom says I'm already too hyper to drink regular."

I agree. "Regular, please."

The girl turned to fill a cup with hot coffee from a silver urn. "I haven't seen you before. You must be new."

"Yeah, I just rode in yesterday."

"Rode? Like on a horse?"

Is this kid for real? Paige shook her head. "The bus."

"Here's your drink. Can I get you anything else?"

The pastries in the glass case drew her eyes. Her stomach grumbled. The exercise had already burnt off her early breakfast. "Those orange scones look amazing."

"They're so delicious. Miss Jenn bakes everything from scratch. She's my boss. And the owner. She's not here today, though."

"Thanks. I'll try one."

"That'll be five seventy-five." Kylie put one of the scones in a brown paper sack and set it on the counter. Paige handed the barista her debit card. She swiped it and handed it back with a pen and the receipt for Paige to sign. "Welcome to Whitman, Paige. I'm Kylie Phillips."

The name was familiar. "Phillips? Like the Mayor?" The town of Whitman was inundated with political signs that read, Mayor Phillips for Governor. A Vote for Phillips is a Vote for Family. Paige scribbled her name across the bottom of the slip of paper and handed it and the pen back to the barista.

"That's my mom." Was that pride in her voice or something else? Paige squelched the urge to ask about Annie. This girl wouldn't know anything. Kylie Phillips looked like she was still in high school. She probably wasn't even alive twenty-five years ago, much less old enough to remember anyone.

The barista returned to her stool and put the ear buds back in her ears. Paige scooted into a bench seat under a portrait of a beaver, or woodchuck, since the water tower read, Whitman. Home of the Woodchucks. The fabric cushion had a rip in the middle, but otherwise seemed sturdy. She sipped her hot beverage, allowing the coffee to not only warm her chilled insides, but release the anxiety from her spirit. Emotionally, this venture had already been a lot harder than she'd expected, and she hadn't even begun her search. She thought on Aunt Hattie's advice. *Take things slow. Find your footing first. Get a feel for the town and the people there. When the time is right, then you can ask about Annie. Don't rush into something you'll regret later.*

Paige put a chunk of the scone in her mouth. It was sweet, tangy, and melted on her tongue. *The barista was right. That's so good.* Halfway through her pastry, the glass door opened, and the bell chimed. The goat-hunting officer entered and went straight for a table in the corner with a view of the whole café. Had he found the animal? He lifted his chin and surveyed the room. Paige caught his eye and gave a little wave. The officer frowned then turned his attention to a lady officer entering the café. She joined him, her back to Paige. He said something, and she glanced over her shoulder, making eye contact.

A familiar fluttering in her stomach began as Paige swallowed the last of her coffee. She grabbed her purse and left the coffee shop, dropping her cup in the trash can on the way out the door. A light drizzle had started while she was inside. *Why are they so suspicious? I haven't done anything. Why am I so jumpy?* She was reading too much into things. She was the one who was suspicious.

Paige sat down on the curb to retie the shoelace on her sneaker that had come undone. A dark shadow blocked the sun as someone stood over her. "Miss?"

The goat-hunter. She remembered his voice. "Yes, officer?" She hopped to her feet and brushed off her bottom. A knot clenched her stomach as her pulse increased. *Calm down. That was a long time ago, Paige, it has nothing to do with the present.* She was running her zipper up and down on her hoodie. She dropped her arms, clenching her palms at her sides.

The cop extended his hand. "Officer Hamilton Bryant. We met a little while ago." He flashed a charismatic smile in her direction. A woodsy oil slicked back his dark hair. Her image reflected in his pupils, like a mirror echoing her inner being. She stepped sideways, removing her reflection from his cornflower blue eyes. "You asked about a place to live?"

Paige nodded, her mouth was suddenly too dry to speak. Something about him stirred her. His uniform was crisp, clean, and well-fitting. His badge and his shoes polished to a shine. The crease down his pants legs formed a perfect perpendicular line. Everything about his image screamed perfectionist. She liked perfection. He was speaking again; his voice like melting butter on a fresh lobster roll from Tony's Crab Shack on the coast. *Stop that. He's a first responder. It's too risky, you know that.*

"My sister and brother-in-law rent out an apartment over their garage. The last renters left a week ago. Would you be interested?"

"Maybe. May I see it sometime?"

"We can drive out there now." He directed her to the police car parked nearby. He moved to the vehicle and opened the passenger door. Paige climbed in, leaving her bike in the rack on the street corner. She had never ridden in the front seat of a police car before, but the smells and the leather seat against her back resurrected a familiar ache. Paige shook off the feeling as Officer Bryant got in. "You all right?" His forehead creased with concern.

Paige buckled her seatbelt. "Just a sense of *déjà vu.*" An odd expression crossed his face, but if he was curious, he didn't ask what she meant.

He turned south onto the main thoroughfare, passing by a theater, the police station, and the "Espresso and Car Wash". *What a strange combination.* Farmland flashed past the tinted windows as they left the city limits and headed into the countryside.

After several minutes, the officer flipped on his blinker, slowed the vehicle, and turned onto a gravel road lined with a white picket fence. An evergreen hedge, large oak tree and an old-fashioned farmhouse came into view, reminding Paige of a story-book home. When the patrol car rolled to a stop, a big dog loped around the side of the house. Officer Bryant opened his door and stepped out, then scuffled his fingers through the labradoodle's tightly-curled fur as the dog licked his face. "Hey, Bruce, how are you today?" Paige opened her door. The dog was panting loud enough for her to hear from the other side of the car. His tail wagged like a windshield wiper during a deluge. He caught sight of Paige and raced around the car, leaping forward and knocking her to the ground. His rough, slobbery tongue removed the makeup from half of her face. "Whoa, boy. Nice to meet you too." Paige laughed and gave the dog a shove. "Friendly, isn't he?"

Officer Bryant offered her a hand. "Probably the friendliest dog in all of Wallowa County, but he makes a good guard dog, too. Dogs have excellent intuitions. He must have a good feeling about you." Paige used her sleeve to wipe the slobber from her face. Officer Bryant gestured toward a two-story garage and she followed. Bruce jogged close to their heels. "The stairs run down the outside here." He pointed at a steep staircase with a railing on the left side of the building, shaded by a line of tall trees and thick bushes. When they reached the top, he removed a key from under the welcome mat and unlocked the door.

Paige stood, flabbergasted. That would never work in a city like Portland. "Do people here always keep their spare keys under their doormats?"

He flashed her a grin. "Whitman is the safest town I know. Crime is pretty rare, if I do say so myself." He dusted his shoulder with a wink. "The Whitman PD is always ready to serve and protect." He pushed open the apartment door with a flourish. Paige stepped onto the tile in the foyer. When her fingers flipped the switch, light flooded the fully furnished room. "Wow." Paige instantly liked what she saw. The apartment was well-kept and smelled fresh.

A living room and eat-in kitchen made up the main room. She found two bedrooms and a bathroom down a short hallway. The apartment wasn't huge, but it was sufficient for her needs, especially with the furnishing. She checked around the kitchen. The cabinets were loaded with pots and pans, and in one of the drawers, she found potholders and towels. "Your sister thought of everything."

Officer Bryant glanced around the room and nodded. "Are you interested?"

"How soon can I fill out an application?" She could hardly contain her excitement. This place was exactly what she was looking for.

Officer Bryant opened the front door and Paige followed him outside, then he switched off the lights and locked the door before he spoke. "My sister is the principal of our school. We can go over there now if you want." He slipped the key back under the mat and led the way down the stairs.

"If it's not too much trouble. I'd appreciate it."

They returned to the patrol car, and Officer Bryant drove back into town. On the way to the school, they passed by Whitman City Hall and Wallowa County Courthouse. The giant building, with its clock tower, filled most of the block. On the opposite side of the street, she caught sight of a hair salon called Curl Up and Dye, and next to that, The

Bookshelf. She'd have to check that one out later for sure. With a quick glance down a side street, she spied the fire department and another interesting store called Junk Monkey Antiques.

A long brick building surrounded by a chain-link fence with several pieces of playground equipment and what looked like a track or football field, or both, came into view. Officer Bryant parallel parked along the street, and Paige exited the car onto the grassy right-of-way. "Which school is this? Elementary? Middle?"

Officer Bryant shut his door. "All of them."

Paige ran her eyes along the building again and stopped at the concrete sign that read, Whitman School. Home of the Woodchucks. "Wait, so this is the only school in Whitman?"

"Only public school."

What kind of bucolic town only needed one school? Paige's graduating class alone had had over six hundred students.

They crossed the blacktop and entered through the glass doors. Officer Bryant waved at the secretary inside the office. Paige stopped. "Do I need to sign in or anything?"

Officer Bryant raised an eyebrow. "I'm pretty sure I can vouch for you."

"No metal detectors? Bag checks?"

"Like I told you, Whitman is a safe place to live," he called over his shoulder as he headed down one of the halls.

She studied the inside of the school as she followed his long-legged strides. Large doors partitioned the building into elementary, middle, and high school. The bulletin boards changed as they crossed from one school into another. They passed a glass cabinet filled with plaques and trophies. Large, framed photos decorated the walls. Paige slowed her steps. "Who are all these people?" She stopped to read. *Graduating class of 2017.*

Officer Bryant walked back to where she had stopped. "Oh, these. Senior photos of every person who has ever graduated from Whitman School. It goes all the way back to the thirties or forties when they started doing this."

Paige's eyes flicked back and forth across the miniature photographs, studying the faces. Had her birth mother attended this school? Was her photo on a wall somewhere? Her nose stung as tears welled up in her eyes. She changed the subject before Officer Bryant noticed. "Is your photo up there somewhere?"

"Yeah, it's there somewhere. I was a dork back then."

"How many students have graduated from Whitman School?"

"All of them."

Bewildered, Paige shook her head. "Huh?"

Officer Bryant puffed with community pride again. "One hundred percent graduation rate, with the exception of the rare expulsion."

"Wow."

"We also have one of the lowest teacher-to-student ratios in the state. One to thirteen." He started moving again, and Paige followed him down to the end of the hallway. A door with black letters. Rebecca Thorne, Principal.

Suddenly, she was in elementary school again, sent to the principal's office for sticking gum in Amanda Pillow's hair. Amanda had deserved it—well, maybe.

They entered what appeared to be a secretary's office, then Officer Bryant opened an interior door. A slender woman with black hair and a black suit sat behind a desk. She stood to her feet as they entered the room. She had the same piercing eyes as her brother. She rounded her desk and gave the policeman a hug. "Hey Hambone." She stepped back. "Who's this?"

Hambone? Paige refrained from releasing the chuckle that was building in her chest. She cleared her throat and held out her hand. "Paige McDonald."

The woman smiled Hamilton's same charismatic smile and squeezed Paige's hand. "Rebecca Thorne. Most people call me Becky. Principal by day. Real estate agent by night."

Officer Bryant leaned on the edge of the desk. "Miss McDonald is needing a place to live temporarily. I showed her the apartment."

Becky returned to her seat. "What did you think?"

Paige remained standing. "I liked it very much. I don't know how long I'll be in town, but I'm interested in renting it while I'm here."

Becky opened a desk drawer and pulled out a stapled bunch of papers. "Sure, we can work something out. I prefer a six-month commitment, but if you pay in advance, I can do month to month. It's six seventy-five a month plus utilities."

That's it? An apartment that nice in Portland would cost an arm and a leg, and probably a kidney, too. "That's doable."

Becky held the papers out over the desk. "This is the application. Just your basic stuff. Credit check. Background check. Previous addresses."

Paige gulped. *Background check. How thorough would Becky Thorne be?* Maybe she was better off at the hotel. However, if she changed her mind now, she would seem suspicious. She'd just have to go through with it and hope Becky abode by privacy laws, especially considering her brother was a cop. She accepted the papers Officer Bryant passed along. "How quickly will I know if I'm approved?"

"How quickly can you write?" Becky smiled. "As soon as you fill out those documents, I can run them through my tenant screening program, but you should be fine. I mean, you're not a felon, are you?"

Paige smiled at the joke, knowing Becky had no idea how close she was to the truth. "I can fill them out right now."

"You can use the teacher's lounge right across the hall."

A garbled voice came over Officer Bryant's radio. He pulled the microphone from his shoulder and stepped outside the door.

Paige shook Becky's hand. "I appreciate the opportunity to rent the apartment. You have a lovely home."

"Thank you. Just drop those papers off with my secretary when you're done. I hope to see you again soon."

Officer Bryant poked his head in the doorway. "Sorry, sis. Miss McDonald. I've gotta run. Becky, could you give Miss McDonald a ride back to the café?"

Paige waved her hand before Becky could answer. "That's OK, really. I'll just walk." Paige followed Officer Bryant out the door. He turned and jogged down the hallway. *I wonder what's come up.* She shook her head, turning her attention back to her own business. She entered the empty teacher's lounge and took a seat. After she filled out the application for the apartment, she dropped it off with the secretary who had returned.

She mapped the way on her phone back to the Rustic Cup to retrieve her bicycle. What to do with herself for the rest of the day? And where should she begin her search for her birth mother?

7

An hour later, Hamilton snapped his laptop shut as he finished typing his report from the traffic accident at the corner of Harwood and 5th Street. The drivers involved had pulled their vehicles into the nearby gas station parking lot, but there was still a dispute over who'd caused the fender bender. After speaking with both drivers and the witnesses, the guilty party was determined, and insurance information exchanged without further disagreement. Another open-shut case typical of the good-hearted citizens of Whitman.

Although, some law enforcement officers preferred the fast-paced, high stress city beats, not him. His was a quiet, predictable career—until today. While he had no aspirations to become a detective, he had to admit that Paige McDonald fired up his inquisitive nature. She seemed like a respectable woman, but then again, there were her comments when giving him her phone number and having a *déjà vu* moment when sitting in the patrol unit. He could see no viable reason to run a background check on her, but he was intrigued. *Who is Paige McDonald?*

Becky's tenant checks were thorough. She wouldn't let

just anyone gain such close access to her home and children. But if she did rent out the garage apartment to Miss McDonald, he was sure to gain the opportunity he needed to find out more about her.

His stomach rumbled, and he glanced at the clock on his dashboard. He was due for a lunch break, but he needed to check back with dispatch first. "Officer Bryant. Patrol Unit Two. Ten twenty-two. Assignment complete. Permission Code seven. Can I go to lunch?"

Kelly at dispatch came over the radio. "Officer Bryant. Negative. We've got a ten ninety-nine at the Whitman Museum."

"Ten seventeen. I am in route. Ten four."

A robbery? In Whitman? Hamilton couldn't recall anything bigger than a convenience store robbery in all his years on Whitman's police force. He put the cruiser into gear and sped toward the museum on Ironwood Street. He pulled into a space in the parking lot, then exited the vehicle, and bounded up the stairs of the stone building, entering through the front door.

Alexander Pendleton, the museum curator, wrung his hands and paced the lobby floor. He stopped in his tracks when he spotted Hamilton. "Aye. Goodness gracious, you are finally here. I'm in such a panic. I don't know what to do. I would never have imagined in all my born days that anything like this would happen in Whitman, of all places on God's green earth."

Hamilton removed his regulation cover and tucked it under his arm, then took his notepad from his duty belt and flipped to an empty page. He pulled the pencil from his pocket and licked the end. "Mr. Pendleton. Can you tell me what happened?"

"Aye. Goodness gracious. They waited until I closed the museum for the dinner. I've been going home every day at the same time for fifty-seven years. My wife, she prepares the best Irish stew in all of Oregon."

"Mr. Pendleton. The robbery?" Hamilton attempted to keep the excitable Irishman focused.

"Oh, of course. When I returned from my dinner, the back door was left ajar. Someone had jimmied the lock. They are old locks, you know. It don't take much—*schoop*—right open they come."

He wouldn't allow the old man's bunny trails to try his patience, but he did need to find some way to streamline this conversation. "Mr. Pendleton, what did they take?"

"Aye. Goodness gracious. They got the journals."

Hamilton raised an eyebrow. "Journals?"

"Aye. The journals of Captain Joshua Gottfried. He fought in the war against the Nez Perce tribe in 1877. He wrote of his experiences in journals and they were donated to the museum in the 1930s by his great-granddaughter Alice Gottfried. The Gottfried's settled this area back in 1890, or was it 1880?"

"Mr. Pendleton." Hamilton spoke with force. "Were they valuable?"

"Aye. Goodness gracious. Of course, they were valuable. Our history is most valuable. Folks don't appreciate it like they used to. We can hardly get folks to visit the museum. Aye. If we could just instill in the young people an appreciation for those who've gone before—"

"Monetarily, Mr. Pendleton. Were they valuable monetarily?" Alexander Pendleton could talk the hind leg off that goat they'd found eating Mrs. Keith's shrubs.

"I dunno. I'll have to check me records. If you'll follow me to the office, I'll take a look-see."

They went through a molded oak door on the left of the lobby into the curator's office. Filing cabinets and boxes of historical artifacts stuffed the chaotic room. Mr. Pendleton dug through a series of folders before finding the right documents. "Aye. Goodness gracious. It says here that the journals value at five thousand dollars."

$5,000. It was enough to open a case file. Was that all that

had been stolen? Certainly, there were other valuables in the museum. Hamilton circled the office, giving everything in the room a once-over. "Mr. Pendleton, are you sure the journals are the only thing missing?" He picked up a wooden box painted as black as a moonless night.

"Aye. Goodness gracious. I keep me 1943 copper wheat pennies in that box. I took it from the safe to show the professor. I'll put it back now." The old man reached out to take the box from Hamilton.

"Just a minute, Mr. Pendleton. Who's the professor?"

"An avid coin collector." Mr. Pendleton reached for the box again.

Hamilton opened the lid. He turned the box to show Mr. Pendleton the empty space inside. "How valuable were those pennies?"

The old man's face paled. He swayed and eased himself into his office chair. "I—I—Goodness gracious—seemed so nice. So professional. I don't—I don't understand."

"Mr. Pendleton, how valuable?" He worked hard to keep impatience out of his voice.

"Aye. Goodness gracious. Each one is selling for sixty to eighty-five thousand dollars at auction."

Bingo. Now that's more like it. "Has this professor visited here before?"

"I've never seen her before."

Her? The earth shifted beneath his feet. "What did she look like?"

Mr. Pendleton leaned back in the chair and pinched the bridge of his nose. "I dunno. If I's remembering correctly, she had hair the color of corn silk and eyes that sparkled like sapphires. She said she was new in town and wouldn't be a 'staying long."

Hamilton had barely finished his report back at the station when Chief House signaled from his office. "Officer

Bryant." The forcible man strode toward him as Hamilton stood to his feet.

"Yes, sir."

"Our victim's name is Mario Montory. The mother saw it on the news and called in this morning. The kid's out of surgery and awake. I want you to head over there now and find out what he remembers about the other night." He dropped a manila folder on Hamilton's desk. "Kid's got a record."

"Yes, chief."

Hamilton entered the hospital room to find the young man propped up in bed, pillows on both sides. The top half of a light blue gown ended where a blanket covered his legs. According to the medical report, one bullet had gone clean through his side while the other had lodged in his upper thigh. The doctor had to remove it surgically. The boy had been running when someone shot him.

Hamilton replayed the police record through his mind. Nineteen years old, Latino, resident of Whitman. Whitman School had expelled him three years ago. He'd had several run-ins with the law: joy-riding, speeding, and possession. Mom was unemployed. Dad worked as a bagger at the grocery store.

Mario Montory fiddled with the edge of the blanket. His eyes stared out the window. The open blinds revealed a rainstorm on the other side, and a grayish cloud cover hid the mountains from view. Hamilton perched on a stool beside the bed and held out his hand. "Officer Bryant. How are you today, Mario?"

The boy turned his head and fixed his eyes on Hamilton's outstretched hand. "Get to the point. I know why you're here."

"Okay then." He crossed one leg over his knee and leaned back on the stool. "Let's cut to the chase."

"I'm not telling you anything."

"How about you tell me what you were doing outside the

church at twenty forty-five Wednesday night?"

"Huh?"

"Eight forty-five pm."

Mario looked back at the window. He muttered under his breath—in Spanish. "I'm not talking." Sweat beaded at his hairline. His fingers continued picking at the fuzz on the blanket.

"What were you doing in the church parking lot? Were you buying drugs?"

The young man turned sharply. "No! I don't do that no more."

Hamilton held up his palms. "Okay. Okay. I'm just trying to get to the bottom of this. Who were you running from?"

Mario didn't respond.

"Are you afraid to talk to me?" Mario's eye twitched. "What are you afraid of, Mario? Did someone threaten you?"

"Get out of my face. I'm not saying nothing."

Hamilton left the room, pulled out his cell phone, and dialed the station. "Hey Lil. Big surprise. Kid won't talk."

"That's not a surprise."

He chuckled at her response. "I've got to think on this some more. I think he was scared to talk to me. Maybe someone threatened him if he goes to the police." He ended the call, then went to the nearest nurses' station. "Hey Rosa, has anyone else been here to see Mario Montory?"

The nurse on duty clicked her tongue. "Let me think. No one yet this morning. His parents came yesterday of course, but they haven't been in yet. One other visitor, I think. Yes, his priest came to see him. Father Hernandez."

He pulled his notepad from his utility belt. "Do you remember what he looked like?"

The nurse raised her eyebrow. "Like a priest?"

"Thanks." Hamilton put the notepad away and snapped the cover in place, then he jogged out to his patrol car and turned on his laptop. A quick Internet search was all he needed. *Father Hernandez?* A quick scan of the screen revealed what he'd already anticipated. There was no record of a Father Hernandez living anywhere in the state of Oregon. Father Hernandez was fake. Who really came to see the boy? And why did they threaten him?

Hamilton leaned back against the headrest to think. Someone had shot the boy while he was running. They shot to slow him down, but not to kill him. Why? Then, they show up at the hospital pretending to be a priest and threaten the boy if he talks to the police. They were missing something important about this case, but what?

Movement at the hospital's sliding glass door caught his attention. Paige McDonald, exited the building, looking pale and disoriented. She had adhesive tape wrapped around her upper arm. He opened his door and called to her over the top of the patrol car. "You feel okay?"

The young woman shook her head and wobbled off the curb. Hamilton stepped out of the car and caught Paige before she fell. "You want to sit down a minute?"

She nodded. "I gave blood. I'm woozier than I expected." The Red Cross was hosting a blood drive at the local hospital. The posters were all over town. He opened the passenger door and guided her into the seat. She let out a sigh, then put her head between her knees. "I don't feel so good."

"Your blood sugar is low. Have you had anything to eat?"

"No. I was going to get lunch afterward."

Hamilton checked the time on his phone. *It's after fifteen hundred hours.* "Let me take you somewhere. Get you some food before you pass out."

She raised her head. Her face was as white as a sheet. "What about my bike?"

"I'll drop you off here after lunch. Will that work?"

Paige flopped toward the floorboard. *I'll take that as a yes.* He jogged around to the driver's side and got in, then he put the car in gear and drove down the street. He parked in one of the spaces on Main Street, then opened the door for Paige. She stumbled out of the car, and he caught her against his chest. Her blue eyes stood out against her pale cheeks. This close he could smell her shampoo. He steadied her and moved away with an awkward chuckle. He had to get some food in her ASAP. They sat at his usual booth, and Kylie met them with her usual plucky self. She reminded him of his sister's dog, Bruce, the blond labradoodle. "Hello, Officer Bryant. What can I get you?"

"Hey, Kylie, may we have some coffee?"

"Sure. Regular or decaf."

"Decaf, with plenty of sugar. And we'll have two of those lunch specials."

"Over and out, Officer Bryant." Kylie giggled and bounded into the kitchen.

Paige spoke from where her head rested on the tabletop. "She's a perky girl."

"She's a good kid. Her mother's the mayor. They live in that mansion you were gawking at this morning."

Her pale cheeks flushed a rosy pink. "Sorry."

"No, it's okay. Lots of people stop and stare at that house. It stands out like a sore thumb."

Kylie brought the coffee, and Paige straightened in her seat. "Thank you."

"Your lunch will be out in a few minutes."

Hamilton sipped the hot coffee. "Mm, thanks Kylie. It's perfect." She blushed at his compliment and fluttered away.

Paige took a drink, then added some of the powdered creamer available at the tables. "The mayor is Kathleen Phillips, right? Isn't she running for governor?"

"Uh huh," he answered before taking another swig of the dark liquid. "She's following her father's career path."

"Her father?"

"Former governor Richard Staten. He was originally from Whitman."

Paige sat her cup down with a thud. A little of the coffee splattered over the edge. She grabbed a paper napkin and sopped up the mess. "Richard Staten. As in Minotaur

Staten?"

Kylie stopped beside the table, her hands loaded with their plates of food. "That's my grandfather."

"Oh, sorry." Paige's neck grew warm. She hadn't meant to insult Kylie's family.

"No problem. Body of a man. Head of a bull. He was a regular beast in the capital and in the courtroom, until he found Jesus, that is."

"Found Jesus?" Paige's forehead crinkled with confusion.

"Became a Christian."

"Oh."

If Paige didn't know what that meant, I wonder if she's not a Christian.

With that, Kylie wandered off to take orders from the other customers.

"Are you a Christian, Miss McDonald?"

Paige's eyes widened. "Me?"

He nodded.

"No. I've never been religious. My grandpa didn't go to church either." She squirmed on the bench. Her skin turned red at her neckline.

He'd made her uncomfortable. He turned the conversation back to Kylie's grandfather. "You're not old enough to remember Richard Staten as the governor, how did you know his nickname?" Hamilton put some ketchup on his fries and stuck them in his mouth. This was his second lunch for today, but he didn't want Paige to eat alone. He'd gone through a drive-through on his way from the museum back to the station.

She seemed to hesitate. "My civics class at college. He wasn't a well-liked man from what I remember."

"No. Mayor Phillips has her work cut out for her. There's a lot of people who don't want to see her win this next election." Whitman PD was attempting to offer protection, but so far, Madam Mayor was being less than cooperative.

As they ate silently for the next several minutes, he

watched the girl across from him, and in his mind drew a quick sketch. Shoulder-length blond hair, bright blue eyes, five feet four inches tall, about one hundred fifteen pounds, willowy, well-toned—like she did some sort of exercise on a regular basis. What was she doing in Whitman? How long did she plan to stay? It was time he found out. "Where are you from?"

She bit the club sandwich, chewed, then swallowed. "Portland."

He picked up his coffee cup and signaled for Kylie to bring him a refill. "What have you been doing this afternoon? Besides giving blood, of course."

"I spent a couple of hours at the library. I can't check anything out yet, but I used the computer for a while, researched some things on microfiche, and checked out the rare book room." Paige chuckled. "I have a thing for dusty, old books."

Microfiche? That's interesting. Not many people use that anymore. Microfiche allowed numerous images to be stored via photographic film. A special machine was needed to view the tiny pictures. People used it for research and to read through old documents like newspapers, catalogs, journals… *Journals like the ones stolen from the museum today?* "What brings you to Whitman?" He watched for signs of distress or dishonesty. She fiddled with her fork and glanced repeatedly around the room. Her voice raised in pitch as she answered, "I'm—I'm—" *She's hiding something, but what?* Hamilton opened his mouth to ask another question.

"Sunday, Monday, Happy Days. Tuesday, Wednesday, Happy Days."

He shut his mouth and glanced around the restaurant. Where was that music coming from?

Paige pulled a cell phone from her coat pocket and swiped across the screen, putting it to her ear. "Hello."

She paused. "Yes." Hamilton could hear a mumbled voice coming from the phone. "Um, well, I…" *Her eyes shifted.*

She's hesitating. Who's on the other end of the line? "Sure, dinner sounds great." Paige ended the call then laid her phone face-down on the table. "Becky said I can rent the apartment. I'm having dinner at their house tonight."

"I'm glad things are working out. You'll really enjoy living in Whitman for however long you decide to stay." He was baiting her. Would she bite? *Give me something to work with here.*

Kylie interrupted. "Are you all finished?"

"Yeah, we're all done. Thanks, Kylie. I'll take care of the bill." *She slipped the hook this time.*

Paige gathered her purse from the bench. "Are you sure? I'm happy to pay for my own."

"Don't worry about it. I've got it."

"Thank you, Officer Bryant. You didn't have to do that, though I appreciate the lunch. I guess I'll see you around."

Hamilton opened his wallet and pulled out his debit card. "Want a ride back to the hospital?"

"No, thanks. I'll manage."

He turned to pay at the cash register. The bell jingled. When he glanced back over his shoulder, she was gone.

Paige kicked herself all the way down the sidewalk. If she rented the apartment, it would guarantee her chances of running into Officer Bryant again. However, another opportunity like this might not come along. The apartment was comfortable, fully furnished, and it didn't have noisy neighbors blasting the TV all hours of the night. Besides, if she backed out now, it was sure to stir Officer Bryant's suspicion, and that was something she wanted to prevent at all cost. How would she have answered if her phone hadn't interrupted at that moment? *I just need to be more careful and limit my interactions with Officer Bryant.*

8

Just before 6:30 that evening, she rang the doorbell on the Thorne's farmhouse. Bruce barked on the other side of the door, announcing her arrival. Mrs. Becky Thorne opened while holding back the excitable canine. "Sorry, he loves visitors."

"It's OK. We've met. Hi Bruce." Paige held out her hand to the dog's nose. Bruce sniffed, then slurped her fingers. When Becky let go of his collar, he jumped up and put his feet on Paige's baby blue sweater and white bohemian skirt.

Becky called over her shoulder. "Tyler, put the dog outside, please."

A teenage boy carrying a handheld gaming system bounded down the stairs two at a time. "Got it, Mom."

"Follow me." Paige followed Becky through the house. The front door shut, then thudding echoed on the stairs. Two younger boys came running around the corner, nearly plowing into the two women. Becky grabbed one of the boys by the collar of his shirt. He stumbled backward as his chase came to a sudden halt. "Hey, what have I said about running in the house?"

"But Mom, Timmy stole my Ducks cap."

Becky called down the hallway where the smaller boy had disappeared. "Timothy, give Tony his hat." She let go of the boy's shirt.

He dodged the living room furniture and ducked around the corner. A "Mom said to give it back!" faded as he disappeared out of sight.

Becky entered the kitchen and opened the fridge. "Can I get you something to drink, a soda pop or something?"

"Sure. I'll have a pop." Becky pulled a cold can from the shelf and slid it across the island in Paige's direction. "How many children do you have?"

Becky snapped open a can for herself. "You've met them all. Tyler, Tony, and Timothy. My husband wanted to keep trying for a girl, but I was afraid we'd end up with a whole houseful of boys. I love them, but some days… you see these gray hairs?" She leaned forward and pointed at the top of her head. "I've got three of them, named Tyler, Tony, and Timothy." Becky was as animated as her three sons. She started pulling bowls from the cabinets and ingredients from the fridge. "I hope you like meatloaf because that's what I'm making." She raised her voice and called out, "David!"

A clean-shaven man wearing sweat pants and a T-shirt popped out of a room adjoining the kitchen. "Yes, honey."

"Would you fetch another bottle of ketchup from the downstairs pantry? The boys finished this one already."

David offered his hand to Paige before he went to get the requested condiment. "Dave Thorne, I'm Becky's husband."

"Paige McDonald. I'm renting your garage apartment."

"It's nice to meet you, Miss McDonald. I'm gonna go get the ketchup before Becky works herself into a frenzy." He grinned lovingly at his wife then disappeared down the basement steps.

Paige perched on an orange plastic stool. "May I help?"

"Can you chop onions?" She set a cutting board and knife in front of Paige.

"Yes."

"Here." She tossed a sweet yellow onion in Paige's direction. Paige caught it just before it rolled off the counter, then she peeled back the skin and worked at chopping the vegetable with the chef's knife. At some point, a bottle of ketchup appeared on the counter. She hadn't seen Dave return from the basement, but TV sounds came from the room she assumed was a den. When she finished chopping the onion, Becky took the cutting board and knife and with a swish swiped the pieces into a big bowl filled with raw hamburger meat.

"Anyone home?" A male voice echoed through the house.

Becky leaned back from the counter where she was shredding cheddar cheese. "In the kitchen, Hambone."

Officer Bryant appeared in the archway between the kitchen and living room. "Hey, who let you in here?" He said to Paige with a grin.

"Ignore him. He's the party crasher."

"I'm not a party crasher. You said I was welcome anytime."

His sister washed her hands under the sink, then dried them on a dish towel. "Did I? I must have forgotten." She winked at Paige. Paige loved the way they bantered back and forth. As an only child she'd spent her days doing solitary activities. If her birth mother had kept her, would she have grown up with siblings, instead of spending so much time alone?

The officer scooted a stool away from the island. Timothy, the youngest Thorne son, raced around the corner and into his uncle's outstretched arms. "Uncle Ham!"

Officer Bryant grunted as he scooped Timmy onto his lap. "Whaddya got there?"

"It's a keychain. Tony traded it to me for a Ducks hat."

"But wasn't that cap already his?"

Timothy nodded his head like a dashboard bobble-head.

"Yep!" Officer Bryant released the boy, and he scrambled out of the kitchen.

"I tell you, Becky, we've got to keep our eyes on that one."

"Don't I know it." Becky scratched her nose on her sleeve. She dropped the grated cheese into the bowl with the other ingredients. "Oh, hey, would you go into my office and get that rental agreement for Paige? She might as well look it over while dinner cooks. It's still going to be a while."

Becky's office was as trashed as her teenage son's bedroom. There were papers scattered everywhere. And the sad part? Her home office was always like this, where she didn't have a personal secretary keeping everything organized for her. *If I was a rental agreement, where would I be?* Hamilton unclipped his necktie and jammed it into his pocket, then unbuttoned his collar. This little room was like an oven all year 'round, but it was the only private room his sister could use for her real estate business. David had claimed the den for his man cave and the boys had commandeered the basement for a playroom. He shuffled through the stacks of papers on his sister's computer desk, but he didn't find anything with Paige's name on it. He turned, and a manila folder on top of the printer caught his attention. He picked it up and flipped the folder open. *This looks like Paige's application.* He rustled through the papers, scanning the documents. His eyes fell on words he'd trained them to spot. Even if he wanted to, he couldn't unsee them. If the folder had been a door, he would have slammed it.

He returned it to its place on top of the printer and stepped back. The contract rested in the printer tray, the blanks filled in with black ink. He snatched the paper and hurried back to the kitchen.

"Did you have any trouble?" Becky asked as soon as he

entered.

"No. No, trouble at all. Here." He jabbed the paper toward Miss McDonald, working to keep the tension from his voice.

"Thank you." Paige took the document from his hand. Without another word, he turned to join Dave in the den watching baseball. Maybe watching his favorite team crush Dave's favorite team would release the tension building in the back of his neck.

An hour later, they sat at the rustic dining table. A buck shoulder mount kept watch from over the doorway. The three young boys all talked at once, their hands reaching in complete disorder for scoops of mashed potatoes, rolls, and corn. David sliced the meatloaf and loaded large squares onto each plate as it was passed.

Officer Bryant seemed to sulk at the foot of the table. His nephews, Tony to his left and Tyler to his right, tried to draw their uncle into conversation, but he answered with more grunts than actual words. Paige accepted the plate offered her, loaded with more food than she could possibly eat, and set it down on the table. She picked up her fork and scooped up the creamy potatoes.

"Miss McDonald, my daddy still has to say grace." Timothy's high-pitched voice spoke from opposite her seat. Paige's cheeks flushed as she laid the fork on her plate. *Say grace? That's what some people call prayer at meals, right?* The others folded their hands and closed their eyes. She followed suit.

David Thorne's voice bounced off the walls as if he wanted it to reach all the way to Heaven. "Dear Lord, thank you for your many blessings and for the bounty you have provided…" Paige peeked under her eyelids. Officer Bryant stared at her, his head neither bowed nor his eyes closed. She squirmed in her seat. She hadn't had an officer scowl at her like that since she'd been ten minutes late to a meeting with her probation officer.

After the prayer ended, Paige tried to focus on her food, taking bites of meatloaf and potatoes. She glanced out of her peripheral. Officer Bryant was eating, but he kept his eyes trained on the side of her face. It was disconcerting the way he glared at her. *What did I do?* She tried to ignore the heat from the cop's eyes. "Everything is delicious. Thank you, Becky."

"So, what brings you to our little town?" Becky asked.

Paige swallowed as the room blurred. "I'm... I'm..." She took a swig of icy water from her glass, giving herself a moment to think. "I'm considering a move here." The total belief on their faces drove a knife into Paige's stomach. She poked at the ketchup topping on the meatloaf with the tines of her fork.

"What can we do to convince you to stay?" David Thorne spoke from the head of the table. He wiped his mouth with a paper napkin and folded it beside his plate. He leaned back in his seat, his gut spilling over his belt buckle.

"Since you all have so kindly provided me with a place to stay,"—she smiled to express her thanks—"I guess it depends if I can find a job."

"What did you do before?" The question came from Officer Bryant. It was the first time he'd spoken to her since bringing the rental contract from Becky's office.

"I was—well, I worked at Powell's City of Books in Portland."

"Powell's Books huh?"

She nodded, then stuffed a bite of mashed potatoes into her mouth. They were softer and creamier than any she'd ever had. Her grandfather, well, Benjamin McDonald had been a decent cook, and Aunt Hattie was—Aunt Hattie. Becky and Officer Bryant exchanged silent looks. Her eyes begged. He shook his head. Paige swallowed. "Did I miss something?"

"No," Officer Bryant answered.

Becky held out her hand. "What my brother means to say?" She shot a frown in his direction. "We have an old family friend who is struggling to run a bookstore in town. I'm sure she could use your expertise."

"I've passed a bookstore, The Bookshelf, on my way around town. Is that the one?"

Becky and David nodded. Officer Bryant looked like a pouty child who didn't get his way. What was that guy's problem? "Thank you. I'll check it out tomorrow."

"Did you shoot any bad guys today, Uncle Ham?" Timothy shot an imaginary gun with his finger.

Officer Bryant turned his attention to the boy. "No. Not today." The little boy's chin dipped.

"Police officers don't want to shoot people, Doofus," the Thorne's oldest boy, Tyler, said.

"Not unless we have to."

"Don't call your brother names. It's not nice."

The middle child, Tony, swallowed a large bite of meatloaf. "Did anyone shoot at you, Uncle Hamilton?" The boys' eyes turned expectedly on their cherished uncle's face, their very breath hanging with anticipation on his next words.

"No. No one shot at me." The boys groaned, but Becky's sigh of relief was heard audibly.

"Have you ever been shot at?" Somehow the question slipped from her lips even though Paige knew the answer. When Officer Bryant's eyebrows arched into his forehead, she wished she could take it back.

"Of course, Miss McDonald. I'm a Law Enforcement Officer. It's part of the risk."

"But why? Why risk it? No one asked you to."

An uncomfortable silence swept over the room. The cuckoo clock on the wall ticked past the minutes. "You're right, Miss McDonald. No one asked me to. I don't have to be a cop, but I don't know if I could look myself in the mirror if I quit. People out there need me."

She couldn't help herself. The pain of loss sprang up like a geyser from the deepest depths of her aching soul. "What about the people in this room? Don't they need you? Isn't your family more important than a bunch of strangers? These people obviously love you, but you would risk your life for those who don't give one hoot whether you live or die?"

Officer Bryant stood to his feet. He tossed his napkin on the table. "My family matters the world to me, but each one understands why I do what I do. Those people out there are not strangers, they are an extension of my family—my community, my neighbors. I care about what happens to them, too."

Tears threatened to spill down her cheeks. She took a slow, deep breath. "Thank you for dinner, Becky. I think I'll head back to the hotel now." She pushed her chair back from the table. David and Becky rose to their feet. The boys watched the adults with wide eyes.

"You're welcome. I can have that key ready for you as soon as your check clears. It'll be Tuesday. The bank isn't open on the weekends and Monday is a holiday, of course."

"That's fine." Paige crossed to the door and set her hand on the handle. "Thank you again. Goodnight." She opened the door, then stepped out into the crisp night air. She went to her bike and leaned against the metal frame.

A voice called out. "Miss McDonald." Officer Bryant strode quickly toward her. Should she make a break for it? Would that be running from the police? Maybe it didn't count if they weren't on duty or trying to make an arrest. Paige swung her leg over and sat on the leather seat. He grabbed the handlebars. "I think we got off on the wrong foot."

"Don't worry about it, Officer Bryant, I—"

"Becky made pie. She wants you to come back in and enjoy some."

"No thanks, officer. I'm going back to the hotel."

He leaned forward. When the sides of his jacket parted, she saw the black grip of his weapon. His voice dropped to a whisper. "Miss McDonald, I know you're up to something. People leave Whitman, they don't move here."

Paige stuttered for an answer. Could she trust him with the truth? "It's personal." It wasn't a lie.

The officer stepped back and dropped his arms. "I've been hearing that a lot lately." He looked far from convinced, but he sighed and said, "At least allow me to give you a ride into town. Becky will murder me if I let you ride your bike in the dark out here."

Beyond the driveway, the countryside was pitch black. "I have lights and reflectors. I'll be fine."

"Will you please come inside and eat pie before you leave? I'm making an effort here for Becky's sake."

If this woman was to be her landlord, she wanted to stay on her good side, otherwise she wouldn't have cared one way or another. "All right. For Becky's sake." She wasn't sure what her next step would be, but one thing was for sure, she needed to avoid Hamilton Bryant as much as possible.

9

Saturday morning, Hamilton woke before his alarm. He couldn't get Paige McDonald off his mind, and her rental of the garage apartment only added to his concern. After Paige had left, he'd tried to reason with Becky and David. He'd admitted to reading the background check, which only fueled his sister's ire. It was against the law for her to discriminate against potential tenants based on their past, but he didn't like the idea of Paige living so close to his family. Something had brought her to Whitman and he was going to find out what that something was.

Opening day of the weekly Farmer's Market was a major event in town each year and it included the annual Vintage Junktique. He personally didn't get the fascination with someone else's leftover junk. Although, he was attached to his grandfather's old truck, it wasn't random. He had a sentimental connection to the rusting heap of metal.

He rolled over and groaned, scrubbing his hand over his face. After a bowl of cereal, he dressed in his uniform, then drove across town to Sacajawea Park. He rolled down the window of his patrol car and breathed in the smell of the overnight rain. The grass was still wet, and puddles spotted the road, but the sun shimmered in a cloudless sky. He parked the cruiser, then unloaded his supplies from the trunk: boxes of McGruff coloring books and honorary deputy badges.

"Mountain's out." Lillian Hurston walked toward him carrying two large coffees.

"Yeah. Going to be a beautiful day." She handed him one of the cups. "Thanks." He took a long sip of the steaming refreshment. The caffeine would perk him up after not sleeping much last night. "Ready for this?"

"Sure, it'll be fun."

While they drank their coffee, they watched the other vendors set up their booths and displays. At ten o'clock, the officers and the taekwondo grandmaster began a self-defense demonstration for a crowd of about twenty kids and their parents. As Hamilton stood on the foam mat, he cast a sideways glance at Lillian on the sidelines. Why did the chief bench her? He racked his brain, but couldn't think of a valid reason, and Lillian seemed reluctant to supply him with one. What wasn't she telling him?

He pushed the nagging thoughts out of his mind and turned his focus to the demonstration seconds too late. The grandmaster flipped him before Hamilton could blink, and he landed squarely on his back. Air raced from his lungs with a hard blast. The Asian stretched out his hand. "Sorry, Officer Bryant. I thought you ready." Hamilton grasped the proffered limb and stood to his feet with a groan.

"My fault. I should've been paying attention." Hamilton brushed the dust off his uniform, then adjusted his stance for the grandmaster's next move.

After the demonstration and a Q&A, Lillian distributed the coloring books and badges, and they both posed for photos and groupies. They repeated the whole thing twice over. At noon, Hamilton was ready for a break. His stomach growled. "Want something to eat?" he asked Lillian.

"No, thank you. I have some errands to run. I won't be back this afternoon."

"Oh, okay."

Lillian hurried to her car without so much as a backward glance. Hamilton tried to bury the uneasy feeling in his stomach. He wandered through the vendors in search of something to eat. He sniffed the air and smiled at the aroma that filled his nose. He was in luck—a troop of boy scouts dished up hot dogs and chips, raising money for their big jamboree this summer. He bought two dogs and threw some extra into the donation jar.

"Thanks, officer," said the lispy boy scout, then he saluted and stood to attention. Hamilton grinned and saluted back. He scarfed down his hot dogs and soda pop. They had about an hour and a half left of the self-defense demonstration, finishing at two o'clock. He was on duty for the rest of the day, patrolling the area for the remainder of the event. He tossed his trash in the receptacle, then returned to the grandmaster and gathering crowd.

Hamilton loaded the remaining boxes of coloring books into the back of the patrol unit, then slammed the trunk shut, and set out on foot to patrol the park. He circled once, keeping his eyes open for any mischievous behavior or suspicious activity. After running some teenagers off the playground equipment, he headed for the Vintage Junktique, an outdoor antique market on the blocked off street. He walked the center aisle, shaking his head. Sellers hawked everything from porcelain figurines to tractor pieces to antique vases and old paintings. The event reminded him of the saying, "One man's junk is another man's treasure." He hoped someone was finding a treasure in this mishmash.

Up ahead, Paige McDonald walked along the booths, wearing a fire engine red sweater, jeans, and sneakers. Her blond hair brushed her rounded shoulders. She paused in front of one of the tables. She tossed a tattered book back and forth in her hands and ran the tips of her manicured fingers along the binding. She returned it to the table and picked up another. Hamilton approached from the right. "What brings you out today? Anything specific?"

Paige startled and dropped the open book onto the blacktop. The inside pages crumpled when they hit the ground. Her jaw clenched as she bent to retrieve the book. Was it the unnecessary damage or his presence that irked her? Paige set the book back on the table. "Old books."

"Huh?" Right. She was answering his question. He straightened his regulation cover. "Oh, really?"

"I find a lot of antique books at yard sales and flea markets. Most people don't realize how much monetary value they can have. They sell them off cheap, not realizing they could get a lot more for them."

"Do you often find profitable ones?"

"Occasionally. Estate sales and used bookstores are the best places to look." Paige waved to the seller and continued down the progression of loaded tables. She kept her eyes on the merchandise and didn't make eye contact with him. "What brings you to the park?" At that moment, she noticed his uniform. "Stupid question. You're on duty."

Patrol. Right. He was supposed to be keeping an eye on the event attendees, not following a book-hunting blond with brilliant blue eyes, skin as smooth as ivory soap, and rosy pink lips like the china doll on the table they were passing. *Where did that thought come from?* Hamilton shook his head. *Get your head back on task.* He opened his mouth to speak when his cell phone began playing a tune. He stepped away from the booths and swiped the phone screen. "Hello."

"Officer Bryant? Pastor Whitestone. I was mowing the church yard today, when I noticed the window to the basement was open. I haven't been down there since I put away the Christmas costumes back in January. I went to shut the window and the basement door was unlocked.

Downstairs, boxes were left opened and moved around. Someone was in the church basement searching for something."

"You haven't authorized anyone to go down there."

"No sir. I keep the only key in my office, but it's been missing since last week." The preacher paused. He swallowed. "I've been thinking about that shooting in our church parking lot…"

Hamilton held his finger to his ear to block out the noise of the crowded park. "Something to report?"

"It took me a while, but something *was* stolen from the church basement. It wasn't a coincidence."

Hamilton's pulse sped up. Beads of sweat formed on his brow. "What was it?"

"A 1535 Coverdale Bible Richard Staten donated to the church about six months ago."

Hamilton puffed out a breath of air. "Is it valuable?" His eyes drifted to the red-sweatered woman crossing the street to her bicycle locked on the bike rack. *No. It couldn't be.* The nagging voice in his head wasn't helping. S*he is into old books.* Her own words echoed through his thoughts, complicating the situation. *Most people don't realize how valuable they can be.*

Pastor Whitestone's voice wavered. "Over a half a million dollars."

Hamilton felt like someone punched him in the gut.

Kathleen Phillips opened the garage entry door, purse and jacket in hand. Her house was dark when she stepped into the foyer. She flipped the switch, bathing the room in warm light. *I guess no one's home.* She dropped her belongings on the sideboard, then walked through the house to the kitchen. A hot pink sticky note was stuck to the center island. "Mom. Went to the movies with friends. Kylie." Her stomach grumbled. Kathleen turned and opened the stainless-steel refrigerator and found a plastic-wrapped plate with a note on top. "Kylie's out. Here's your dinner." *Thank you, Matilda.*

Matilda Brownly had worked for the Staten family for thirty-five years. Kathleen couldn't imagine functioning without her. The woman cleaned, did laundry (ironing and steaming), homework with Kylie, and she was a pure genius in the kitchen. She'd done the same when Kathleen and Erik were children, practically raising them when their parent's schedules kept them too busy. She was an icon in their home. However, the woman had to be over sixty years old. Was she ready to retire? Kathleen would speak to her as soon as possible. She'd ensure Matilda had a padded retirement. It was the least she could do after all they had put her through, especially Erik.

Kathleen removed the plastic wrap and stuck the plate in the microwave. She pressed several buttons and the machine reheated her dinner. A light blinked on the answering machine. Kathleen tapped the button. Her brother's voice came over the speaker. "You know, Dad has had this same phone number since we were kids. Anyway, my phone died, and I don't have your cell number memorized. Business takes me back to Portland. I'll see you again in a couple of days. Have a good one." The machine beeped to signal the end of the message.

She took a seat on one of the bar stools, propped her chin on her hand, and stared at her black cell phone screen. The house was silent except for the humming microwave. Too quiet. An eerie kind of silence that sets your skin on edge. How had her father lived in this big house all by himself for all those years? *If I win the election, I'll sell it before I move to Salem. Or sooner.* Once her dad's estate was settled. When would Don send her a copy of the will? She thought again of their conversation at the funeral. *Dad altered the will. Why would he do that? What did he change?*

The microwave beeped, startling her. Kathleen removed the steaming plate and returned to the stool with a heavy sigh.

She'd spent the day at the school in Joseph, speaking to the electorate about the upcoming elections, and the event had been a complete disaster. Without warning, the stage lights exploded. Glass fragments showered over the crowd, sending citizens screaming and running for cover. The stage curtains caught fire, and security had escorted her to her vehicle as if there had been a terrorist attack. It was clearly an electrical shortage. Incompetence. She was surrounded by incompetence. Could this debacle affect the election? At the very least, it made her appear inept in front of the electorate. Chief House would have a hissy fit come morning when word of this hit the news. He had already been on edge leading up to the primaries, and now that she'd won the candidacy, he was sure to be on her case.

When she finished her meal, she dropped her plate in the sink, then removed a glass from the cabinet and filled it with lukewarm tap water. She turned and leaned against the counter. The house phone rang. She picked up the receiver. "Hello." *Nothing*. How strange. "Hello."

Beep. beep. beep. The call ended. *Bad connection? If it's important, they'll call back.* She finished her glass of water, then carried her cell phone through the house, turning off the lights as she went. She climbed the carpeted staircase. It was late, and she was tired.

An odd noise came from her father's personal office as she passed. She paused, straining against the silence that pounded her eardrums. There it came again. Faint, but someone was in there. Her pulse quickened, and a shiver ran through her body. She gripped the golden door knob and threw open the door. A blinding flashlight turned her direction. She covered her eyes and swung her arm at the light switch. After the third swing, her hand connected, and the overhead light fixtures chased away the darkness. "Erik!"

It was her brother's turn to shade his eyes. "Sis!" In a

second, he recovered. He folded a piece of paper and put it in his jacket pocket.

"What are you doing here? You scared me."

"Sorry, sis. I didn't know you were home. How was the rally?"

"Something short-circuited the stage lights, but you know, same old, same old. I thought you were in Portland."

"I'm headed there, but I wanted to stop by and see the old place again before I left." He gave a sweeping glance around the room and gestured with his arm. "It's hard to believe he's gone."

"Sometimes I still hear his voice."

Her brother moved closer and put his hand on her shoulder. His woodsy cologne calmed her senses. "Hey, it's only been a week. It'll take time. You were a lot closer to Dad than I was."

"That was as much your fault as it was his." Erik's jaw clenched. She'd hit a nerve. "I miss him." She hadn't admitted that to anyone, even herself. Being in this room, without him, made it so real. Until the day of his death, he'd spent hours inside these hallowed walls. Even when he was too weak to walk alone, Kathleen brought him and sat him in his chair and then fetched his cup of coffee.

And that's where he'd died.

Masculinity bathed the room furnished with black leather furniture, a solid oak conference table, bookcases filled with law books, and old wooden filing cabinets. She caressed the top of the worn desk and traced the multitude of water spots on the mahogany top, inset from the years of a lack of coaster use. When she came to the edge, she applied just a little pressure and the desk wobbled. *Oh, Daddy.*

Men had cowered at the sound of his voice. His presence commanded attention, like a raging bear or a roaring lion. She'd always admired him. He'd been a tough father. His rod had attempted to beat them into submission. Kathleen had complied to his iron hand. Erik, on the other hand, had revolted against the authority. The stricter the rules and the more painful the whippings—the harder her brother had rebelled.

She moved to the bookcase and ran her fingers across the spines of the books. Moonlight spilled through the arched glass panels. Her fingers sunk in a gap on the shelf. She ran her hand around inside the empty slot. Something was missing. "Erik. Did you borrow one of Dad's books?" There shouldn't be a gap.

Her brother appeared at her side, his eyebrows narrowed. "No. This is the first time I've been in this room in, oh, probably twenty years. Could Kylie have taken something?"

Kathleen shook her head. "Kylie hasn't stepped foot in this office. Ever. She didn't like this side of her grandfather."

"Well, something is missing."

But what? She left the bookshelves and waded through the filing cabinet for the lists of his books. She found the correct manila folder, spread it across the desk, and then sorted through the lines and lines of black type. Her father had categorized each book by shelf and had listed each with author, publisher, and value. She ran her finger down the names, matching them to the books on the shelf. Erik watched over her shoulder. Her eyes grew wide and a knot formed in her stomach. The missing book was *The Federalist*, a collection of essays Alexander Hamilton and James Madison wrote in 1788, valued at $450,000. *That's not possible.* No one in the house had any reason to remove it from the bookcase. Someone had stolen it. Someone had broken into her home, pawed their way through her father's personal library, and had walked off with a valuable piece of American history. Erik paled and dropped into one of the massive leather chairs. "Oh my."

Kathleen tossed aside the papers in her hand, grabbed the phone receiver, and dialed 911.

The dispatcher's voice spoke from the other end. "This is 911. What's your emergency?"

"Kelly. This is Mayor Phillips. I'd like to report a robbery."

10

A light drizzle teased at the hotel window as Paige dressed. A hodgepodge of outfits, her mother's Bible, and the bookmark from the Wallowa Mountains Baptist Church lay spread out over the comforter. It was Sunday morning, and that bookmark was the only other link she had to her birth mother's identity, besides the name, Annie. If she could speak with this Pastor Whitestone, maybe he could tell her something, anything, that would get her closer to the truth. Paige wasn't a church-goer, hadn't really had much use for God, especially the strict Judge the chaplain at juvenile hall had described, but if it helped her find her mother, she could endure one service.

She leaned into the full-length mirror and slid the post of a pearl earring through her left ear, then stepped back and smoothed her sleeveless, knee-length black dress. She might be too dolled up for a country church, but the little black dress was the only dressy thing she'd packed. She slipped her black pumps onto her stockinged feet, then checked the time on her cell phone screen. When did worship services start? She hadn't checked. She'd have to walk. She couldn't pedal in her pumps and short skirt. She reached for her purse, but her attention turned to the pile of scattered laundry. She didn't want to be late, but the mess pulled at her like a magnet to metal. She moved to the bed and began folding. It couldn't hurt to spend a few minutes straightening up the room.

At eleven o'clock, she scurried up to the Wallowa Mountains Baptist Church. The white steepled building, with its bell tower and stained glass windows, rested at the end of a country lane, surrounded by budding oaks, maples, and dogwood trees. She jogged up the staircase, then pulled open the wide, polished oak door. The foyer was warm, but empty, when she stepped inside.

She peeked through a window in the interior double-doors. A man in a black suit stood behind a podium. She was late. She would make a scene if she entered now; everyone turning in their seats to observe the stranger intruding upon their solemn worship. She should come back next week and be punctual.

A toilet flushed, and Timothy Thorne stepped into the foyer from the door marked, Men, still stuffing his dress shirt into his slacks. His face registered surprise, then recognition. "Miss Paige," he said, a little too loudly.

"Shh." Paige pressed her finger to her lips and glanced nervously toward the auditorium.

"Miss Paige," Timmy began again, this time keeping his voice at a loud whisper. "Did you come for church?" Before Paige could respond, he heaved open the interior door and said, "You can sit with me."

She felt obliged to follow the little fellow down the center aisle. Becky and Dave looked up in surprise when Paige and Timmy stopped next to the pew. The preacher continued with his sermon, but she sensed that all eyes had turned in her direction. The small boy climbed over his parents' legs, then patted the crimson cushion beside him. Paige's cheeks flushed as she gestured into the pew. "I'm sorry. May I?" Dave slipped into the aisle. Paige stepped passed Becky. The older boys scooted over. She settled onto the pew and turned her attention to the speaker.

"We are all sinners. We are all condemned before a Holy and Righteous God. We all deserve eternal punishment in the Lake of Fire."

Oh great. Another Bible-thumper yelling about God's judgment—how the big man upstairs just couldn't wait to squash his errant creation. She let her mind wander back to her days at the Juvenile Detention Center, like a zoo of caged animals or a nature conservatory—days on end of slop food, chore inspections, rehabilitation classes, and once a week—mandatory chapel. The preachers stood high and mighty over the little sinners and poured God's wrath on them. Hellfire and brimstone. "Repent," they'd yell and scream, "Repent!"

"You can't do one single thing to make God love you more."

A sharp pain jabbed her side. *Ouch.* Timmy frowned and pointed at a page in the book on his lap. He whispered, "Romans, chapter five. Right here." To appease the child, Paige found the place at the back of her mother's Bible. Her eyes scanned the print. *There are so many passages. Which one is he on?* She cast a questioning glance in Becky's direction, who leaned over and pointed to the sentence marked with a number six. It was highlighted with a hot pink highlighter. *Did my mother highlight this?*

"You can't do one single thing to make God love you less."

The preacher paused for dramatic effect. Paige lifted her chin and met his eyes. Had she heard right? "Let's read these verses aloud together." She read the words along with the preacher. "For when we were yet without strength, in due time Christ died for the ungodly. For scarcely for a righteous man will one die: yet peradventure for a good man some would even dare to die. But God commendeth his love toward us, in that while we were yet sinners, Christ died for us."

The tall man walked down from the stage to mingle with the audience. Was that allowed? "He already gave His Son for you. He already paid the highest price to show you how much He loves you. 'For God so loved the world that He gave His only begotten son.' If I had a son, I would not sacrifice him for the world. I don't love the world that much. But He gave His Son for the world, all the while knowing that many would reject Him, that they would spit on Him and mock Him. It says here that 'scarcely for a righteous man will one die.' That means that few people would be willing to give their lives for a good person, someone that society believes deserves to live. But Christ died for sinners, those whom society believes deserve their punishment. Murderers, child molesters, rapists, kidnappers, even thieves or drug addicts. Are they not worthy of Christ's sacrifice? The Apostle Paul said, 'Christ Jesus came to save sinners, of whom I am chief.' He died for the chiefest of sinners."

The preacher's words faded. God loved sinners? She'd never heard this before. A God of love? If she'd thought about it, she would assume that God loved the good people. The people who gave to charity, and went to church, and helped old ladies cross the street. But the thought that God loved those who'd made a mess of their lives… If this was true, was it possible that in spite of everything, God loved… her?

"Please stand for the invitation."

The audience rose to their feet and bowed their heads. Paige followed their example. A piano played softly. A woman's voice rose with a sweet timber. The music was unlike anything she'd heard before. Was this how the angels sang? All too soon the song ended. The temple of worship still echoed with the music, while the preacher prayed aloud. As soon as he said, "amen," Becky and David's boys bolted for the door along with the other children. Paige turned to Becky. "Thank you for letting me join you. I wasn't sure what to do, coming in so late and everything."

Becky placed her hand on Paige's arm. "No problem. I'm glad Timmy found you. Did you enjoy the service?"

Her mind raced to find a truthful answer. Her thoughts during the preaching were far too personal to share. "It was interesting," she ventured.

Becky's smile didn't waver. "Good. I'm glad. Do you have lunch plans?"

Paige scanned the auditorium. "Sort of. I'm hoping to talk with Pastor Whitestone. Could you maybe point him out to me?"

Becky turned and spoke to Dave, who was standing in the aisle. "Go on out. I'll help Paige, then join you all in a moment." David nodded and headed toward the rear door. Paige followed Becky into the aisle. "Pastor Whitestone is the pastor of our little church. He was the one preaching. He usually greets the congregation in the foyer after services." Paige and Becky joined the crowd of worshipers gathered in the space making small talk, but the tall preacher was nowhere in sight. Becky tapped an elderly woman on the shoulder. "Have you seen Pastor Whitestone?"

"He left right after service. He'll be back this evening."

They have church twice on Sunday? Paige's shoulders drooped. She would have to wait until this evening for her chance to speak to Pastor Whitestone. She lifted her chin, squared her shoulders, and gave Becky a crooked smile. "Is that invitation for lunch still open?"

Dave Thorne went to the den for an afternoon nap. The two older boys disappeared somewhere in the house. Becky filled the sink with soapy water to wash the lunch dishes. Her son, Timmy pulled on her arm. "Please Mom, I need someone to get the box of clay off the top shelf."

"Go ask your dad. He's not doing anything." She waved him away. "Or ask one of your brothers. I'd like to talk to Miss McDonald." She held out a dish towel to Paige. "Dry?"

"I can handle that." Paige took the cloth, her fingers digging into the fabric with nervousness. What did Becky want to talk to her about?

Becky plunged her hands into the steaming water and began scrubbing a porcelain plate. "I apologize for my brother's behavior the other night. He's very protective when it comes to his family."

Paige took the dripping plate from Becky and ran the terry cloth over the glass. "That makes him a good brother."

"True, but sometimes he gets carried away."

"I should apologize for being so—so opinionated."

"Paige." Becky's voice adapted a motherly tone. "If you don't mind me asking, what are you doing in Whitman?"

Her eyes searched Paige's face. She'd been so kind, opening her home, allowing her to rent the apartment. Paige owed her the truth. "Do you promise not to tell your brother?"

Becky's wet hand squeezed hers. "I promise."

"I'm searching for my birth mother, but I don't have much to go on. Just a name and a bookmark."

"What was on the bookmark?"

"It's from Wallowa Mountains Baptist Church. Her first name is or was Annie, that's all I know."

Becky leaned against the counter, her hands dripping soapy water on the tile floor. "Annie?" She pressed her lips together and stared at the ceiling. "I don't know anyone in Whitman named Annie. How long ago was this?"

"I'm twenty-five years old, so about that long."

"I would have been eleven. I'm trying to think…" Becky tapped her chin. "Maybe it'll come to me later. I can ask around if you'd like."

"No, please. I want to do this myself."

"Okay. If that's what you want." Becky turned back to the sink. She rinsed the rest of the plates and handed them to Paige, one at a time. "What was it like living in Portland? I've lived here all my life. I've never even been passed the county line."

"Crowded and expensive." Paige dried and stacked them on the counter.

"Have you always been into books?"

Paige took hold of a drinking glass and rubbed the towel over the etched design. Becky was brave to use such nice dishes with three boys in the house. "Pretty much. I guess my adopted grandfather passed on his love for old books to me. A substantial portion of my collection once belonged to him."

"Jessie, the owner of The Bookshelf, is a sweet Christian woman and she's always been like an adopted grandmother to Hamilton and me. She's an *important* part of this family. I don't know what we'd do if anything happened to her." Paige didn't miss Becky's emphasis on the word, *important.* She caught the sharpness in her tone and the glint in her eyes. Becky's voice dropped to a whisper. "I'm trusting you. Don't give me a reason to regret my generosity."

Hamilton stifled a yawn. His shift had officially ended at four o'clock yesterday, but after clearing the park, he'd headed over to check out the church building. Martin had finished his investigation by the time Hamilton arrived on the scene. No damaged locks. No sign of forced entry. Someone had told the boy exactly where to find the key and where to find the Bible, but who could have known? It's not like the book was kept in a glass case with a sign posted that read: Ancient Bible worth half a million dollars. Officer Martin had dusted for fingerprints and collected several. They would have those results back in a couple of days.

After leaving the church, he and Martin had examined the mayor's home late into the night. There was no sign of forced entry. He'd checked every door and every window in the entire mansion. It had taken until 4:00 this morning to complete the paperwork. He'd climbed into bed at 4:30 and had slept through church services. He would still be sleeping if Chief House, who had yet to arrive, hadn't ordered this mandatory meeting.

Several minutes later, the chief stormed through the secure door, waving his coffee cup-laden hand. His bloodshot eyes and disheveled uniform spoke volumes. "That woman makes me so mad."

Hamilton jumped out of his chair and snatched the Styrofoam cup before the chief spilled its contents. "She won't agree to tighter security?" He set the cup on the edge of his desk.

"No!" Chief House slammed his fist on the metal desk, sloshing the coffee. Hamilton grabbed tissues from the box on Lillian's desk and mopped up the spill. "She insists the fire at the rally in Joseph was an accident and not a targeted attack."

"There was a fire in Joseph?" He'd obviously missed something. His superior quickly filled him in on the details.

"What about the robbery?" Martin asked.

"She insists that it has nothing to do with the elections. A random theft."

Random? Third robbery in as many days and it's random? "What do you think?"

Chief House dropped into a swivel chair and plowed his fingers through his hair. "I think both were intentional. Either someone is trying to injure Mayor Phillips or at the very least make her look incompetent. But who?"

"What about that new girl, um…" Officer Martin propped his chin in his hand. "Paige McDonald. We don't know anything about her."

Hamilton sprung to life at the mention of Paige's name. "How'd you hear about her?"

"Kylie Phillips mentioned her the other day when I was out for coffee. I assume you've already met."

"I have. She's renting Becky's garage apartment. She

doesn't seem like the type." Hamilton didn't believe the words even as he spoke them. He'd seen the background check.

"Think about it, Bryant. Who else could it be? We have no idea why she's here in town. This trouble all started about the same day she arrived." Officer Hurston interjected.

"Lillian, come on." *Why am I defending her when I've had the same thoughts?*

Chief House tapped his fingers together. He rested them on his chin, and a thoughtful expression crossed his face. He walked around the desk, then sat on the edge. "Officer Martin is right. We don't know anything about this woman."

"We can't just run a background on her without probable cause." Hamilton couldn't bring himself to mention her past arrests. That was sure to make her a person of interest. He swallowed. *Should she be?*

"I want you to get close to her, Bryant. Find out more about her and why she's in Whitman." Chief House's statement caught Hamilton's attention.

"How? Date her?" He meant it as a joke.

"Something like that."

He shot forward in his chair, his eyes wide. "No. No way."

"Why not?"

"Why can't Officer Hurston just become her new BFF, or whatever women do?" Hamilton gestured in her direction. Lillian folded her arms over her chest. "What if she's guilty? How would that look to the community and the media?" He was grasping at straws and they all knew it.

"If she is guilty, we'll explain to the press that you went undercover for the sake of the investigation."

Hamilton flopped back against the office chair. The movement twisted the seat to the side and he shifted back. "Why can't Lillian do this again?"

"Officer Hurston has her hands full with something else."

Hamilton opened his mouth to comment, then changed

his mind. He sighed, then ran an agitated hand over his amassing facial hair. He needed a shave. And a bath. And a bed. His eyelids drooped. He was too tired to argue anymore. "If I say yes, can I go home and get some sleep? I'm supposed to be off-duty."

"Yes. We're done here. You're still working the Memorial Day event tomorrow, right?"

"Yes, sir. Goodnight." Hamilton rose from his chair and removed his weapon, wallet, and keys from the desk drawer.

Once he reached the minivan, he opened the door and plopped down on the leather seat, then laid his head on the steering wheel. What had he gotten himself into? He didn't date in real life, now the chief ordered him to fake date? The worse part of the whole thing? If he wasn't careful, he could see himself falling for the book-loving blond from Portland.

After the evening worship service, Pastor Whitestone led Paige into his office. A large desk occupied the center of the small, crowded room along with a computer, a copy machine, a metal filing cabinet, a spinning office chair, and several bookshelves. Paige took the seat the preacher offered. She sat her purse and Bible on the desk and tucked her hair behind her ears. She crossed her legs and self-consciously tugged at the hem of her short skirt. The preacher sat in the chair opposite her. From this close distance, she got a better look at the man. He was tall and lean with narrow shoulders, a strong back, and salt and pepper hair. He wore a two-piece suit and a navy tie. He was clean-shaven with expressive eyebrows. His voice was confident and deep. "You wanted to speak with me, Miss—"

"McDonald. Paige McDonald." Paige leaned forward and shook the preacher's hand.

"What can I do for you, Miss McDonald?"

"Please call me Paige."

"All right, Paige. How can I help?"

"Two weeks ago, I came across this Bible in our attic." She laid her hand on the leather binding. "I found a bookmark inside from this church." Paige paused. Her pulse thrummed in her temples. Her breaths grew rapid and shallow. She flexed her fingers. "I'm sorry. I'm just a little nervous."

He leaned back in his chair and crossed one foot over his other knee. "Take all the time you need, Miss Paige."

A knot formed in her throat. She opened her mouth to speak, but nothing came out. She took a deep breath. "I'm hoping you might know my birth mother?" There, she'd said it.

"Your birth mother?" The pastor dropped his leg and leaned forward, resting his hand under his chin. "I'm confused. Why come to me?"

She removed the bookmark from inside the Bible and pushed it across the desk. "This has the church's address on it. It's my only other clue to who she might be. I was hoping that if she visited this church or maybe lived here in Whitman, that you might recognize her name."

"What is her name?"

"Annie."

Something flickered across the pastor's face. "What year was that?"

"1992."

"My father was the pastor then. He passed away about ten years ago. I only recently moved back." Pastor Whitestone gestured toward the Bible. "May I see?" He set a pair of reading glasses on his nose.

She nodded. The preacher lifted the sacred pages and opened to the front cover. His lips slightly mouthed the words written there.

"She abandoned me at a fire station in Portland and left a note in that Bible." Tears welled up in her eyes. "It says there that she loved me, but if she really loved me, why would she just leave me?"

"Have you considered the possibility that she didn't have a choice?" His tone was soft but held a hint of a reprimand.

She stared down at her hands unsure of how to respond. It was possible that her mother didn't have a choice. *But isn't there always a choice? Couldn't she have kept me? Or at the very least found me a loving home? Abandoned on the steps of a fire department? It was so cold. So heartless. Wasn't it?*

When she raised her chin, the pastor was flipping through the pages of the Bible. Finally, he stood to his feet and stepped around the desk. He held the Bible out where she could see a highlighted verse. "Did you do this?"

Paige shook her head. Some strands of hair got stuck in her lipstick. She brushed them away with her fingertips. "It was that way when I found it." The pastor grew silent. The only sound was the flipping of the pages. He perched on the edge of the desk and handed the book back to her. She hugged the Bible to her chest. "Did you know my mother?"

Pastor Whitestone stared down at his shirt and played with his tie clip for a long time. Would he answer? He shuffled back to his chair, removed his bifocals, folded them up and laid them on his desk, then he leaned back. For several minutes, he stared at the tiles on the ceiling. She fought the urge to see what drew his focus.

Finally, he spoke. His words were so faint, Paige had to lean forward to catch them. "I knew a girl named Annie—once—but I'm not sure she still exists."

11

"Paigey!"

Aunt Hattie flung her arms wide as she exited her station wagon. She grabbed Paige's cheeks between her hands and smooched her on the forehead. "I've missed you so much. Gerald, Delilah, and the dogs send their love. How are you?"

Paige stepped sideways and ringed her arm through her aunt's elbow. It surprised her how much she had missed the older woman. "I'm good. Come on inside." The Thorne's had invited Paige and her aunt to their home for a Memorial Day picnic.

A minivan pulled into the gravel driveway. Officer Bryant shut off the engine, then hopped out, shutting the door behind him. He slipped his sunglasses over his eyes, like the model on a magazine or a CIA spy. Paige let out a gasp as Aunt Hattie's elbow connected with her ribs. "Who's the hunk?"

"Aunt Hattie!" Paige's face grew warm.

He walked up and extended his hand. "Hamilton Bryant. You must be Paige's aunt."

Aunt Hattie giggled and stretched on her toes to kiss him on the cheek. She winked at Paige. "You never told me about this cutie. Do I hear wedding bells?" Hamilton covered a cough. Paige averted her eyes and tucked her hair behind her ear. The silence grew awkward.

She was relieved when the screen door opened, and Becky's head stuck out around the frame. "Welcome. Come inside and meet my parents."

The officer crossed the yard in wide strides and grabbed the screen's door handle. "Ladies first." Aunt Hattie and Paige entered the house, but not before Aunt Hattie whispered into her ear loud enough for him to overhear. "He's a gentleman. Don't see many of those nowadays."

Paige ignored her aunt's remark and instead turned her attention to the man and woman in the living room alongside Dave and his boys. Timmy perched on the woman's lap, jabbering away like a little bird.

Becky made introductions. "Mom. Dad. I'd like you to meet our guests." The woman moved Timmy from her lap as she and the man both stood to their feet. "This is Paige McDonald. She'll be renting the garage apartment. And this is her great-aunt Hattie. Paige. Hattie. My parents, Wade and Jessica Bryant."

They exchanged pleasantries, then Aunt Hattie settled onto the couch next to Mrs. Bryant. She asked Aunt Hattie about a peculiar piece of jewelry she wore, and the two women began talking as if they were old friends. Officer Bryant stepped forward and slapped his dad into a man hug. "Hey, how's it going?" They moved off to the side and joined Dave. A moment later, the three men disappeared.

Becky touched her arm and nodded toward the kitchen. "Help me with lunch?"

"Sure." In the kitchen, celery stalks and bottles of soda pop stuck out from inside the brown paper shopping bags. "Are you feeding an army?"

Becky laughed. "Almost. Here. Start peeling potatoes for

an army's worth of potato salad, Private Paige." She handed her a ten-pound bag of potatoes.

"Yes, ma'am, Captain Becky." Paige saluted, then set to work with the vegetable peeler.

Several minutes later, Aunt Hattie poked her head around the corner. "Do you all need any help in here?"

"No!" Paige shouted. She blushed and lowered her voice. "That's OK, Aunt Hattie. We've got everything under control."

"All right, dear. Let me know if you need anything." Her aunt returned to the living room. Becky stared hard at her, waiting for an explanation.

"Aunt Hattie can't cook. Like, at all." She whispered. She didn't want to offend her aunt, just protect everyone's taste buds from torture. She finished peeling the potatoes, then chopped them into cubes before swiping them from the cutting board into a stock pot full of water.

"I have these hamburger patties done." Becky slapped the last one onto the platter. "Dave! Time to light the grill."

After stuffing their stomachs, the guys began a game of touch football in the front yard. After several touchdowns, his sister joined in. Paige took a seat on the front steps, while his mom and Paige's aunt carried the empty plates and platters inside. His dad left the game and climbed into a hammock suspended between two large trees. He dropped his hat over his eyes and the gentle breeze rocked him to sleep.

Hamilton dusted his pants off, then joined Paige on the front stoop, watching his family finish the game. He loved these people more than anyone else in the world. Becky grabbed her youngest son around the waist. Their laughter carried across the yard. Dave tossed the football to the other two boys. Tony and Tyler both tried to catch it, Tyler pinning

Tony to the ground. When his big brother climbed off him, Tony twisted in the grass and groaned. Tyler gave him a hand to his feet and a pat on the back.

"How do you do it?" Paige's soft voice caught him off guard. She stared off into the distance where the rolling farmland met the snow-peaked Wallowa Mountains.

"Do what?"

Her blue eyes met his as Mom's and Hattie's voices floated from the open kitchen window. The two women were getting along well. "How do you risk your life every day knowing what your death would mean to these people?"

He took a deep breath and dropped his hands between his knees. He really had only one answer, one that he'd prepared many years ago. "Hereby perceive we the love of God, because he laid down his life for us: and we ought to lay down our lives for the brethren." This scripture was his lifeline, his motivation for doing what he did.

"Did you read that on an inspirational calendar or something?"

"No. It's found in the Word of God. The Bible. It means, God showed his great love for me, so the least I can do for my fellow man is share His love to them by laying my life on the line for them. My family's trusting God to protect me and when it's my time to die, it's my time. That's true whether I'm a LEO, an accountant, or a librarian."

"A librarian?" Paige arched her eyebrow.

He chuckled at her reaction. "It was the most risk-free job I could think of. Besides, I know what will happen to me when I die. Do you?"

Paige cleared her throat. "I think I'll show Aunt Hattie around town, then go back to the hotel to change before tonight's event. See you there."

"I'm working security, but I'll see you around."

Sacajawea Park surged with patriotic energy when Paige rode in on her bike and locked it in the bike rack under the large shade trees. Aunt Hattie was worn out and chose to remain back at the hotel.

Paige sat on a park bench and hugged her arms across her chest. A cloud cover dropped the temperatures and blocked the stars. She had an unobstructed view of the temporary stage set up by the pavilion. Buntings of red, white, and blue, American flags, and silver stars trimmed both the stage and pavilion. Large black speakers blasted the music and lyrics to "I'm Proud to be An American".

A large black sedan pulled next to the curb. The rear door opened. A woman wearing designer sunglasses, a stunning 1950s black cocktail dress and overcoat, and knee-high boots stepped out of the vehicle. She straightened her collar and smoothed the wrinkles in her dress with manicured hands. Her makeup was flawless, and every hair seemed tamed into submission. Behind her, emerged Kylie Phillips, the young barista from the Rustic Cup. Kylie wore a patriotic ensemble complete with star-spangled pumps and dangly star earrings. She'd pulled her blond hair back in a ponytail and it swung like a pendulum with every movement. "Hi." She called to Paige and waved enthusiastically. She grabbed the stiff arm of the woman in black. "Mom, this is Paige McDonald. The girl I told you about. Paige, this is my mom, Mayor Kathleen Phillips."

"How do you do?" Paige stood to her feet, extended her hand, and fought the urge to curtsy. "It's very nice to meet you, Madam Mayor."

The queenly woman turned her direction. "So, you're the girl who likes grasshoppers in her coff—"

Paige couldn't see the mayor's eyes behind the sunglasses, but she could've sworn the woman flinched. Her extended hand hung in the air, momentarily suspended between earth and sky. Just as quickly, she recovered and clasped Paige's hand with a practiced greeting. Without another word, she moved toward the stage with elegant strides. "Bye, Paige." Kylie called over her shoulder as she scurried after her mother.

Well, that was weird. Paige shrugged off the strange feeling and returned to her seat just as the Thorne family walked toward her across the grass. Becky carried a tattered quilt and a grocery sack overflowing with snacks. Dave carried two bag chairs while Timmy rode on his shoulders. "Hi Paige." The little boy waved.

"It's Miss Paige." Becky corrected.

"Hi Miss Paige. Can I get down?"

"Sure, buddy. Give me a hand, Tyler." The Thorne's teen son held the chairs while Dave lowered Timothy to the ground.

"Look what we got." The little boy stuck a package of glow sticks in Paige's face. "You can have one if you want."

"Thank you, Timmy. That's very sweet—"

"There's a clown! Can I go see the clown? Please! He's doing face paintings. Can I have my face painted? I want to be Spider-man." Dave dug into his pocket and pulled out his wallet. He fingered through the billfold and handed Tyler several one-dollar bills.

"Here. Take your brother to get his face painted." Tyler groaned audibly but still reached for Timmy's hand.

"Come on. Let's go." The two boys walked off, Timothy dragging his reluctant older brother.

"Want to share a blanket with us? I brought snacks." Becky held up the plastic grocery bag and waggled her eyebrows.

Paige laughed and slapped her knees. "OK. Sure."

They found an empty spot in the grass near the stage, then they spread out the quilt and set up the chairs. "Chair or blanket?" Dave offered.

"Blanket." Paige folded her legs under her and sank into the soft material.

Dave sighed in relief and dropped onto the red folding

chair. Becky patted his hand and teased. "He's too old to sit on the ground anymore. Popcorn?"

Paige waved her hand. "That's all right. Thank you, though."

Becky sat back in her chair and tossed a handful of popcorn into her mouth. Paige shifted and pulled her knees to her chest, wrapping them with her arms. "Becky, I just had the strangest encounter with—"

The music quieted, and the VFW Honor Guard mounted the stage and presented the colors. Several people walked on stage, then one of the men grabbed hold of the microphone. "Please stand for the singing of the National Anthem."

The crowd rose to their feet as the music began to play. Becky whispered in Paige's ear. "That's the County Commissioner." When the music stopped, he spoke. "Welcome to our annual Memorial Day event. Our speaker is none other than your very own Mayor Kathleen Phillips. Please welcome her to the stage."

Mayor Phillips stepped on stage and accepted the microphone from the man. Applause broke out from the crowd. "Thank you. I am honored to be here tonight to celebrate with my neighbors and my community. Memorial Day is a special opportunity for us to honor the men and women who gave their lives for our freedom in the branches of our military. We humbly thank you for your sacrifice. The city council members and I have a special treat. As soon as it gets dark—"

Pop! Pop! Pop! The sudden noise sent panic sweeping over the crowd. A woman screamed as fireworks detonated and shot toward the stage. Sparks showered the spectators. The officials on stage covered their heads and stumbled down the stairs. Someone shuttled the mayor through the crowd. Officers from the Whitman Police Department took control. As Paige turned to follow the others, there came a loud explosion. Dangerous flare-ups sent the community running for cover. Firefighters moved in, dragging hoses as the streamers caught fire and the flames licked at the pavilion. In the chaos, Paige lost sight of Becky, Dave, and their children.

A hand grabbed her arm. "Are you all right?" Officer Bryant shouted over the noise of the fleeing audience.

"I'm OK. What's going on?"

"We don't know yet. Our priority is getting everyone safely away from the fire. The volunteer fire department is already on it."

"Was it an accident?"

Before he could answer, a voice came over his radio. "Officer Bryant. Direct traffic heading east."

"Copy. Over and out." He turned his attention back to Paige. "Gotta go. Get a ride with Becky and Dave back to the hotel. Please, don't try to ride your bike with all the nervous traffic out tonight."

Paige nodded as he jogged off. She dialed Becky's phone number. She answered, and Paige arranged to meet them by the playground equipment. She hung up her phone, then retrieved her bike from the rack. She last saw Hamilton directing traffic on the corner of Cedarwood and 3rd.

Her daughter, Kylie, had gone to bed. The police officers had left, although one of them was posted in a patrol car right outside. This was no accident. Someone had deliberately messed with the fireworks. It meant the fire in Joseph was most likely on purpose, too. Adrenaline pulsed through her veins as Kathleen sat alone in the dark, still coming to grips with what had happened. There were those who couldn't stomach the idea of another Staten in the state office. Someone was out to kill her or make her look foolish, but which was it?

Her short encounter with Kylie's friend had shaken her far more than the fireworks debacle. Something about that girl had touched a nerve, almost as if… Kathleen shook her head at the ludicrous thought. *You're tired and stressed, and now you're hallucinating. Your fear of scandal is making you see things.*

Without thinking, her hand slid to her abdomen. Her father had convinced her that giving the baby up for adoption was the best thing for everyone. She'd had dreams, plans, and they hadn't included motherhood her senior year of high school. She'd been so young. So scared. So foolish.

Unanswered questions burned through her mind like a blaze. Who had adopted her baby girl? What kind of people were they? Where was she raised? Was she well-loved? Well provided for? What kind of woman had she become? Had she gone to college? Was she married? Did she have children of her own?

More than just the unknown fueled the bitter ache in her heart, but all that she'd missed over the past twenty-five years.

Her little girl's first steps. Her first loose tooth. Her first day of school. Her first crush. Her first date.

The chink in her armor split open and her soul laid bare and vulnerable. A low moan slipped from Kathleen's throat. Her nose burned. She sunk her head into her folded arms and wept for all she'd lost. All that had been taken from her. All that she'd given up.

Moments later, the tears dried. She straightened her shoulders and considered all that she'd gained. If she could go back and do it all over, would she have chosen a different path?

Probably not.

12

Tuesday morning, rain clouds hovered over town as Paige left the hotel on foot. The blustery wind invigorated her spirit, and despite the impending storm, she walked with a skip in her step. It was about a ten-minute walk to The Bookshelf bookstore. She pulled on the handle, but the door refused to budge. She cupped her hands against the glass and peered inside. Dark and empty.

A car horn sounded behind her. Paige spun on her heels as a minivan pulled alongside the sidewalk, facing the wrong direction. The window lowered, and Officer Bryant stuck out his head. "Morning, Miss McDonald."

She stepped across the sidewalk to the grassy right-of-way, hugging her cardigan to her chest as a chilly breeze sent goosebumps down her arms. "Morning."

"Mrs. Faye will be in a little later. I've got to help her with her car battery after I drop Tyler at baseball practice." Officer Bryant's nephew slouched in the passenger seat fully engrossed in something on his cell phone screen.

"Thanks." She turned to walk away, heading for the Rustic Cup. She could use a cup of hot coffee to warm her insides. She glanced over her shoulder at the handsome police officer. *A nice strong cup of coffee.*

"Wait. Miss McDonald. Paige." The van rolled forward. Paige paused as Officer Bryant hemmed and hawed, fiddling with the end of his clip-on tie. "Would you allow me to buy you dinner tonight? Offer my apology?"

Paige cracked her neck to the side. It was her turn to hem and haw. "I don't know. I don't think. I… No." Officer Bryant set the van in park. She stepped back as he joined her on the sidewalk. He racked his fingers through his hair, leaving several strands standing on end. The endearing mess he left behind warmed her to her toes. *Stop that.* She scolded herself.

"Please. Becky said you could rent the apartment. If you want, I'll help you move in after we eat."

She didn't really have much to move, but the expression on his face was pitiful. She shouldn't, but she caved with a groan. "OK. One dinner. One apology. And you better make it a good one."

"Ten four." He saluted like she was an army general and returned to the minivan. He did a U-turn in the middle of the road and headed west. Paige shook her head. She must be daft to agree to a dinner with Officer Bryant, or she was just lonely. The next thought froze her to the sidewalk. Maybe, despite her vow to stay away from first responders, she was attracted to the man wearing the uniform. Paige blew out a frosty breath, straightening her shoulders. Ridiculous. Absolutely ridiculous. One dinner. It was just one dinner. No need to start mailing the "save the date" cards.

Inside the Rustic Cup, a crackling fire in the wood stove brought a homey glow to the café and nipped the morning chill in the bud. Paige breathed in the earthy aroma of roasted coffee beans. An unfamiliar woman worked the counter: taking orders, filling cups, and making lattes. Kylie delivered the orders to the tables. Paige waved at the teen girl, then waited in line at the counter. When the others finished, she stepped up. Before she could order, the barista spoke. "Hi. You must be the girl who likes grasshoppers in her coffee."

Did Kylie tell everyone that story? Warmth crept up her neck. "Paige McDonald." She offered her hand to the barista.

She gave it a gentle shake. "Jenn McMillan. Kylie told me about you. I'm the owner."

"Nice to meet you. I don't really drink grasshoppers in my coffee. I wanted a grasshopper iced mocha, you know, mint." Paige pulled her hand back and fished in her purse for her wallet. "I'll just take a black coffee today."

The barista moved to fill the order. The dark liquid simmered into the cup when she pulled the handle on the stainless-steel coffee urn. "Uh oh, a mocha girl who's drinking black. Something's up? Boyfriend trouble?"

Paige shrugged. "Something like that."

Jenn snapped a lid on the paper cup and handed it over the counter. "On the house, sweetie. And if you need any man advice, don't hesitate to stop in and ask. My husband and I have been married for twenty-five years, and we haven't killed each other yet, so I guess that's saying something."

A smile spread over her lips. Jenn's warm personality made it impossible to stay glum. "Thanks, Mrs. McMillan."

"Call me Jenn"—she emphasized her first name—"and you're more than welcome, sweetheart."

Paige sat at a table near the front window, but The Bookshelf was over a block and a half farther down the street. It was unlikely she could see anyone coming or going. The aromatic steam squeezed through the hole in the lid of her cup. She lifted it to her lips and sipped the hot liquid, allowing it to warm her freezing hands and her nervous stomach. Vehicles moved through the traffic light and pedestrians milled around the shops. It wasn't as busy or as crowded as Portland, but the town seemed to take on a life of its own.

"Do you need a refill?" Paige turned her head. Kylie waited beside the table, coffee pot in hand.

"That's OK. Thanks, Kylie."

"Sure, no problem." Paige's cell phone buzzed, causing it to jump on the table like a Mexican jumping bean. "You should probably get that."

Paige stood. "I'll take this outside." She glanced at the screen, then smiled at the familiar number. She hit the answer button as soon as she stepped out of the noisy café. "Hello, Aunt Hattie."

"Hello, Paige McDonald."

The deep voice sent shivers up her arms. Her pulse quickened. "Who is this? What do you want?"

"I want you to leave Whitman"—the voice started giggling—"and come back home. Oh, Paigey. It's not the same here without you."

"Aunt Hattie. You scared me to death." Paige touched her hand to her chest. She took deep breaths to slow her heart rate.

"I'm sorry. I miss you."

"I miss you, too. But we just saw each other this morning when you left."

"I know. Do you need money?"

Paige laughed. "You gave me fifty thousand dollars less than a week ago. I'm fine."

"Okay, dear. If you need anything you will call, won't you?"

"Of course. I love you."

"I love you too. Bye."

The call ended. Paige's vision momentarily clouded with tears. Dear, sweet Aunt Hattie. If there was anyone in this world Paige could count on, it was her. Paige sniffled, wiped away her tears, and scanned the street. An elderly woman unlocked the door to The Bookshelf and went inside. *Mrs. Faye?* Paige tossed her empty cup into a trash can, then jogged to meet up with, hopefully, her new temporary employer.

A bell jingled over the door when Paige entered The Bookshelf. Her eyes widened, and she pursed her lips to hold back the explicative that threatened to bubble out. Posters from the early nineties, tack holes, and leftover pieces of tape decorated the bare walls. The ceiling had faint yellow stains where the roof had leaked, and a few metal shelving units ran down the center of the bookstore, dividing the space into two indistinguishable sections. Overflowing boxes clustered against the walls and stacks of books filled every available space. The Bookshelf could only be described as the biggest mess Paige had ever seen.

A fragile, elderly woman about four foot five with a head of thinning white hair, a cane, and a wobble in her step appeared from a doorway in the back of the store. She clasped her chest when she spotted Paige. "Oh, child. You scared the living daylights out of me." Her voice was low and gravely, reminding Paige of the grandmother from the *Walton's* reruns Aunt Hattie liked to watch. "May I help you find anything?"

Paige stepped aside as the little lady hobbled to a chair behind the checkout counter—if it could be called that. A white card table sat in the corner topped with a cash box, an adding machine, and a receipt book. No computer or cash register in sight. "Are you Mrs. Jessie Faye?"

"I am. Oops. Forgot the sign." Jessie Faye hopped from her chair and carried a chalkboard sign outside. Through the window, Paige read the words: Come on in and smell the books. Paige didn't smell books. She smelt bleach, cardboard, and bankruptcy.

"Mrs. Faye. Please, Mrs. Faye." The old woman piddled around the store, doing nothing in particular. "I'm here about a job."

Jessie Faye froze mid-step. The crow's feet around her eyes pulled tight as she squinted at Paige and frowned. Suddenly, she looked more like the gun-toting granny from *Beverly Hillbillies*. "What makes you think I'm hiring?"

"Becky Thorne and Officer Bryant mentioned you might be in need of some assistance with the bookstore."

At the names of Becky and Hamilton, Mrs. Faye's worry lines faded. She looked twenty years younger. "Sweet things. Always looking out for old Jessie Faye. Well, since they sent you… You got any experience?"

Paige nodded. "I worked at Powell's City of Books in Portland for two years."

Jessie Faye let out a low whistle. "Powell's Books. I am in the presence of literary royalty."

"No, Mrs. Faye. I'm just a humble shelf organizer and book sorter, but I know a thing or two about bookstores and business in general. The store could use a facelift. It's quite run-down and outdated."

Jessie Faye pressed her fingers to her mouth. A soft cry escaped her lips. Tears brimmed at the corners of her eyes. "My Lawrence would be ashamed if he could see this place now. He ran it with such love and passion. I've tried to keep up with it, but I'm just not a business-minded woman."

Good going, Paige. You made the old lady cry. "If you don't mind me asking…" A metal folding chair leaned against the wall. Paige's heart felt heavy as she opened it and offered the old woman a seat. "Where is your husband now?"

"Six feet under. He passed away 'bout twenty years ago."

"Oh, I'm so sorry." That did nothing to ease the weight on Paige's chest. *This poor woman.*

"No matter. I'll be joining him soon enough." Mrs. Faye released a shuddered breath. "You've got the job if you want it. I can't pay much, but you'll have the pleasure of seeing this little place returned to its former glory."

How much was "not much"? Would it be enough to live on? Mrs. Faye looked so depressed and the store was in such disrepair, Paige couldn't resist. "Do I need to fill out an application? Get a background check? A drug test?"

"That's not necessary."

Paige was grateful, but she didn't want to take advantage

of an old lady. "I feel I should tell you"—she swallowed—"I used to be a thief."

Paige's confession didn't appear to faze the woman in the least. "My Lord died between two thieves and he took one of them to paradise with him."

"I—I don't understand."

"Never mind. If Becky Thorne trusts you, that's good enough for me."

"Thank you, ma'am. I'll do what I can."

Paige spent the morning sorting and arranging books into more organized piles. Jessie Faye sat in her chair, nodding off now and then, her gentle snore mixing with the whine from the heater and clanging from the water pipes. Only a few customers patronized the store. At noon, Paige walked down to the Rooster Café and brought back two roast beef sandwiches. She gently shook Jessie Faye's shoulder. "Mrs. Faye. I've brought lunch."

The old woman opened her eyes and yawned. "Thank you, dear. I am getting a bit pekish."

Pekish? Who even uses words like that anymore? Paige moved the equipment from the card table and spread out the sandwiches and bottles of water. They sat in two metal folding chairs. Mrs. Faye's wrinkled hand clasped hold of Paige's across the table. "I'll say the blessing." The white-haired woman bowed her head. Paige closed her eyes and tipped her chin toward her chest. She'd prayed more since she'd arrived in Whitman than she had in her entire life.

"Jesus, thank you for giving me another day to live. Thank you for sandwiches. Thank you for bringing Paige here to help me. She is a blessing sent straight from you. And tell Lawrence that I miss him very much, but I'll be seeing him soon. Amen." The prayer finished. Mrs. Faye nibbled on her sandwich.

Blessing. Mrs. Faye thinks I'm a blessing from God? "God

didn't bring me here, Mrs. Faye. Becky mentioned you might have a job opening. I needed a job. That's all."

The old woman's impish smile puzzled Paige. "Believe what you will, child. Believe what you will. And please call me Jessie. Mrs. Faye was my mother-in-law."

Paige opened her mouth to argue but thought better. She'd let the old woman think what she wanted, but Paige wasn't a blessing—to anyone. She ate a few bites of her sandwich and took a couple sips of water. "I've been thinking about your store, Mrs.—Jessie. It really needs a lot of work."

Jessie's shoulders drooped. "Don't I know it. I should sell it, but I can't bear the thought of letting this old place go. Lawrence, my husband, loved his little bookstore. He always said, "There's no better place to find God than in the pages of the Book.""

Paige didn't know what the old lady meant by that, but she did feel sorry for the woman. She wanted to help if she could. All morning while she'd worked, she'd been brainstorming. "I have a suggestion." She waited until she had Mrs. Faye's full attention. "We should close the store, renovate, and have a grand reopening. If we do it right you will easily make back the money we spend on the overhaul, along with a substantial profit."

Mrs. Faye washed down the first half of her sandwich with a long drink of water. She wrapped up the second half of her sandwich and wiped her face with a paper napkin. "It sounds like a wonderful plan and I wish I could afford it, but I don't have the money for such a spendy endeavor." She stood to her feet, groaning and stretching. "Thank you for the lunch." She carried the leftover sandwich to the back room where Paige had spotted a mini fridge earlier in the day. Her aged footsteps shuffled across the floor and into Paige's heart. When the "employee only" bathroom door clicked closed, Paige removed her cell phone from her pocket. She swiped across the screen and tapped on the contact she wanted. Her aunt answered on the second ring. "Hi. Aunt

Hattie. I've got a question…"

Late that evening, Paige sat cross-legged on her bed, wearing a tank top and shorts. The television played a rerun episode of her favorite show. Her cell phone and a hotel notepad, that she'd been scribbling on for over two hours, laid on the comforter. Getting The Bookshelf ready for a grand reopening was not going to be an easy task. She thumped her pencil against her lip, sure she was still missing something. She read over her list again.

1. Remove books
2. Remove dust bunnies, cobwebs, and posters
3. Paint walls, ceilings, and trim
4. Purchase shelving and furniture
5. Purchase computer and set up POS system
6. Catalog inventory
7. Arrange store
8. Market for grand reopening

Someone knocked on the hotel door. Paige crawled off the bed and called through the door. "Who's there?"

"It's Hamilton Bryant. We had dinner plans."

Paige face-palmed her forehead. She'd forgotten about dinner. She unlatched the chain and opened the door. "I'm sorry. I forgot all about it." Hamilton's face flushed, and he looked away. Paige grabbed her hoodie off a hanger and pulled it over her head.

He turned back. "No problem. We can go now if you're ready."

She groaned. "I don't know. I'm—It's been a long day."

"I promised to move you into the garage apartment."

While she didn't want to go to dinner, she did want to get moved. "OK. Let me change and we can leave."

She closed the door, then quickly changed into a sweater and jeans and threw everything else into her duffel bag. Ten minutes later, Hamilton loaded her bag and her bicycle into the trunk of the minivan and they drove down the street. "Where are we going?" She asked.

"El Bajio. Have you tried it yet?" Paige shook her head. "Hope you like Mexican. Not much is still open this time of night."

"Sounds fine."

He pulled into a parking space in front of a building painted like a stucco structure from Old Mexico. He opened the door under the welcome sign and they entered the restaurant, where Paige admired the wall murals that furbished the ambiance of an outdoor Mexican courtyard. Brilliant parrots, nestled on tree branches, were painted so life-like, she half expected to hear their calls. "It's beautiful!"

"How many?" The hostess addressed Officer Bryant.

"Two, please."

They followed the young Latino woman to a teal corner booth under a painted cherry blossom trellis. Paige scooted onto the cushion. Officer Bryant sat across from her, and the hostess handed them menus. "May I get you something to drink?"

"Water with lemon." Officer Bryant spoke first.

"Same, please." Paige opened the trifold and scanned the choices as the hostess left to retrieve the drinks. She peeked over the top of her menu. "Are you sure this is OK? This place is kind of spendy for an apology."

"You said to make it a good one. Besides, they have really good chips and salsa."

A server brought their waters, an overloaded basket of chips and a bowl of salsa. "Are you ready to order?"

"Not yet." Paige looked back at the menu. "What's good here?"

"I usually order chicken fajitas," answered Officer Bryant.

"OK. I'll get those too."

The server wrote down their order, then left. A door swung behind him as he entered the kitchen.

Officer Bryant squeezed his lemon into his water and stirred it with a spoon. He took a drink, then returned the glass to the paper coaster. "So, about that apology?"

Paige's face grew warm. "It's OK. I get it."

"I'm not sure that you do. This is not just a job to me. This is my life, and I take my responsibilities seriously."

"I'm sorry. I didn't mean to insinuate—"

"Who's apologizing to whom? I brought you here to make amends not to start another argument. I'm sorry for upsetting you the other night, and for my rude behavior. I was caught off guard."

Caught off guard? She was almost afraid to ask. "By what?"

Officer Bryant fiddled with the paper ring around the napkin and silverware. He peeled it off and laid the rest on the table. "I have a confession. When I went to Becky's office for the lease agreement, I may have seen your background check."

"Oh." Paige's heart sank. "So, you know?"

He nodded his head. "You want to tell me about it?"

Not really. But the words poured from her lips anyway. "When I was twelve, my grandfather passed away. I was angry, and I started taking stuff. Nothing big, but enough to get community service every time I got caught. I think, I just wanted to be in control of something. When I was fifteen, I spent six months in juvenile hall for a crime I didn't commit. I was framed, but with my prior infractions, they threw the book at me."

"What happened?"

"Someone I thought was my friend stole three thousand dollars from the school office—cash collected for the spring formal from various fundraisers. When the police started asking questions around school, she stashed the money in my backpack."

When she finished her story, his forehead crinkled.

"Those weren't juvenile arrests on your record, Paige."

"I know." She took a drink of her water, giving herself a moment to think. She'd come this far, she might as well tell him the rest. She nervously traced the pattern on the table.

When she finally raised her head, Officer Bryant met her eyes. "Go ahead."

"Once I was released from juvie, I made a decision. If they were going to label me a thief, I might as well be one. I started stealing more valuable stuff and selling it to a fence. I didn't get caught for another four years. I was good at what I did. When I was twenty, I was finally arrested, and the judge gave me probation instead of incarceration, but only if I got help and cleaned up my act. I still don't understand why he showed mercy. I certainly didn't deserve it." Paige shrugged. "I chose to change my life. I saw a counselor for two years and went to business school." *What does he think of me now? Is he itching to get away from me?*

The server approached the table with a large round tray. He set two steaming cast-iron skillets loaded with grilled chicken, peppers, and onions on the table, then two plates of lettuce, cheese, sour cream, and *pico de gallo*, and two tortilla warmers. "Can I get you anything else?"

Paige shook her head and Officer Bryant answered, "No, thank you. I think we're good."

She opened the tortilla warmer and took out a flour tortilla. "Officer Bryant, I'd appreciate it if—"

"I'll keep it to myself. Yeah, I will. And call me Hamilton. I think you deserve it after that confession." He gave her a crooked smile before filling a tortilla shell with chicken and veggies.

For the next several minutes, they ate in silence. She licked sour cream off her fingers and filled another tortilla. She opened her mouth for a bite when her phone starting ringing. "Sunday, Monday, Happy Days." She wiped her greasy hands on a napkin and grabbed her phone, swiping her finger across the screen and pressing the glass to her ear. "Hi,

Aunt Hattie."

"Hi, dear. I've been thinking about your idea, and I can't think of a better use of the money."

"Great. Can I call you back later? I'm having dinner right now."

"Sure, Paigey. Call me tomorrow. It's late and I'm going to bed."

The parrot squawked in the background. "Goodnight, Hattie. Goodnight, Hattie."

"OK. Aunt Hattie. I'll call you tomorrow."

"Bye, Paigey. Enjoy your dinner."

Paige hit the end button and laid her phone on the table. "My Aunt Hattie."

Hamilton quirked his eyebrow. "Happy Days?"

Paige laughed and ducked her head. "Yeah. Happy Days. My grandfather and I used to watch reruns on his days off. The song reminds me of him, even if it is a little cheesy." She picked up her fajita wrap and stuffed the remainder in her mouth. "Are you finished?"

Hamilton dropped his napkin onto his empty plate and signaled for the server. "Check, please."

After paying for the meal, Hamilton drove out to the Thorne house. He rolled her bike into the garage through a side door, then carried her duffel bag up the metal stairs. When they reached the top, he pulled the brass key out of his pocket. "Here you are. Keys to your new home."

Paige accepted the key and unlocked the door, surprised that he was still allowing her to stay so close to his family. "Thank you for dinner."

"You're welcome. I hope we can do it again sometime."

She was glad he couldn't see her red cheeks in the dark. "I'll see you later." She lifted her duffel and carried it through the door.

"Tomorrow?"

"Tomorrow. Maybe."

"I'll take that as a yes."

13

"I wish you'd been at Bible Study tonight, Mom." Kylie set the ceramic plates on the dining room table. "Jenn does an excellent job explaining the verses."

Kathleen nodded her head and murmured a response. She tapped her pen against the stack of papers and continued reading the document in front of her.

"And then she said that Jesus was born on Thanksgiving Day and someday the great turkey is going to come and set us all free."

"That's nice." *Why don't these figures match? I thought Bennett and I went over these last week.*

"Mom! You're not listening to a word I'm saying."

"Excuse me. What?" She removed her reading glasses and looked up from the papers strewn across the table. "Did you want something?"

Kylie folded the napkins in half and tucked them under the edge of the china plates. "I wish you'd go with me to the women's Bible study." She arranged the flatware onto the cloth napkins.

"I'm sorry. You know I'm busy. Preparing for the

election is a lot of work."

"But that's all you ever do."

"Kylie." She snapped. Her daughter's whiny voice grated on her nerves. She put her glasses back on and returned her attention to the list of campaign contributions.

The ringing of the doorbell echoed through the house. "Would you get that?" She didn't take her eyes from the contribution statements.

Kylie set something heavy on the table with a *thunk*. Her response oozed with sarcasm, "Sure, Mom. I'm not doing anything."

"Hey, kid." Kathleen looked up as her brother strode into the room, as suave and confident as ever. He embraced Kylie and swung her around. "How's college?"

"Fine. I only hate one class."

"Hey, that's better than high school. What smells so good in here? Surely, your mom's not cooking."

Kathleen set her mouth in a hard line. "I see your manners are as bad as always. Don't you wait for someone to greet you at the door before entering?"

"Not always." Erik kissed the crown of her head with a loud smack. "Where's Matilda?"

Kylie emptied a sauce pan into a glass bowl on the center island. "Tuesday's are her night off now, so I'm getting to practice all those things I learned in Mrs. Pendleton's Home Ec. class."

"Mrs. Pendleton still teaches home economics." Erik's eyebrows raised with surprise. "I figured she would've retired a long time ago."

Kathleen scoffed. "I was in her class when I was in school."

"That's exactly my point. A long time ago!" Erik pulled out a chair and sat at the table. "Mind if I join you for dinner?"

Kylie shook her head.

Kathleen rolled her eyes at her brother's teasing. "From

what I recall, you were in her class, too."

Kylie brought the bowl to the table and took a seat on Erik's right. She scooted her chair forward, tucking her knees under the table top. "Really, Uncle Erik? You took home economics?"

"In my defense, shop class was full. Besides, it was a classroom full of girls!"

Kylie laughed, and Kathleen reveled in the sound. Her daughter had had little joy since her grandfather's funeral. She was happy that Kylie's zeal for life seemed to be returning.

"Mom, would you put that stuff away so we can eat?"

"It's not *stuff*." Kathleen stood and cleared her work documents from the table. Kylie handed her a plate, drinking glass, and flatware. Kathleen arranged them on the quilted placemat, then her daughter extended her hands to both her mother and uncle and bowed her head. Kathleen knew what Kylie expected them to do. She nodded her head at Erik, silently begging her brother to participate. He obliged and clasped their hands. Kylie prayed out loud.

How long had it been since Kathleen had prayed for anything other than a blessing over a meal? She knew the exact date: April 22, 2009. She'd begged God to spare the unborn child she'd carried in her womb, but her supplications had gone unanswered. If her daughter chose to believe in God, she wouldn't prevent her, but she'd given up on her own faith. He didn't hear. He didn't care.

"Mom, would you pass the salad?"

Kathleen's thoughts returned to the present. "Oh. Here." She handed Kylie the chilled bowl, then held up her plate for Erik to serve her a scoop of Kylie's boeuf bourguignon. "How goes business in Portland?" She asked her brother.

"Profitable." He took a bite of roasted carrot. "Wow, kid. You outdid yourself. I think this is the best boeuf bourguignon I've ever had."

"Thanks, Uncle Erik."

"Of course, it's the only boeuf bourguignon I've ever

had."

"Uncle Erik!"

"Sorry, just kidding."

Kathleen chewed a tender chunk of beef, then took a sip of lukewarm water. "Wasn't Mrs. Pendleton's home economics class the one you were always trying to get out of?"

Erik nodded his head and swallowed. "That's right. I couldn't stand her voice. 'Now, class if you turn to page two thousand ninety-seven in the recipe book, we'll see the steps to make the most amazing, perfect, out of this world cheesecake that you've ever tasted in all your natural born days.'"

"You do that perfectly!" Kylie applauded.

Erik stood and bowed from his waist. "Thank you."

"Your uncle always did have some unusual talents."

"Like what?"

As humorous memories flooded her mind, Kathleen tried not to choke on her food. "Erik learned how to forge Dad's signature in middle school. He wrote doctor's notes for us whenever we wanted to skip out of class. Do you remember that?"

"Yeah. The good old days. There was also that time I picked the lock on the principal's office door and put all the furniture on the track field."

"Then it rained, and you got suspended."

"Oh, yeah. Remember what I did while I was suspended?"

"Poor Matilda. Dad was so mad."

Kylie's expression urged her uncle to tell the story. "Every Friday, Matilda would…" Kylie leaned forward, hanging on her uncle's every word while the boeuf bourguignon grew cold and forgotten.

"Bennett!" Kathleen shouted the next morning, as she bulldozed through her desk drawers. She wet her fingers and flipped through a file she'd ripped from the lowest drawer. "Jeremiah Bennett!" She hollered again.

Her administrative assistant entered the room carrying his tablet and wearing a headset. "Yes, Madam Mayor?" He raked his fingers through his flaming red hair.

"Did you take care of my travel arrangements like I asked?" She'd hired Jeremiah Bennett as her assistant the same day she took office three years ago. He'd started out as an incompetent college student and worked his way to becoming the most trusted member of her staff.

"I did, but there's been a slight correction." He winced and squinted his eyes.

"A slight correction?"

"Yes, Mr. Donahue asked me to—"

"I asked him to arrange a rental car for you." Joe Donahue, her campaign manager and press agent, entered the room. He wore Oakley's, Levi's, and a Ralph Lauren polo shirt and jacket. He took off his sunglasses and hooked them on his shirt. Still in his early fifties, Joe's hair was a little gray around the edges, but he wore it with class and it somehow only made him that much more attractive, if that was even possible. Like George Clooney.

She cocked an eyebrow as agitation flavored her words. "A car? It's an eight-hour drive from here to Salem. I thought I was getting an air taxi from Bend."

Joe folded his arms across his chest. "Yes, that was what we'd discussed. However, the more I thought on it, the more I felt that driving was the better option. Traveling by car will give you the chance to see the sights along the way. We can get the newspapers to print the story. Gubernatorial candidate takes in Oregon countryside." He marked the air like he was already reading the headlines.

Kathleen sighed and surrendered. Joe was right. He usually was about these things. "How are you getting there?"

Joe slid on his sunglasses and spun on his heel. "I'm taking my plane."

Kathleen shook her head, then turned her attention back to her assistant. "You have everything you need to take care of things while I'm gone?"

"Yes, Madam Mayor."

"What time is it now?" She grabbed his left wrist and jerked it toward her.

"My watch is over here, ma'am." Jeremiah extended his right wrist in her direction. She'd forgotten he was left-handed. "It's eight forty-five."

"Thank you, Jeremiah. I'd best be on my way."

"Yes, Madam Mayor. You have a long day of driving ahead of you."

Kathleen tightened her jaw and gathered her things. "Would you put those bags in the trunk?" She gestured toward her suitcase, makeup bag, and garment bag draped over the chair in the corner of the office.

"My pleasure."

Kathleen followed Jeremiah out of her office. She paused at the doorway and gave everything a cursory glance, then with a satisfied nod, flipped the light switch off and locked the door behind her.

He confirmed that the Hawthorne District neighborhood was quiet and deserted, then jogged up the stairs to Hattie McDonald's Foursquare and rang the doorbell. A week had passed since his last sighting of Brooklyn McDonald and he needed to verify her whereabouts. He straightened the cap on his head and tucked the pencil stub behind his ear. Several minutes later, the front door cracked open. A white-haired woman peeked around the frame. She didn't remove the chain, but kept it stretched across the gap like a suspension bridge over a river full of alligators. Hattie McDonald squinted and pursed her lips, eying him as if he were one of those alligators. He relaxed his face and spread a toothy grin from ear to ear. If he was going to get anything from this woman, he needed her to trust him. He kept his voice upbeat and cheerful as he introduced himself. "Hello, Miss McDonald. I work with Brooklyn at Powell's City of Books. I haven't seen her in a while and I wanted to stop by and check if she was okay."

The door opened a little further. "You work with Paige?"

"Yes, ma'am."

"You're a man, so I guess you can't be that abominable Cat." The old lady dropped the chain and opened the front door the rest of the way. "Paige doesn't work at Powell's Books anymore."

Well, this is news to me. "I'm so sorry. Has she managed to find other employment?"

"Not yet. Paige has taken a sabbatical to go on a journey of sorts. She's in Whitman searching for her birth mother."

His mind whirled with the news. He struggled to keep his voice steady. "Thank you for telling me. Let her know that I wish her the best of luck. Good afternoon to you." He turned as the door closed behind him, and he clomped down the stairs much slower than he'd jogged up.

Brooklyn McDonald was in Whitman? This was an unexpected twist.

Kathleen made a pit stop at the halfway point to stretch her legs and catch a bite to eat. Her stomach had been protesting for the last hour, and she needed to use the restroom. Joe had been right, of course. Driving across the countryside had given her a new appreciation for her home state. She sat on a park bench with a to-go salad container on her lap and a plastic fork in her hand. While she ate, she watched the small-town citizens around her as they went about their daily lives.

While campaigning, it was easy to focus on the big cities, but these were votes—people she needed to win over, too. Out of the 4.2 million people who lived in Oregon, less than half of the population lived in the major cities. Much of the state was rural. She tapped her fork against her lips. Rural areas usually meant strong families. Old-fashioned values. They'd want someone who'd protect their beliefs, their values, and their farmland. She set her salad to the side and dug through her purse until she found her cell phone. She popped in her Bluetooth and dialed Joe.

"What can I do for you, Madam Mayor?"

The background was noisy and chaotic. "Are you still in the air?"

"No. I landed a while ago. I'm here at the hotel. Let me step outside." She waited while he moved. She heard him speak to someone, maybe the doorman, then the background grew quiet. "There, that's better. You were saying?"

"I'd like to have a rally at home in Whitman. I've done several in other locations, but not in my hometown. I think it would be good for the rural voters to see that I come from a small town, too. I would have their best interest at heart because of my background."

Joe whistled on the other end of the line. "Nice. Wish I'd thought of that." He paused. "Like a political rally?"

She shook her head even though he couldn't see her. "No. I'm thinking bigger. Like a family-centered type thing. With balloons, clowns, bouncy houses… I don't know… music, carnival games, the store owners could get involved with raffles or something like that. I haven't thought it all through yet." For a moment there, she was sounding a lot like her daughter, Kylie. Kathleen coughed and straightened her spine. She blew out a breath and collected her thoughts. "Do you think this is something we should pursue?"

There was silence on the other end of the line. Kathleen waited. The only sound was a crow cawing in the distance.

Even the town around her had grown sparse in the last few minutes. "Joe?"

"It's a doozy of an idea." His voice startled her. "One I think we should consider. When were you thinking about hosting this event?"

"Is a month too short of notice?"

"What if we made it part of the town's Independence Day celebration?"

"That might work. After the Memorial Day fiasco, I've been seriously reconsidering fireworks."

"Can't cut fireworks. We want to secure the support of the local families, not make enemies of them."

"Right, we'll figure it out. I need to hit the road. I still have a long way to go."

"Drinks tonight at eight?"

"I don't drink."

"That's right. You don't drink, smoke, or chew or run with those who do."

Kathleen ignored his sarcastic remark. "I'll meet you around eight this evening. We can get coffee."

"Coffee before bed? I'll stay up all night."

Kathleen chuckled. "Not me. Coffee has never had that effect on me. See you in Salem."

"Bye."

She tapped the end call button on her phone and removed the Bluetooth, then glanced over at the remains of her salad. It looked a lot less appetizing than it had a few minutes ago. She picked it up and walked it to the trash can, tapped the salad pieces into the bin, then dropped the plastic container and the fork into the recycling bin. She needed to get back on the road. She still had several hours to go before she reached her destination.

He hung up the phone call from his contact in Portland and smirked. With Kathleen out of town, he could execute the next part of his plan. He scanned the park area surrounding the Bowlby stone building, then slipped inside the dark stairwell. He climbed the stairs to the second floor and peeked through the window at the dark, empty hallway, checking the positions of the security cameras and the door to the mayor's office. 3…2…1… Just as he expected, the generator kicked on and the lights flickered, then turned on. He checked his watch. Four and a half seconds since he cut the power. It wasn't enough. These stairs and the bathrooms were the only areas of the courthouse not under surveillance. No, for this to work, they'd have to take out the generator, too. Unless he could think of another way. It was a lot of work, but it'd be so worth it. Richard Staten was a connoisseur of fine art and collectibles. The paintings in his former office were worth millions on their own, not even counting the pieces in the Mayoral mansion. He was going to take back every cent he was due. His cell phone vibrated in his pocket. He checked the caller ID. His contact. Hopefully calling with the information he needed, but he couldn't answer here. His voice would echo. He didn't relish the thought that the camera downstairs would capture his exit, but what else could he do? He walked down the stairs and out the door, keeping his face turned from the camera, but not shielded. He kept his movements predictable and mundane. Once out of sight of the camera, he answered on the last ring. "Whaddya got?"

Kathleen pulled up to the entrance of The Grand Hotel at a quarter of seven. She had just over an hour until she was to meet Joe for coffee. The valet opened her door. "Good evening, ma'am. Welcome to The Grand Hotel." She exited the car and opened the trunk of the rental, then handed him the keys. A bellman waited at the curb with a cart for her luggage. "Please enjoy your stay."

"Thank you."

The doorman held the door as she passed through the entry and headed straight for the registration desk. Her heels clicked on the marble floor overshadowed by glitz and glamour. The check-in clerk greeted her with a friendly smile. "Do you have a reservation?"

"Yes. The name is Kathleen Phillips."

The woman tapped on her keyboard. Her eyes flickered as she viewed the screen. She frowned. *Frowning? That can't be good.* "I'm sorry, what did you say your name was?"

"Kathleen Phillips. My assistant made all the arrangements."

"I don't have anything for a Kathleen Phillips. Could your assistant have reserved the room under his own name by mistake?"

"I suppose that's possible. Jeremiah Bennett." *This is odd.* Surely, Bennett wouldn't have made such an error. She'd asked him this morning if he'd made all the arrangements and he'd confirmed.

The woman pecked on the keyboard, then shook her head. "I'm sorry."

Kathleen sighed and removed her wallet from her purse. "Do you have any rooms available that I can reserve right now?"

The woman shook her head again. "No, I'm sorry. We're booked up for the week. There's some sort of political event in town."

Kathleen pursed her lips together. "I'm aware."

"Is there some sort of trouble here?"

Kathleen spun on her heel at the deep voice. Senator Chatham stood directly behind her, a concerned expression on his usually smug face. "It appears the hotel has lost my reservation." She couldn't keep the annoyance and frustration from her voice, exhausted from driving all day and her shoes were killing her feet. She just barely refrained from flinging them across the room, one by one. The clerk at the counter stuttered and muttered an apology. "I've also been informed that the hotel is booked solid because of the rally. What are you doing here?"

Senator Chatham reached out and squeezed her arm. "I'm here to support an old family friend. I'm certain there's something we can do about this little mix-up." He snapped his fingers. "My suite has an empty bedroom. It's completely at your disposal."

She frowned and drew her eyebrows together. A sudden stone sunk to the bottom of her stomach. "I don't think that's such a good idea. What would people think?"

Senator Chatham released his grip on her arm. "Nonsense. There is nothing untoward about aiding a friend. Where else would you go? Everything in town is filled."

She glanced back at the clerk, who stuck out her lip and shrugged. "It's true."

Kathleen sighed and dropped her shoulders. "Fine. Thank you." *I'm certainly locking my door tonight. Besides*—she handed the clerk her identification—t*here is always that adage, 'Keep your friends close and your enemies closer'.*

14

"I've made a list of everything that needs to be done, starting with emptying the store. My new apartment has a second bedroom I'm not using, so I thought we could move everything there for the time being. Then we'll paint, buy shelving units and a computer. I'll set up a database and a point of sale system. Before you know it, this store will be back to running the way she did in her glory days." Paige tapped her pencil on the card table in a stroke of victory. Aunt Hattie had loved her idea—investing the $50,000 into The Bookshelf. Jessie Faye sat across from her in the storage room/office space that Paige envisioned as being divided into a real office with a storage room.

The old woman dabbed her eyes with a tissue. She sniffled. "I still can't believe you would do all this for me."

Paige rested against the cold frame of the brown metal chair. "You're welcome, Jessie, but like I explained, it's an investment. After we get the store running again, you will pay us back with eight percent interest."

"I know. Well, I think, I know. My old brain can't quite keep up with all those new-fangled ideas, but if you say so. Is eight percent enough?"

By the time, I'm done with this place, 8% interest is going to be more than enough. Paige nodded.

"We'll do it, but you must see the project through to completion."

"You'll also have enough profits to hire a manager to run this place for you, so you won't have to come in every day." *You'll need a replacement for me if this whole family reunion doesn't work out.*

Jessie patted her white curls with bent fingers. "What do we need to do first?"

Paige checked the time on her phone. The front bell jingled in the main room. She smiled. "Here comes phase one."

"Phase one?"

Paige just grinned as Jessie followed her into the store front. Officer Bryant stood in the entry holding an armload of flattened cardboard boxes. "Where do you want me to put these?"

She froze in place. *What is he doing here?* She tried to mask her surprise. She'd expected Becky or Dave to drop off the boxes, not Hamilton. *Why does it have to be him?* She couldn't stop thinking about their "date" last night. Her confession hadn't scared him away? *Becky must have roped him into helping.* It was the only logical explanation she could think of. She swallowed and pointed at an empty area she'd cleared first thing this morning. "Is there more?"

Hamilton dropped the boxes on the floor with a groan. "More?" He laughed. "Becky must have called every merchant in town. The back of the minivan is loaded with these things. I had to fold down the seats to make them all fit."

"Perfect. Let me help."

Hamilton had parallel parked along the curb. After pushing, pulling, and making several trips back and forth, they managed to transport all of the boxes from the minivan into the store. "Thank you, Officer Bry—I mean—Hamilton. I appreciate you bringing those by." Paige stuck her hands into her jeans' pockets.

"You're welcome. I'll see you later. I've got to get to sleep. I'm on night shift starting tonight."

Paige returned his wave as he drove away, then she cracked her knuckles and headed inside. She had a lot of work ahead of her. Anything to keep her mind off the adorable, yet puzzling Hamilton Bryant.

Hamilton sat in his patrol car at two o'clock Thursday morning, coffee in hand and a bag of mini donuts from the convenience store propped on the dashboard. He took a sip of the hot liquid, then leaned back against the headrest. The streets of Whitman were quiet. That's why he loved the night watch. It gave him time to think. To pray.

Lord, I don't know what to do about Paige. She's an enigma, a puzzle. An ex-con, for goodness' sake. I shouldn't be attracted to her and yet I am. She's not a Christian. If we were to—uh, marry—we'd be unequally yoked. What about my vow to remain single? How do I reconcile my own fears, my own feelings, with your path for my life? Is Paige a part of that path or merely a distraction that I need to avoid?

He lowered the cup into the cupholder in the console, then put the car into drive. Time to make his rounds. He pressed on the gas pedal and rolled forward. His eyes flittered back and forth. All was just as it should be.

Mr. Haberdeen waved from his front yard as his bulldog, Puggles, nosed in the bushes. A light shone from college student, Peter Brunner's upstairs window. He must have waited until the last minute to do his homework. Again. *Does he need help with his classes? I should check in with him and see how it's going.* He'd tutored Peter before. Hamilton turned the corner onto Ironwood Street, passing the Keith's Victorian. Mrs. Keith paced in front of the lighted bay window, swaying and bouncing her colicky newborn in her arms.

Flashing lights on a stalled vehicle up ahead drew his attention. *What's going on up here?* He pulled behind the disabled vehicle, opened his door, and removed the flashlight from his duty belt. He flicked it on and shone the beam toward the driver's window. The running car appeared abandoned. The hairs on his neck stood on end. His hand reached for his weapon. He turned to return to his cruiser just as something connected with his face. His head snapped back as searing pain ripped through his cheekbone. He blinked and shook off the disorientation. With quick reflexes, he dodged the second punch, but he dropped his flashlight and it rolled under the car. His assailant wore all black with a hood shadowing his facial features. He was a foot taller and more than fifty pounds heavier. Hamilton jerked sideways trying not to engage in a fight. He kept his right hip tilted away, making sure his weapon stayed out of the guy's reach. "Sir, you need to calm down." The big man charged him, but Hamilton stepped aside and drew his gun. "On the ground. Hands behind your head." The attacker turned and charged a second time. Hamilton stuck out his foot and the oaf toppled to the ground like the giant, Goliath. Hamilton kept his gun trained on his back. "Hands behind your head." He yanked the handcuffs from his belt and clasped them over the guy's meaty wrists. He scanned the area for anyone else, then holstered his weapon. He hauled the suspect to his feet and forced him to spread eagle while he frisked him for drugs or weapons. When he came up clean, Hamilton shoved him into the back seat of the squad car, then did a search of the suspect's vehicle, finding nothing except for an ID. Satisfied, he shut off the car, took the keys out of the ignition, then returned to the patrol car to haul the guy to the station for processing. He'd call for a tow later.

A sly grin spread over Jerry's face. The distraction worked according to plan. His cohort, Ike, would occupy the cop for hours. He picked the lock and opened the door, then entered the alarm code. The police cruiser pulled away as he slipped inside. If it wasn't so cliché, he'd say this was easier than taking candy from a baby. To be accurate, it was as easy as taking cell phones from an electronics store. Which was exactly what his boss had in mind.

Hamilton's cell phone startled him awake. He groped at the night table, knocking his keys and a lamp onto the floor. He yanked the phone and charger from the wall. The caller ID read Dave. Hamilton groaned and ran his hand over his face, wincing when he touched his bruised chin. "Hello." His voice was gravely from lack of sleep. *What time is it?*

"The store's been robbed."

Hamilton's eyes shot open. He threw back the blankets and jolted to his feet. "How much did they get?"

"They cleaned the store out. I'm down thirty-to-fifty thousand dollars' worth of merchandise."

"I'll call it in on my way. Don't touch anything."

Hamilton tossed on a polo shirt and jeans, then called dispatch while he drove the minivan to his brother-in-law's electronics store on Ironwood. He'd just been by here last night. Everything had gone smooth until his altercation with Ike Simmons. When he'd run the ID through the database, he got zero hits, which probably meant it was a fake. Simmons' blood alcohol level had been zero, which had left Hamilton perplexed most of the night. He would charge him with assault which would at least keep him in jail for a little while. Anger and frustration grew in his stomach. Was Ike merely a diversion? A distraction? As Hamilton began putting the pieces of the puzzle together, he didn't like the picture they formed.

Officers Martin and Stone had arrived and were roping off the sidewalk with police tape. A curious crowd gathered outside the storefront. Hamilton parked in the alley behind the stores. Chief House approached him as he entered through the back door. "Nice shiner. Shouldn't you be sleeping?"

Hamilton ignored the chief's question. He couldn't sleep now even if he tried. "Whaddya got so far?"

"Our suspect or suspects picked the lock, then turned off the security system. Time stamp shows zero two sixteen hours. They picked the locks on the display cases and stole fifty-thousand dollars' worth of cell phones and accessories, all while wearing gloves and not getting picked up by the officer on duty. Now why is that?" The veins on the chief's neck bulged like lava flows from an erupting volcano.

So, the robbery *had* happened during the arrest. Hamilton raked his hand through his hair and twisted on his heel. "Ike Simmons. The guy I hauled in last night for punching me in the face. Whoever robbed this store was conspiring with Ike. They knew I'd have to take him to the station for processing and they used my absence to their advantage."

Chief House groaned audibly, then left Hamilton and joined Officer Martin, where he was taking a statement from Hamilton's brother-in-law. This made four robberies in less than a week. What was going on here? Why the sudden rise in criminal activity?

The image of a blue-eyed blond formed in his mind. She'd admitted to being a former thief, to selling to a fence. Had she suddenly found herself in need of cash? He thought of The Bookshelf's renovations. Jessie went on and on about how Paige had donated money for the project. That had to be expensive. She had means, motive, and opportunity, but was she guilty? He had to get to the bottom of this. One way or another.

"Miss Paige! Miss Paige!"

Paige flung open her apartment door. "Timmy. Are you OK?" He stood on her front stoop. His face was flush, and he was panting as if he'd run up the staircase. She looked him over but didn't see any gushing blood.

"I'm fine. Are you fine?"

She tucked her hair behind her ears and sighed with relief. "Yes, I'm OK, but *you* scared *me*. I thought something was wrong."

"Sorry." Timmy pointed down the stairs. Hamilton and Timmy's brothers loaded the back of Becky's minivan with bag chairs and a cooler. "Uncle Ham is taking us to see a movie in the park. Do you want to go with us?"

Paige grimaced. "I don't know. I don't want to impose. I wasn't invited." *Do I really want to spend an entire evening with Hamilton?*

"You wouldn't be 'posing. Uncle Ham sent me up here to invite you."

"I don't know…" Timmy was sweet, but every time she and Hamilton got together, they either fought or disaster ensued. Besides, she wasn't interested in dating a cop and she needed to stay away before he asked her out again. She'd made a promise to herself. A promise that was getting harder and harder to keep the more she got to know Hamilton Bryant.

Timmy's eyes grew as big around as pancakes. "Please, Miss Paige."

His bottom lip pooched out, tugging at Paige's heart. No matter how much she resisted, she couldn't stand the thought of breaking the little boy's heart. "Give me five minutes." She held up her palm with all five fingers outstretched.

The towheaded boy shouted as he galloped down the metal stairs. "She said she'd come." Paige shook her head and closed the door, then went for her shoes and backpack. After she was ready, she jogged down the stairs to Becky's minivan.

Hamilton leaned across the seat and opened the door from the inside. She climbed in and dropped her backpack onto the dirty floorboard. A purplish bruise and split lip decorated the left side of the officer's face. She gasped. "What happened to you?"

Hamilton glanced at the boys in the back seat, then cleared his throat. "I had a bit of an altercation last night."

"Yeah, Uncle Ham got pummeled in the face!" Timmy shouted from the back.

Paige and Hamilton chuckled. "I see," she said. "Sorry about that."

He put the van in gear and pulled out of the driveway. "It's okay. Just part of the risk." She sucked in a sharp breath and turned her head. *Part of the risk?* Wasn't that the problem? This time it was a punch in the face. What if his attacker had drawn a knife or a gun? Would his family be planning a trip to the park or the hospital? Or the morgue?

Fifteen minutes later, they parked in one of the parking spaces surrounding Sacajawea Park. Dozens of families milled around a large blow-up screen. Colorful chairs and coolers spotted the green grass. "What's playing tonight?" Paige asked as they exited the minivan. The older boys slammed the rolling door shut and ran off.

Hamilton pulled the handle and raised the hatchback. "Cars four or five, something like that." He answered.

Timmy snorted. "It's *Cars 3*, Uncle Ham." He bumped against her leg and reached for her hand. Her heart melted as his soft palm and dirty fingernails melded with her manicured fingers. She met Hamilton's twinkling eyes.

"I think he likes you," he said with a chuckle. He then pulled the cooler from the back and shut the door. He slung the chair straps over his shoulder.

"Can I get something for you?"

Hamilton angled his chin toward his nephew. "You

already have your hands full." *He really loves these boys. He's going to make a great dad someday. Maybe he'll have a little towheaded boy just like Timmy.* Paige's cheeks flushed. Hamilton was focused on choosing a place to sit and didn't seem to notice her embarrassment. They found an open spot under a shade tree and set up the chairs. A curly-haired boy wearing a Batman T-shirt ran up to Timmy. After a moment of conversation, they ran off together toward the swings leaving Paige and Hamilton alone. He opened the cooler and removed a dripping ice-cold water bottle. "Want one?"

"Sure."

He wiped the condensation off with his hand and flung it to the side. Droplets sprinkled across her arm. "Hey!" She laughed. He grinned and dried the bottle with the edge of his T-shirt then handed it to her. When Paige unscrewed the lid and took a swig, a cooling sensation washed over her tongue and down her throat. She dropped the bottle into the cupholder on the arm of the chair and wiped her forearm across her mouth. Hamilton downed an entire water bottle. He crushed it with his hands and tossed it like a basketball into a nearby trash can. "Nice."

"Thanks."

They sat in awkward silence for several minutes until Paige couldn't take it any longer. "How—how are the investigations going?"

"Nowhere." Hamilton leaned forward and propped his elbows on his knees. "Sorry. I can't really talk about open investigations."

"Oh." What could they talk about? It seemed every subject was either off limits or taboo.

"My nephew has really taken a liking to you." He didn't turn his head or even look at her.

"He's really sweet. They're all very fond of you."

No reply.

She glanced at the cooler. Food was always a safe topic for conversation. "Did you bring anything to eat?"

A smile spread across his face. "Becky packed her famous homemade ice cream sandwiches." He popped open the cooler and fished out a Tupperware container.

Homemade ice cream sandwiches? She's the principal and a real estate agent. She's raising three boys and she had time to make dessert. Who is she? Wonder Woman?

"Try one. They're amazing."

Paige helped herself to one of the chocolate cookie sandwiches. Sweet vanilla ice cream dripped down her fingers as she licked the side. Out of nowhere, all three boys appeared. Paige watched in horror as their dirty hands clawed at the sweets. In seconds, the container was empty, and they sat in the grass licking their fingers like hyenas after a kill.

"Wow! It's like a shark feeding frenzy."

Hamilton leaned over until his warm breath brushed her ear. Her stomach did flip flops. "There's a second container hidden in the cooler just for us. Becky knows how they can be."

"Oh. That's nice of her." She fought against the disappointed feeling that settled over her. *What are you thinking? You don't even want his attention. He's keeping things on a friendship level and so should you.*

"My daddy's store got robbed."

The words from Timmy's mouth flashed like a lightning bolt into Paige's thoughts. "What?" *Another robbery? What's going on here?* "When?"

"Last night." Hamilton answered. "Someone broke into Dave's store and lifted fifty thousand dollars' worth of merchandise."

"Oh, no. I'm so sorry."

"You're going to get them, right, Uncle Ham?" Tony spoke up.

Hamilton tussled his nephew's hair. "You've got it, kiddo."

Paige leaned back in her picnic chair. Officer Hamilton looked much less certain than the promise to his nephew indicated. He'd clenched his jaw and his shoulders sagged under the weight of the recent crime spree. He turned and met her eyes. Her cheeks flushed again under his gaze, until the setting sun broke through the line of trees and illuminated the ugly blue bruise on his face. She broke eye contact. She was right to stay away. Her heart would never survive the loss of another man in uniform.

The movie ended at nine o'clock. He drove them back home to Becky's before his shift started at ten. Timmy fell asleep in the backseat. "Thank you for a fun evening." Paige's voice was soft as she exited the minivan.

"You're welcome." He unbuckled the little boy's seatbelt and lifted him into his arms. The screen door slammed behind the two older boys. She stood beside him, looking like she had more to say. She fumbled with her keys and tucked a stray hair behind her ear. "Hamilton, about tonight—"

"Hold on a minute. I've got to take him inside. I'll be right back. Wait for me?"

He hurried into the house and deposited the sleeping child on his bed. After a quick word with Becky, he returned to the driveway. Paige was gone. A light appeared over the garage.

He'd wanted to question her about the recent robberies, but that would only serve to put her on the defensive. Too many questions and she'd feel like a suspect under interrogation. His sister would have his head if he did that. Clearly, she felt that Paige deserved their trust. But the woman was, without a doubt, hiding something. She'd yet to answer his question of why she'd come to Whitman. Lillian was right. Paige's arrival in town and the start of this string of robberies had occurred about the same time, but that didn't necessarily make her the thief.

Did it?

Saturday morning, Paige ambled through town, her purse over her shoulder and a coffee cup in her hand. Blinding sunlight bounced off the blacktop as she pushed on the glass entrance to Sam's pawn shop where a little bell signaled her entrance. Shelves of old clocks, guitars, weapons, and all manner of valuables cluttered the open space. Paige breathed in and sneezed. The store smelled of desperation and dust. A bald man wearing reading glasses, a sweater vest, and a scowl stood behind a glass display case, winding the gears of an antique cuckoo clock. She dodged a rack of DVDs and approached the counter, setting her purse on top with a *thud.* "Good morning."

The broker frowned and peered over his glasses. "Yes?"

"I'm in the market for antique books or first editions, do you have any?"

"Have you checked the floor?" He didn't bother to raise his head.

She turned 360° and glanced around. "No. I thought I'd save the trouble and just ask."

He rested his tools on the countertop, then wiped the beading sweat from his forehead with a yellowed handkerchief. "There's none on display. I'll have to check the back."

"If you knew there wasn't—"

"I'll be right back." He disappeared behind a half-height swinging door.

His attitude was infuriating, especially toward a potential customer. Paige strolled around the store, attempting to "fizzle her sizzle" as Aunt Hattie always said. She stopped beside a cabinet of jewelry, careful not to touch the clean glass and leave smudgy fingerprints. She squatted down to admire some of the pieces. A pink and clear diamond bracelet caught her attention. The bell jingled as another patron entered. She glanced his direction and then paid the man little attention. She stood to her feet just as the rude broker returned.

"Nope, none in the back either. Can I show you anything else?"

"May I see this diamond bracelet?" She pointed into the cabinet.

"Why? You can't afford it. I'm taking it to Portland next week to find a rich buyer in the city." His tone was sharp and condescending.

Paige was taken aback by his total lack of customer service. "Never mind. Have a good day, sir." She couldn't help taking on a bit of a sarcastic tone herself. She stormed out the door and down the sidewalk, thinking—I can't believe he'd treat me that way—and plowed directly into the rock-hard chest of a man, spilling hot coffee all over the front of his… navy blue police uniform? "Oh, I'm so sorry."

He stepped back and brushed at the scalding stains. "Wow. That's hot."

That voice. She raised her head and came eye-to-eye with Officer Hamilton Bryant. "I'm so sorry. I wasn't looking where I was going." She waved her hand at the store she'd just left. "That man has really got my goat."

"Who? Sam?" He continued brushing at the wet spots on his shirt.

"I think so."

"Don't pay him any attention. A bit cranky, but he's harmless." Hamilton unbuttoned his shirt revealing the white T-shirt underneath. Brown stains spotted the area around his stomach. "Wow, that was hot," he repeated. He untucked the T-shirt and flapped the end. Paige tried not to stare at the ab muscles exposed every time he raised the fabric.

"I'm really sorry." *Will he mention last night?* The second he'd been out of sight, she'd bolted for her apartment. *I don't know what I was thinking.* She wasn't sure what she'd wanted to say to him before he went inside with Timmy.

"It's okay. I'm finished with my shift and heading home anyway." They'd been walking while they talked. They now stood beside the police car. "I'm working nights, so if you need any help with the bookstore, just let me know."

Paige's heart fluttered. *It's nothing. He's thinking of Jessie Faye.*

Without a word of how she'd disappeared on him, Hamilton climbed inside the patrol car. He put the key into the ignition and started the engine, then he keyed into his microphone and talked to dispatch. With a *whoop whoop*, he drove off. Just before he turned the corner, he raised his hand to wave. She waved back, then grabbed hold of her wrist. *Seriously?*

She continued her walk down Main Street, trying to get the handsome officer out of her thoughts. Her shoelace slapped against her leg. The left one had come untied, so she paused at a cement bench in the community park surrounding the courthouse. Frustrated groans came from a car down the street. The trunk stood open and someone was attempting to load something inside. Paige tied the laces, then dropped her foot to the ground and jogged over to lend a hand. Kylie Phillips precariously balanced a plastic tote spilling over with wads of brightly colored materials. She'd already loaded two more totes into the trunk. "Kylie? Do you need help?"

The poor girl whimpered and shoved down on the bin. "I need to take these over to the school, but I can't seem to fit all three buckets in the trunk." She stomped her foot, then rushed to steady the tote as it slid sideways on the bumper.

Paige leaned around the trunk lid. "Is anyone riding with you?"

"No. I'm all by myself. Except for Matilda. She's our housekeeper. And cook. But she's at home. My mom's been in Salem since Wednesday. She won't be home until late tonight or maybe tomorrow."

"Have you tried putting the last tote inside the car? Like

on the backseat?"

Kylie face-palmed her forehead and groaned. "Why didn't I think of that?" Paige opened the door and Kylie easily slid the tote into the back seat. She squealed and threw her arms around Paige's upper torso. "Thank you. Thank you. Thank you."

"You're welcome." Paige peeled the ecstatic girl from her mid-section. "Have a nice afternoon." She turned to walk away.

"You want to go with me? See the school?"

She'd already seen the school with Hamilton a week ago. She couldn't see any reason to return. Kylie's eyes grew big and her lips pouched out. "OK." Inwardly, she sighed. What was wrong with her? She couldn't even say no to a simpering teenager. She rounded the vehicle and slid onto the grayish suede seat. She stoked her fingers over the polished wood dashboard. "Nice." She commented as Kylie bounced under the steering wheel.

"It belonged to my grandfather. He gave it to me when I learned to drive two years ago."

"Richard Staten, right?"

Kylie nodded as she pulled onto the street. When they arrived at the school, she parked, then turned off the car and removed the key from the ignition. "Will you help me carry this stuff inside?"

"Sure."

They entered through a side door. The school was dark and quiet, and their footsteps echoed in the empty hallways. Kylie flipped a light switch on the wall and the florescent lights flickered on. The walls of framed photos gave Paige reason to pause. Graduates gazed down on her, some with smiles, some without. *Annie's photo must be up there somewhere.* She hoped, anyway. She'd yet to find actual evidence that Annie had ever lived in the town of Whitman.

Last Friday evening, before dinner at Becky Thorne's, she'd gone to the records department at the courthouse.

When she'd explained what she was looking for, the sympathetic registrar shook her head. "Without a last name, there's not really anything I can do."

"Could you run a search for the name Annie and see what comes up?"

Run a search? She chuckled again at the woman's response. No one had digitized the city of Whitman. Hundreds of thousands of forms and certificates filled document boxes in a warehouse sorted by the first letter of the last name. Without that information, it would take a year to dig through each box.

Paige turned from the photographs and followed Kylie backstage of the auditorium. "We can set these boxes over here."

The heavy curtain parted, and Paige stared out across the stage. Her feet froze in place. Blood pulsed in her temples. Her heartbeat thumped against her ribcage. *"You'll be there, won't you Grandpa?" She'd giggled as the bristles of his mustache tickled her nose when he leaned down to plant a kiss on her forehead. "Of course, I'll be there. I wouldn't miss opening night, my little star."*

"Are you okay?" Kylie's voice broke through her thoughts.

Paige closed her eyes to shut out the memories. She took a deep breath and nodded. "Yeah. I'm OK, but I could really use the restroom."

Kylie grabbed her hand. "Come on, we'll use the teacher's bathroom. It's cleaner." Kylie dragged Paige down the hallway and into a stark-white concrete block room. Floor to ceiling, 1950's green metal dividers separated two stalls. Graffiti covered the doors and walls. Kylie spoke from the other side of the divider. "These were student bathrooms until they remodeled and built the bigger ones. I think this was the girl's room."

Paige slid the bolt on the stall door into place. As she sat, she caught sight of something scratched into the door. The names "Annie + Ryan" surrounded by a heart. *Annie? My mother? Maybe she did live here. Maybe she went to this school.* She looked at the second name. Ryan? Was that someone Annie had a crush on? Had they dated? Paige sucked in a breath. Was that her father?

She flushed the toilet and unlocked the slip lock, but the door didn't budge. *Odd.* "Hey, Kylie? I need help. The door's stuck." She hit the door with her hip. Nothing happened. "Kylie." She pulled on the top of the door and shook it. She tried again. She looked down at the door. There was a second lock. Turned around backward. And locked from the outside. "Kylie!" Silence. Paige squatted and peeked under the gap. The next stall over was empty. Had the toilet flushed? When did Kylie leave? "Kylie! Help. Kylie!" Paige wrapped her arms around her ribcage and squeezed. "Kylie?" She whimpered.

The lock clicked. She pushed, and the door opened. Kylie stood outside the stall, laughing. Paige's heart pounded in her chest.

"Sorry. I didn't mean to scare you. It was just a harmless prank. Someone mounted the original lock backward. Instead of fixing it, they added the bolt."

Paige took deep breaths to slow her pulse. "I thought I was stuck in there."

"Someone would have found you, eventually."

The two girls left the school building and headed back into town. Kylie dropped Paige off where she'd left her bike. Paige waved and pedaled back to her apartment. She'd had enough excitement for one day.

She'd settled onto her sofa with a cup of coffee and the television remote when she remembered the letters on the back of the bathroom door. Was "Annie" her mother? Was that proof she'd once lived in Whitman? And who was Ryan? Was he her father? Would she ever learn the truth?

15

Kathleen tucked her legs under the steering wheel of her rental. The service station noises muted when she closed the car door. She'd made a quick pit stop inside to use the restroom, and purchased some snacks and a bottle of pop, while the attendant filled her gas tank. She clicked her seatbelt into place, then with a glance in all directions, pulled out onto the access road and worked her way back to Highway 84. It'd been a long three days of campaigning—speaking at the convention center in Salem, followed by a reception and press conference. She hated carbonated beverages but needed the caffeine to keep her going. She'd tried the service station coffee, and it had tasted like mud. She'd been on her feet most of the weekend and her high-heeled shoes pinched her toes. She kicked them off and drove in her stockinged feet. She pressed the OnStar button on her steering wheel. "Call Joe Donahue," she told the hands-free system.

"Dialing Joe Donahue," said the computerized voice. The phone began ringing.

Joe's voice carried over the speakers. "Madam Mayor. What can I do for you?"

"Would you get me those numbers from our last contributions statements?"

"Sure. What's up?"

"I was going over the files earlier. Something doesn't add up. How many pledges did we receive this week?"

There was a moment of silence on the other end of the line. "Eighty-seven thousand dollars was pledged."

That's it? Gubernatorial campaigns take millions. What's going on here?

"Do you want those numbers now?"

Brake lights flashed ahead. Traffic slowed. Kathleen tapped her brake pedal, then stopped as the line of cars in front of her came to a complete standstill. "No. Have those numbers on my desk by morning. I'll be back late tonight. I'm meeting Dad's attorney in La Grande to discuss the will."

"Will do. Safe trip."

Kathleen pressed the end call button and focused on driving through the heavy traffic. As the cars crept forward, she caught sight of flashing lights. The police were directing traffic into one lane to pass a motor vehicle accident.

He watched from the shadows. It wasn't difficult to find her car. Kathleen Phillips was as predictable as the tide. Every time she was in La Grande, she ate at this same restaurant and parked in the same spot. The parking lot was empty on a Sunday night, and a shade of trees hid the driver's door from prying eyes. He glanced at his watch. She'd been inside for fifteen minutes. The lawyer had shown up just after she did. He moved forward, crouching out of sight. Her car alarm wasn't set. The indicator light wasn't blinking on the dashboard. *Stupid woman. So trusting. It will be her ruin.* Without touching the car, he stuck the key into the lock and turned. The door unlocked. He opened the door and slipped into the seat. With gloved hands, he lifted her half-consumed soda pop bottle from the cup holder. She wasn't finished. She preferred her soda pop and her water to be lukewarm. He pulled a plastic bag from his jacket pocket and removed the small white pills. He dropped them in the soda and gave a small shake. The pill would dissolve by the time she left the restaurant. She'd never notice the slight change since she already despised the taste of pop. He returned the bottle to the console, then slipped out of the car, locking it behind him.

Kathleen tuned in to a channel on the radio. Clouds covered the moon. The two-lane county road wound its way through farm country. She rolled down the window and cool air rushed into the car. Without taking her eyes from the road, she opened a bag of peanut M&M's and tossed a handful into her mouth. The sugar should help keep her awake. She took a swig of soda pop and shivered as it went down her throat. She smacked her lips and stuck out her tongue. *Yuck.* She twisted the cap back in place and dropped the bottle into the console.

A while later, her eyelids drooped. She shook her head and yawned, then she groaned and blinked. Her meeting with Don Wall had been successful. Don assured her that she'd be getting a copy of the will in the mail soon. She hoped probate wouldn't take too long. She needed her inheritance to invest in her campaign. The contributions were much lower than she expected. This trip had nearly depleted her own resources. She had enough funds to last until payday, but she was relieved that that day wasn't far off.

Something moved in her peripheral vision. A deer stepped out of the shadows. She swerved but managed to stay on the road. She ate another handful of M&M's, washed them down with the last of her pop, and turned up the music. She glanced at the green lights on her dashboard. It was midnight. She passed through the town of Lostine. *Almost home.*

Gloved hands dug through the files inside the drawer. He heard a noise and flicked off the flashlight. He waited. Silence. He clicked on the small LED beam and continued his search. *It's here somewhere.* His hands didn't quiver, his knees didn't shake, nor did his pulse race. Not like those fool amateurs he'd hired. He'd done things like this before. Worse things before. He was hardened against the anxiety. Nerves of steel, some would say, but not for useless things like diving off cliffs or jumping out of airplanes. Power, prestige, wealth. That's what he needed his confidence for.

Finally. He held the manila envelope in his hand, the one that would define his future. He opened the metal bracket and removed the stapled papers. His eyes skimmed the paragraphs as his clenched fingers left crinkle marks on each side. The scorch of the betrayal surged through his veins and clouded his thoughts. How could they do this? It was the final blow. The straw that broke the camel's back, per se. They wouldn't get away with it. They'd pay. No member of the Staten family would ever blacklist him again.

The office door opened. He closed the drawer, turned off the mag light, and slipped into the shadows.

A dark figure entered the room.

He pulled a gun from his belt. He wasn't above using it but preferred not to. Murder was so messy. Keys jangled. Desk drawers opened. The office chair swayed with the figure's weight. Would he remain long? The room grew warm. A bead of sweat ran down his hairline. He blotted it with his jacketed shoulder. Even one drop of sweat would leave DNA at the scene. He was careful. Always vigilant. No hair. No sweat. No fingerprints. No skin flakes. All of which could identify him and destroy everything he had worked for.

This was taking too long. Every second increased the odds of discovery. His fingers gripped the trigger. He stepped from the dark corner. Adrenaline surged through him as he raised the gun.

Tap! Tap!

Kathleen stretched her neck to the side. She wasn't ready to get up. She had a pounding headache.

Tap! Tap!

"Go away, Kylie. I'm sleeping."

Tap! Tap!

She opened her eyes and bit back a scream. A bearded man in a straw hat and overalls stared in the window of her car. What in the world? The fog slowly cleared from her mind as she rolled down the window. She must be having a strange dream.

The farmer spoke before she could. "Good morning, ma'am. Are you all right?"

Kathleen nodded. A swelling pain took her breath away.

"My name is Moses McCall. I was just wondering why you're sitting in the middle of my cow pasture?"

Despite the pain, Kathleen jerked forward, banging her chest into the steering wheel. Several brown and white cows lowed as they chomped on the grass surrounding her car. "What? What happened?" The exploded airbag draped over her lap. White powder coated the interior of the car.

"That's what I'm wondering. Certainly is a strange place to take a nap." Kathleen opened the car door and stepped out. She grabbed the edge to steady herself. "Are you sure you're all right?"

"I. Don't. Know."

Every direction she turned, pasture surrounded her. The road set back about one hundred feet on the other side of a flattened barb wire fence. "I was driving home last night, but that's all I remember. Where am I?" A wave of lightheadedness and nausea washed over her body. The stranger grasped her arm and eased her back into the driver's seat. "Just outside Wade's Point. Have a seat. I've called 911 and they're sending an ambulance."

She laid back against the headrest. "I'm fine. I don't need an ambulance."

The farmer chuckled. "I think your face would disagree."

Kathleen lowered the sun visor and grimaced at her reflection in the mirror. A large black and blue bruise spread across the left half of her forehead and down her cheek and across her nose. A line of dried blood ran from a split lip. *No wonder I have a headache. This will look great on the front page.*

Sirens echoed in the distance. The gentle farmer squeezed her hand, and she closed her eyes to await their arrival.

"Mom." Kylie burst into the room wearing tennis shoes and a hoodie, looking far more like a twelve-year-old than a freshman in college. Kathleen leaned forward on the hospital bed and embraced her daughter. "You're okay."

"I'm fine, Kylie. It looks worse than it is."

"Not really." The curtain moved, and Doctor Zuckerman entered. He ran his finger over a piece of paper on a clipboard. "You've got a nasty concussion, and your nose is broken. We did some blood analysis. Your blood alcohol level was zero."

"Andrew. You know I don't drink."

The doctor cleared his throat. "As I was saying, your blood alcohol level was zero, but you did have trace amounts of Zolpidem in your system. Why would you take a sleep aid before driving?"

Sleeping pills? "That's ridiculous. I don't use insomnia medication. Especially not while I'm on the road."

"Can you explain how it got in your bloodstream?"

Kathleen shook her head. "I don't have any idea."

"Zolpidem works fairly quickly. Did you stop somewhere before your accident? Have a bite to eat or something to drink?"

Kathleen shook her head again. "No. I don't think so. Well, I had a late dinner in La Grande with Don." She gasped, touching her fingers to her lips. "You don't think someone at the restaurant would hate me enough to attempt to kill me, do you?"

The ER doctor shrugged. "I'm a doctor, not Sherlock Holmes. But I do suggest you take this very seriously, Madam Mayor."

"Please, Mom."

Kathleen leaned back against the pillow and squeezed her daughter's hand. "All right. For your sake." Her eyes closed, and she drifted into a restless sleep.

Kathleen's cell phone rang. She heard the playful tune through a fog. She rolled over on the mattress and picked up her phone from the nightstand and put it to her ear. "Morning, Don."

Her eyes flickered open and she looked for the large red numbers on her alarm clock. But, her clock wasn't there. Her nightstand wasn't there. In their place, hung an intravenous drip and a pulse oximetry monitor. She blinked twice. Fear twisted her gut. She was in the hospital. With a concussion. She'd run off the road. Someone had drugged her. She swallowed as her chest tightened. Someone had tried to kill her.

"Your father's will was stolen." The lawyer's words were blunt, without fanfare or pleasantries.

Kathleen's eyes widened, and she sat up with a sudden burst of energy. "What?" Her scrambled thoughts tried to register his words. Someone stole her father's will? But how? Why? "What are you saying?"

"Late last night, someone was in my office. They hit me

over the head with something. They stole Richard Staten's Last Will and Testament from the filing cabinet. The whole folder, actually."

"What does that mean for the estate if we can't procure a will?"

"Everything will be held in probate. If a will cannot be presented to the court, a judge will decide who gets what. It can take months, sometimes years."

"Don?"—a sudden question came to mind—"What were you doing in your office in the middle of the night?"

No answer except for the *buzz* of the dial tone.

16

Monday afternoon, Hamilton made notes on a scratch pad at his desk in the bullpen. He hadn't bothered to ask Paige about disappearing on him the other night and he hadn't seen her since, except for when she'd spilled hot coffee on his shirt. He smiled to himself at the memory. *Paige McDonald is adorable when she's embarrassed.* He groaned and combed his fingers through his freshly-cut hair. If Paige had noticed, she didn't comment. *Why do you care? She's a person of interest. Well, not exactly—yet. You made a commitment to stay single and you need to stick with it. And if you did decide to marry, it certainly wouldn't be to an ex-con.* He shook his head. He needed to get back to work. His vexing thoughts weren't getting him anywhere with the recent cases.

Officer Martin spun Lillian's empty office chair and straddled it backward. "I need a favor."

"Sure."

"Would you switch shifts with me on Thursday? I'm scheduled for graveyard, but my wife just reminded me that I have a court hearing at zero nine hundred hours on Friday. It's about the kids we've been fostering, so it's important that

I stay awake. I'd rather switch than take a personal day, you know."

"Yeah, I can do that. I'll be praying."

Martin stood and moved Lillian's chair back into place. "Thanks, man. I owe you one." His desk drawer slammed shut. The bullpen door beeped as he left.

Hamilton returned to his notes and reread what he'd written on his tablet. On his way into work, he'd given out a ticket for running a red light. Unfortunately, the young speeder had become belligerent and had forced Hamilton to arrest him. For now, he sat in holding, waiting on his lawyer, while Hamilton typed up his report.

Chief House stopped at Hamilton's desk and dropped a manila folder. "Check this out." Hamilton opened the folder and read the report. They'd removed two sets of fingerprints from the case that had held the valuable Bible. One belonged to Michael Whitestone, the former pastor of Wallowa Mountains Baptist Church, but he'd been dead for ten years. The second belonged to Mario Montory.

"He stole it."

"Looks like it." The chief went into his office and closed the door.

Hamilton leaned back in his chair and rested his arms on top of his head. This didn't make any sense. The man shot Mario in the church parking lot. Martin had recovered three shells. Two bullets went into Mario and they'd found a third stuck in a brick on the side of the church building. Hamilton dropped forward and opened a file on his computer. He scanned the digital image with his eyes. The trajectory indicated that the shooter was across the street to the northeast of the building. That would indicate he was shooting in the direction of the church. If Mario had been running away from the church with the stolen Bible, wouldn't the shooter have been shooting from the other direction? They should have found the stray bullet somewhere else. *Is it possible Mario was running toward the church and not away?* But if he stole the Bible, why?

Hamilton stood to his feet, opened the drawer, and removed his wallet, keys, and weapon. It was time he had another talk with Mario Montory. Hopefully, the boy was in a chattier mood than his last visit.

Hamilton drove to the Montory's residence. He parked along the street and surveyed the block before he climbed the rickety porch. The east side of town kept the police on their toes more than the rest, reporting more than a few drug busts, domestic violence cases, and destruction of property incidents each year.

He opened the screen and knocked. Mrs. Montory opened the door. Crow's feet and worry lines made the woman appear older than her years. "May I help you?"

"Patrol Officer Hamilton Bryant." He held up his badge. "I'd like to have a word with Mario if I may."

"My son has nothing to say, officer."

"Maybe so. Maybe not."

Mrs. Montory sighed. "Come in."

He stepped inside the modest house. The screen door slammed behind him, then she closed the interior door and folded her arms across her chest, a common motion people made as a shield against whatever he had to say to them. As a police officer, he seldom brought good news.

The first thing he noticed was that the living room was cold. Too cold. The recent storm had brought the outdoor temperature down into the fifties. *Is their heat broken or shut off?* Goosebumps formed on his arms despite the standard issue coat and peaked cap. Mario Montory lay under a faded quilt on a worn-out couch. The stained carpet was freshly vacuumed. The television hummed in the background where rabbit ears topped with aluminum foil struggled to catch the channels, resulting in static and a fuzzy picture. Hamilton removed his cover and gestured toward the furniture. "Please take a seat, Mrs. Montory. This won't take long."

Mrs. Montory eased into the rocking chair and crossed her slippers. Hamilton remained standing, keeping both the front door and the kitchen entryway in his line of sight. "Mario. I've gone over the evidence multiple times and no matter how I look at things, there's just something that doesn't add up." He paused. The young man didn't take his eyes off the "snow" on the television screen. "You weren't running away from the church that night, were you? You were heading toward it."

A heavy silence hung in the room.

"I-I don't understand." Mrs. Montory moved to the sofa and laid a trembling hand on the figure under the blanket.

"We know you stole the Bible from inside the church. Your fingerprints were found on the glass case. The nurse said a priest came to visit you at the hospital?"

Mario shook his head. "He was dressed like a priest, but he wasn't no priest. He threatened to kill me if I talked to the police."

"But he wasn't trying to kill you before, was he?"

"They was two different guys. The guy at the hospital wasn't the same guy as shot me."

Two different guys? "If you tell me what happened, we might work out a lighter sentence. Maybe even without jail time."

"Please, Mario." His mother's voice pleaded.

"A man, I don't know his name, paid me to get that book from the church. He told me right where to find it, too. I came in after church started, took the book, and left through the basement window."

So far, his story was holding up. No one had seen the boy enter the church and Pastor Whitestone had said he'd found the basement window left open.

A cuckoo clock chirped the hour in the background. "I was supposed to meet the man in the alley behind the supermarket, but I started feeling bad about robbing the church, so I started back. He caught up with me and said I had to give it to him. I started running. One bullet flew over my head. Then, he shot me in the side, but I kept going until he shot my hip. He took the book from me in the parking lot of the church."

The shooter was just slowing him down. Hamilton scribbled notes as fast as he could. "Can you tell me anything about the man?"

"He wore a red shirt and baseball cap."

Same thing the witnesses had noticed when he fled the scene. "Anything else? Even the smallest detail can help with our investigation."

The young man tilted his head as he thought for a moment. "Yeah, the guy held the gun in his left hand."

A gentle knock rapped at the apartment door. Paige switched off the TV and left the comfort of her knitted throw, then flipped on the porch light. She opened the door. The air chilled her bare feet. Becky Thorne stood outside in the pouring rain, wearing a hooded raincoat and high heels. "I know it's last minute, but I need a favor."

"Step inside. It's cold out there." Paige moved aside as Becky entered dripping water onto the tile floor. Paige closed the door behind her. "What's up?"

"It's Dave's birthday tomorrow, and we have reservations at the lake for dinner. My babysitter canceled on us at the last minute, Hamilton is on duty until eleven, and Tyler's already at a friend's house for the night. The other two boys are too young to stay home alone. Would you come over and watch them? It's just until Hamilton goes off-duty."

Paige hesitated. As much as she wanted to help Becky out, she'd never babysat anyone before. Although she'd taken the Red Cross babysitting course when she was twelve, she'd never actually had the opportunity to practice those skills. As an adult, she'd spent little time around children, preferring to leave "Story Time" up to the other employees. "I'll try. I can't guarantee anything."

Becky shrugged. "Don't worry about it. Just keep them alive till my brother gets here."

Paige put on her jacket and tennis shoes and followed Becky across the soggy yard. Bruce jogged along beside them, his tail wagging. The kitchen was warm and cozy when they entered through the back door. Video game noises came from inside the den. "Tony. Timothy," Becky called. The noises ceased, and the two boys stormed into the kitchen. "Hi, Miss Paige." Timmy hugged Paige around the middle, catching her off guard. She awkwardly patted his back.

Tony sulked and flopped into a chair. "I'm too old for a babysitter."

"You've made that very clear." Becky ignored his eye roll. "Miss Paige is going to stay with you until Uncle Hamilton gets here. Be respectful. We'll see you tomorrow." She kissed both boys on the head.

"What time do they need to go to bed?"

Becky waved her hand. "They can stay up until their uncle gets here. They've started summer break."

"Yes!" Both boys pumped their fists.

David came around the corner, wearing a suit and tie. Becky whistled. He grabbed her hand and spun her in a circle, then pulled her into his arms and kissed her. Paige averted her eyes and flushed warm. Becky pushed from her husband's chest and grabbed her purse off the kitchen table. "Don't play video games all night," she shouted over her shoulder as she passed through the screen door Dave held open for her. It slammed shut when he let go. A moment later, the truck engine roared, then grew faint as they drove away. Both boys turned their eyes on her. Paige swallowed. "What do you guys want to do?"

"I'm hungry," Timmy said, rubbing his stomach. Tony disappeared into the den. Paige heard the video game noises start again. She removed her cell phone from her pants pocket. "We could order pizza." She wiggled the phone in Timmy's direction, hoping for a smile.

He didn't. Instead he groaned and dropped cross-legged to the tile floor. "They don't deliver out here."

"Oh." Paige scratched her head. What did kids like to eat? She opened the freezer and found a package of frozen fish sticks. She cringed but pulled them out anyway. She held out the cardboard box. "How about these?"

With a grin, Timmy sprang from his spot on the floor. "Yeah! Can you make mac n' cheese too?" He scrambled to the pantry and removed two boxes of prepackaged noodles and powder.

Her nose wrinkled again. "Are you sure?"

Timmy tossed the boxes on the counter, then scurried into the den. "Paige is making fish sticks and mac n' cheese." Paige couldn't hear Tony's reply, but she set about making the boys' dinner. She would rather starve than eat prepackaged food. The directions were easy to follow, and twenty minutes later, she was pulling the cookie sheet from the oven. She stirred the cheese powder into the noodles, then set the table.

"Dinner, boys."

Both boys scrambled to the table. Timmy bowed his head and prayed over the meal. When he said, "Bless this food to the *nourishnent* of our bodies," Paige nearly laughed out loud. It would take a miracle for God to bless frozen fish sticks and boxed macaroni and cheese, but Timmy was so adorable that maybe God would make an exception in this case. Before Paige could blink, the boys scarfed down the food. *What now?* She checked the time on her phone. It was only seven o'clock. "What do you guys want to do now?"

"Can we watch a movie?" Timmy licked unnaturally yellow cheese sauce off his lips.

Paige looked at Tony. "Want to watch a movie with us?"

"As long as it's not a baby movie."

"OK. What do you all want to watch?"

Timmy named an animated cartoon that Paige had heard about but hadn't seen.

"That's for babies!"

"It is not. Dad likes it and he's not a baby."

Paige fought the urge to pull out her hair. "Whoa. OK. Let's try to find something we can all agree on."

Tony named another film. This one Paige had seen. She raised her eyebrow. "I don't think your parents would approve. Pick something else." Timmy chose another movie. This time, Tony shrugged and grunted. *I'll take that as a yes.*

Faint thunder rumbled in the distance as they settled in the den. Tony rocked on a banana chair in front of the television. Paige popped in the DVD, then dropped onto the thread-bare couch. It was an eyesore, but comfortable, which explained its position in the den. Becky probably wouldn't allow it anywhere else. Paige picked up the remote and turned on the screen. Timmy snuggled up beside her and pressed his nose against her sleeve, then leaned his head back. "You smell good."

Paige chuckled. "Thank you." The movie started and the next hour and a half swept by. When the movie ended, they played the *Mario Kart* video game for an hour, then they started a second movie. This time the boys agreed much quicker. Paige made microwave popcorn and returned to the couch just as the movie started. The thunder grew louder. The storm moved closer. The film had them fully engrossed when Bruce jumped up and started barking at the back door. Paige paused the movie. The door squeaked open. Timmy jumped up from the couch and ran into the kitchen. "It's Uncle Ham!"

Paige set the popcorn bowl on the coffee table and joined them. "I guess it's time for me to head out."

Timmy pulled on her shirt. "But Paige, we haven't finished the movie. You have to watch the best part."

Hamilton unzipped his sopping jacket and hung it on the coat hooks by the back door. He hadn't changed out of his uniform. "You don't want to go out right now. You'll get drenched just getting from here to the garage." Lightning flashed outside the window and thunder echoed, as if agreeing with his analysis. "Besides, I brought dinner." He held up a brown paper sack. "I know the things my nephews eat. I figured you would prefer something a little healthier." He sat the bag on the counter and unloaded two Styrofoam boxes. He opened the lids. Steam rose, and an amazing aroma wafted to where she stood.

Her stomach growled. "Thanks. That was nice of you." *He paid attention to your eating habits. That's sweet. No. It's part of what makes him a good cop.*

Hamilton took plates from the cabinet and dumped the containers onto them. He handed one to Paige. "This one is yours."

She raised the plate to her nose and inhaled. "Oh, that smells so good."

Paige and Hamilton followed Timmy into the den, where they sat on the couch with the little towheaded squirt between them. Paige hit the play button on the remote and the movie continued. A crack of thunder startled Timmy, and he scooted closer to Paige, curling up against her side.

An hour later, when the credits rolled, Hamilton carried their dishes into the kitchen. "Time for bed, boys," he called out.

Tony rose from the banana chair as Hamilton stepped back through the doorway. "Goodnight, Uncle Hamilton. Goodnight, Miss Paige." His footsteps thumped on the stairs as he retreated to his bedroom. Timmy hadn't moved. Paige looked down at his little head. He was asleep in her lap.

Hamilton scooped him up and carried him upstairs. While he was gone, she washed the dishes and set them in the drying rack. She wiped down the table and countertops. Hamilton returned as she was shaking the crumbs from her rag into the trash can. "All tucked in?"

"Yeah. Want some coffee?"

"No thanks. I should be headed home now." She put on her jacket and opened the back door. Heavy rain splattered mud as it hit the grass. The wind blew cold raindrops across her face and hair. Lightning lit the sky. Thunder echoed. She sucked in a breath and prepared to make a run for the garage.

Hamilton reached around her and closed the door. "You'd better wait. It'll let up eventually."

Paige shivered. She wasn't sure if she was cold or if she shivered at the prospect of being alone with Hamilton again. She removed her coat, took a deep breath, and wrapped her arms across her chest. "I guess I'll take a cup of that coffee." She perched on the stool at the kitchen island.

He poured water into the Keurig and added a K-Cup. After a moment, the hot water dribbled through the cup and into the coffee mug underneath. He handed her the first one, then made one for himself. He removed the creamer from the fridge and set it on the counter.

She added some to her cup, then took a sip. "Thank you."

"No problem." He joined her at the island but didn't add creamer. "How's it going at The Bookshelf? Making any progress?"

"All the books have been moved into the spare room in my apartment. I'm working from home while the contractor does the renovations for the plumbing, electric, and drywall."

"That's got to be pretty expensive."

"It's fine. It's all taken care of."

They talked about Paige's plans for The Bookshelf while they drank their coffee. Hamilton asked her about her interest in books. She asked about his interest in police work. The more they chatted, the more Paige relaxed.

"I watched this documentary last week."

She stuck out her tongue. "Ugh. A documentary. I'd rather stick pins in my eyes."

"Oh, OK, what do you like to watch?"

"*American Pickers*." Hamilton's forehead furrowed. "You

don't know what that is, do you?"

He shook his head and laughed. "No. I'm afraid not. I suddenly got this image of people picking their noses."

"Yuck." She suppressed a shudder. "Anyway, on the show, these guys visit collectors and search for rare artifacts or valuable pieces of American history. They sell them in their stores or keep them for their own collections."

He shifted on the stool. "Now, see that's something I can't understand. Why would anyone want someone else's junk?"

"They're not junk. They're pieces of the past. They tell us stories of those who came before us."

"If you say so." Hamilton stepped down from the stool. He carried their coffee cups to the sink and rinsed them out. He paused and tilted his head. "Hey, listen. I think the rain stopped."

"I should get going before it starts up again." She moved to put on her jacket.

He put on his coat as well. "I'll walk with you."

"You don't have to. I'm not afraid of the dark."

He opened the back door and held it for her. "It's okay. I want to."

At her door, Hamilton stuffed his hands into his pockets. "I had fun tonight."

"Me too." The rain had brought down the temperatures even lower and she longed to rush inside her warm apartment, but he looked like he had more to say. The cloud covering began to clear. Moonbeams illuminated his face. He scratched the back of his head. "Thanks for helping Becky with the boys. I know she appreciates it and I do too. You seem like a nice girl and I hope we can be friends."

Friends? Their eyes met and held. Paige's heart skipped a beat. He was kind, good with his nephews, exactly the type of man Aunt Hattie wanted her to find, except he had one flaw. "Friends." Paige nodded her head and entered the apartment. She watched as he descended the staircase and thumped his hand on the patrol car as he passed on his way back to the house. Paige sighed as she closed the door. *If only you weren't a first responder.*

17

It was almost midnight before Kathleen left the courthouse, locking the front door behind her. As always, she was the last one out. Her feet ached. Her head ached. Everything ached. The monthly council meeting had taken longer than she'd expected it would. All members were present including the Police Chief, Fire Chief, and City Attorney. They'd discussed the recent crime wave at length and the threats against herself as the mayor.

First, the fire in Joseph, then the fireworks explosion on Memorial Day, then the sleeping pills after the trip to Salem. Chief House wanted her to let him assign her a bodyguard, but Kathleen wasn't ready to admit defeat. If she thought about it too long, she might become paranoid, but she couldn't let whoever this was push her around. Staten's don't require bodyguards and she wasn't about to start now.

They'd also discussed funding for the political rally scheduled for the end of June. She'd been frustrated that they'd denied her petition to use city funds for the event; however, she'd been more stunned to learn that the town of Whitman was going broke. Over fifty grand was unaccounted for. The treasurer had assured the council that he was looking into the disappearance, but the reporter from the Wallowa County Chieftain had taken special interest in the missing funds. Kathleen was already picturing the headline that would appear in tomorrow's paper, Whitman Runs Dry as Mayor Lines Pockets. It wasn't true, but that wouldn't stop the supposition.

Silver moonbeams lit a path to her car parked in the Reserved for Mayor space. She paused at the base of the courthouse stairs and fished in her purse, searching for her car keys. A movement out of the corner of her eye caught her attention. Someone stood in the shadows of the courthouse. It was too dark to make out anything more than a silhouette. Her head swelled and the pounding in her temples increased. Her pulse picked up speed. She'd never reach her car first if he intended to harm her.

"Why didn't you tell me about Paige?"

She knew his voice. The strangle of fear melted away and left confusion in its place. "Paige who?"

"Paige McDonald."

"What about her? I don't even know the girl. I only met her once. At the Memorial Day event. Why would I tell you about her? You're not making any sense."

"Why didn't you tell me you were pregnant?"

The parking lot swirled around her. She turned her back so he wouldn't see her angst. Her secret was out. He knew the truth. Hot tears streamed down her cheeks. Guilt consumed her from within. She felt vulnerable and she hated that feeling. She was strong and perfect, but not anymore. There it was, that glaring chink in her well-crafted armor.

If her secret leaked to the public, everyone would know how she'd failed—how she'd succumbed to a heated moment of passion. How, that in his embrace, under the stars, in the back of his pickup, she'd forgotten herself. She'd felt nothing but the strength of his arms around her and she'd given herself to him in every way. As much as she aimed to be, she wasn't perfect after all, but she didn't want anyone else to know that. A strong resolve settled in her heart. "I couldn't. It would have changed everything."

"I would have helped you, Annie. We could have gotten married."

"That's exactly why I didn't say anything. A baby didn't fit into our plans. You had your dreams. I had mine."

"But how could you abandon her? Couldn't you have put her up for adoption? Found a loving home for her?"

Kathleen wheeled around to face the father of her firstborn child. His words struck fear into her heart. Confusion. Disbelief. "What do you mean? I did put her up for adoption." She remembered it as if it was yesterday, placing the baby in her father's arms, handing him her Bible and asking him to give it to the new parents. She'd run away then. She couldn't bring herself to watch him load her baby into the car, couldn't watch him drive away.

"She claims she was abandoned. On the steps of a fire station."

She choked back the bile that rose in her throat. It had to be a trick. Her father wouldn't have deceived her like that. Would he? "I don't understand. You've talked to her?"

"She deserves to know the truth. She's here in Whitman, trying to find her birth mother. You."

My daughter's in Whitman? No, that can't be. "What does this have to do with Paige McDonald?"

He stepped into the streetlight. "Paige is our daughter."

"What? What makes you think that?"

"She's the right age. And she looks just like you did. Except for the blond hair. Are you going to tell her who you are?"

Kathleen didn't answer him. Her silence confessed the undeniable truth. She was just like her father. This person… This girl… This Paige McDonald could undo everything she'd worked for—everything she'd accomplished.

Somehow, he read her thoughts. He always could.

"Elections, Annie? How could you? You're better than that."

"Don't call me Annie. It's Mayor Phillips. What I decide to do about Paige is my business. Some strange girl rides into my town claiming she's my long-lost daughter. Now. With elections and my father's will pending. I'm suspicious of her dubious intentions."

He stood close enough to touch her. He reached out and brushed her hair behind her ear. "What happened to you, Annie? What happened to the wide-eyed, innocent girl I fell in love with? You were so carefree, so full of life. You bubbled over with the joy of the Lord. You're not the girl I remember. Everything changed."

Kathleen shifted as warmth gathered under her collar. "Not everything?"

"Everything. What did you do with her? What did you do with my Annie?"

She lifted her chin, determined not to let his sappy sentiment affect her. "She died when I left this place. If it hadn't been for my father's illness, I—I never would have come back here."

"I still love you, Annie. I never married. I kept—kept hoping that she'd—that you would come back to me."

Her nose burned as her vision blurred. "I don't think she can come back."

With a firm tug, he pulled her into his arms and pressed his lips to hers. She returned his kiss with a fervency that frightened her. He had such control—such power over her. Her face hardened. She wouldn't let any man control her—never again. She pulled away. "Did you tell her that you're her father?"

The spell broke. He stepped back, dropping his arms to his sides in defeat. "It wasn't my place."

Kathleen sighed with relief. "Will you keep it a secret for now?"

"Annie—Mayor Phillips. I want to get to know my daughter."

"I know. But please, not yet. I need time to…" She left the words hanging.

"I'll be silent. For now."

"Thank you. It's better this way."

His shoes scraped across the gravel parking lot. Footsteps paused. His voice carried back to her on the night air. "By the way, Annie, if you're still unsure of her claims, I should tell you—she has your Bible."

The Rustic Cup was as quiet and as peaceful as it was every day at this hour of the morning. The sun was just rising, giving off the first rays of dawn. Kathleen loved this time of day when all the world was still. Bird songs filled the valley. The front window gave a picturesque view of the snow-peaked mountains. Everything was still except for her heart.

No one else occupied the café. The owner, Jenn McMillan, piddled in the kitchen, gracing her mouth-watering pastries with their finishing touches. She'd previously ground the fresh coffee, and the whole place adopted a warm, earthy aroma. Kathleen had already ordered a cup and it sat in front of her, steam rising in delicate swirls. Kylie's shift didn't start until eleven, so she could speak freely without fear of her daughter overhearing. She traced the gingham pattern on the tablecloth with her French-tipped fingernail. This rustic booth with its deer antler light overhead was her booth, her spot. The mayor's spot.

A mayor was in control and possessed an air of authority. Citizens looked to the first family of their town for guidance and leadership. However, for the last twenty-four hours she hadn't felt much like a paragon, not with memories of a frightened teenager bouncing around in her head like that chaotic ball found in the game of Pong.

Autumn of 1991. The trees on the foothills had turned to yellow, brown, red, and gold. The days were short, and the smell of woodsmoke hung in the air as if the whole town was on a camping excursion. Her senior year in high school. Homecoming. A beat-up pickup truck. Shivers while watching the stars. Not knowing if those shivers came from the night chill or the closeness of her boyfriend.

Tears of frustration dripped off her chin and made ripples in her coffee cup. She leaned over, opened the snap of her black leather purse, and dug through the contents, searching for a tissue. The irritating bell on the café door jingled. Kathleen raised her head. Her brother entered the café and waved when he made eye contact. He paused at the counter to place an order. If his taste hadn't changed, he would request a caramel cappuccino and a hot buttered crescent with strawberry preserves. The Rustic Cup had been in business since they were children, Jenn's parents having run it before her.

Erik slid into the bench opposite her and smoothed his Armani tie against his chest. His dark cowlick swooped to the right, and his polished teeth stood out against the bronze of his skin. "You look nice." She tried to smile, while stashing the tissue back into her purse.

"Business in Portland. It's a beautiful morning, isn't it? We're in for some more storms this next week though. Did you see the weather report?"

Kathleen nodded. *Smooth talker. Good conversationalist. Just like our mother.* She and her father were their complete opposites. Bulls in a china shop, he'd always said. Direct. To the point. No grace. No poise. And it suited them. Politics were not for pansies.

But as she sat across from her brother now, she felt worse than when she faced a roomful of reporters at a press conference. "I, um…" She warmed her nervous hands on her coffee. "I wanted to talk to you about—" She paused as Jenn brought Erik's order, napkins, and the bill. Her brother nodded his thanks, then began adding sugar packets to the already sweet drink. Kathleen wrinkled her nose and shuddered. "Do you ever see Mom?" That was a safe topic.

"Yeah." Erik bit into his pastry. He chewed and swallowed before continuing. "I stop in every now and again, if I'm in California."

"Do you think Dad left her anything in the will?" The same will that was still missing.

Her brother shook his head. "Doubt it. They were unhappily married for thirty-five years. It's not like Mom needs his money anyway. Did you call me here to ask about Mom?"

Kathleen nervously glanced around the room.

"No one's listening. What's going on?"

She sucked in a deep breath. "Twenty-five years ago. My senior year of high school. You were in juvenile detention for—well, you know…" She stopped again. Did she really want to tell him? She blurted out the words before she changed her mind. "I got pregnant."

Erik choked, and a spray of liquid shot from his lips. Kathleen handed him a paper napkin and he dabbed at the stains sprinkled across the silk noose around his neck. "I didn't know."

"No one did except for Dad. And the midwife. And they're both dead." Her forehead creased. At least she thought the midwife was dead. It had been twenty-five years and the woman was elderly even back then. "Anyway, I didn't know what to do. Dad was running for governor, and I was headed to Stanford. I wasn't ready to be a mother. Dad arranged for a family to adopt my baby. At least that's what he said, but I have reason to believe he lied."

Erik took a bite of his crescent. "Is that really a surprise?" He said with his mouth full.

"No. I guess not. But there's a young woman recently come to town. She's searching for her birth mother."

He raised an eyebrow. "Why do you think that's you?"

"She has a Bible. With a note. Signed by Annie."

Her brother choked on his pastry. He coughed and waved his hand. "Water," he rasped and signaled to the barista. Jenn brought a glass. Erik took a sip before he spoke. "Annie. Wow. I haven't heard that name in a long time."

"I know. A quarter of a century." Kathleen paused. "This girl claims she was abandoned on the steps of a fire department."

"I see your dilemma. Either Dad lied about the adoptive family and dropped your baby off at a safe haven location, or this girl is fabricating a story to make you look bad."

"Neither option is a good one."

Erik popped the last of his crescent into his mouth and washed it down with his coffee. He glanced at the gold watch on his wrist. "Sorry. I've gotta run. My meeting's at eleven." He pushed away from the table and dropped a fiver on top of the bill. "I'll see you later, and good luck. Keep me posted."

Her brother left, the little bell signaling his departure. Jenn returned to the table with a tray to clear Erik's dishes. "May I get you anything else, Madam Mayor?"

"Thank you, Jenn. That'll be all. I need to get over to City Hall."

"Have a blessed day."

Blessed? Kathleen gathered her purse and jacket. She didn't feel blessed. She had the feeling she was standing on the edge of a precipice, staring at the jagged rocks below. The café began filling with the regular customers seeking their daily coffee fix. She slid out of the bench, slipped her purse strap over her shoulder, and slung her jacket over her arm.

Outside the café, the town of Whitman was waking up. The grocer and florist set out displays meant to advertise their sales and lure customers inside. Sam Harris washed the windows of his pawn shop. Several cars crisscrossed this way and that on Main Street. A blustery wind blew through the center of town. Dogwood petals showered the square and blew along the blacktop. Kathleen crossed her arms over her chest, wishing she had chosen to don her jacket rather than carry it.

She stepped into the crosswalk and headed for the large

Bowlby stone building. A grounds man swept the sidewalk, and another mulched the flowerbeds blooming with tulips and lilies that lined the concrete walkway and surrounded the staircase. Kathleen marched up the stairs, opened the heavy wood doors, and entered the lobby. The tile floor was freshly polished and smelled like lemon. A yellow wet floor sign still sat in the middle of the room. The fountain bubbled and gurgled. She entered the left hall and waved at the security guard as she passed the window of his office. She rode the elevator to her office on the second floor. Her assistant sat at his desk, wearing his headset. She opened the door to her inner sanctum and hung her coat and purse on the rack next to the window. Her assistant followed. Kathleen opened the window shades, then sat behind her desk. "What have we got today, Bennett?"

Bennett swiped the screen of the tablet he held in his hand. "You have a meeting at ten thirty, a luncheon at the Historic Society at noon, then you need to review the renovation plans for the old hotel."

"Thank you. Any calls?"

"Not really, Madam Mayor. Just Miss Bittern complaining about the noise the children make while they play in Sacajawea Park."

Kathleen shook her head, slightly baffled, slightly humored. "If she doesn't like children, she shouldn't have bought a house right next door to the park. Get your steno pad. I need you to take dictation."

"Of course, Madam Mayor."

When Bennett left the room, Kathleen let out a sigh. She crossed to the window overlooking her little town. Her little kingdom. If the voters elected her as their governor, she'd move to Salem and leave this quiet little sanctuary for the second time in her life. It was what she'd always wanted, but Paige McDonald's appearance had thrown a monkey wrench in her plans. What did she want more—to connect with a daughter she never knew or to be governor of Oregon, potentially launching a political career that could end with her as the first female president in the White House?

If the press sniffed out this story, they'd smear her name and label her a baby abandoner. She'd be forced to withdraw from the gubernatorial race in shame. She tapped her fist on the glass and laid her forehead on the cool window panes. It should be an easy decision, but was the longings of one stranger worth losing a lifetime of dreams and the adoration of millions?

18

Paige worked at the kitchen table, typing on her laptop. Stacks of books surrounded her. She was building an adjustable database for the store's inventory, complete with their ISBN numbers and monetary value. She'd taken a special interest in the stack of books beside her on the tabletop. These were first editions, possibly valued into the thousands of dollars.

She clicked on the screen and typed the next book title into her spreadsheet. Then she switched back to the previous Internet window, checked the dollar amount on the screen, then flipped back and added the number to the line. She set that book aside, then read off the next title and began her research. After checking several websites, she added the information to her growing list.

She covered a yawn, then took a swig from her water bottle and checked the time on her phone. Was it only eight o'clock? She rubbed her tired eyes and stretched her aching back. The wooden chair wasn't the best choice of seating.

She took a break from cataloging to check her email, moving the mouse to click on the message from Banner

Books, a store in the Portland mall. It was going out of business and everything in the store was for sale for a discounted price. Her eyes scanned the page. "Yes," she cheered out loud. Her cheeks grew warm as she glanced around. She chuckled at her insecurity. There was no one to hear her.

According to the email, Banner Books had what she needed, but she had to come pick them up at the mall. How was she going to get twenty bookshelves all the way from Portland to Whitman? On her handlebars?

Tap, tap, tap. The light knock on the glass door startled Paige from her concentration. She stretched her back again and blinked her blurry eyes. She'd been sitting in front of the computer screen for far too long. Officer Bryant waved at her through the window. Paige unlocked the door, and he stepped back as she pushed it open. A gust of cold air blasted into the room dropping the temperature by several degrees. Hamilton came inside, blowing on his bare hands. He removed his peaked cap. "Cold night. I thought it was springtime, not second winter."

Paige closed the door behind him. The heater kicked on. "Do you need something?" She rubbed the goosebumps on her arms.

"Just finished dinner at Becky's. I was headed back into town, but I saw your light and thought I'd stop by. Keeping busy?"

Paige nodded as she walked back toward the table. She secured her cardigan across her chest. "I'm pricing these books. Some of them are really old and really rare. A few are even first editions."

Hamilton followed her into the kitchen and picked up the one on top of the pile. He peeled back the spine that was coming apart. "Is that good? The rarity, I mean."

Please don't do that. She stilled his hand. "That one's worth about six thousand dollars even with the busted spine."

He dropped it back on the stack like it bit him. "Wow."

"I don't think Jessie realizes what treasures her husband had in that store. She's been practically giving them away."

"People around here can't afford books that expensive." He pointed at one of the prices on her computer screen.

"I didn't think so. I'll speak to Mrs. Faye first, but I'm hoping she'll let me find a buyer in the city or maybe online." She gestured toward the boxes stacked around her apartment. "I have no idea what else might be in here. I still have all of those to get through."

"How much more is there to do over at the store?"

"The contractor is supposed to finish the plumbing on Thursday or Friday. The commercial carpet gets installed early on Monday, so I'm hoping to paint the store sometime between there."

"If you'd like some help, I'm pretty handy with a paint brush."

"Thanks. After painting, we'll be ready for furniture: a desk, tables, chairs, bookshelves. A bookstore in Portland is going out of business. They're selling everything including the fixtures. I've reserved the bookcases, but I don't have a truck to go get them."

"I've got a truck."

"Really?"

He combed his fingers through his hair. "I'm happy to help. I'm off this weekend if that works for you."

"I'll have to call and ask. Could we go Friday?" A feeling of excitement fluttered in her chest.

"Sure."

"Yes! Thank you." Paige threw her arms around his neck.

His eyes widened. "I didn't know you were so eager to spend time with me."

She dropped her arms. *What came over me?* "No. I mean—I'm just…" She stuttered, and her face grew warm. "I'm excited about the bookcases. That's all." He didn't look convinced. "Portland is four hours away. Are you sure you don't mind?"

"Not as long as you drive. I'm taking Officer Martin's shift Thursday night, so I'll need to sleep on the way."

"No problem. Thanks."

Dispatch spoke over his handheld radio. "Attention. Patrol Unit Two. Please respond. We've got a four fifteen. Address nine seven three two Fish Hatchery Road."

Hamilton moved toward the front door, speaking into his radio as he walked. "This is Officer Bryant. Roger that." He turned back to address Paige. "I've gotta go. Duty calls. See you on Friday."

Paige closed the door behind him. Why had she reacted like that when he offered to help? Had she just been excited about getting the shelves or was something else, something deeper, going on? Something that wasn't supposed to be happening? She'd promised herself that she wouldn't love another first responder. Not again. Her cheeks felt flush. She needed some fresh air. Needed to cool off. Needed to think. Her fingers trembled as she slipped her feet into her sneakers, grabbed her coat and backpack, and then bolted out the door, locking the apartment behind her.

Two hours later, Hamilton headed out on his last patrol before calling it a night. Officer Stone would take over at eleven o'clock. Hamilton drove the police cruiser down Main Street, then made a right turn at the corner. Cedarwood Street had fewer street lights, and a crime was more likely to occur in the dark alleys that ran behind the businesses. He parked his car at the corner of Cedarwood and Third, then exited the vehicle, carrying his flashlight. He moved along the storefronts, checking locks and peering inside the glass windows. He neared the end of the block and turned down the side street to go around back and clear the alley. Before he rounded the far corner, a piercing alarm desecrated the stillness of the night. Voices grew frantic and metal clanged in the alleyway. Hamilton drew his weapon as he rounded the corner of the building. His flashlight illuminated the darkness. Teens fled the scene, struggling to climb the wooden fence that separated the alley from the residents' backyards. Cans of spray paint littered the dirt road. Wet paint tagged the weathered fence boards. He bolted forward with a shout, just missing the hood on the jacket of the last kid.

He would have gone after the vandals, but his attention turned to the pawn shop's rear door hanging open. The alarm came from inside. He stepped inside, weapon drawn. "Police." He flipped on the light switch and cleared the backroom and then the showroom. Shards of glass and a variety of trinkets covered the floor, but the burglars had only smashed one of the three glass cabinets. Hamilton dialed his phone. "Sam, you're gonna want to get down here," he shouted over the alarm. When he hung up with the broker, he dialed Chief House. "We've got another robbery."

"Where?"

"Sam's place. They ransacked a jewelry case. Sam's on his way."

"Ten four."

He stepped back into the alley as a car peeled around the corner, heading straight for him. It skidded to a stop, and Sam Harris jumped out. "What's going on?" He entered the store, spitting and fuming.

"First, turn off that alarm." Sam muttered as he crossed to the panel and entered the correct code. Hamilton took a second to relish the quiet. "That's better." He pointed to the smashed glass cabinet. "What was in there, Sam?"

"Mostly jewelry, watches, stuff like that."

"Anything missing?"

Chief House and Officer Stone entered through the back door. Broken glass crunched beneath their shoes.

"I don't know. I'll have to check inventory." The broker ran his fingers through his gray hair in frustration. He stooped down and picked up several pieces of costume jewelry off the floor. His knees popped as he jerked to his feet. He muttered something under his breath.

"What's wrong?"

"There used to be a diamond bracelet in here. I was talking to Charlie just yesterday about taking it to Portland and selling it to a bigger store. No one in this area can afford it."

"Are you sure it's gone?"

"Sure as I'm standing here."

"Where did you get it?"

"Old Staten brought it in here about a month ago and put it on consignment—meaning I paid him when I sold it. But now that he's dead…"

Hamilton shook his head and raised his eyebrow. "Richard Staten's portion of the proceeds will belong to his estate, Sam."

The old man grumbled but didn't reply.

Hamilton moved around the store, looking for anything else out of place. "Have you seen any suspicious behavior in here lately?"

"Not off the top of my head."

"We can dust for fingerprints, but considering this is a busy store, I'm not sure it'll be worth it. We'd probably have to question everyone in town."

Sam moved a stool out onto the floor. "How about that newcomer?" He perched on the stool, reminding Hamilton of a sharp-eyed hawk searching for a free meal.

"You mean Miss McDonald? She's not a thief." Even as he said the words, he knew the possibility was there. But that was all behind her. Right?

"She was in here the other day. She asked if I had any old books. I went to the back to check if I had any. When I returned, she was staring at the diamond bracelet. She even asked to see it."

Officer Stone pulled out a notepad and started writing. Hamilton held out his hand. "Wait. Now Sam, women are always admiring diamonds. You can't seriously think she lifted the piece, do you?"

"Well, how about all that other stuff? The phones from Dave's store. The journals and coins from the museum. And then there's the Bible from the church and that book from the Staten house? She obviously has a thing for old books. This all started when she came to town."

"That's circumstantial evidence. There's been nothing to put her at the scene of any of these crimes."

Sam folded his arms across his chest and harrumphed. "Alexander Pendleton said it was a woman."

Alexander Pendleton talks too much. This conversation was getting him nowhere fast. *Was it possible that Paige was the thief?* He took a deep breath and shook his head. S*top listening to suspicious old men.* A crowd had gathered outside on the sidewalk. Several of the onlookers cupped their hands against the glass trying to get a better look inside.

Jerry watched from outside the pawn shop, mingling with the crowd. The alarm code hadn't worked. He'd only had time to smash the cabinet and grab the one bracelet before the alarm started announcing his presence. His boss would not be pleased. Frustration growled in his chest and the hot jewelry burned a hole in his pocket. He needed to stash it somewhere for now. The blond woman carrying a partially opened backpack was an easy target. No one would even notice. He took several steps, slipped the jewelry inside the backpack, then continued walking along the sidewalk without looking back. Officer Stone came outside and dispersed the crowd.

He would wait for the girl to leave and then follow her home. He'd retrieve the bracelet as soon as she fell asleep.

Paige's eyes flew open. She lay still, not hearing anything other than her own heavy breathing. A noise came from outside the apartment. Her pulse quickened. It sounded like someone was climbing the metal staircase. She rolled to a sitting position and waited. A faint clicking sound. She slipped off the bed and crossed to the open bedroom door. The carpet was cold beneath her bare feet. She leaned on the door frame and listened. Movement caught her eyes. The handle on the front door jiggled and rattled. Someone was there. Someone was breaking into her house. She gasped and scrambled to her bedside, grabbing her cell phone off the nightstand and jerking the power cord from the wall. Her hands trembled as she tried to find the phone app. Where was it? She couldn't focus beyond the pounding in her chest. *911. I need to call 911.* She found the right icon, pressed on the screen, and began typing the numbers.

Loud, deep barking shattered the quiet. The metal staircase clanged, and a male voice shouted. She dropped the phone on the comforter. The growling and barking grew louder and more insistent. Paige left the safety of her bedroom and tiptoed to the front door. Trying to control the shaking in her hands, she flipped on the porch light and peered out just as a man jumped into the driver's side of a dark vehicle and peeled down the driveway. She ran back to the bedroom, and instead of dialing 911, entered Hamilton's number.

"Hello."

"A man tried to break into my apartment." Something banged on the apartment door. Paige let out a piercing scream.

"What's wrong? Are you okay?" Hamilton spoke from the other side of the line.

Be still my heart. Paige put the phone to her cheek. "Someone's at the door."

"Go see who it is, but don't open it."

Paige peeked through the window from behind the curtain. Dave Thorne stood outside the apartment door, a flashlight illuminating his face. Relief swept over her. "It's your brother-in-law."

"Let him in."

The door was already unlocked. The man had been so close to getting inside. She shivered. Dave entered the apartment with Bruce at his heels. The dog whined and pressed its wet nose into Paige's hand. "Are you all right?" Dave asked, concern written on his face. "I heard you scream."

"Yeah. I'm fine. Thanks to this big guy." She knelt and scratched the labradoodle behind his ears. "I don't know what I would have done if he hadn't scared that man off." As the adrenaline wore off, tears clouded her vision. A lump caught in her throat. "I was so scared."

"He was barking at the back door. I just thought he wanted out. I had no idea someone was out here." Dave squeezed Paige's shoulder. "Come into the house. Becky will make some coffee or hot chocolate." Paige moved to put on her shoes and jacket. A voice came from the phone in her hand. She put it to her ear. "Sorry. I forgot you were there. Dave's taking me into the house with them."

"I'm on my way over."

"That's not necessary." The only answer was the dial tone.

Paige sat at the island counter in Becky's kitchen, drinking a cup of hot coffee. Her hands had stilled, and her pulse was back to normal. The steaming liquid warmed her from the inside out. Becky and Dave waited up with her, all three dressed in robes and slippers. Becky had brought down an extra set for Paige. Something hit the door, jiggled the handle, then knocked. Dave unlocked the back door. Hamilton bolted inside, wearing sweats and sneakers. His dark brown hair stuck out in random tufts. Paige pressed her fingers to her lips, hiding a smile. He looked boyish and endearing, though his facial expression was serious. "I checked around the property and didn't see anyone. I'm sure they've hightailed it back into town for now. Whoever it was." He laid his gun and keys on the counter. Becky handed him a cup of coffee. "Thanks." He turned his eyes on Paige. "Are you all right?"

Paige nodded. "Just shook up."

"Know anyone who'd want to break into your apartment? Crazy ex-boyfriends? Unpaid contractors?" His eyes twinkled. He was teasing her. Well, mostly.

"No. I don't know of anyone who'd want to hurt me. I don't even own anything valuable except my bike. My laptop is about ten years old and no offense, but I think that TV in the apartment is older than that."

The Thorne's son, Timmy, stumbled through the arched doorway, rubbing his sleepy eyes and wearing Spider-Man pajamas. "What's everyone doing awake?"

"A bad man tried to break into Miss Paige's house." Becky answered.

"Was it the one with the red baseball cap?"

Hamilton's eyes grew wide. "Have you seen him before?"

Timmy hopped up on a barstool. "Yeah. At the picnic when the fireworks 'sploded. Can I have hot chocolate?"

Becky pulled a mug from inside the cabinet. "Where at the park did you see him, Timmy?"

Dave handed her a package of hot chocolate powder from the pantry and she poured it in the mug and added hot water from the Keurig.

"He was doing something with the fireworks. His baseball hat had the Trailblazer's thingy on it. I tried to tell him I liked his hat, but he ignored me and walked away."

Fireworks? Does whoever tried to break into my apartment also have something to do with what happened on Memorial Day? One look at Hamilton's face and she knew he was thinking the same thing.

"Here's your cocoa." Becky handed him the mug.

Timmy wrinkled his nose. "No marshmallows?"

"No marshmallows. You need to drink it and get back to bed."

"But it's hot," he whined.

Dave opened the freezer, popped an ice cube out of the tray and dropped it with a plop into Timmy's cup. "There, that'll help."

"Do you remember anything else? Where did he go after he left the fireworks?" Hamilton asked.

Timmy sipped his cocoa. He sighed and smacked his lips. "I don't know where he went, there was too many people."

His uncle's voice took on a tone of frustration. "What did he look like?"

Timmy shrugged. "I don't know."

"How tall was he?"

"About as tall as daddy."

"Was he wearing a coat? A uniform? Was there anything strange about him?"

Becky grabbed Hamilton's arm. "That's enough. He's six."

"You're right. I'm sorry." He sank onto a stool. His shoulders drooped. His chest rose and lowered as he took a deep breath. "Thanks for the info, little man."

The room was silent except for the sound of Timothy slurping down his drink. He gasped with delight. "That was yummy." He wiped his mouth with his pajama sleeve. "Goodnight," he said, then jumped down from the stool and dropped his mug in the sink. It clinked against the other dishes.

"Goodnight." The adults called after him.

Becky gathered the other empty cups and sat them on the counter next to the sink. "I'll make you a bed on the couch. I don't want you to stay in that apartment alone until they catch this guy, whoever he is."

"Thanks, Becky. I'll feel better knowing she's safe."

Paige cut her eyes at Hamilton. He was worried about her? *He's only doing his civic duty. Besides, if someone is after me then that puts his own family in jeopardy. He's only concerned with their safety, right?*

19

Eight o'clock Friday morning, Hamilton arrived at Becky's house, driving a beat-up pickup truck. Its exterior was more rust than baby blue paint. "Are you sure this thing is safe?" Paige asked him. He left the truck idling while he walked around to the passenger side.

"Of course it's safe, it's been running since 1962." He leapt up on the bench and grinned.

"Why doesn't that make me feel any better?" Paige climbed inside like she was on a trek to the peak of Mount Everest. She dropped her purse on the seat between them. "Do you mind if we stop by my house? Aunt Hattie's house. There's a few things I would like to pick up."

"No problem. I have a couple errands I need to run, too."

She waited for him to expound further, but he didn't, so she pressed on the clutch, put the truck into gear, then watched over her shoulder as she backed down the Thorne's driveway. She drove through town and then turned on the county road that would take them to Interstate 85 and then on to Portland. Hamilton folded his coat and stuffed it under his head as he leaned against the window. She adjusted the air and turned on the radio. "This is KHPE Hope 107.9. Bringing hope to life." Paige reached for the dial to change the station, but a soothing song began playing. *I'll just let it play for now.*

Several minutes later, the song ended. "Love paid a price so hope could become a reality," said a male voice. "I'm just amazed at this thought. Jesus Christ. The God of Heaven. The God of love paid the highest cost so that you and I could have hope. Hope for a better future. Hope for forgiveness of sin. Hope that even when this world beats us down until we barely have strength to stand, Someone, who knows all things, is right there just waiting to take your hand and walk with you."

Hope.

That was something she could understand. She hoped she would find her birth mother in Whitman. She hoped her mother would want her in her life. She hoped she would learn the truth about where she came from. She hoped she would finally feel like she belonged. She hoped she wouldn't lose her heart to the LEO on the bench beside her.

Why was he being so nice to her? He knew what she was and yet he'd continued to lend a hand with the bookstore. Of course, that had to be the reason. It was all for Jessie Faye. Becky and Hamilton were very close to the old woman. Paige glanced over at the sleeping officer. He shifted and scrubbed his hand over his face. *What if he's hanging around to keep an eye on you?* He knew the things she'd done. Was he afraid she'd rob the old lady blind? Or was he afraid she'd steal from his sister? Her eyes stung as hot tears formed. *He's not your friend. He's a cop and nothing else. Don't forget that.*

Paige pulled into Aunt Hattie's driveway and turned off

the engine. Hamilton stretched and yawned. He blinked and rubbed the sleep out of his eyes with the back of his wrists. "Did you sleep well?"

"I did. Thanks for driving." His deep, gravelly voice made Paige's heart flutter.

"You're welcome." Her words squeaked out and her cheeks grew warm. *Stop it. You're acting like a silly school girl.* Paige let herself out of the truck. She buttoned her coat against the sudden gust of wind and slung her purse strap over her shoulder.

"I'm impressed that you know how to drive stick-shift."

"I learned in my Aunt Hattie's old station wagon. It has a manual transmission."

He studied the house through the windshield. "So, this is where you used to live?"

"All my life."

Hamilton slid across the bench. "I'll be back in about an hour."

"OK." Paige slammed the heavy door, then skipped up the steps to the house. She unlocked the door and entered. The house was dark and quiet. No excitable Dalmatians or friendly Persian. No parrot squawking a greeting. *No one's home. Not even the animals. Maybe they have vet appointments.* Paige glanced in the kitchen and spotted Aunt Hattie's cell phone on the counter. "Aunt Hattie, I wish you wouldn't go out without a phone." Paige picked up the cell phone and dialed the vet's office just to ease her concern. *Please be there.*

"Dr. Rose's office, how can I help you?"

"Hi. This is Paige McDonald. I was just checking to see if my aunt, Hattie McDonald, is there."

"Hi Paige. No, she's not here."

The line went quiet. Paige's heart pounded against her rib cage. If Aunt Hattie wasn't at the vet, where was she?

The receptionist spoke again. "Oh, hold on. She just walked through the door. Looks like a neighborhood boy helped her with the animals."

Relief washed over Paige. Everything was normal. "Thanks. Bye." She pushed the end call button and returned the phone to the counter so Aunt Hattie would find it when she returned home. She opened the fridge and found a bottle of water hidden behind the orange juice. Aunt Hattie would be so disappointed that she'd missed her. Paige was a little disappointed herself. She needed one of her aunt's bear hugs and inspirational philosophies.

She took a couple of drinks from the water bottle, then set it on the counter and jogged upstairs to the attic. She grabbed two empty boxes and a small suitcase and carried them to her bedroom.

Everything was just as she'd left it. Her brown teddy bear sat on top of the pillows. His big, round eyes looking sad and alone. Paige dropped to the mattress on her stomach and grabbed the bear with two hands. She hugged him against her face and sniffed the familiar scent. One of the EMTs at station #9 had given him to her when she had her tonsils out as a six-year-old. The bear had been her constant companion from that point on, until she became too old for stuffed animals. After which, she gave him a prominent place at the head of her bed. "You want to go to Whitman, old bear?" She held him to her ear. "OK." She rolled over and tucked him into the corner of the suitcase. *I need to get busy. I've only got an hour.*

She grabbed some extra pairs of clothes and undergarments and stacked them beside the bear, then she pulled a list of books from her pocket. These books were the missing volumes to several series already found in The Bookshelf's inventory. Complete series were worth a lot more than partials. It wasn't hard to find what she needed and there were only two books on her list that she couldn't find on her shelves. It didn't bother her to give them up. Selling them was why'd she collected them in the first place.

She stacked the books into one of the boxes, then carried that box and the suitcase downstairs and set them by the front door. She used the second box to load up on anything else she thought she might need: DVDs, spare toiletries, office supplies… She'd just finished raiding the pantry for snacks when she heard a knock. She carried the second box to the living room, set it on the floor, and then opened the front door.

"Ready?"

"Yeah. Would you load the boxes and the suitcase into the back?"

'Absolutely." Hamilton moved to lift the first box.

"Let me write Aunt Hattie a note, and we can be on our way."

Traffic was as bad as usual. It took them an hour to drive across town. By then, it was 2:30 and Paige's stomach started protesting. They parked in the mall parking lot, then entered through the main entrance. Paige was familiar with the layout and knew her way around. They agreed to eat lunch in the food court before heading to Banner Books. She placed an order for a plate of Mediterranean cuisine at the Pyramid Café, while Hamilton disappeared into the crowd, heading for The Sub Shop. When her order was ready, she took the tray and found a seat at one of the tables.

Palm trees surrounded a waterfall fountain. Pennies, nickels, dimes, and the occasional quarter rested on the bottom of the wishing pool. A vivacious hum filled the area. Hundreds of voices. A hundred different conversations. She had a good view of most of the food court, except for the Jamba Juice behind her on the lower deck. A bearded man in his late thirties, early forties, sat alone at a table to her left. His stained T-shirt boasted the name of some nerd convention or video game advertisement. He wore glasses, and his blond hair stuck out in wild patches. His thumb scrolled the screen of the latest smartphone. His right hand gripped a set of wooden chopsticks, and with ease, he munched a plate of Japanese food.

A Latino, eating Chinese food with a fork, sat at a table to her right. He wore a leather jacket and had parted his greasy hair. He'd nearly finished his plate when a girl in a tight skirt appeared and sat across from him with a bag from the chicken place. His phone buzzed and he answered. "What? We'll be there. No, no problem. I said we'd be there."

He hung up the call. "Will you finish already?" He snapped at the girl across from him.

Something sharp poked Paige's back. "Put your hands where I can see them," said a deep, unfamiliar male voice. Paige eased her arms onto the table. Her pulse raced. She slowly turned her head. Hamilton stood behind her wearing a mischievous grin and sticking the edge of his tray into her back.

Paige blew out a breath. "You scared me!"

"I was just messing with you. Sorry. Who'd have thought a simple cheese steak would take so long?" He slid his tray onto the table as he sat in the chair opposite her. He pointed at her plate. "You haven't eaten much."

"I got distracted people watching." She picked up her fork and stuck a scoop of basmati rice into her mouth.

He unwrapped his cheese steak. Grease dripped from the corners of the bread. Paige wrinkled her nose and shivered. He raised his eyebrows at her reaction. "What? Something wrong with my sandwich?"

"No. I guess not." She paused. "How do you eat that stuff?"

He took a big bite. The sandwich filling squished out the side. "Years of practice." He spoke with his mouth full. An orange streak ran down his chin.

"You got a little something?" She touched the spot on her own face.

He grabbed his napkin and wiped the grease off. "You're not one of those vegans, are you?" He dipped a French fry in ketchup and stuck it in his mouth.

Paige gestured at the pile of grilled chicken on the Styrofoam plate. "No. I just prefer healthier choices. I do love a good pizza, though."

"This is healthy. I've got meat. Cheese. Bread. Veggies."

"French fries don't count." She said with a laugh.

"I meant the onions and bell peppers on the sandwich."

Paige shook her head and returned to her plate of cucumber salad, grilled chicken, basmati rice, hummus, and pita. They finished their lunches and threw the trash in the garbage, then they walked through the mall to the bookstore. A bright yellow and red "going out of business" sign was plastered on the front glass and a big "60% off" sign hung from the tiles on the ceiling.

Hamilton paused at the entryway. "Go ahead without me. I'm going to get a cup of coffee so I can stay awake to drive home." He walked off and she entered the store.

After paying for the bookshelves she'd reserved, she returned to the concourse to find Hamilton with his back against the wall, one foot propped up on the beige ceramic tiles. He sipped from a steaming paper cup, but he'd fixed his eyes on something across the way. "What are you looking at?" Paige tipped her head, trying to see what had caught his attention.

He gestured with his cup. "Check out that store."

J.R. Electronics, a retail store on the opposite side of the concourse, had black tiles with gold trim and gold lamp sconces on the walls. A tall desk with a computer monitor occupied a corner toward the back of the store. Two men, one African American and one Caucasian stood at the desk looking at the computer screen. On the opposite side of the store, a giant TV stood on a white folding table. Two well-dressed men sat in folding metal chairs, absorbed in watching a football game on the TV. Three TV boxes sat in the middle of the floor, all different brands and sizes. A floral bed sheet was draped across the back of the store.

"Go over there and ask if they have any cell phones?"

"Huh?" Paige turned her attention back to Hamilton.

"Just do it."

She crossed the open concourse, dodging shoppers, then glancing over her shoulder before entering the store. Hamilton followed at a distance. The two men at the desk saw her approaching and smiled. "May we help you?"

"No. I mean, yes. Uh, I was just wondering if you all carry cell phones." Paige stumbled over her words.

The store attendant's eyes lit up. "We had a new shipment come in this week. What brand are you looking for?"

Hamilton crept closer to the curtain, trying to remain unnoticed. *What is he doing?* He caught her eyes and rolled his fingers. He wanted her to keep distracting the men at the desk. She stepped to the left, drawing the clerks' attention away from the right side of the room. "Um, I don't know. What kind do you recommend?"

"Let me see what we have in stock."

The man typed a few buttons on his keyboard. He whispered to the man at his side, like a training session. He pointed at the screen and whispered again. Paige twirled her hair around her finger and batted her eyes at the second man. A grin spread over his face and he leaned forward. "Do you have a preference?"

Hamilton was at the sheet. Paige sucked in a deep breath

"Excuse me, sir, only employees are allowed behind the curtain." One of the men from in front of the television stood to his feet and stepped toward Hamilton, his sheer size alone was intimidating. "I'm going to have to ask you to leave."

Hamilton held up his hands. "Sorry. You guys have a nice day." He walked over and grabbed her arm. "Let's go, darling." She slipped her hand through his elbow. Before they walked out of sight, she glanced over her shoulder. All four men stood together at the desk, scowling. The one she'd spoken with had his cell phone to his ear. When he made eye contact, a shiver ran through her body. *Something isn't right.*

Hamilton drove the pickup around to the loading docks

at the back of the mall. Paige checked the bay number on the piece of paper the manager had given her. "Number 12."

He backed the truck up to the bay door. The manager stood in the wide doorway, waiting with a stack of bookshelves. He'd broken down the shelves into manageable pieces. They loaded the units into the truck bed, then they returned to the cab. Hamilton started the engine and put the truck into gear. Instead of heading for the exit, he circled the mall, studying the cars and vans parked in the loading areas. "What are we doing?"

He didn't answer. After several minutes, he shrugged his shoulders and turned toward the mall exit. "Just doing what I do best."

"Which is?"

"A little investigating." The traffic light turned red, and he stopped. He glanced in the rearview. His eyebrows pulled toward the center, and he frowned. When the traffic light changed to green, he turned right and headed down the wrong street. "You're going the wrong way."

"I know."

He was silent again. *Why is he acting so strange?*

"That store is a front."

"That store is a front."

They spoke at the same time. He furrowed his brow. "How did you know?"

It wasn't the first one she'd seen. She cast her eyes toward the floorboard. She couldn't answer him. Her face grew warm. Like it or not, she'd been a thief.

"Oh." Her silence spoke volumes. "You…" Hamilton let his words trail off.

"Yeah. I was. How did you know? Did your Spidey sense tingle?"

He glanced sideways at her with a crooked smile. "If something appears suspicious, it usually is." He checked the mirror again.

"You don't give people much benefit of the doubt, do

you?"

"Trust but verify."

He glanced into the rearview mirror. Again. "Why do you keep looking behind us?"

"Are you hungry? I could really go for a burger right now." Hamilton jerked the steering wheel and turned into a McDonald's parking lot.

"We just finished lunch less than an hour ago. How can you be hungry?"

He parked in a space near the door and turned off the truck, then unbuckled his seatbelt and slid across the seat until his leg touched hers. His arm reached over her shoulders. His face inched dangerously close to hers. Paige pressed her back against the door. *What is he doing? Why is he acting so weird? Is he going to kiss me?*

He spoke slow and enunciated. "A van has been following us ever since we left the mall. Without arguing, we are going to slide out your door and go into the restaurant." His left hand unbuckled her belt. "Right. Now." He opened the door at the same time he shoved her out of the truck. He grabbed her hand and bolted for the entrance. No one noticed their rushed entry and they found a seat in the busy restaurant. Seconds later, a dark van pulled into the parking lot, circled the building, then came to a stop directly behind Hamilton's vehicle. The van had a logo on the driver's door. An encircled *JR*, though the two letters were blended to appear as one. *JR* for J.R. Electronics.

Paige's heart thumped against her ribcage. "What happens now?"

"We wait until they leave. I'm hoping they won't enter a public building with all these witnesses." His jaw was tense. He spoke without taking his eyes off the van outside the window.

Her whole body trembled. She held her breath as she peeked over her shoulder. Two men climbed out of the van and looked around. *The men from the store.* Her head swam, and a cloudy feeling washed over her. Hamilton reached across the table and squeezed her hand. His other hand removed his cell phone from his pocket. One of the men outside put a cell phone to his own ear. His lips moved as he spoke with someone on the phone. With a nod, he hung up. The men returned to the van and drove away.

Hamilton's shoulders dropped as he let out a deep breath. He released her hand. Then he swiped his finger across the screen of his phone and tapped the glass. He put it to his ear. "Hi. This is Patrol Officer Hamilton Bryant from Whitman PD." He stated his badge number. "May I speak with your police chief, please? Thank you."

Paige traced her fingertip along the stenciled pattern on the table, still feeling the pressure of his hand on hers. His touch had comforted her, strengthened her. *How can that be? How is this happening?* She lifted her chin and allowed her eyes to trace the contours of his face. *He's only doing his job. He didn't mean anything by it.* But it felt like so much more.

He continued to speak on the phone, most of the conversation in some sort of police code she couldn't follow. While she waited, her thoughts turned to their current predicament. *What will happen now? Why were those men following us? Are we in danger?*

Hamilton tapped the screen again, ending his phone call. His lips twisted into a weak smile. "I feel like we deserve some ice cream. Would you like anything?"

Paige tried to ignore the pounding in her chest. "Sure. I'd love a hot chocolate sundae."

The next afternoon, Paige covered a yawn, hoping Hamilton wouldn't notice. She'd put on a brave face for him on the way home yesterday, but in the dark last night, fear gripped her heart and had refused to let go. She'd barely slept at all. Her temples ached and her eyelids drooped. She'd arrived early this morning with paint cans and drop cloths, but Hamilton had already been waiting at the door. The contractor had finished the bathroom and loft renovations on Thursday, then he'd stripped out the carpet while she and Hamilton were in Portland.

She couldn't stop thinking about those men who had been following them. Who were they? What did they want? It must have had something to do with that farce of an electronics store at the mall. Before they left McDonald's, Hamilton had given the van's license plate number to the Portland police department, but he'd turned down the escort back to Whitman. She hadn't realized he was armed until he laid his weapon on the dashboard of the truck within reach as he drove home. He'd assured her the police were aware of the situation and had encouraged her to trust the system. That was easier said than done when you'd been to juvenile hall for a crime you didn't commit.

Putting yesterday out of her mind, she turned back to preparing the walls of The Bookshelf for painting. She slid her hand along the window frame, pressing green tape firmly to the plaster. "Thank you for letting me rope you into this."

"You didn't rope me. I volunteered." He spoke from somewhere in the room.

She turned around and saw him taping the other window. "I hope you know what you're doing. I tend to be a little bit OCD." She walked to his side and straightened the piece of tape he'd just stuck down.

Hamilton chuckled. "I see that."

"Sorry." Paige blushed, and went back to taping her own window.

"Portland PD phoned late last night. By the time they got to J.R. Electronics, the store was abandoned."

"They're still out there." It wasn't a question. They both knew it to be fact.

"I won't let anything happen to you."

Paige glanced over her shoulder. Hamilton's large hands stroked the tape as he melded it into the trim. If only she could read his thoughts. It was his job to protect people. Did he consider protecting her as more than just his job?

After they'd covered everything, they opened the paint cans: a cheery butter yellow and a cornflower blue. *Like the color of Hamilton's eyes.* Paige blinked. *Why did I think that?*

Hamilton laid out the paintbrushes and trays. "Which color is for what?"

"Blue for the walls. Yellow for the trim," Paige answered, then poured blue paint into her tray. She grabbed a roller brush and started on a wall without a window.

They painted in silence for several minutes. She glanced his direction. His muscles flexed as he stroked the paintbrush on the trim. Her face grew warm when he caught her staring. She returned to rolling the wall and tried not to look at him again.

His voice carried to her from the other side of the room. "I was thinking about going on a hike to Sacajawea Peak tomorrow, do you want to go with me? Beats going by myself."

"Isn't it dangerous to hike alone?" She kept her eyes on her task.

"My point exactly."

Paige turned. "But weren't you going before—never mind." Amusement danced in his eyes. She jerked her head.

"Will you come?"

"I…" She searched for an excuse. Any excuse.

"Come on. You owe me for fetching those bookshelves."

"OK."

"Great. I'll pick you up after church. We'll take a picnic lunch."

Was this a date? Hiking. Picnic lunch. Together. It sounded like a date. Did she want it to be? *Dates lead to falling in love. Falling in love leads to heartache. Don't think of it as a date. You promised yourself. Just think of it as an outing between friends. You can be his friend.*

"Do you want the window frames yellow, too?" She

turned to answer, then gasped as his dripping paintbrush swept across her nose. Hamilton lowered the brush and put his hand over his mouth. "Oh, Paige. I am so sorry." His words bounced as he held back a chuckle. "That was a complete accident."

"I bet it was." She raised her paint roller and rolled blue paint down his T-shirt.

Hamilton flicked yellow paint into her hair. "I said I was sorry."

Paige dropped her roller, grabbed a paintbrush and marked an x across his face. The yellow paint seeped between the stubble of his facial hair. She turned her back to grab a towel. A smooth coolness ran down her shoulders. She wheeled around. Hamilton held a paint tray in his hands and grinned like a mischievous school boy.

"Seriously?" She grabbed the blue paint can and charged at him, ready to pour it over his head. Her foot caught in the drop cloth. She released the paint can as she tumbled forward into his chest. His arms encircled her frame. The paint flew from the bucket and splattered across the wall. When she raised her chin, his lips hovered inches from hers. His eyes crinkled with laughter. Her fingers toyed with his shirt pocket. She sucked in a breath as he leaned closer. He was going to kiss her. She wanted him to, oh, how she wanted him to. She pushed away from his chest, lowering her gaze to the floor. "We should clean up before Jessie sees this."

"Paige." She heard the longing in his voice. The pleading. She turned her back to him. Hot tears stung her eyes and ran down her cheeks, blending with the streaks of wet paint. She grabbed a towel from the floor and hid her face.

When she lowered the terry cloth, he was gone. The faucet in the bathroom was running. She gathered the brushes together and refilled the paint trays. The blue can was mostly empty. She clicked her tongue at the geometric splat on the wall. *At least we'd already planned to paint the walls blue.* The bathroom door opened, and Hamilton stepped out, drying his hair with a wad of paper towels. "You're turn. I'll finish cleaning up out here." He spoke softly, almost remorseful. Paige gestured toward the back of her shirt. "What do I do about this? Everyone will see it if I bike back to my apartment."

"We could ask the firefighters to hose you off." A chuckle escaped his lips and he gave her a weak smile.

"That's not funny." A giggle bubbled in her chest. It grew until she couldn't hold it back any longer. Laugher spilled from her lips. Hamilton stepped toward her, releasing a belly laugh. "You have paint in—in…" He reached out and touched her hair. It was an innocent gesture, but Paige froze.

"I'm going to go clean up." She ducked under his arm and scurried to the bathroom. She slammed the door, turned and rested against it, forgetting about the paint on her back. Every synapses of her brain warned her to stay away from him, not to fall in love with a hero. But for some reason her heart wasn't listening.

20

After yesterday's paint incident, Hamilton wouldn't have blamed Paige if she'd changed her mind about going on the hike with him. He'd attended worship services this morning at his church. He'd hoped she would come, but she hadn't. Was that a sign that she didn't want to see him?

He breathed easier when she jogged out of Becky's house wearing tennis shoes and a bright pink jogging suit. She carried a water bottle in her hand and had a backpack over her shoulder. He opened the passenger door of his truck, waited for her to climb inside, then shut it and ran around to his seat. He turned the key in the ignition. "Mountain's out. For now." He watched out his rearview while he backed out onto the county road. "Hope we don't get too wet. It's supposed to rain later this afternoon."

They talked while he drove, but instead of heading into Joseph, he veered onto a dirt road and parked in an empty turnoff. He grabbed his backpack from behind the driver's seat. "Ready?"

The hiking trail traveled uphill through an evergreen forest until it reached Sacajawea Peak. Hamilton had hiked here often as a boy and had camped at the lookout point each year with his Boy Scout troop. He'd loaded his backpack down with water, first aid supplies, and a picnic lunch of local favorites.

They hiked in companionable silence, concentrating on their steps. The trail was steep, but eventually it plateaued at the picnic area. Paige stopped to catch her breath, bending at the waist. She straightened and wiped her forehead on her sleeve. "That's quite a climb. Is this Sacajawea Peak?"

He took a swig of water before he answered. As he screwed on the cap, he pointed over a wall of trees. "No. That's Sacajawea Peak." She followed his point to where the tip of the mountain touched a darkening sky. Rain clouds gathered on the horizon.

Her lips parted and she groaned. "We're not going to hike up there, are we?"

"No. This is as far as we'll climb. You ready to eat?"

"Absolutely. I worked up an appetite on that last hill. What's for lunch?" They sat at one of the picnic tables. Hamilton opened his backpack and began pulling out colorful Tupperware containers. Paige raised an eyebrow. "Tupperware. How domesticated of you?"

He chuckled at her observation. "Sometimes I bring food with me to work. Especially when I'm on the graveyard shift and all the restaurants are closed, including Casa Thorne."

Paige tipped her head. "Casa Thorne?"

"AKA my sister's house."

"May I help?" He handed her a couple of containers. They removed the lids, revealing a spread of various cheeses, grapes, cherries, cold cut sandwiches, pretzels, and Oreo cookies.

"You've got to try this cheese." He removed a chunk from the container and held it out. She leaned forward. He set it on the edge of her lip. She tipped her head back, her fingers pushing in the bite sticking out of her mouth.

She swallowed. "That is so good."

"Local and organic." He took a bite. Smooth, creamy, and tangy on his tongue.

She popped a juicy grape into her mouth. "You sound like a commercial." She tossed one across the picnic table.

Hamilton caught it in his mouth. "Can't help it. I love Whitman."

"Have you lived here all your life?"

He chewed another chunk of cheese before answering. "Except for the stint I spent at the Police Academy. I've never wanted to live anywhere else." And he would protect it with every fiber of his being as long as God allowed him.

"I dated a cop—excuse me—an officer once. He was cute. Sweet. I thought we were growing close, so I told him about my past. He dumped me over text message, saying it wasn't fitting for a civic role model like him to be seen with an ex-con."

"I'm sorry, Paige." *Is that why she's not a fan of first responders?* Paige was a nice girl. A girl whose company he found himself enjoying more and more all the time. He didn't even need the chief's order to spend time with her because he woke up every morning wondering if they'd cross paths. If only things were different. If only she were a Christian. If only officers won't being killed all over America.

"So, how does a handsome guy like you manage to stay single?" She clapped her hand over her mouth. Was she embarrassed that she'd called him handsome? Or because she'd asked such a pointed question about his love life? "I'm sorry. I shouldn't pry. It's none of my business."

He ran his finger along the weathered crack in the picnic table. The sun went behind the clouds. He drew a long breath before he spoke again. His eyes met hers. His voice still tremored with memories. "I had a friend. Will. We grew up together. Good man. Better cop. In 2010, when he married his high school sweetheart, I was his best man at the wedding. Two months later, on Thanksgiving Day, he died during a drug bust gone wrong. I stood beside his wife at the graveside. She was so young—too young to be a widow." His words increased in speed, volume, and conviction. "I'm single because I choose to be. Law enforcement has always been dangerous, but never more so than in recent years. One hundred and thirty-five officers were killed in the line of duty in 2016."

"Then why continue? Why keep risking your own neck? Why not retire and settle down?"

"Being a police officer—it's not a job. It's a calling. This community—they need me to keep them safe. If I quit, I would be letting everyone down. I would be letting myself down."

Paige took a couple bites of her sandwich. Hamilton watched her face. *What's going through her mind?* He chewed a cherry and spit the pit on the ground for the squirrels. He started working on his sandwich. *She's not saying anything.* He grew nervous. Had he been wrong in sharing his heart? He'd only told her the truth.

"I was raised by a firefighter." Hamilton jerked his head, startled by the sudden admission. "At first, the whirling sound of the fire alarm was like the Batman signal. My grandpa was a super hero in my eyes. As I grew older, I came to understand what that meant. He was putting his life at risk for the sake of others, even if it was their own stupidity that had put them in jeopardy in the first place."

Hamilton reached across the table and squeezed her hand. "What happened to him?"

"He retired from the station when I was ten but continued to work as a volunteer. Two years later, a roof caved in under him."

"Paige, I'm so sorry for your loss." A gloomy cloud descended over the picnic table. Her shoulders drooped under the weight of her grief. Emotion welled up in his heart. He suddenly wanted to do whatever was required to make her smile again. The view from Lookout Point was both majestic and inspiring. "Walk with me?"

"Sure."

"Leave our stuff here. We'll get it when we come back." Paige followed him with her arms crossed over her chest. At the top of the hill, the wind blew uninhibited, and it started to drizzle. The view was as beautiful as he remembered. Over the edge of the rocky cliff, the Wallowa Valley spread out below them. Rolling hills surrounded by growing farmland extended as far as the eye could see.

Paige gasped. "It's amazing." She stepped closer to the edge and pointed to the right. "What's that?"

He leaned out to see what she meant. "That's a dirt road that goes from Wallowa Lake to the picnic area."

"A road? There was a road?" She waved her arms and wheeled around to face him. Her feet skidded on the wet rocks like a cartoon character going for a run. She tumbled backward until her spine connected with the ground.

"Ouch? You okay?" Hamilton knelt beside her.

She took a deep breath, wheezing as her lungs inflated. "Yeah, I'm OK." She squeaked. She slowly rolled to her side. Blood and spit dribbled down her face. He helped her sit up. She spat bloody saliva on the ground. "I bit my tongue."

"I've got instant ice packs in my first aid kit." She started to stand, but Hamilton pressed on her shoulder. "Stay here. I'll get it."

As the rain picked up speed, he half-ran, half-skidded down the muddying path to the picnic table where they'd left their packs. He dug in his backpack until he found the first aid kit, then he snapped open the plastic container and withdrew the ice pack. He popped the cell inside and ran back to where Paige waited. She had scooted back against a boulder. Wet hair clung to her face and neck. He handed her the ice pack. "Here. This should help with the swelling." She stuck her arm in the air and mumbled something unintelligible. "Huh?"

She moved the ice pack. "Help me up."

"Oh sure." He gave Paige's hand a tug. She stumbled and

fell against his chest. Rain dripped from her hair down her face. Her cheeks were red from the cold air. A streak of bloody saliva tinged her chin. He tucked his hand in his sleeve, cupped her face, and wiped away the stain. She was warm and soft in his arms. She was still holding his hand. Her palm was smooth compared to his calloused one. He had faced down criminals with guns and yet, somehow, this woman made him more nervous than he'd ever been before. He gazed into her eyes and longing spread from his head to his toes. Had he ever seen eyes that blue before? What was this feeling? It was stronger than an urge to protect her, to shelter her from all that would seek to harm her. It was greater than any sensation he'd ever felt before. Was there even a name for what he felt? He tangled his fingers in her golden hair. She moved the ice pack. His eyes flickered to her lips. Pink and soft. He bent toward her until their faces nearly touched. Her breath caressed his stubbled chin. Did she want this as much as he did? Would she push him away? Her body molded into his. Her long dark eyelashes lay against her cheeks like butterflies on summer blooms. He kissed her. Her hands crept around his neck and his arms encircled her waist. Their lips parted, and her head dropped to his chest. One thought and one thought alone consumed his thoughts. He never wanted to let go. Never, ever wanted to let go.

The spell broke when she stepped away and ran her hands over her sleeves. "I'm freezing. Would you get my jacket from my backpack?" She stuck out her split tongue and held the cold pack to it, then she leaned back and sat on the edge of the boulder.

He jogged back down the path, then unzipped Paige's backpack, pulled out her jacket, and gave it a shake. Something heavy dropped to the ground. He leaned over to retrieve whatever had fallen and froze midway. Diamonds glistened in the dirt. His breath caught in his throat and dread squeezed his heart. *No way.* The bracelet looked very similar to the one Sam had described. *Is this the stolen bracelet? What is Paige doing with it?* He knew the answer and it hit him like a kick in the head. He used his sleeve to pick up the jewelry, so as not to smudge any fingerprints. She couldn't be the thief. There must be a misunderstanding. Maybe it wasn't even the same bracelet.

"Hamilton!"

He stashed the bracelet in his pocket. Should he confront her about it or check with Sam first? If it wasn't the stolen piece, he could always tell her he found her bracelet on the ground. Which he did. Technically. "Hamilton!" She called again. He jogged back to Lookout Point. *Dear God, please don't let her be the thief.*

He dropped Paige back at her apartment, then swung by the station and put the bracelet in an evidence bag for safekeeping, then he headed for the pawnshop. The sign said closed, but the door was still unlocked. Sam Harris came around the corner from the back and stopped behind a newly installed glass cabinet, grumbling and running his hands down the length of his chest. "We're already closed, Officer Bryant. Did you want something?"

"Just information, Sam. This isn't a social call." He reached into his pocket and pulled out a zip-lock bag holding the diamond bracelet. "Is this the stolen piece?"

The cranky old man moved out from behind the counter. He raised his glasses from where they hung on his shirt collar and put them on. "Where did you get that?" He tried to snatch it from Hamilton's fingers. He held it out of reach of the much shorter man.

"Just answer the question."

Sam folded his arms across his chest. "Looks like the right one, but I can't tell without a closer look."

Sweat beaded on Hamilton's forehead. *Sam's wrong. This can't be the same piece.* He released the evidence into the man's outstretched hand.

Sam studied the bracelet. He turned the bag back and

forth in his hand. "I think this is the one."

"I need more than that. A *think so* won't hold up in court."

"I take photos of the more valuable pieces that come in here. For insurance purposes."

"Get them."

Hamilton followed Sam through a narrow trench of boxes and plastic totes to a cluttered desk in the corner of the back room. Sam touched his mouse and the computer screen lit up. He typed in a password. A few clicks later and he gestured toward the screen. "That's the one."

Hamilton stared at the photograph, his mouth too dry for words. A lump formed in his throat. There was no doubt about it. The bracelet in the photo was the same one in Sam's hand. The same one he'd removed from Paige's backpack that afternoon.

He'd stolen her heart. There was no doubt about it. Paige stopped typing on her keyboard and pressed her fingers to her lips. His kiss had felt like sunshine after a string of cloudy days. A fresh flush warmed her face. *It isn't supposed to be this way.* He was a LEO, a first responder, and a self-proclaimed bachelor. He'd even stated as much only minutes before he held her in his arms. He was everything she'd vowed to avoid, and yet, he attracted her like a sunflower follows sunlight. She could only hope she wouldn't be burned.

She left her laptop on the kitchen table and dropped to the couch. She kicked off her tennis shoes and propped her feet up on the coffee table. Her calves burned from the exercise of hiking. *I guess you use different muscles when riding a bike.* She covered her mouth to stifle a yawn. She still needed to shower and change clothes before heading to the Thorne's for the night. She hopped up from the couch and went into the bedroom, stripped out of her jogging suit and reached into her pants pocket for her cell phone. She wiggled her fingers. The pocket was empty. *Where's my phone?*

She removed her backpack from the coat closet and combed through the contents. It wasn't there either. *I must have lost it on the hike.* It was growing dark outside, but she didn't want her phone rained on all night. She'd have to ride back out to the picnic area and find it. *I should call Hamilton and ask him to drive me up there.* She glanced around for her phone to call him. *Duh? It's not here.* There wasn't a land line in the apartment and the Thorne's weren't homc. *Never mind. I'll just go look for it myself.* Her heart thumped under her ribcage. What about the trespasser who tried to break into her apartment or the men who'd followed them at the mall? *It's fine. There's nothing to be afraid of.*

Hamilton drove to the station in a daze. He'd trusted her, and she'd betrayed his trust. He should have seen this coming. He knew she'd been lying to him about her purpose in Whitman. Why had he doubted his instincts? *I let her steal my heart, but I guess that's not the only thing she stole.* How many of the recent robberies had Paige committed? Was she guilty of more than one? Anger and frustration built up in his chest. He'd let down his guard and it had cost him.

The light in the chief's office glowed under the door. He tapped on the wood and waited.

"Yes?"

Hamilton stepped inside, shutting the door behind him. "Hey, chief. Got a minute?"

Chief House leaned back in his chair and laced his hands behind his head. "What's up?"

Hamilton tossed the zip-lock bag on the chief's desk. "I confiscated this this afternoon. It's the bracelet stolen from the pawn shop. Sam confirmed it."

"Did you make an arrest?"

"No sir." As angry as he was, he couldn't bring himself to arrest her.

Chief House's forehead wrinkled with confusion. "Care to explain?"

"I found the bracelet in a backpack."

"Who's backpack?"

"Paige McDonald's."

The chief blew out a breath. "I see. Is there a conflict of interest?"

"Excuse me?"

"Do you have feelings for the girl and that's why you can't arrest her?"

Hamilton swallowed and tried wishing away the warmth climbing his neck. "Yes, sir." He'd always been honest with the chief. He wouldn't start lying to his superior now.

"We could test for fingerprints. Unless she used gloves, or her prints aren't in the system."

"They are." Hamilton pursed his lips. Why did he have to say that?

The chief raised an eyebrow. His chair creaked as he leaned forward. "She's been arrested before?"

"Yes, sir."

"For?"

"Theft."

Jerry slipped into the leather seat and shut the car door, trapping the bitter breeze on the outside. He couldn't make eye contact with the man next to him. His boss looked chill, but in his eyes, all he saw was ice. They'd agreed to meet at Sacajawea Peak. He was supposed to turn over the diamond bracelet. Except he didn't have it anymore. Most likely, the girl had already found it and turned it over to the police. He'd been careful, though. Well, almost. At least he didn't leave fingerprints like that kid Montory, even if he had set off the alarm and had to stash the bracelet in a backpack.

"Do you have it?"

"I couldn't get it. There was this big dog."

His boss sighed and rubbed his forehead. "You're an idiot, you know that?"

"I could try to retrieve it again."

"Don't bother. It's lost now." The fence pulled an envelope from inside his coat and handed it to him. "Here's your take from the phones. Where's the coins?"

"I have them in my coat." He reached in his pocket. His empty pocket. "Um, I don't have them anymore."

"Fool! Have you been carrying them around with you?" The fence withdrew a gun. "Can't you do anything right? First, you nearly let Montory get away. I had to threaten him to keep him from talking to the police. You should have just shot him dead."

Jerry pressed his back against the door. "I've never used a real gun before. I set the fire, though, like you asked. And the fireworks worked like a charm. And I got the phones and the coins."

"The coins don't count. You lost them."

"What about those journals?"

"They're worthless to me."

"You got the money, right? From the city accounts. They were empty when Madam Mayor met with the city council."

"I didn't take that money. Someone else got it first." The fence narrowed his eyes.

Jerry didn't like the insinuation in the other man's voice. "It wasn't me."

His boss lowered the gun. "I've got one more job for you, if you can keep from botching it up."

"I can do it. I promise."

Paige switched on a flashlight, then hiked to where she and Hamilton had picnicked earlier that afternoon. As she climbed, she waved the light beam back and forth on the ground hoping it would reflect off the cell phone screen if she'd dropped it along the way. When she reached the plateau, she headed for the pavilion. The flashlight beam glinted off something on the picnic table where they'd eaten lunch. Her phone. Voices carried on the still night air. A car was parked in the shadows with its windows down. She switched off the flashlight and crept closer.

"I can't do that."

"Every man has his price."

"That may be, but what you're asking me—where did you get those?"

"Never mind. The point is that they exist. I can give these to"—the next words were unintelligible—"or I can make them disappear. What will it be?"

"Happy Days" rang out in the darkness.

"Hey, who's out there?" The car door opened. A shot rang out.

Paige lunged for the picnic table, dropping her flashlight. She grabbed her phone, and then scrambled down the path. Her tennis shoes skittered and slid on the mud and gravel. The clouds moved. A beam of moonlight lit the steep trail.

The ground leveled out as she reached the bottom. She mounted her bike and pedaled toward town, listening for a car giving chase. She pulled into the Thorne's driveway and skidded to a stop. The porch light shone like a beacon. She was safe. Her heart raced from pedaling.

Another, much brighter, light clicked on. She squinted in the blinding headlights. An officer stood next to a police cruiser. She dropped her bike and walked toward him. "Excuse me, officer. Can I help you?" He dangled a pair of handcuffs. Paige stepped back. "What's going on?" Her knees buckled. She couldn't catch her breath.

"Paige McDonald, you're under arrest. You have the right to remain silent. Anything you say can and will be used against you in a court of law. You have the right to an attorney. If you cannot afford an attorney, one will be provided for you." Cold metal clapped around her wrists.

No. Not again.

21

"I didn't do it."

Her voice traveled through the halls of time and bounced off the jail cell walls. Fifteen-year-old, Paige jerked from the principal's grasp, her ponytail swinging in frustration and fear. Principal Taylor's other hand clutched the wad of cash he'd just removed from her distinct lime green Lisa Frank backpack. "If you didn't do it, why do you have the money for Spring Formal?"

She wasn't sure, but she had a good guess. "It wasn't me. I swear."

"Your hoodie is on the security footage." The same hoodie she wore at that very moment. The same hoodie she now wanted to throw into the incinerator behind the school. She and her bestie, Samantha, had bought matching hoodies at the mall. The bedazzled BFF on the back made them unique. Had it all been a setup? How could she tattle on her best friend? Who would believe her anyway? She had a record and it would be her word against that of the vice principal's daughter.

When she'd stood in front of the judge a couple of days

later, she'd kept hoping that Samantha would confess, but she didn't. Paige had chewed on her bottom lip and bit back the tears as he'd pronounced her guilty. Guilty of a crime she hadn't committed. Her previous infractions made it an easy decision to send her to juvenile detention and throw away the key.

Here she was again. This was worse than *déjà vu*. This was a living nightmare. Paige rested her face in her hands and let the tears fall. What was the sense in stopping them? She rotated on the uncomfortable cot and laid on her back with her knees in the air. She stared at the tiles on the ceiling. What had she done to deserve this? Who would do this to her? Bitterness crept through her heart like the English ivy that the State of Oregon had banned several years ago. It was all coming back. The hurt. The pain of being falsely accused. She was fifteen all over again. But this time, it was worse, because she'd fallen in love. How could Hamilton do this to her? How could he have even thought she was the thief? Her overwrought emotions threw out all logic. She didn't want to analyze the situation or weigh her feelings against the truth. *I've worked so hard these last five years to be something else, but it's still true. I'm a thief, and once a thief, always a thief.*

He didn't sleep all night. Hamilton leaned back in his desk chair in the bullpen and propped his regulation boots on his desk. He covered his eyes with his hands, failing miserably to block out the florescent lights. His head pounded. Turning Paige in was one of the hardest things he'd ever done. The betrayal in her eyes as she'd passed him on her way to the holding cell would haunt him for the rest of his life. If there ever was a time in his life when he wanted to be wrong, it was now, but there was no denying the evidence. Paige broke into the pawn shop, smashed the glass case, and stole the diamond bracelet. What else could it be? The bracelet was in her backpack.

The door beeped. The receptionist let someone into the restricted area. He rotated his chair. His sister entered the bullpen, dragging his nephew, Tyler, by the ear. Hamilton dropped his feet to the floor as Becky shoved her teenage son toward him. "What brings you out this morn-"

"Tell him." Becky interrupted.

He wrinkled his forehead. Was there something he forgot to tell Tyler? The woebegone expression on his nephew's face told him that wasn't the case. "Tell me what?" It must be important for Becky to drag Tyler to the station so early in the morning.

"Uncle Ham, I—um—I…"

Becky's face flushed. She pressed her hands to her lips and stomped her foot. "Tell him." Hamilton hadn't seen his sister this mad since, in the fourth grade, he'd made copies of her diary pages and had passed them out at the school.

"We—I mean, I…" Tyler glanced over his shoulder at his mother and pleaded for mercy.

He didn't find any. "He and his friends were the ones who tagged that fence the other night. I found the leftover cans in his backpack."

Hamilton stood and took a step toward his nephew. Tyler looked sick with fright. "Vandalism, Tyler, really?"

Tyler fell to his knees and clasped his hands under his chin. "I'm sorry, Uncle Hamilton. I'm sorry. I'll never do it again. I promise. Please don't throw me in jail." Hamilton glanced over at his sister. She was barely holding back a snort. Her sides shook. She clasped her hands over her lips and turned her head the other way. Hamilton looked back at his nephew kneeling on the tile floor and looking every bit the repentant sinner.

His nephew had never gotten in trouble before. Hamilton was apt to let his first offense slide; however, it wouldn't hurt to put a little fear of the law in him first. He straightened his tie and narrowed his eyes. "I don't know, Tyler. Vandalism is a pretty serious offense. You could be looking at ten to twenty." He meant, of course, days of community service, but it achieved the impact he wanted.

Tyler's eyes grew big as saucers. "Years?" The word croaked from his throat. The poor kid looked like he might pass out.

It was Hamilton's turn to hold back a chuckle. He put his hands on his hips. "Since this is your first run-in with the law, maybe I can be lenient."

The boy's head bobbed like a bobble-head on a dashboard. "Please, Uncle Hamilton."

"You're free to go, but if I see you in here again…" He slit his finger across his throat. Tyler grasped both hands around his neck. Hamilton stepped forward and mussed Tyler's thick blond hair. "I'm just messing with you." His nephew relaxed, and he grasped his uncle's hand. Hamilton pulled him to his feet. "Vandalism is a serious crime, though. I don't want to see you in here again. I mean it."

"Thanks, Uncle Hamilton. You won't, I promise."

Hamilton walked Becky and Tyler out to their van. Tyler jumped in the passenger side. Becky opened her door and started to get in, then stopped and stepped out again. "Hey, I heard rumor that you caught the pawn shop thief."

"Yeah, unfortunately, I guess. She's locked up in the back."

The passenger door opened, and Tyler's head appeared over the top of the van. "She?" Tyler jumped down and circled the van. "It couldn't have been a girl, Uncle Hamilton. I saw the thief running from the store. It was a man."

"Are you sure?"

"Yeah. Whoever it was, they were too big to be a woman."

Hamilton felt the breath whoosh from his lungs. Relief washed over his body. And then, fear. *I'm an idiot. What have I done? Paige is never going to speak to me again.*

She came to the cell door as Hamilton pulled a set of keys from his pocket. "A witness come forward putting a man at the scene of the crime. You're free to go."

"That's it. No apology. No reimbursement for emotional trauma. How about you spend the night in here for false imprisonment?" Her voice was steaming with anger and he deserved every bit of it.

"I am sorry, Paige. If there is anything I can do to make this up to you—"

"Forget about it." She stepped out of the cell and into the hallway.

"I know you're mad at me, but I was only doing my job."

She stomped a few steps away from him. "Of course, I'm mad. I said I was innocent."

He chased after her. "So does every prisoner we haul in here. Jails are full of *innocent* people." He made finger quotes around the word, innocent. "I'm so sorry."

"Sorry!" She spun on her heels. Her eyes flashed. "You only thought it was me because of my record."

He wanted to say that her past hadn't crossed his mind, but he'd be lying if he did. "You were in possession of the stolen bracelet. The evidence was pretty convincing." He shuffled his feet. He'd moved based on facts, and they had failed him.

Paige paced the tight hallway, swinging her hands wildly. She huffed and leaned against the wall. She clutched the zipper of her jacket in hand and slid it up and down. The longer she thought, the faster the zipper moved. It froze halfway up. "All the time we spent together, you were watching me, weren't you?" Tears pooled in her lower eyelids and threatened to spill down her flushed cheeks. Her voice cracked. "I knew better than to get involved with a police officer. I thought maybe you cared, but none of it was real. You were playing undercover cop and I was the schmuck who trusted you."

He grabbed her arm, wrapping his fingers around her pale, slender wrist. "Please, it's not like that."

She jerked from his hold. "Stay away from me."

Paige left the police station on foot and wandered through town not knowing where to go. She couldn't go home to the Thorne's house and face Becky's disappointment. Did they think she was a thief, too? What was the point of staying in Whitman any longer? She hadn't gotten any closer to finding her birth mother, and it was starting to seem like the whole search was for nothing. She should give up and return to Portland. Aunt Hattie missed her. She'd made a good life for herself there. It had only been a couple of weeks, maybe Cat Bastille could get her old job back for her. Things could go back to the way they were. Staying in Whitman just wasn't worth the heartache. She'd taken a risk, and someone had hurt her. Again.

She walked to the Rustic Cup and ordered a drink at the counter. When she went to pay for the coffee, Jenn reached out and squeezed her hand. "I heard what happened. Are you all right?"

"I don't want to talk about it." Paige took her steaming cup and sat at a table in the corner. *Is everyone staring at me, or is it just my imagination?* The police had acquitted her of any charges, but would the good citizens of Whitman continue to be suspicious? She laid her cell phone, wallet, and keys down on the tabletop; the personal effects she'd had on her person when they'd arrested her. She raised her coffee cup to her nose and breathed in the comforting aroma. *What do I do now?*

He sat alone on the ripped leather booth. His coffee had grown cold as he stared at his cell phone screen, waiting for it to ring. That little bell on the door grated against his nerves, setting his teeth on edge every time a customer entered the café. The wind sent chills crawling beneath the sleeves of his expensive sports coat every time the door opened. His phone buzzed. He put it to his ear. "Yes?"

"We need to move the stuff, boss. Po-Po's hot on our tails here in Portland. Have you got a place?"

He tapped his pen on the tabletop. He'd expected as much, which is why he'd already scoped out the hangers at the old unmanned airport. It was abandoned. Secluded. No one had bothered with it since the county had built the new one east of town. It was the perfect hideaway for their cache of merchandise. "Load the stuff and bring it here tonight." He tapped the end button. He was about to pull off the biggest heist of his career. This was bigger than the one they'd done in London. Bigger than Pittsburgh. If they could pull this off, he was expecting seven million dollars in revenue, possibly ten. If that red-headed southpaw could keep from messing it up.

Richard Staten's personal library had some of the most valuable books he'd ever laid eyes on. The collectors would pay through their noses to get ahold of those collections. He'd taken a sampling to wet their interest. But it wasn't just the books. Historical artifacts filled Staten's mansion. The courthouse and city hall, too. The paintings in the mayor's office weren't replicas. They were the genuine thing.

And no one would be guarding those two locations the night of the political rally. They'd all be at the school protecting Kathleen. Making it appear like she was in mortal danger was the most ingenious stratagem he'd ever concocted. Staten had betrayed him and now he would return the favor.

"Sunday, Monday, Happy days. Tuesday, Wednesday, Happy days." The oldies music came from the other side of the café. A blond girl answered a cell phone. He recognized her ring tone. She'd been the one last night at Sacajawea Peak.

There was no telling how much she had overheard of their conversation. He squinted his eyes to get a better look at the girl. *Why does she seem familiar?* No matter. He'd have to eliminate her. She was a risk he wasn't willing to take.

"Can I warm your coffee?"

He pushed the mug to the edge of the table. "Thanks, Kylie."

"You're welcome."

He pointed across the room. "Do you know that girl?"

"That's Paige McDonald. She's new in town."

Paige McDonald? That's a name I haven't heard in a long time. What's she doing in Whitman? He removed his wallet from his pocket and licked his fingers, preparing to withdraw a couple of ones to leave a tip. He froze mid-lick. *Paige McDonald? As in the girl claiming to be Kathleen's abandoned child?* Things just got more complicated than he'd ever imagined.

Paige pushed the end button on her phone and sighed. Jessie asked her to come in as soon as possible. *She's going to fire me. I just know it. I guess I can't blame her.*

The store smelled fresh and clean when Paige entered The Bookshelf, several minutes later. Someone had finished painting the walls and trim. The carpet was installed, and the metal shelving units were in place with some of the books already loaded. Jessie Faye hummed as she emptied a box labeled 'mysteries' onto one of the shelves. *When did all this happen?*

"Hello, Jessie." Paige approached the woman and clasped her hands behind her back. "I'm out." The woman had to have heard where she'd spent the night. There was no way she would keep her employed now.

"Good morning, Paige. You can start with those boxes over there on the other side." She smiled and gestured around the room. "Do you like it? Becky and her family spent all afternoon and evening working in here. Isn't it wonderful?"

Paige swallowed and furrowed her brows. It did look wonderful, but Jessie was avoiding the obvious. "I spent the night in jail." The elderly woman continued her work without a word. "Do you think I'm a thief?"

Jessie met Paige's eyes. Her features softened. The corner of her mouth turned up. "It doesn't matter what I think."

But it did. Paige hated the thought of this sweet woman thinking ill of her. "I didn't take the bracelet. I'm not guilty."

"We're all guilty, honey."

"I don't understand."

"For scarcely for a righteous man will one die: yet peradventure for a good man some would even dare to die. But God commendeth his love toward us, in that while we were yet sinners, Christ died for us."

That was the text Pastor Whitestone had preached her first Sunday in Whitman. The same verse her mother had highlighted in the Bible. *What does it mean? God commendeth His love toward us? How did He do that? By dying? But if a god could die, that wouldn't make him much of a god, now would it? Besides, why would anyone think a god would love people? The gods in ancient myths and legends didn't give love, they demanded the humans' devotion. They were often angry, jealous, and difficult. Selfish beings, really, but a God of love?* "Does God love you?" The question slipped from her lips.

The old woman poked her head around the metal shelving unit, her reading glasses propped on top of her white curls. "Yes. He does. He loves me very, very much."

Of course, He did. Jessie was a good woman, kind to others, and benevolent. Paige knelt by a box on the floor. She cut the tape and opened the flaps. She took a deep breath. "Jessie?"

"Yes?"

Paige picked up a book and flipped through the aged pages. She traced her fingers over the raised letters on the cover. "Does God love me?"

"He does."

"How do you know?"

"He died for you."

That's stupid. "Why would anyone die for me?"

"Because He loves you."

"Why would He do that? I'm not worthy of anyone's love." *Jessie's wrong. God doesn't love me. He might love those who are good, but He doesn't love me. No one can love me.*

"But that's the beauty of it all. God doesn't love us because we're worthy. He loves us in all of our unworthiness."

The store grew quiet. The only sound was the books tapping the shelves as the two women settled them into place.

"Jessie." Paige paused. "I'm going back to Portland. I can't stay here any longer."

There was silence, and then a *groan* came from the other side of the room. A stack of books crashed onto the floor. "Jessie? Mrs. Faye?" Paige darted around the shelving unit. Her heart plummeted. The elderly woman sat on the floor slumped against the wall, clutching her chest and moaning. Paige dropped to her knees and touched the woman's shoulder. "What's happened? What's wrong?"

Jessie groaned. Her eyes rolled back in her head and closed. Paige felt her throat for her pulse. *Still strong. That's good. Shallow, but steady breathing.* She jumped up from the floor, grabbed her phone, and dialed 911. *Dear God. Don't let her die.*

Hamilton left Paige pacing the waiting area and entered the Emergency Room. He pulled back the curtain of the exam room where Jessie reclined on a gurney with a hospital gown hanging loose on her thin frame. Her eyes were closed, and her face was as white as the sheet under her. He sat on the edge of the bed and called her name in a hushed voice.

"Who's there?" Her voice trembled as she squinted through transparent eyelids.

He squeezed her wrinkled hand. "It's Hamilton."

"Oh, dear boy." Her gnarly fingers brushed his shaved face.

"You can cut the act. I know you're faking."

Jessie opened her eyes wide and pushed her body to a sitting position. "How'd you know?"

"I just talked to your doctor. He said your heart is as strong as an Olympian. Why the dramatics?"

The old woman folded her hands in her lap and sighed. "Paige."

"What about Paige?" Maybe she was ill. Jessie wasn't making any sense.

"She's leaving."

Hamilton stood and moved away from the bed. "Leaving? Why?" He turned his back on the old woman, hoping she wouldn't notice his distress.

"She's fallen in love."

He spun on his heel. "With whom?"

"You."

Me. No way. She's made it clear that she's not interested in a relationship with a first responder. "I think you're mistaken. Paige wouldn't date me if I was the last man on earth." Especially not now, not after he accused her of stealing and had her arrested.

"Do you have feelings for her?"

"It doesn't matter how I feel. My job is too dangerous. I can't ask her to endure that. It's too risky. You of all people should know that."

"It's time you stopped blaming your lack of faith on my grandson's death."

"Jessie—"

"I'm not finished." She held up her wrinkled hand. He bit his bottom lip to keep from interrupting. "William died doing what he loved. His job was dangerous, and Gracie knew that when she married him. She's not bitter or angry at God for taking her husband. She's grateful that God allowed them to have any time together. She would rather have been married to him for a short while than not at all. None of us know how much time we have on this earth. You could just as easily die from cancer or in an automobile accident. Does that mean we sit around waiting to die? Of course not. It means we get out there and live by faith the life that God intends for us to live. It's not for us to know how much time we'll have. We're only required to wisely use the time He's given us."

Hamilton had no response. The old woman was right. He'd been hiding his lack of faith behind his grief. If God was leading him and Paige together, wasn't it disobedience to ignore God's direction? Could he trust God? Could he enjoy whatever time they would have together instead of worrying about the future?

He returned to the edge of the bed. "But what do I do? Paige has no faith in God. We'd be unequally yoked if we got married, and I can guarantee she feels nothing for me now but disdain. I betrayed her trust. She'll never speak to me again, much less go out on another date."

"She needs Jesus, Hamilton. You must find a way to keep her here in Whitman. If she returns to Portland, I'm afraid she'll never find salvation."

"I'll see what I can do, Jessie. Thanks for the dress down."

"You're welcome. Anytime."

Hamilton returned to the waiting area. Paige peeked around him as the emergency room door closed. "How—how is she?"

He hesitated. He couldn't tell Paige the truth about Jessie's condition. That would give her a green light to leave town. But he couldn't lie to her either. "She's going to be fine," he answered.

Paige's shoulders lowered as she sighed with relief. She

touched her hand to her chest. "I'm glad she's OK. Is there anything I can do?" Her voice pleaded with him. Here was his opportunity to convince her to stay in town.

"She asked if you'd finish getting the store ready for the grand reopening while she takes some much-needed time off."

"Sure. Sure. I can do that."

Hamilton squeezed her shoulder. "Thanks. I know it means a lot to her." Paige looked at the place where his fingers touched her shirt. "Sorry." He moved his hand. They made eye contact, but what he saw in her eyes was not anger. It was hurt.

The next morning, Hamilton rose early and drove out to the cemetery. The grass sparkled like diamonds in the morning dew. American flags fluttered in the breeze created as the sun warmed the earth. He took a seat on the bench and bowed his head. He couldn't get Jessie's reprimand out of his mind. *"It's time you stopped blaming your lack of faith on my grandson's death."* Was that really what he'd been doing? Was this more about trusting God than about protecting a wife from the pain he saw Gracie go through? Wasn't he doing the honorable thing, staying single? Did God have a different plan for his life? Plans that involved a spouse? Children, maybe? Was he allowing his fear to keep him from living the life God had for him?

He closed his eyes, and a prayer rose from his lips. He startled when a hand squeezed his shoulder. "I thought I might find you here. I stopped by the hospital to see Jessie Faye last night and she told me she'd raked you over the coals." He opened his eyes. Lillian joined him on the bench. "Beautiful up here, isn't it?"

He didn't answer. Not at first. His focus remained on the granite gravestone in front of him, his elbows propped on his thighs. Lillian's finger brushed a tear off his cheek, leaving a cold mark where she'd touched him. "I miss him too."

He leaned back against the wooden slates. "It still feels like yesterday. I can't believe he's gone."

"I know. Me neither."

"I used to love Thanksgiving Day when I was growing up. Family. Food. Football." He chuckled and playfully bumped Lillian's shoulder. She was a much bigger football fan than he was. "But ever since Will died, it's just not the same."

"Any one of us could have been on that task team that day. I was offered that position and I turned it down so I could move back home. That could have been me. Maybe it should have been me."

A dark cloud passed over the cemetery. Lillian shivered. Hamilton removed his coat and wrapped it over her shoulders. Her words stuck him like a knife. *It should have been me.* They were both single. It should have been one of them. Not Will. Gracie shouldn't have been widowed so early in her marriage. Why did it have to be him?

Hamilton turned his head to see his partner. Tears glistened in her eyes. Wisps of hair clung to her wet cheeks. "Lil, we've been friends forever, haven't we?" They'd grown up together, played cops and robbers in the woods, graduated the Academy… They understood each other. Most of the time. "What's going on? You've been distant and vague. You keep disappearing without a word, and Chief House put you on the desk."

Lillian bent over her knees and broke into sobs. The sound rattled him to his core. "Lil, it's fine. You don't have to tell me if you don't want to. I'm sorry for pushing."

She sat up, sniffling and wiping her sleeves across her face. "No. No. I want to tell you. I just—I need a moment." He turned away and gazed out over the valley. Lillian squeezed his hand. "Hamilton?" He turned to face her. "I've been diagnosed with breast cancer."

Silence. What could he say? A heavy weight settled into

the pit of his stomach. He swallowed the knot in his throat before he spoke. "How bad is it?" He choked on his words. This was one of those times when knowing the truth was worse than not knowing.

"We caught it early. I've had several appointments with the doctors. I need surgery and several rounds of chemotherapy. The oncologist is optimistic." She put on a brave smile. "Nothing to worry about."

"Are you sure?"

Lillian put her hand to her lips. He pulled her into his arms and held her while she cried. Jessie's words echoed through his thoughts. *"None of us know how much time we have on this earth. Does that mean we sit around waiting to die? Of course not. It means we get out there and live by faith the life God intends for us to live. It's not for us to know how much time we'll have. We're only required to wisely use the time He's given us."*

22

Later that same morning, Hamilton drove Jessie home from the hospital, though the cardiologist had been willing to release her the previous night. Hamilton chuckled at the memory of the way she'd carried on until she'd convinced him to let her stay in the hospital overnight.

A white van followed close behind them. He flicked on the blinker and slowed his truck to turn into Jessie's driveway, but the driver of the van laid on his horn and swerved around the pickup. If he'd been in his patrol unit, he would have pulled it over and given the driver a citation. As it was, he simply parked on the gravel, then helped Jessie into her house. After she unlocked and opened her front door, she shuffled across the floor, dropped into her rocking chair, and pointed to an afghan hanging over a nearby quilt rack. "Would you get that blanket for me? I feel a draft."

Hamilton retrieved the blanket and tucked it across her lap. "Can I do anything else for you while I'm here?"

"Would you make me a cup of tea?"

"Of course." He went into the kitchen and prepared the tea without further instructions. He knew exactly where she kept everything in her cabinets. When the kettle whistled, he poured hot water over the tea bag, and brought the steaming mug into the living room, and set it on a coaster on a table next to Jessie's chair.

"Would you open the curtains and let the sunlight in? That hospital was too dark and dreary."

"You were only there for one day, and that was at your request." Hamilton loved teasing the old woman, but he went to do as she had requested. He pushed open the drapes on the front windows. Sunlight flooded the room. The same white van passed the house, heading in the opposite direction as before. Jessie was speaking, but Hamilton barely heard her. A Dead End sign stood just beyond the driveway. The time between coming and going had been much too long for just a simple turnaround. "What's down this road? Anything?"

"There's nothing down that way except for the old airport. It's been out of use ever since the town built that new one."

How odd. I think I'll drive down there and scope it out. He turned around to face his old friend. "Is there anything else you need before I leave?"

"No, thank you. I'll be fine." She tapped her wrinkled cheek. He leaned over and gave her a little peck.

"I'll see you later."

"God bless you, Hamilton."

He left the house, then pulled the door tight behind him. He jiggled the handle just to be sure it was secure. It bothered him to have a defenseless elderly woman living alone at the far edge of town. *Defenseless?* He chuckled to himself. Not Jessie Faye. The good Lord in Heaven gave her all the defense she needed.

He climbed into his truck, put the key in the ignition, and backed out of the driveway, then drove past the Dead End sign and around the corner. The road followed a creek for two or three miles, then crossed a bridge. Another half-mile and the road entered a neglected clearing.

Two rusty airplane hangars stood parallel to an overgrown landing strip. The asphalt ended and became a dirt road filled with muddy potholes. A vehicle had recently driven through the mud. Wet tracks led all the way to the door of one of the hangars.

Hamilton parked at the end of the paved road and walked the rest of the way, avoiding the puddles in order to keep from leaving visible footprints. A padlock fastened the hangar door. He checked the side doors. Both were locked tight. He tried peeking in the windows, but black paper covered them. He checked the second hangar and found the same thing. He circled the airport, looking for anything out of the ordinary, but after seeing nothing unusual, he headed back to the pickup truck and drove back the way he'd come.

Paige stacked several more books onto their new shelves and aligned the spines with the edge of the shelf. Working kept her from thinking too much, and she'd kept as busy as possible over the last few days. She'd promised that she would stay in town until after the grand reopening. It was the least she could do after Jessie had been so kind.

Oldies music streamed from her cell phone on the brand-new reception desk that had replaced the old card table. A desktop computer and credit card machine topped the desk. She'd arranged the loft upstairs into a quiet reading area with plush chairs, and tables with electrical outlets for laptops and USB ports for charging electronic devices. Another computer had been set up in the brand-new office in the back. New shelving had been added in the storage room to hold extra office supplies and extra inventory, and it was all labeled and organized. She still had to catalog about twenty-five boxes of books that remained in her apartment, upload all the inventory information into their brand-new POS system, and then design a website so Jessie could sell the books online as well as in the store.

The music paused. Her cell phone rang. She rushed across the room and snatched it up on the last ring. "Hello." *I hope it's Becky with an update on Jessie.* Paige hadn't heard anything since Jessie had left the hospital on Tuesday.

"Miss McDonald. This is Mayor Phillips. How are you this afternoon?"

Paige hesitated. *What is this? A welfare check? How did she get my number?* "I'm fine. Uh, thank you." *Why would the mayor be calling me?*

"Would you come and meet me here at City Hall?"

Can people refuse a mayor? Or are they like royals? Off with your head or run you out of town if you anger them? "Sure. I can do that." Butterflies flittered in her stomach. *The mayor wants to meet with me? Why?*

"Excellent. I'll see you here at three o'clock." A click, then the line was dead.

What was that all about?

At a quarter till three, Paige grabbed her cardigan and purse, then jogged down the sidewalk to the imposing building made of Bowlby stone. She didn't know what that was, but the residents of Whitman were proud of it. Whitman City Hall and Wallowa County Courthouse occupied the same building. She gripped the strap of her leather purse and opened the molded oak door. It banged shut behind her and echoed in the empty marble hall.

A security guard indicated for her to hand him her purse, then signaled for her to pass under the metal detector. He sifted through her personal belongings. "Have a nice day, ma'am." She nodded and grabbed hold of the straps as he handed her bag back, then she crossed to the glass barrier on the far side, her heeled shoes clicking on the polished tile floor. A young woman spoke into a headset and rapidly typed on a keyboard. With a flash of her hand, she signaled the universal sign for "wait a minute."

"Yes, sir, Mr. Brighten. I have you down for an appointment with the commissioner for two o'clock, June eighteenth. That's next Monday. Yes, sir. Yes, sir. Have a good afternoon. May I help you?"

Paige waited. The receptionist's eyebrows raised. "Oh, you were talking to me."

She nodded.

"I'm supposed to meet Mayor Phillips."

"Down the hall. Elevator to the second floor."

"Thank you."

The receptionist waved her hand and spoke into her microphone. "Good afternoon. Whitman City Hall and Wallowa County Courthouse, how may I assist you?"

Paige rode the elevator, then turned the handle on a door with gold letters on the glass that read, Mayor Kathleen Phillips. A man in his early twenties reclined in an office chair with his feet propped up on a polished desk. "Puh, puh, puh. I've got you now." He shouted. His thumbs flicked the screen of a cell phone in his hands. There was no one else in the room. A potted ficus grew in one corner and the open window blinds allowed sunlight to illuminate the dust in the air.

"Hello?"

The young man's head shot up and he scrambled to his feet. His chair tumbled backward. He jumped from the floor and straightened his tie, then he stepped around the desk and extended his hand with a broad smile. "Jeremiah Bennett, Mayor Phillips' assistant. Do you have an appointment?"

"She asked me to be here at three o'clock." Paige brushed her hair behind her ear and shifted her purse strap to the other shoulder. Mr. Bennett glanced at the watch on his right wrist.

"Have a seat." He pointed to several plushy chairs in the corner with a table of magazines and a replica of a Monet painting on the wall called, *Wheat Stacks at the End of Summer*, fitting for the farm country surrounding Whitman. "Mayor Phillips stepped out for a quick meeting with Public Works. She'll return any minute."

Several minutes later, the door opened, and Mayor Phillips stepped in, a stack of manila folders on her arm. "The Water Commissioner says we can raise taxes or raise water prices, but something has to go up. Blackguard."

Paige stood to her feet. "Mayor Phillips?"

The mayor turned sharply and peered over her reading glasses. "Miss McDonald. Do come in." She didn't smile.

Paige followed the woman through the door into an office about the size of a hotel suite. The walls sported several more replicas of famous paintings: a Van Gogh, another Monet, and a Rembrandt. A gurgling sound came from a tabletop waterfall. Solid oak bookcases and filing cabinets filled the spaces between the massive windows. Mayor Phillips opened one of the drawers, dropped the files into place, then sat in the leather office chair behind the enormous desk. "Please, have a seat." She folded her reading glasses and set them aside.

Paige's pulse fluttered in her chest. Jitters ran up and down her arms and legs. Was she excited to meet someone so important or scared by what the city official might have to say? Both, she decided. The woman hadn't taken her eyes off Paige since she'd entered the room. Paige shifted nervously.

A car horn honked outside the window, jarring the mayor from her fixation. "Well," Mayor Phillips leaned forward, and rested her clasped hands on top of a desk calendar. "Are you enjoying your stay in our little town?" Her voice dripped with implication. She was fishing for information.

Paige skip-walked to a chair, sat, and placed her purse underneath. "Yes, ma'am." She gestured toward the paintings. "I love your choice in artwork."

"Thank you. Where are you from?"

"Portland, ma'am."

"What, may I ask, brought you to Eastern Oregon?"

"I, uh—" What could she tell the mayor? She remembered Hamilton's words. *People leave Whitman. They don't move here.* Paige bit her lip. Her mind raced for an answer.

Mayor Phillips walked around the desk and balanced on the corner, crossing one pantyhose-clad leg over the other. "I hear you've been inquiring about your birth mother?"

How did she know that? "Yes. Yes, I was. Am. I am."

"And you believe she's here in Whitman?" The city official drummed her fingers on the desk.

Paige clasped her hands together until her knuckles turned white. She didn't feel comfortable sharing her personal history with a stranger, but what choice did she have? "I learned of her existence only a few weeks ago. A firefighter adopted me after he found me abandoned on the front steps of a fire department." The woman's expression remained unchanged. "I found a Bible in my attic. My adopted great-aunt explained that it was found with me. Inside was a note signed, 'Annie'. A bookmark from the Wallowa Mountains Baptist Church jump-started my search."

"How interesting." Mayor Phillips stopped tapping her fingers.

She might as well ask. The worse she could say was no. "Do you… I mean, have you ever…" Paige groaned in frustration. "Is there a woman named Annie in town?"

The older woman returned to her chair. "I've been mayor for three years. I don't recall hearing of an Annie in that time."

"How about when you were younger? Back when you were growing up."

"I'm sorry. I can't help you."

"I tried checking for birth or death records, but…" She left the sentence hanging. Without a last name, it was an impossible search. Besides, Annie might be her mother's nickname and not her legal name at all. Paige stood. "I'm sorry for having bothered you, Madam Mayor."

Mayor Phillips extended her hand. "Nonsense. I invited

you here. Have a nice evening. Bennett will walk you out."

Paige followed the assistant through the empty halls. She was halfway down the street before she realized she'd forgotten her purse under the chair.

🚔 🚔 🚔

Kathleen paced up and down the large area rug. Her campaign manager braced himself against the window and lit a cigarette. "Are you sure?" He let out a puff of smoke. Kathleen crossed the room, yanked the cigarette from his fingers, and ground it into the floor under her pump. "Don't smoke in my office."

Joe Donahue raised an eyebrow and slipped the lighter back into his jacket pocket. "Touchy, aren't we?"

Kathleen sent him a look that said, "Shut up or you're fired."

The campaign manager held out his hands. "You're the one who never mentioned this possibility. You might have said, 'Hey Joe, I've got a"—Kathleen flinched at his crude language—"who just might pop out of the woodwork someday'. Again, I ask, are you sure?"

Kathleen stopped pacing and dropped into the chair behind her desk. "I'm sure. It was like looking in a mirror." She met Joe's eyes. "A mirror with a blonde wig."

It was the manager's turn to pace. He crossed the room. Once. Twice. He stopped, turned, and leaned over the desk, slapping his hands against the wood. "It's a trick."

Kathleen shifted. She'd already considered that possibility, but after her late-night conversation with the father, she doubted the validity of that claim.

"It's a political tactic. Someone's dug up some dirt. They paid this girl to pretend to be your daughter. Your opponents are hoping that the fear of scandal will be enough to make you back out of the race."

Kathleen leaned forward. "Is that possible?"

Joe flashed a cocky grin. "Sure. It's possible. When have I ever been wrong?" Kathleen raised an eyebrow. "Okay, Okay. Once or twice. Call her bluff. You'll see that I'm right."

"I'm not the first candidate to have a child born out of wedlock."

"No, but you may be the first to abandon a newborn on the steps of a fire station."

"I didn't do it. My father did."

"Won't matter. The good citizens of Oregon will place the blame squarely on your shoulders."

If her father had abandoned the baby, it meant that he'd chosen political power over his own granddaughter. In her heart of hearts, she knew it was a possibility. More than a possibility. A reality. He'd lied to her and left her child on the steps of a firehouse. She should be grateful he thought to leave her at a safe haven drop-off. *I guess he wasn't completely heartless. Could that new will have something to do with Paige? Did he regret his decision? What could it all mean for Kylie? For Erik and me?*

Kathleen took a deep breath. There was one more piece of information she had yet to share with her campaign manager. It was the one piece of the puzzle that completely undid all of his conspiracy theories. "She has my Bible."

Joe's forehead furrowed. "What are you trying to say?"

"I'm saying that I left my Bible with my baby to be given to her adoptive parents. I wrote a letter in it, but only signed it with a nickname. There's no way someone could have found that in a thrift store and connected the dots back to me. It had to have been given away along with her."

"Have you seen the Bible? With your own eyes?"

Kathleen shook her head. "No." *Where is he going with this?*

"Then it could still be a hoax."

"Maybe." Her campaign manager was in denial. She had more pressing concerns. "What if Paige McDonald goes to the media?"

"We'll have to make sure that doesn't happen."

Paige doubled back and hurried to the mayor's office to fetch her purse. The assistant was not at his desk, and the interior door was closed. Voices carried from inside. She considered knocking but didn't want to interrupt an important meeting. She could wait until they finished.

She circled the room, stopping to get a closer look at the haystack painting. She'd always admired Monet's work. The bouquet of sunflowers was her favorite painting. So bright and cheerful. She turned and spotted a bookcase she hadn't noticed before. Most of the books were crisp-new, but one stood out. The binding was stripped and frayed as if it had been read over and over. She removed it from the shelf and caressed the hardcover like a lover's face. She flipped through the yellowed pages. Highlights, pen marks, sticky notes—this was a well-used book. She turned back to the front page.

Annie,
You're a girl after my own heart.
Go get 'em and show the world what we Staten's can do.
Dad.

Why does Mayor Phillips have a book given to Annie? Unless… Paige's heart thumped louder. A dizzying sensation spread over her body. The interior office door opened. She wheeled around. Mayor Phillips' eyes zeroed in on the book in Paige's hands. She read the truth in the mayor's expression. "You're Annie."

There was a long pause. And a sigh. "I'm Annie."

She wasn't going to deny it? "You're… You're my mom."

Mayor Phillips made eye contact with a man inside the room behind her before answering. She turned back and nodded.

"But your name…"

"Is Anna Kathleen. No one called me *Annie* except for

my father, my brother, and your father Ryan. I guess the only other person who knows is our housekeeper Matilda."

The writing in the bathroom stall at the school. Ryan *was* her father. Paige's temples throbbed as her initial shock gave way to anger and betrayal. "You… You lied to me. I sat in your office only minutes ago… I told you my whole story and you said nothing. Worse than nothing. You denied even knowing Annie. Why did you lie? Why did you abandon me? Why didn't you want me?"

"I didn't *abandon* you, Paige. I was seventeen and a senior in high school. Stanford University had accepted my application. I was planning to graduate with degrees in political science and civil law. I revered my father and trusted his judgment. When I got pregnant, he convinced me that the best thing to do was to let a family adopt my child. He was running for governor that year and I guess he was afraid that having an unwed mother for a daughter would ruin his chances for election. I don't know if he fabricated an adoptive family or if he chickened out at the last minute." Mayor Phillips rested her hand on Paige's arm. "Please. Will you keep this a secret?"

Paige ignored the pleading in her eyes. "I don't understand. I thought you'd be happy to see me."

"I need you to keep this to yourself. Just for a while. We'll talk soon. I promise."

What else could she say? Paige turned to go. "Here's your book." Her mother took it. "Oh, and I left my purse in your office, that's why I came back."

The man in her mother's office retrieved it. "Here's your purse. Do we have your promise to keep this under wraps?"

Paige bit her lower lip. With a nod, she turned and left. She collapsed on a park bench outside the courthouse and tried to process what had happened. *Mayor Phillips is my mother?*

She'd finally found her birth mother. Wasn't that her whole purpose in coming to Whitman? Her heart should be exploding with joy. Why wasn't it?

23

"Whaddya got there, Timmy?" Hamilton squatted next to the front stoop of his sister's farmhouse where his nephew fiddled with something in his lap.

The towheaded boy held up his treasure for his uncle to get a better look. "There's money in these little cards, but I can't figure out how to get it out."

"Let me see." He held out his hand, and Timmy placed the small white cards in his palm. Immediately, Hamilton realized what he was seeing. The stolen coins from the museum. "Where did you get these?"

Timmy pointed at the hedge along the driveway. "I found them in the bushes. Can you get the money out, Uncle Ham? I want to buy an ice cream cone."

"I'm afraid these belong to someone else. I need to give them back." Hamilton took his wallet from his pocket and fished out a five-dollar bill. "You can have this to buy your ice cream, if you'll trade with me."

His nephew snatched the bill from his fingers. "Sure. Thanks." The hyperactive little boy scrambled into the house, waving his money like a captured enemy flag. "Mom, look what Uncle Ham gave me!"

Hamilton removed a handkerchief from his pocket and wrapped the coin cards to preserve any fingerprints. Not that it would do any good, his nephew had certainly smudged out any useful prints on the coins. He put the cloth back into his pocket and walked over to the hedge.

Alexander Pendleton stated that he'd taken the coins out of the safe to show "The Professor", a blond woman he'd never seen before. Hamilton's investigation assumed that she'd been the one to steal the coins as soon as the old curator went home for lunch. But why would she have pitched the coins into the Thorne's bushes? Why hadn't she fenced them?

Hamilton glanced toward the garage apartment. A blond woman with a penchant for the five-fingered discount lived on the very same property where his nephew had found the coins. *No. It couldn't have been Paige.* He'd already been down that road. It was the bracelet all over again.

He caught sight of something else hidden underneath one of the bushes. He leaned closer and moved the branches with a stick. Cigarette butts. Paige doesn't smoke. No one on the property smokes. Someone else had been standing there. What were they doing? Watching the house? Watching Paige's apartment? Someone who'd tried to break into the garage apartment? Had they dropped the coins in their haste to escape the jaws of a certain labradoodle? Or were they planted there to set Paige up—again?

Hamilton left the yard and entered the kitchen, where his sister was washing the dinner dishes. She jumped when the screen door slammed. "Have you heard from Paige?"

"You didn't have to give Timmy that money." Becky turned from the sink, the plate in her hand dripping soapy water on the floor.

"You're dripping."

"Thanks." She dropped the plate back into the soapy water and dried her hands on a dish towel. "Did you say something when you came in?"

"I asked if you had heard from Paige."

"I haven't seen her since Monday. I think she's staying busy at The Bookshelf. What happened with you two anyway?"

He looked at his sister as if she'd suddenly grown three heads. "Uh, she was falsely arrested, and it was my fault. The only reason she's still in town is because of Jessie's fake heart attack."

"Leave it to Jessie Faye." Becky chuckled. "I guess Paige does have the right to be upset with you, but if she didn't steal the bracelet, how do you think it got in her possession?"

Hamilton shook his head. "I have no idea." He unfolded his handkerchief and held out the coins for Becky to see.

"Are those…"

"The coins from Mr. Pendleton's collection. Timmy found them outside in the hedge."

"Our hedge?" She sank onto a stool at the island. "But how?"

He shrugged and tapped his hand on the counter. "Thanks for dinner. I'm going to head back to the station, give Lillian a call, and see if we can't make heads or tails of what's going on around here."

"No problem." Becky stood to her feet. "Dairy Barn has a two for one special tonight. I guess I'll take Timmy out for ice cream. Dave said he and the other boys wouldn't be home until late."

"Is Tyler almost finished painting Mom and Dad's house?" His brother-in-law had punished Tyler for tagging public property by volunteering him to paint the interior and exterior of his grandparent's twenty-two hundred square foot farmhouse.

"I don't think he'll be interested in painting anything else anytime soon."

"That's good. I'll see you around."

"See you later."

Mayor Phillips is my mother? Paige locked The Bookshelf door behind her and laid her head against the cool glass. She was still reeling from this afternoon's revelation. In all the time she'd been in Whitman never once had she considered that possibility. She'd think, "is that her?" for every woman she passed on the sidewalk, except Kathleen Phillips. *Anna* Kathleen Phillips. She arched from the door and hurried to her bike. She wanted to catch the florist before they closed and take some flowers over to Jessie. She still hadn't heard an update on her condition.

A half hour later, with a bouquet of Gerber daisies in hand, Paige knocked on the front door of Jessie Faye's little bungalow on the edge of town. She expected the woman to call out to her from inside, but instead the door opened and Jessie stood before her, wearing an apron and her hair in curlers. The aroma of cinnamon and ginger wafted from inside the house. "Paige. I'm surprised to see you."

Paige extended the bouquet. "These are for you."

"How nice. Come in."

"You're looking well." She stepped inside, and Jessie closed the door. "I was worried about you. What does the doctor say?"

"I'll be right as rain as long as I don't overdo it. I need to take it easy for a while longer. How are things at the store? Here. Have a seat. Would you like some homemade gingersnaps?" Jessie headed out of sight to the kitchen.

"Yes, thank you." Paige called after her, then she sat on the 1980s sofa and spoke loud enough for the old woman to hear. "The Bookshelf is looking nice. The furniture I ordered came in and I've hooked up the computers. There's only about twenty-five boxes left in my apartment, but I'm hoping to get them moved over soon."

"Glad to hear it." Jessie wobbled into the room, carrying

a plate of cookies. "No more thoughts of running back to Portland?"

Paige accepted a cookie from the plate and nibbled on the side. She hadn't been running away, had she? She thought of Hamilton's kiss and the hurt of his distrust and betrayal. She'd given herself little time to think about it over the past couple of days. She was avoiding her feelings for the policeman. Was she still angry? With surprise, she realized she was not. He was only doing his job and the evidence had overwhelmingly pointed in her direction. And he'd apologized for not believing her. *Why am I so willing to forgive him? Because you've fallen in love with him. That can't be. He's a first responder. I promised myself.*

"Paige?" Jessie's voice drew her back. The woman had settled into a rocking chair with an afghan over her legs. "Have you found a reason to stay?"

Besides Hamilton? Should she tell Jessie what she'd discovered about her birth mother? She'd never even revealed her purpose for visiting Whitman in the first place. "I was adopted by a firefighter twenty-five years ago. I came to Whitman to find my birth mother." She explained about the Bible and the bookmark, then paused waiting for Jessie to process what she'd said. "I discovered her identity only a few hours ago. My mother is—"

"Little Annie Staten. Also known as Mayor Phillips."

The world spun, and Paige's heart tried to beat its way out of her throat. "How did you know that?"

"I was the local midwife up until the town built the new hospital in 2007. The summer of 1992, I got a call from Mayor Staten. He said Annie was in labor and could I come deliver the baby. I brought you into this world a few hours later. Mayor Staten tried to give me hush money to keep quiet about the whole thing, but I wouldn't take it. You were a miracle from God. How you came to be was none of my business. Two days later, Annie's baby simply disappeared as if she'd never been born. Two weeks later, the town held a going-away party as Annie headed off to Stanford University. Four months after that, Mayor Staten became Governor Staten. It wasn't too difficult to figure out what had happened. As soon as you said you came here to find your birth mother, I realized who you were."

"She didn't seem very happy to see me. It wasn't quite the reunion I dreamed of."

Jessie reached across and squeezed Paige's hand. "Give her time. Annie's not the same girl she used to be. I can see it in her eyes. She's carrying a lot of pain and bitterness, and it might take a while before she can open her heart to you."

"Thanks, Jessie." Paige helped herself to another of the homemade cookies. She took a large bite and savored the snappy flavor on her taste buds.

"When are you going to tell Hamilton that you're in love with him?"

Paige coughed and sent cookie crumbs flying from her mouth. She swallowed. "Excuse me?"

"It was a simple question."

"I'm not in love with Hamilton."

The old woman raised an eyebrow.

"Jessie, when my grandfather died, I made a vow never to marry a first responder. I already lost one loved one because they wore a uniform. I'm not going to risk that again."

"Oh, well that's a shame."

"Why is that?"

"Hamilton's in love with you."

The sun had set by the time Paige pedaled home. Her conversation with Jessie kept circulating through her mind like a popular library book. *Hamilton's in love with you.* It just wasn't true. Jessie was confused or had misunderstood. Hamilton had told Paige very clearly that afternoon at Sacajawea Peak that he had no intentions of ever marrying. And then he'd kissed her. Paige's cheeks flushed warm at the memory. It was crazy, but what if the old woman was right? Could they overcome their mountain of fears and live happily ever after?

Hamilton Bryant was a good man. Easy on the eyes. Great with children. If she was perfectly honest with herself, he was everything she wanted in a husband. Could she live with the risks that came with his chosen profession?

When she reached the Thorne's house, Paige stored her bike in the garage, then jogged up the metal staircase to her apartment. The door hung open. The lock was visibly broken. Paige froze. She gave it a push but didn't step inside the foyer. She flipped the light switch. Ravaged book pages littered the carpet like snow. Angry red letters desecrated the wall behind the sofa.

Leave Whitman Before Someone Gets Hurt.

"Thank you, officers. Have a nice night." Becky said as she wrapped her arm over Paige's shoulders.

The vandal's *modus operandi* was completely different than at any of the rest of the recent crime scenes. Whoever had been in her apartment had wanted her to know that they'd been there. Officers Martin and Stone loaded boxes of evidence into the back of their patrol car. Evidence that included her mother's Bible, torn to shreds. She felt nothing but anger. Anger at whoever did this to her apartment. Anger at whoever planted that bracelet in her backpack. Anger at her past decisions that made her who she was.

She was a thief. It was time to admit it. It was time to embrace it. And it was time to do something about it. "Do you know where Hamilton is tonight?"

"He said he was going back to the station. I suspect he's still there."

Hamilton leaned back in his chair, his feet propped up, and his arms suspended over his head. Before him, spread out across the desktop, was a plethora of notes, tagged evidence, photographs, six empty bottles of root beer, and a cardboard pizza box filled with the crusts from all eight slices of a large Hawaiian pizza. He was no closer to solving the cases, but a lot closer to a bad case of indigestion.

His gut told him that all the robberies were connected: the Coverdale Bible from the church, the journals and coins from the museum, the Separatists documents from the mayoral mansion, the phones from David's store, and the diamond bracelet from the pawn shop. Five similar cases—but even his over-sugared brain could see that the jewelry and cell phones were the odd ones out. The books were all valuable and had historical significance. Why historical documents, then common, easily fenced items? Was something else in that glass case at Sam's or was it merely a coincidence?

The doorbell in the front lobby buzzed. The other officers all had their own passes. Unless Lillian had her hands full from the coffee run she'd gone on. He opened the door to the bullpen. Paige stood in the lobby, looking sheepish, soaking wet, and holding a large pizza box. "Hi."

"Paige. What are you doing here?"

"Can I come in? I brought pizza."

He glanced over his shoulder at the piles of reports. She was a civilian, she shouldn't see this stuff. But—he had a thought—she'd been a thief. Was it possible that she could shed some light on the crimes that he was missing? Besides, she did have pizza, and it could be a long night. He opened the door further. "Come on in."

"Thanks." She stepped into the bullpen and handed him the pizza box. As soon as he took it, she laced her arms across her chest. "Someone broke into my apartment and destroyed all the books that hadn't been moved to the store yet."

Hamilton grabbed his phone and turned it on. It took several seconds, but then the text app showed seven alerts, all from his sister. "I turned my phone off so I wouldn't be disturbed. I had no idea." He was a total *dummkopf. Paige might be a thief, but she would never destroy a book*. He'd seen the way she handled them with absolute care. "Are you OK?"

"Yeah. Just angry."

"At me?" He grimaced and steeled himself against her reply. "Honestly, I'm surprised you're even talking to me right now."

"No, I'm not mad at you. I'm mad at the person who did this. You were only following the evidence. You didn't put that bracelet in my backpack. I want to know who did. I want to know who turned thousands of dollars of literature into confetti."

"The truth is I could use your help."

"What can I do?"

Hamilton swallowed. He hated to say it. *Please don't be angry*. "I need the viewpoint of someone who…" He rubbed the back of his neck and groaned.

"Was a thief." She stated it so matter of fact it pained him to hear her say it.

"I'm so sorry, Paige."

She reached out and squeezed his arm. "It's OK."

"All right then. Let's get started, but first I need to say this: all evidence and reports are the property of Whitman Police Department. Everything we discuss is off the record and must remain inside this room. You cannot discuss these cases with anyone else. I'm pretty sure I can get in trouble for just letting you see this stuff."

The bullpen door opened. Lillian stepped inside and shook the rain from her hood. "It's raining buckets out there, but I brought coffee." Her eyes immediately went to Paige. "What's she doing here?" Then the pizza box. "She bribed you with pizza."

Hamilton scoffed. "She didn't bribe"—Lillian raised an

eyebrow—"She bribed me with pizza."

"She's a civilian. She shouldn't be here."

"She can be trusted."

Lillian didn't look convinced. She pinned her eyes on Paige. "Anything we discuss inside this room is off the record. If you leak—"

"I've already given her the rundown, Lillian." Hamilton grabbed her elbow. "I don't think you've officially been introduced. Paige, this is Officer Lillian Hurston, my partner—" He almost added, "in crime." *How weird would that have been?* "Lillian, this is—"

"Paige McDonald." Lillian said and leaned forward. Paige gingerly shook her hand.

"Coffee?" He asked Paige, trying to ease the tension in the room. "Let's get back to work, shall we?" The three took seats around Hamilton's desk. "Where do you want to start?"

"Start in order. What happened first?" Paige answered.

"The church robbery was first. The thief stole a Coverdale Bible worth about a half a million dollars. Two days later, the museum was robbed, and a five thousand dollar set of journals from some unknown was taken and several 1943 wheat pennies each valued around sixty thousand dollars. The very next day, the mayoral mansion was robbed, and historical documents were taken."

"Do you know the mansion was robbed that day or is that when the crime was reported?"

Hamilton's eyes widened. "Reported, actually. That was when Mayor Phillips noticed that the book was missing."

"What if the mansion robbery actually happened between the church and museum robberies? Or even before?"

"That's an interesting idea." Hamilton scribbled it down on his notepad.

"OK, what happened next?"

"It was five days later before Dave's electronics store was broken into and then another seven days before the pawn shop robbery."

"Has anything else been taken?"

"Not that we know of. At some point, after they broke into the pawn shop, someone planted that bracelet in your backpack. That same night, someone tried to break into your apartment."

"Today, more than a week later, someone does break into my apartment and destroyed all the books left from The Bookshelf. And what about that weird store in the mall, J.R. Electronics? Those guys were following us, and it wasn't to get your autograph."

Paige took the last two reports and lined them up side by side on the table. "The MO doesn't line up between these two cases. The alarm was blaring at the pawn shop."

"How did you know that?" Lillian asked.

"I was on a walk and stopped when I saw the crowd."

"You walked from Becky's house?"

Paige nodded.

"Did you have your backpack with you?"

"I. Did. What if the thief was in the crowd and stashed the bracelet in my bag before I left? Then they showed up late that night to retrieve it, but Bruce chased them away."

"So, the person who broke into your apartment tonight was after the bracelet."

Paige shook her head. "I don't think so. They didn't just break into my apartment. They shredded every book in there, including one that belonged to my mother." Paige's brow furrowed. She looked lost in thought for a moment.

Lillian picked up the police report about his brother-in-law's store. "Martin's report states that the security system at David's store was turned off sometime in the middle of the night."

"Why turn off the alarm at one location and leave it on at another?"

"Do these other places have alarms?" Paige asked.

Hamilton and Lillian exchanged looks. "I'm pretty sure the church doesn't, and the mayoral mansion does."

"What about the museum?"

"I don't think so. There isn't anything valuable there except for, obviously, Alexander's coin collection."

"How did someone rob the mayor's house without setting off her alarm? Or Dave's store for that matter? Unless, they knew what the codes were. What about accomplices?" Paige asked.

"Mario Montory assisted with the church robbery. Ike Simmons distracted me just before the electronics burglary." He rubbed his chin, remembering Ike's painful right hook.

"Was there an accomplice at the museum?" Paige asked.

"It's hard to tell. Maybe. Maybe not."

"Why?" Paige looked at Lillian.

Lillian pulled out the report and handed it to Paige. "According to Mr. Pendleton's description, the museum thief could have been you."

"What?" Paige's eyes scanned the paper in her hand. "Blond hair. Blue eyes. Calls herself *The Professor*. Lots of blonds have blue eyes, and I would never call myself professor. That's just weird."

"I found the coins from the museum today."

Lillian jolted in her seat. "Where?"

"Actually, Timmy found them. In the hedge at my sister's house."

Paige blanched. "You don't think I—"

"No. No." Hamilton was quick to reassure her. "I also found a pile of discarded cigarette butts. Someone was standing there a long time. I'm sending them out in the morning for DNA analysis."

"What about the guy who shot Mario?"

"Left-handed guy wearing a red hat." Lillian read off the report.

"Timmy saw a man with a red hat messing with the fireworks just before the explosion on Memorial Day." Paige reminded him.

Hamilton tapped his chin. "Could the attempts on the mayor be connected to the thefts? A book was stolen from her home and, according to Chief House, someone gave her a sleep aid before she drove home from Salem two weeks ago."

"Why would random burglaries and attempts on the mayor's life be connected? That makes no sense." Lillian cracked her neck and stretched out her back.

"The mayor's assistant is left-handed."

"What did you say?"

Paige glanced back and forth between the two officers. "Mayor Phillips' assistant, Jeremiah Bennett. I met him earlier today. He wore his watch on his right hand, so I'm assuming he's left-handed."

"Really? That's interesting." Hamilton wrote a note on a legal pad.

Lillian frowned. "Just because he's left-handed doesn't make him the shooter. That guy is as squeaky clean as a boy scout and underwent an in-depth background check before getting hired at City Hall."

Knots plagued Hamilton's stomach. All that pizza and soda was finally getting to him. "If you girls will excuse me for a minute."

As soon as Hamilton left the bullpen, Paige studied the lady officer across the desk. She wore civilian clothes that hung loose on her thin body. She had short brown hair and pale skin. Officer Hurston closed her eyes and sighed. "Are you OK?" Paige asked.

She opened her eyes. "Yeah. I'm fine. Just tired."

"Have you known Hamilton—Officer Bryant—long?"

"My whole life. We played together as kids and then went to the Academy together."

"He's—He's a really great guy."

"He is."

Paige's shoulders dropped, and her heart sank to the floor. Those two had so much in common, and they'd known each other forever. Surely, if Hamilton was interested in getting married he would choose someone like Lillian who understood his job.

"Don't look so forlorn. We dated a few times, but he's like a brother to me. We're partners, and we have each other's back. That's where our relationship ends. Besides, he's got his eyes set on someone else."

"Who?"

"You, silly. It's as obvious as a two-headed turtle at a turtleneck convention. When he looks at you, there's no one else in the room. Ever since he lost his best friend, Will, he's been too afraid to consider having a future with someone. I just want him to put his fears aside and live the life he's meant to live, you know?"

"He told me about Will. Did you know him?"

"The three of us did everything together. Three peas in a pod. The Three Amigos. The Three Musketeers. Hamilton took Will's death the hardest. It tore him apart. For a while, he considered leaving the force—"

"Whaddya girls talking about?"

Paige's heart leapt into her throat. "You scared me."

Hamilton dropped into his chair. "Did you solve the mystery while I was gone?"

"No. Not yet."

"And I don't think we're likely to, not tonight anyway. I'm beat." Officer Hurston stood to her feet and hung her purse strap on her shoulder. "I'll see you tomorrow, Hamilton. Nice to meet you, Paige." With that, she left.

Hamilton hid a yawn behind his hand. "Lil's right. It's late. You want to take the rest of this pizza home?"

"No, you can have it."

"Grab your stuff and I'll drive you back to Becky's."

Paige watched him as she put on her coat. *"I just want him to live the life he's meant to live."* His broad back and wide shoulders were toward her as he finished typing something on the computer. *"It tore him apart. He considered leaving the force."* But he'd chosen to remain a police officer. He'd chosen to remain a hero. *"He's been too afraid to consider a future with someone."* She walked up behind him and laid her hand on his shoulder. *I should have told him about the note on my wall.* His muscles tightened underneath her palm. *I'm so sorry for your pain.* He looked over his shoulder. The florescent light overhead twinkled in his eyes. Or was it the sight of her that brought that gleam to his face? Was she willing to find out?

24

Kathleen eyed her campaign manager as he lit a cigarette, puffed, then blew, leaving a wisp of smoke to curl toward the ceiling. She wrinkled her nose and scowled. "How many times have I asked you not to smoke in my house?"

"This would be the first." He turned his head back and forth, searching for a place to dispose of it, then shrugged and dropped it into the empty soda bottle on the end table beside him. "What were we talking about?"

"You were telling me all the reasons why I shouldn't reunite with my firstborn daughter."

"Madam Mayor, let's be honest. Your campaign slogan is, A Vote for Phillips is a Vote for Family. The press would have a field day with this story. They'll say, 'Twenty-five years ago, Mayor Phillips abandoned her newborn infant outside a fire department rather than let a loving family adopt her. What kind of heartless woman would leave a baby alone on a cold, dark night? Is this the kind of person we want running our state? A woman who claims to put family first, but has, in fact, done the complete opposite?'"

His words stuck her like a knife to the heart. Those claims

weren't the least bit fair or substantiated. "It was summer. And I had nothing to do with it. My own father deceived me."

Joe shook his head. "That's not how the public will see it."

"What do you mean?"

"I'm just saying, the electorate are a fickle lot. They tend to hear what they want to hear. I said it once, and I'll say it again, they'll place the blame squarely on your shoulders. Of course, there is another possibility."

"What's that?"

"I told you. She's a fraud and your opposition sent her here to throw you off your game or go as far as to convince you to quit the elections. She'll ruin everything we've worked for if she's allowed to continue. You must put a stop to this. The way I see it, you have two options: either deny your relation and send her packing before this story leaks to the press or accept her as your long-lost daughter and drop out of the race. Your choice. You'll never win the election with a scandal like this following you to the polling booth."

Joe's phone started ringing. "Donahue." He left the drawing room, phone to his ear.

Her press agent and campaign manager was right. He had experience piloting the media's formidable bailiwick. Who was she to think that this could have any positive outcome?

All she needed to do was deny any relation to Paige McDonald. Any relation to the babe that had formed under her heart, that had grown in her womb soothed by her heartbeat.

Kathleen sucked in a breath. Could she do it? Did she really have a choice? Her lifelong dreams hung in the balance. She sank into the plush armchair and raised the receiver on the old-fashioned rotary phone. Richard Staten chose power over family, and she was about to do the same thing.

The girl answered on the first ring. "Hello, Paige. This is Mayor Phillips. I'm ready to talk."

🚓🚓🚓

Heavenly's Restaurant was deserted when Paige stepped inside. The dinner rush was long over; even the late diners had left. Only her mother—her chest swelled with excitement—her mother, Annie, sat alone in a booth at the rear of the restaurant with her back to the door. This was it. The moment she had waited for her whole life.

"Hello, Mom." She slid into the leather booth. She laughed awkwardly and shifted, feeling school-girl giddy inside. "I've waited twenty-five years to say that."

Annie lifted her head. Her lipstick stood out against the pallor of her skin. "You can't call me that."

"Do you prefer mother? I think I'm too old for mommy. Or would you prefer I called you Annie?"

"I can't be your mother."

Paige deflated like a balloon. "What?"

Annie put her finger to her lips and nervously surveyed the room. "Do not call me mom or mother. I am Mayor Kathleen Phillips. You cannot show up in my town and expect me to drop everything to welcome you into my life."

That's exactly what Paige *had* expected.

"I've worked hard to get where I am. One slip-up could—would ruin everything. I won't let an orphan girl from Portland destroy everything I've worked for."

"What about your Bible?" She stammered. What was happening? Her hands began to shake, and her pulse sped up. "I don't understand, please…"

"How do I know you didn't find that thing at a thrift shop or maybe my opponent put you up to it? Go back to Portland, Paige. Forget about me. Please." Mayor Phillips grabbed her coat and purse off the bench, dropped a dollar bill on the table for a tip, then left the restaurant without looking back.

Paige's heart broke into a million pieces. Her vision

blurred. Sobs threatened to burst from her lips. She wanted to crawl into a hole and die. It wasn't enough that her mother gave Paige away in the first place, but then to reject her a second time hurt more than Paige could have imagined.

Why did she come here? Why did she have this desperation to meet a mother she never knew? Why was it so important that her mother love her, that she be cherished by the one who had given her birth?

Memories flooded her thoughts like a rush of waters from a cracked dam. Feelings of shame and regret squeezed her soul like the deadly grip of a python.

"Why don't I have a mother?"

The question had caught her grandfather off guard. He'd stopped stirring a pot on the stove and stared at her. She'd continued setting the two place settings. She now knew that the words that had poured from his mouth that day had been nothing but lies. Lies about her parents. Lies about her beginning. Lies about everything. She'd built her entire identity on false information.

Every year, in school, they'd design cards or paint their handprints onto pretty paper with poems for their mothers for Mother's Day. Only, she didn't have a mother. Didn't even have memories of having a mother. When she'd arrived home from school that day, she'd searched the house. No photos of a mother. If her mother didn't exist, did she? If she didn't have a mother to love her, then maybe she was unlovable. Her heart had shriveled up like a plant in the sun with no water.

She'd had her grandfather's love, but then, he wasn't really her grandfather at all. Aunt Hattie loved her, but it wasn't enough. Her spirit cried out for unconditional love. She had sought that. Starting with Whitman. Starting with Annie.

What had she expected? Was her mother supposed to welcome her with open arms? Too many movies. Too many novels. This wasn't how it was supposed to be. Within the pages of a fairytale, her mother would have accepted and loved her, but this wasn't a story. This was real life. And real life didn't always have happy endings.

She should go home to Portland and forget she ever came to this place or met Mayor Anna Kathleen Staten Phillips. Her mother had made it clear that she wanted nothing to do with Paige. Feelings of abandonment welled up within her soul. It was pointless to stay around. *I'm sorry, Jessie. I can't do it. I don't belong here.*

Her cell phone dinged. She took it from her coat pocket, then tapped the home button to light up the screen. A text from a blocked number. She held her breath as she read the cryptic message. It was all in code. Code, she knew only too well.

Shivers ran down her entire body, and the hair on her arms stood on end. Her phone made a whooshing sound as another text appeared. A photo. The screen cracked as her phone hit the tiled floor.

The evening was still and quiet. The only sounds were the chains on her bike, the clicking from the walk/do not walk sign on the traffic light, and an old crow sitting on top of the power lines. A sudden breeze blew a plastic grocery sack across the black top and sent goosebumps up Paige's arms. She shivered.

She turned right at the corner of Main Street and Cedarwood. Officer Martin waved as she passed the police car parked in front of Harvey's Pet Emporium. She pedaled down Cedarwood until she got to 5th Street, then she cut through the back alleys until she ended up back at the rear entrance to The Bookshelf. She took out her keys and with shaking hands unlocked the deadbolt and went inside, taking her bike with her, and then locked the door behind her. It took a minute for her eyes to adjust to the darkness.

As she crouched out of view from the front window, her eyelids sagged, and she covered a yawn. At nine o'clock, she opened her backpack and ate two of the protein bars she kept inside for emergencies. An hour later, headlights passed the window as thc officer went on patrol. Everything was going according to plan. A few minutes later, the rear door handle rattled as he checked the locks. She held her breath and waited in the darkness. He would be back at two. With shame burning her eyes, she unzipped her backpack and began stuffing it full of the rarest books. She had unlocked the deadbolt and turned to gather her backpack, sweater, and bike, when she heard a sound at the back door. She ducked behind the bookcases. A figure came into view and a flashlight beam searched the room.

It landed on her backpack. "Paige. Are you in here?"

Hamilton. What is he doing here? He wore civilian clothes. She stepped out from behind the bookshelf and shielded her eyes from the bright light. "I'm here."

"A note on my apartment door said you wanted to meet me here. Why didn't you just text? Are you working late?"

Think fast. "I am. I mean, I was. I headed home, but then I realized that I left my phone." She pulled her cell phone from her pocket and wiggled it in the air. The lies burned her tongue like a cinnamon fireball candy. She grabbed her heavy backpack, swinging the strap over her shoulder. *Wait. A note? I didn't send him a note.*

"How did you get here? Your bike wasn't outside."

He wasn't letting her off that easy. He was good at his job, she'd give him that much. "I—" A book fell from the backpack. The noise drew Hamilton's flashlight.

"What's that? Paige? What's going on?"

Her knees trembled. She didn't know what to say. Would he even believe her?

A clanking noise came from the back of the store. Hamilton cupped his hand over her mouth and flicked off the flashlight. "Shh." Her breath came in sharp, quick gasps.

Her pulse raced. He grabbed her arm and pulled her behind the loaded metal shelves.

Two masked men came into view. *Wait. What are they doing here? That's not the plan.* They didn't carry flashlights, but used the street lamp from outside the window. Hamilton pressed her body against his, his solid chest and muscular arms like a fortress of safety. She became chilled when he moved away, creeping down the bookshelf to circle around the other way. *He'll never forgive me when he finds out about this.*

The dust from the old books tickled her nose. A sudden twitch worked its way through her sinuses. *No. Don't sneeze.* She pressed her finger to her nose. *Where did Hamilton go?* His silhouette had disappeared into the darkness.

She set her hand on the shelf and leaned forward. The shelf tipped. Books crashed to the floor. The two men bolted out the back door. Hamilton jumped up and ran after them. *Where's he going? Is he even armed?*

Paige tossed aside the pile of books and hurried after Hamilton. She found him standing in the empty alley. The two masked men were nowhere in sight. Hamilton ran his hands through his hair with an irritated groan. Without his weapon or Kevlar vest, it would be foolish for him to give chase.

The ear-splitting squeal of rubber tires shattered the night. Paige spun on her heel. A dark van turned down the alley and headed right for them.

Tires squealed on the pavement, leaving behind rubber tracks. The passenger leaned out his window, aiming a handgun in their direction. "Get down." His only thought was to protect the girl beside him. Hamilton knocked Paige to the ground and shielded her as bullets ricocheted off the bricks and shattered the windows. One pierced his shoulder. The tires squealed again as the van drove off. He lay still on his stomach, breathing heavy as Paige wiggled out from under him. He pivoted his neck to look at her. Horror radiated from her eyes. Blood tinted her fingers as she covered a gash on her upper arm. He gritted his teeth as the pain overwhelmed him. "Call the ambulance." He whispered. His eyes closed as conciseness faded.

🚓🚓🚓

A sharp stinging sensation burned her upper arm underneath the gauze wrap, but she, otherwise, escaped unharmed. *Because of him.*

He lay deathly still, his eyes closed and his face pale from the loss of blood. He was lucky to be alive, according to the ER nurse. Jessie Faye would say he was blessed. Blessed? What blessing? This was a nightmare. It was everything she had feared, and it was all her fault. He'd saved her life—by risking his own. He was a police officer. A first responder. He would always put his life on the line for strangers, friends, loved ones… *and even crooks, like me.*

The metal bed squeaked, and Hamilton's eyes fluttered open. The corners of his mouth tipped up when he saw her. "That's some good stuff." His voice came out slurred from the pain medicine. He patted the edge of the mattress beside him. Paige took a seat but couldn't meet his eyes. A tear ran down her cheek. "Hey, it's all right." His calloused hand squeezed her bare forearm.

"You could've died."

"But I didn't."

"Not this time." An angry edge slipped into her voice. He tried to hold her hand, but she jumped to her feet, crossing her arms over her chest. "But what about the next? Or the next?"

"Only God knows tomorrow, Paige. I have to trust that He's in control of my life." He sounded more awake and alert now. His intense gaze landed on her bandage. "How's your arm?"

"It'll heal." She paused and tipped her chin toward the tile floor. "I'm sorry."

"Sorry? For what?"

"You covered me. You got shot because of me." Those words had been hanging over her like a thunderstorm, threatening to rain painful memories down on her fragile heart. She ducked her head, twisting her hands together like pretzels. She still had more she needed to say, but how could she admit to what she'd done?

He fought the urge to ask questions. There was a long moment of silence. The clock ticked on the wall. He could hear her anxious breathing. She raised her head, tears brimming in her eyes. "When I was twelve-years-old, I started hanging out with some troublemakers. I knew they liked to shoplift, skip school, and stuff like that.

"One night, they—we were playing with matches in the basement of an abandoned apartment building, setting stuff on fire, then stomping them out. I should have told someone right away, but I didn't want to be a snitch. The flames got out of hand, and we got scared, and ran out of the building. I didn't realize then that fire station number nine would be called—that my grandpa would be the one…" She took an audible breath. "He died when the roof collapsed, and it was all my fault."

What a heavy burden to carry. "Paige, you were a child. You can't blame yourself for—"

"There's more. Last night, I was supposed to rob The Bookshelf of its most valuable books. I was getting ready to leave when you showed up. Then they showed up, and then they shot you. I don't know what happened. They weren't supposed to be there. It wasn't part of the plan."

"I don't understand. What are you talking about? What

do you mean, supposed to?"

"I—text message—rob The Bookshelf. I should have—you almost—because of me. It's all my fault."

Hiccupping sobs broke up her words, but Hamilton got the gist. The air rushed from his lungs, like someone had punched him in the gut. Tremors shook his body. "Paige, how—how could you?"

"They—he—threatened my mother."

"Your mother? I don't understand."

"My birth mother. That's why I'm here. In Whitman."

Hamilton tried to follow. "You found her?"

Paige nodded.

"And someone threatened her—your mother?"

"I received a text message. It said someone would hurt my mother if I didn't rob The Bookshelf Sunday night."

"Why didn't you come to me? I could have helped you."

"I don't need your help."

"Paige—"

"And you didn't have to be a hero."

Hamilton tried to sit up. He winced and laid back against the pillow. "Paige…" He groaned more than spoke.

"You will always put the safety of others before your own. I can't. Live. Like. This. I'm not—I'm not strong enough." She clasped her hand over her mouth as a sob escaped her lips, then she ran from the room.

Hamilton squeezed his eyes shut. The pressure inside his chest yearned for release. He wanted to howl, to run, to kick something. He'd protected her. Why did that make her so mad? Her words echoed. *"You didn't have to be a hero."* Wasn't that what he was supposed to be? It was his job—his life. He expected a girl who was raised by a firefighter to understand that.

A crushing weight smashed down on his chest. *She does understand that.* She understood all too well. His career had unfathomable risk, a fact he'd come to terms with a long time ago. It was exactly why he'd avoided romantic entanglements. *Dear God. How can we ever be together?*

"Are you leaving Miss Paige?"

At the sound of the squeaky voice, she stopped jamming her clothes in her duffel bag. Timothy stood in the doorway of her bedroom. Muddy footprints left a trail down the hallway from the front door. She dropped the cardigan in her hands and sat on the edge of her bed. She must look a sight. She wiped at the tears on her face. "Timmy, what are you doing in here?" She was glad she'd scrubbed the nasty words off the wall in the living room before he saw them. Timmy sniffled. *Has he been crying?*

"Are you leaving because Uncle Ham got hurt?"

When did a six-year-old get so perceptive? Paige stood and began folding her clothes again. "It was my fault."

"But you didn't shoot him."

He wouldn't have been there if it wasn't for me. I as good as pulled the trigger. And it didn't matter that she hadn't been the one to light the match thirteen years ago, either. The guilt she carried was still the same. She hadn't stopped the others. *It just got out of hand. It wasn't supposed to happen that way. No one was supposed to get hurt.* No one… Especially not Benjamin McDonald. She'd just as sure killed him, and it was her fault Hamilton was shot. They'd come to her rescue. They couldn't help it. They were heroes.

The Bible verse Hamilton had quoted on Memorial Day echoed through her thoughts. *"Greater love hath no man than this, that a man lay down his life for his friends."*

She heard Mrs. Faye's gravelly voice. *"But God commendeth his love toward us, in that while we were yet sinners, Christ died for us."* No one had to convince her that she was a sinner, but the thought that a Holy God would, could love her was just ludicrous. Why would a being so far off devote any attention or affection on her? Why would Jesus give His life for her? She needed answers, and she knew just where to find them.

She slowed her pedaling as she approached the church building. Pastor Whitestone was just descending the stairs from the front door. He carried a briefcase and wore a crisp collared shirt. His tie blew cock-eyed and he just caught his fedora before it blew away in the sudden breeze. "Pastor Whitestone."

He paused on the stairs, his eyes wide. "Paige. Miss McDonald. What can I do for you?"

"Do you have a minute? I'd like to talk, if you have the time."

"Sure. Not a problem." He placed his briefcase and hat inside the car parallel parked along the curb, then motioned toward the steps. Paige sat on the cold concrete and Pastor Whitestone sat beside her, his lanky legs hanging two steps further down. Paige pulled her knees to her chest and picked at her nail polish, then she turned her head and fixed her eyes on his smoky gray ones. "I want to know why?"

The older man shifted on the uncomfortable step. His Adam's apple bobbed when he swallowed. "Why what?"

"Why would God love me? I've never done anything for Him. In fact, I've pretty much done the opposite."

Pastor Whitestone closed his eyes. Was he praying? Did God hear spontaneous prayers? Of course, He heard the preacher's prayers, but what if she prayed? Would God hear her?

"But God commended his love toward us, in that while we were yet sinners, Christ died for us."

There's that verse again.

"There is no answer to your question." Her eyebrows lowered in confusion. "I don't understand why God would love us. We certainly don't deserve it, but that's the beauty of His entire plan. God loves us in spite of ourselves. Despite every wicked thing we've ever done. And the best part is that He doesn't just love us. He gave His life for us."

"Why did He have to die?"

"Do you know what sin is?"

She nodded. She knew. The chaplain at juvie had repeatedly condemned her as a sinner fit for hell. He hollered about something called repentance, but never explained what that meant.

"Sin has to be paid for. The scriptures tell us that the payment for sin is death. But thank God He didn't leave us with that; 'the gift of God is eternal life through Jesus Christ our Lord.' We don't have to die to pay for our sin. Jesus did it for us. He took our place."

"How do I accept that gift?"

"All you have to do is ask."

"It's really that simple?"

"It's really that simple. 'For whosoever shall call upon the name of the Lord shall be saved.'"

"Would you mind if I went inside the church for a little while?"

"Not at all. I'll swing by later and lock the door."

"Thanks."

The setting sun beamed through the windows and lit the auditorium with an orangish hue. The pews shone like a golden path to the altar. The cross carved into the pulpit drew her eyes. She sat down on one of the benches and bowed her head, then folded her hands and pressed them to her lips.

A tear rolled down her cheek as she thought about the words of Pastor Whitestone. She didn't bother to wipe it away. It dripped off her chin and left a dark mark on her jeans. All her life she'd been missing something. Even without knowing the truth of her birth, she'd struggled with feelings of insecurity, of being unwanted and unloved. She'd tried to be a good person, but it wasn't enough. Nothing filled the longings of her heart. And now she knew what would.

God loved her and wanted her. He died for her—with all her anger, fear, and resentment. He loved her anyway and He was extending exactly what she needed most: peace, love, and a sense of belonging.

"Dear Jesus," she prayed aloud. Her voice echoed in the empty sanctuary. "Thank you for dying on the cross for me. Thank you for loving me. Thank you for wanting me. Please forgive my sin. Wash me clean and give me a new heart and a new life."

He stood watching, waiting, counting her breaths. He shivered with anticipation. She would pass only inches from his fingertips. If he reached out his hand, he could touch the wayward strands of yellow hair as she pedaled down the sidewalk. He smirked when she stopped, her tennis shoes skidding on the concrete. She dismounted her bike, propping it on the kickstand, and bent to tie her shoelace. Her back faced him. Timing was on his side, and timing was everything. If he stepped out now, she'd never see him coming. It was too easy. He could rid himself of this pest, this menace that threatened everything. Everything he desired. Everything he'd worked so hard to obtain. His entire future hung on her existence. The note hadn't scared her away. Shredding her books hadn't scared her away. He'd even shredded that incriminating Book. Kathleen could thank him for that later. If Paige wouldn't leave town, he'd have to kill her. It was the only way.

He moved closer, the weapon poised. Moonlight glinted off the steel barrel. Each step brought him closer to redemption, to relief.

Headlights rounded the corner. She straightened, her eyes following the vehicle as it approached. He slipped into the shadows and hid the gun inside his coat. An opportunity lost. The car pulled alongside the sidewalk. A police cruiser, no less. Her guardian angel sent to safeguard her from demise. He shielded his face from view by the collar of his jacket and slunk into the darkness. *Another time, Miss McDonald, another time.*

25

If his sister fluffed his pillow one more time, Hamilton was going to lose his last shred of sanity. He'd been home from the hospital for only twenty-four hours and he was already tired of doing nothing, surrounded by Spider-man posters and Captain America bedsheets. He was under strict orders to take it easy for as long as humanly possible. The 9-millimeter slug had entered just below his shoulder blade, barely missing his spinal cord and right lung, then exited through his pectoralis major.

The bullet wound was painful, but his emotional misery was far worse than the physical discomfort. Paige lived only one hundred feet from the back door, and he had yet to see her. Becky said Paige hadn't left town, but neither had she been back to visit him at the hospital, so the only other alternative was that she was avoiding him.

The bedroom door opened. Becky entered, carrying a lunch tray and a long cardboard box under her arm. "How are you doing?"

"The same I was the last time you were in here. How many times are you going to ask me that?"

"Until I get a better answer." She set the tray in his lap. The smell of homemade fish and chips and a slice of Heavenly's marionberry pie wafted to his nose. He licked his lips and grinned. "You know just how to cheer me up."

"Lean forward. I'll fluff your pillow for you."

"Oh, no, you don't." He shook his head and stuffed a wad of French fries, coated in ketchup, into his mouth. "What's in the box?" He chewed and swallowed.

"I don't know. It's addressed to you. Tyler brought it home when he went by your apartment to pick up the mail." She sat on the edge of the bed and set the box in her lap. "Want me to open it?"

"Please."

She tore off the tape and opened the flaps. "Oh, Hamilton. It's beautiful."

"Jessie asked me to pick it out that day I went with Paige to Portland. It turned out pretty nice, don't you think?"

"She'll love it."

If only she'll stay. Please Lord, I want her to stay.

Paige sat in a window booth of the Rustic Cup, sipping a cup of hot coffee. Her newfound faith in God brought a peace she'd never had before. She'd changed her mind about leaving town before the grand reopening. As much as her heart was hurting, she still wanted to follow through for Jessie's sake. It had been nearly a week since she'd seen Hamilton or Mayor Phillips. She'd spent that time finishing up around The Bookshelf, then designed posters and fliers advertising the event. After the bookstore's big day, then she could return to Portland with a clear conscience. Nothing else held her here.

Kylie Phillips slid into the booth bench across the table from her. "Are you okay? You look heartbroken."

A lump formed in Paige's throat. *Kylie and I are sisters. Does she know? Of course she doesn't, and it's not my place to say anything.* "I'll miss this place when I return home."

"Do you like living in Portland? I used to live in Indianapolis. We moved here when I was thirteen after my dad died and my grandfather got sick."

"I'm so sorry. What was your dad's name?" *Do we have the same dad, too?* She knew nothing about Kylie's father.

"Lionel Phillips. He was a Formula One driver. He got killed during a race."

Lionel, not Ryan. We're half-sisters, but still sisters. I always wanted a sister. "Do you miss him?"

"Not really. He wasn't around very often, and when he was, he wasn't a nice person. Are you going to the rally tonight?"

"Probably not. I'm not feeling up to socializing."

"It'll be a lot of fun. The high school band is playing, and there'll be free food. The speeches might be boring, but there's supposed to be door prizes and a raffle. That sounds cool. Please come. It would mean a lot to me. And my mom."

I don't think your mom cares whether I'm there or not. "I'll think about it, but I'm not making any promises."

A customer waved from the other side of the restaurant. "Miss? Can I get some more coffee?"

"Coming." Kylie left the booth and hurried back to work.

Paige took out her cell phone to check the time. She tapped the home button. Nothing happened. *The battery's dead. I'll plug it in when I get back to my apartment.*

The energy in the cafeteria was electric. Kathleen strolled through the crowd enjoying the carnival games and band music. She wore business chic, an all-black pantsuit with a single button jacket, a red scarf, belt, and high-heeled pumps. She'd curled her hair and arranged it to frame her face. Bright red lipstick completed the overall look.

Red, white, and blue streamers hung from the ceiling and Vote for Phillips posters decorated the walls. The air smelled like the Dungeness crabs flown in from Portland and the marionberry pies from The Willamette Valley Pie Company in Salem.

Guests had traveled from all over to take part in the event, including several from the Executive, Legislative, and Judicial branches of the state government. Whitman police monitored the goings-on, providing protection for her and their special guests. Chief House had taken the threats against her person very seriously and had required all officers to be available for security detail.

Whitman's Fire Chief, Neal McMillan, Master of Ceremonies for the evening, introduced the next speaker. The Deputy Secretary of State. After they shook hands, Neal left the stage and headed to where Kathleen stood watching the proceedings. "Madam Mayor. You're up next."

"Thank you, Neal." Kathleen ducked behind the makeshift stage to where she'd stashed her attaché. She opened the snaps and sorted through the papers inside, searching for her speech. *I know I asked Bennett to print it out this afternoon.* "Bennett!" She waved and called to her assistant.

He ran over, licking melted butter from his fingers. "Yes, Madam Mayor?"

"Have you seen my speech?"

"Yes."

Kathleen's shoulders sank with relief.

"I printed it off and put it in your briefcase."

"It's not there."

"I printed it just like you asked, then I put it in your bag with your copies of the program and schedule for the evening. It should be there."

She checked the attaché case a second time, finding both the program and schedule, but no speech. "Well, it's not here."

"I'm so sorry, Madam Mayor, I don't know how—"

Kathleen held up her hand. "Never mind. I'll just walk over to City Hall and print off a new one."

Bennett turned pale. "I don't think that's a good idea."

"Nonsense. It won't take long."

"It's raining again. I can drive you if you'd like."

"Thank you, Bennett. How thoughtful. I appreciate that."

At the entry to the school building, her assistant pulled his suit jacket up over his head and ran for his vehicle parked in the lot. He pulled it around and stopped as close as possible. The cold rain dampened her stockinged feet as she stepped from the curb and into Bennett's two-seater Mustang.

Paige lurched into the teacher's bathroom and escaped into the corner stall, locking the bolt behind her. She dropped the toilet lid and sat atop it, drawing her knees to her chest. She'd thought she could handle seeing her mother again, but she was wrong. *Oh, Mother. Why? Why can't you love me?* She traced the pen marks on the back of the door with her fingertip. "Annie + Ryan". Her mother and father. *Is this as close as I'll ever be?*

Masculine boots appeared beneath the door. The handle jiggled. "Sorry, this one's occupied." The boots retreated.

Attending the rally had been a big mistake. She would just go back home. Kylie would be disappointed, but she'd made no promise. She'd rather be curled up at home with a Grande cappuccino and a movie. Paige wiped the tears from her eyes and stood to her feet. She unlocked the door and tried to open it. The door wouldn't budge. *Not again.* She tried pulling on the top. Maybe Kylie had followed her into the bathroom, playing a prank on her as before. "Not funny, Kylie. Let me out." No answer. Nothing but the gentle buzz of the exhaust fan.

"Hey. You out there. Can you help me? I'm locked in the

stall." Again, there was no answer. *I'll just call for help.* She stuck her hand in her pocket and wiggled her fingers in an empty hole. *Where's my phone?* She groaned in frustration. It was still plugged in, charging.

Paige yanked off her high-heeled shoes, then climbed on top of the toilet. She could see the rest of the bathroom. Empty. *Wasn't someone just in here? Where did she go?* Panic coursed through her veins. *They weren't trying to open the stall, they were locking the door.*

She grabbed the top of the wall and tried to pull herself over but slipped and slid to the floor. She banged on the door. "Help. Someone help me!" She tried to climb out a second time but wasn't strong enough to lift herself over the wall. Could she squeeze underneath? The stall doors were too low, she'd never fit. What's going on? Who would do this?

The room went dark. *That's just great. The lights must be on an automatic timer.* She sat on the toilet, arms wrapped around her knees. She was stuck. She could yell until she grew hoarse or wait and hope someone came to use this bathroom soon.

Bennett dropped her off at the curb. Kathleen fished out her keys from her purse, then unlocked the front door of the courthouse. She stepped inside and tried to turn on the light. Nothing happened. *The storm must have knocked the power out. Shouldn't the generator have come on?* She shook her head and pulled out her cell phone, turning on the flashlight app. *I don't have time for this.*

Bennett stumbled through the door, shaking the rain from his coat.

"The power isn't working. We'll have to take the stairs."

They climbed the stairs to the second floor. Bennett unlocked the office door and held it open. "I'll check in here and see if I misplaced your speech somewhere."

She unlocked the door to her inner office and entered the

dark room. *Without power, I'll be unable to print a new copy. I have to find the one Bennett printed earlier.* Using her phone flashlight, she searched her suite, hoping to find the speech set aside and forgotten.

Something didn't look right about the room. She turned her head and pivoted on her heels. The faint beam highlighted empty spaces on the walls. Where were the priceless paintings?

"Bennett! I've been robbed. Someone stole the paintings." She sprinted to the interior door and jerked it open. A masked man stood on the other side. "Excuse me, what do you think you're doing? Where are my paintings?"

He held a gun. "Hello, Madam Mayor. You need to come with me."

Paige wasn't sure how long she'd sat there on top of the toilet, but her legs had cramped, and her tail bone had begun to ache. Why didn't anyone come?

She heard a creak. The light turned on as the bathroom door opened. Paige painfully unfolded her legs and scrambled to her feet. "Help. I'm locked in the stall. I thought I'd be stuck forever. Can you please open the door? It's locked from the outside."

The handle jiggled, and the lock turned. The stall door opened. Paige's eyes widened. She sucked in a breath. Before she could scream, a meaty hand clasped over her lips.

All through the Deputy Secretary of State's speech, Hamilton kept hoping to spot Paige in the crowd. He needed to see her. Needed to talk with her. He stood up to go search for her, but Becky pushed him back into his seat. "You promised if I let you come tonight, you would take it easy."

"I am taking it easy. Can't I walk around a bit?"

"Fine, but don't take long. Mayor Phillips will be speaking soon."

"I won't." He was more interested in finding Paige than listening to the mayor, but he didn't tell his sister that. He rose from the metal chair, as smooth as possible without jarring his shoulder, then he weaved his way through the room. Paige wasn't in the cafeteria. He checked the lobby. No Paige.

Disappointed, he took a seat on a bench next to the water fountain. From this vantage point, he could see the student bathrooms, the front doors, and the cafeteria doors. He pulled out his cell phone and checked the time, then he swiped his finger across the screen and dialed Paige's cell phone. Her voice came over the line. "Hello."

"Hey, I've been looking everywhere—"

"I'm not able to come to the phone right now. Please leave a message after the beep."

Voice mail. "Hi. Paige. It's Hamilton. Haven't seen you since the other day. Hoping we could talk. Give me a call when you get this message."

When he returned to the cafeteria, people were preparing to leave. *What's going on? What's happening? Did I miss the mayor's speech already?*

Becky was helping Timmy into his raincoat. "Mom said we're getting pizza!" Timmy pulled on Hamilton's shirt, wiggling until his mother lost hold of the zipper.

"Timothy, hold still." She straightened the boy and finished zipping his coat.

"Where's everyone going? Is it over?"

His brother-in-law answered. "It was just announced that the mayor was called away on urgent business and is unable to speak this evening."

"I thought I saw her here earlier."

"Apparently, it was sudden."

Kylie, the mayor's daughter, was leaving the cafeteria on

his right. "Hold on a minute." Hamilton held up his pointer finger to his family. He elbowed through the crowded entry. "Kylie? Is everything okay?"

The teen girl shrugged. "I guess so. Mom didn't say anything to me. It must have something to do with work."

"Do you need a ride home? We have an extra seat."

"No, thank you, Officer Bryant. We're going over to Peter's house for games." She pointed at a group of college students heading out the main doors. She shifted her purse and turned to follow her friends.

"Oh, wait, Kylie. Did you see Paige tonight?"

"No. I was hoping she would come, but I guess she decided not to."

"Thanks, anyway. Have fun." Hamilton popped his knuckles and headed back to his family.

"Ready to go?" Becky asked.

"You look worried, Uncle Ham." said Tyler.

He hadn't realized he was frowning. Hamilton smiled at his nephews. "Hey, nothing to worry about. I have something I need to do. I'll meet you at the pizzeria." He turned to Dave. "Can I borrow your truck?" His brother-in-law had driven to the school straight from work, while Becky, Hamilton, and the boys had taken the minivan from the house.

"You shouldn't be driving." His sister's lips pinched in a tight line.

Dave squeezed Becky's shoulder. "He'll be fine. He's a big boy. He can take care of himself."

"All right. But be careful out there."

Dave tossed him the keys. Hamilton caught them with his left hand and went out to the pickup. He unlocked the door, then used the handle to haul himself into the cab. A burning spasm wracked his chest muscles. He closed his eyes against the wooziness, laid his head on the wheel, and waited for the pain to pass. Becky was right. He shouldn't be driving, but he needed to talk to Paige. *Lord, please let her be open to what I have to say. Show us a way to get past our fears. Help her to find peace. I'm afraid too, but I want her in my life.* He tried to recall his life before she came to Whitman and suddenly, he couldn't remember anything but her sapphire eyes, toothy smile, and the way her cheeks flushed when she was nervous or embarrassed.

As he drove, he dialed Paige's phone again. It rang and rang without answer. "It's me. Again. I'm heading out to your place. I was really hoping we could talk about the things you said the other day. Call me."

The garage apartment was dark when he pulled into the driveway. Hamilton maneuvered down from the truck, trying not to jar his shoulder, then he jogged up the metal staircase and knocked. Bruce barked from the yard below. It was obvious Paige wasn't home. *Where are you?* He walked back down the stairs and patted the labradoodle on the head. "Have you seen Paige?" Bruce licked his fingers in reply.

His cell phone rang. "Paige?"

"Hamilton. A bike. There's been an accident."

Lillian? She sounded out of breath. "Where?"

"Corner of Greenwood and Glenn."

"I'm on my way."

"No, Hamilton, that's not—"

He hung up before she could finish. Ignoring the fire roaring through his upper torso, he drove to the scene of the accident.

Boxes surrounded Paige as she huddled on the van floor, her hands and feet tied with tight, rough ropes. She'd struggled against them for a long while, but only ended up chaffing her wrists and ankles. The van swerved on the wet road, knocking her sideways. She struggled to sit back up. Tears crept into her eyes as the ropes burned her irritated skin. At least they had removed the sack from over her head.

She chewed on her lips. The hard metal scraped her shoulder as she bounced along. The van swerved again. *Where are we going? What are they going to do with me? Jesus, help me. I don't know what's happening. I need you, Jesus.*

The van pitched hard to the left. Brakes squealed. The boxes slid and crashed. With a hard jerk, the van hit something and stopped. Paige's head smacked the floor. *Ouch. What's going on? What happened?* The vehicle hissed but didn't move.

Suddenly, the back door jerked open. The pudgy bulldog man jumped inside and dragged her to her feet. She stumbled over the bumper and hit the ground with a thump. He squatted beside her, untied the ropes around her feet, and hauled her vertical. The front of the van was crunched against a tree trunk. Steam hissed from the engine block. Behind them, swirling tracks led through the mud from the road. The pouring rain soaked through her clothes, leaving her chilled. The dark woods loomed like a scene from her worst nightmares.

The man yanked open the driver's door and let go of her wrist. "Stay here." He commanded, but the instant he turned his back, Paige tried to run. Her leg connected with something hard and she fell face first onto the ground, her tied-up hands unable to break her fall. Pain shot through her nose. Something warm ran down her upper lip. The man hauled her to her feet and shoved her back against the van. "I told you to stay put." She licked her lips and tasted blood. The man helped his partner down from the driver's seat. "Follow me," said the man. "If you run, I won't hesitate to put a bullet through you."

Paige swallowed against the lump in her throat. "Yes, sir."

A fire truck, the ambulance, and Chief House were present. Hamilton slammed the door of Dave's truck, wincing at the pain that vibrated through his chest. He jogged to the police chief, skidding on the slick blacktop. "Where is she, chief?"

"She who? And what are you doing here? You're on leave."

"Paige. Miss McDonald. Lillian said a bike was in an accident."

"Bike as in motorcycle, Bryant." Relief flooded his mind, but Paige's disappearance still nagged at his thoughts.

"What happened?" He asked as he approached Officer Martin. Martin had his notepad out and was copying down a testimony from a young lady.

"That's all I saw."

"Thank you, miss. We'll keep in touch if we have any more questions." He turned to Hamilton. The girl walked back to a vehicle parked along the side of the road. "Hit and run. The witnesses say a van practically ran the motorcycle off the road."

"A van? Did anyone get the license plate?"

"No. But one person mentioned a logo on the door."

"What did it look like?"

"Like a fancy capital *R*. Well here, let me draw it for you." The design appeared on the scratch pad. "Do you recognize it?"

"Yeah, I do." It was the same logo he'd described to the Portland PD. Not a fancy *R*. *JR*. The logo for J.R. Electronics. Hamilton shuffled back to his brother's pickup.

Lillian ran up to him, the rain soaking her jacket. "You know that BOLO you sent out a couple weeks ago. Sheriff's got it."

"Where?"

"In a tree. The bumper's busted pretty bad."

"Anyone inside?"

"Nope. No passengers, but the back's loaded with hot stuff. The rain's washing away any tracks and the dogs probably won't get a good sniff either."

"Thanks, Lillian. I'll head there now."

"Sheriff said he'd meet you there." She gave him the location.

He climbed inside the truck and put it into gear, then focused on driving on the wet road. *Hang on Paige. I'll find you. Please, Lord, keep her safe wherever she is.*

Deeper into the woods they trudged. *Do they have any idea where we're going?* Paige took a step, and her foot kept on going. Sharp pain surged up her leg. They didn't even stop to help her. She hobbled after them, trying to keep the weight off her ankle.

Finally, the outline of a large building appeared. Her abductor opened a door and a bright light pierced the darkness. *An airplane hangar?*

Two men unloaded cardboard boxes from a windowless van. One of them was one of the men who'd followed them to the McDonald's. The other seemed familiar, too, but she couldn't place him. *Where have I seen you before?*

She did a double-take when she spotted her mother on the concrete floor. Someone had gagged her mouth and tied her hands and feet with zip ties. Murmuring voices echoed, but she couldn't make out the words. A small single prop Cessna blocked Paige's view. A young man stepped from behind the plane. His flaming red hair was unmistakable. *Jeremiah Bennett?* Her mother's personal assistant. He paced the floor, fidgeting with something in his hands.

A second man appeared from behind the plane, wearing a leather jacket and gold watch. Paige had seen him around town, but she didn't know his name. Her kidnappers shoved her toward him. "Here she is, boss."

"Oh, look, sis. It's your mini-me."

Muscled arms grabbed her from behind and hauled her across the hanger, then dropped her next to her mother.

Paige cried out as her knees connected with the concrete floor. The bulldog man and the van driver headed for a door in the wall. She caught a glimpse of a gash in the driver's forehead. She tried to keep calm as she surveyed the hangar. What was going on here? Who was this man who called her mother, sis? Was it really Kathleen's brother? Did that make him her uncle? Her mother and the man were still talking. It was clear, Paige's arrival had interrupted a previous conversation.

"Why did your goons kidnap me?" Mayor Phillips asked. "What did I ever do to you?"

A storm cloud passed over the boss's face. "You? Everything was always about you. You were Dad's apprentice. He focused all his attentions on molding you into the perfect image of himself. All I wanted was a moment of his time, but he never had time for me. In the end, he couldn't even bother to put me in his will."

"How do you know that? Dad's lawyer said the will was stolen a few weeks ago. I never even saw a copy. How did you?"

He laughed. He must have found the expression on her mother's face hilarious. "Because I stole it."

"You stole Father's will?"

He grinned like the Cheshire cat. "Sis, I've stolen a lot of things."

"That's not funny. I thought you learned your lesson. Dad had your juvenile record expunged, so you could go out and make something of yourself without that following you. You were supposed to stay out of trouble."

"Ah, but here's the funny thing. I have made something of myself."

"Why am I here? You still haven't told me why I've been kidnapped."

"You got in my way."

"In the way of what?"

Paige looked over at the men unloading the white van.

That's a lot of boxes. The van she'd been in had been full of boxes, too. One of the guys handed a painting to the other. *That's the haystack Monet from the mayor's office.* "You stole that from City Hall."

Erik smirked. "Good detective work, Sherlock. I'll be sure to put that in your obituary."

"Obituary!" Kathleen shrieked.

"If only you knew the irony of this whole situation. I was going to take what Dad owed me and be on my merry way. All you had to do was stay at your little rally. I even guaranteed police presence to protect you. Of course, you do realize you are both witnesses…"

Guaranteed police presence? But how? Unless he…

Her mother must have had the exact same thought. "Erik! *You* put sleeping pills in my soda that night?"

The grin on his face verged on wicked. "No. I didn't. Neither my men nor I would ever use sleeping pills. Too unpredictable." *If this man didn't use the sleeping pills, then who did?*

"I did, however, arrange for your little assistant here to mess with the fireworks on Memorial Day and start a little electrical fire in Joseph. He also helped me gather a few things around town and was paid well for them I might add."

Kathleen spun her head and glared at her assistant. Jeremiah Bennett blanched. "There's one thing I still don't understand." She jerked her head at Paige. "Why is she here?"

"Ah, yes. Paige McDonald." The man called Erik squatted eye level with Paige. "You don't know me, but I know you." Shivers ran up her arms as she edged away from his face pressing inches from hers. "You were good. I still can't believe you got caught with the diamonds."

"I didn't steal the bracelet." He raised an eyebrow. His meaning registered. Paige lowered her eyes. "Oh, those diamonds."

"What diamonds? What are you talking about?"

Paige swallowed and made eye contact with her mother. "I used to be a thief. This man was my fence. We never met in person. He only ever contacted me by text." She turned back to Erik. "I almost got fifteen to twenty years in jail because of you." She gasped as realization washed over her. "You sent that text. You told me to rob The Bookshelf. Hamilton got shot because of you. You threatened to kill your own sister."

Erik pulled a weapon from underneath his jacket. "And now I will."

"You never said anything about killing anyone. You can't do this."

Erik aimed at Jeremiah and cocked the hammer. "Shut up, you stupid fool. We wouldn't be in this mess if you hadn't brought her to City Hall." A bullet shot from the gun and a split second later, a glass panel shattered and showered fragments. Jeremiah dropped to the floor and crab-walked to the wall. His chest heaved up and down with heavy breaths. Paige's uncle turned the gun on his sister. "You're next." He cocked the hammer a second time.

"Boss." The bulldog man called to Erik. "I think Reese needs a hospital." Erik lowered the gun and strode across the hanger. Bulldog man followed. They entered a door in the back and closed it behind them.

Jeremiah Bennett crawled close, withdrawing a pocket knife from his pants. He began sawing at the zip ties around her mother's hands. "Bennett, how—how could you? We worked together every day for the last three years."

"I needed the money." The zip ties around her wrists snapped. She rubbed at the red marks as he started on the zip tie around her ankles. "You both need to get out of here." The second tie snapped. Kathleen and Jeremiah stood to their feet.

"Why are you helping us?"

"Erik said no one would get hurt. I can't let him kill you. I may be a thief now, but I'm not a murderer. Hurry. Your brother will be back any minute."

"He's no brother of mine." Kathleen reached for Paige's

hand.

Paige moved to stand. Her ankle was sore, but she would be able to bear her weight on it. She met her mother's eyes, and in that instant, she knew what she had to do. She sank back down to the floor. "I can't. I hurt my ankle. Please, go for help. I'll only slow you down."

"Then you have to say that you cut her loose." Jeremiah handed Paige the pocket knife.

"Where are you going?"

"I'll go with Madam Mayor for help."

The two men unpacking the van paid no attention and the other men still had not returned. Kathleen and Jeremiah slipped out the side door unnoticed.

I love you, mother. Hurry.

Kathleen's legs ached, and her lungs burned. The soaking rain chilled her to the bone. Both heels had snapped off her shoes, and she was running barefoot. Sticks, rocks, and prickers damaged the sensitive skin on the soles of her feet. She pressed forward through the woods. She couldn't follow the road for fear Erik was coming after her. The lights of town appeared through the trees. She gasped with relief. "We're almost there." When there was no answer, she paused and looked around. Bennett was gone. "Coward." She whispered under her breath. He knew if he went into town, he'd be arrested as well as fired.

She stepped out onto the road. Headlights blinded her. Brakes squealed. A pickup came to a stop, and Officer Bryant jumped out. "Madam Mayor, what are you doing out here?" He removed his coat and laid it over her shoulders. "Come get in the truck where it's warm."

"They've still got Paige."

The officer's head jerked. "Paige?"

"She's in the hanger at the old airport."

"Tell me what happened."

Kathleen rehearsed the events of the last couple of hours.

He dialed his cell phone. "Chief. I've found Paige McDonald. She's being held by Erik Staten in a hangar at the old airport. At least one or more of the suspects are armed. I have Mayor Phillips in the vehicle. She needs medical attention and possibly Miss McDonald will as well. Yes, sir. I won't sir." Officer Bryant put the truck in gear and stomped on the accelerator.

Several minutes passed. The office door opened. "Where is she?" Erik roared.

Paige lifted her chin. "I helped her escape. She's going for the police."

His hand sprang out and slapped her across the face. Her head snapped. Her cheek stung. Tears burned her eyes. "Where's that idiot, Bennett?"

"I don't know." She choked on the words and rubbed the painful welt on her face.

He drew the weapon and cocked the hammer. "I should get rid of you now."

Paige whimpered as he aimed. She felt around for one of the pieces of broken glass, wrapping her fingers around the sharp edge. Ignoring the stinging in her palm, she lunged forward and drove the glass into his upper arm, forcing him to drop his weapon. Erik cried out. Adrenaline pulsing through her veins, Paige scooped up the gun and pointed it at her uncle. The other men came running, weapons drawn.

Hamilton leaned against the patrol car. Fresh blood seeped through his shirt. All of the moving around had torn open his wound. No one had entered or exited the hanger since his arrival. The police cruisers sped onto the muddy field and skidded to a stop. Officers Martin and Stone, Lillian, and Chief House exited their vehicles. A second later, the County Sheriff Gaines and his deputy arrived. The ambulance was close behind. The EMTs began attending to the mayor's injuries. Hamilton briefed them on the situation, then the sheriff took over. The airport was outside of city police jurisdiction.

"I want Martin and Hurston to cover this exit here. Stone and I will enter here. Chief House, you and Deputy Brown cover the rear entrance. According to Mayor Phillips, there are at least four suspects and one civilian."

"What do you want me to do?" Hamilton addressed the chief.

"I want you to sit down somewhere before you pass out. And get the paramedic to look at that." He pointed at Hamilton's chest.

The officers took their positions, weapons drawn. Sheriff Gaines shouted through the door. "This is the police. Come out with your hands up." Nothing happened. They looked to Chief House for direction. He nodded his assent. Officer Stone kicked the door open and the officers rushed inside.

26

Paige gazed around the room full of laughter and celebration. Everyone seemed to be having a good evening. A local touched her arm. "I'm going to check back every week for new books." She thanked the woman and smiled to herself. She'd succeeded. The grand reopening was a success. The Bookshelf would be a success. Jessie Faye beamed as she mingled and accepted congratulations.

Paige slung her purse strap over her shoulder. She was done here. It was time to go home. She made eye contact with Kathleen standing by the window with a glass of punch. She had one regret from her time in Whitman—that her mother had not opened her heart and accepted her as her daughter. She'd thanked Paige for assisting in her escape but made it clear that it did not change anything between them. Paige's heart was broken, but she resolved to respect her mother's wishes, no matter how disheartening they might be.

She turned her head at the sound of the bell. Hamilton entered through the store front. Okay. She had two regrets. They hadn't spoken since his injury. The terrible things she'd said continued to plague her thoughts. She'd prayed for courage to apologize, but in the end, it seemed better to let sleeping dogs lie.

She'd spotted him only briefly after the police had stormed the airplane hangar. Erik Staten and his cronies were arrested without further incident, and millions of dollars' worth of stolen goods were recovered, including the journals, Coverdale Bible, and Separatist Papers. Collections from as far away as Pittsburgh and London were among those seized that night. The cell phones, of course, had already been fenced. Jeremiah Bennett was arrested while trying to skip town. It turned out that he was thousands of dollars in the hole from online gambling.

As Paige had suspected, she'd only bruised her ankle. Ice, heat, and staying off it for a day had done the trick, and she was back to normal. Mostly normal. Nightmares interrupted her sleep each night, but the trauma therapist assured her that they would lessen over time and eventually fade. The deep cut in her palm, however, would not. She would always have a scar as a reminder of that night. The night she finally understood.

As she'd watched her mother and Jeremiah escape out the side door of the airplane hangar, a mind-boggling peace had settled over her. She'd known that when Erik found them missing, he would kill her; yet, it didn't matter. She'd done the right thing. God would take care of her. And he had.

Paige climbed the stairs to the loft lounge. Her sister, Kylie, reclined in one of the eclectic chairs. "I couldn't leave without saying goodbye."

"But I've barely gotten to know you yet. I've always wanted a sister." Kylie jumped to her feet, throwing her arms around Paige.

If you only knew. Paige embraced the flamboyant teen girl. "We can email and text. If you're ever in Portland, look me up."

Kylie's round eyes brimmed with tears. "I'll miss you."

"I'll miss you, too. You've been a good friend."

"Goodbye, Paige."

"Goodbye, Kylie." She turned so the girl wouldn't see her cry, then she walked back down the circular staircase. Jessie stood at the bottom, her wrinkled hand on the rail. "So, you're leaving us." It wasn't a question.

"There's no place for me here. I need to go back where I belong. Thank you for everything."

The old woman smiled. She reached out with her gnarly fingers and stroked Paige's cheek where the blueish bruise still marred her ivory skin. "I should be thanking you. You saved my business. In fact, if you'll stay until the party's over, there's something I'd like to show you before you leave."

Later that evening, after the guests had left and they'd cleaned up the discarded paper products, Paige followed Jessie into the brand-new office converted from half of the old storeroom. Jessie lifted a large book from off her desk and handed it to Paige. "This is for you." War and Peace. A first edition copy.

"That's so sweet. You didn't have to get me anything." Paige took the book in her hands, expecting it to be heavy. The volume was light. Lighter than it should be. "What?" She opened the front cover. The middle was carved out, and a manila envelope was wedged inside. Paige looked to the old woman for an explanation.

"About six months ago, Richard Staten brought this to me. He and Lawrence were long-time friends, and he had a strange feeling that his son might try something to swindle his girls out of their inheritance. Just in case, he wanted to have a second copy of his Last Will and Testament hidden somewhere where Erik would never find it."

"I don't understand. Why give it to me? This belongs to Kylie and Kathleen."

Jessie motioned for Paige to open the envelope. Paige pried it out, laid the book aside, then opened the metal clasp and withdrew a stack of papers. She read the top page aloud.

To Whom It May Concern,

I, Richard M. Staten, being of sound mind and in my own hand, do write this last will and testament, to state the manner to which my estate shall be distributed upon my death. Primarily, all debts and taxes are to be paid from my accounts by the executor of the estate, my legal representative, Don Wall. This nullifies all previous wills and/or amendments. To my daughter, Kathleen Staten Phillips, I do solemnly bequeath the sum of ten million dollars and two million dollars to each of my granddaughters, Kylie Michelle Phillips and Brooklyn Paige McDonald. To my son, Erik, I leave nothing but my regrets that I wasn't a better father. All other monies are to be donated to the town of Whitman, Oregon, a place I have loved all of my life. My personal belongings are to be divided between my daughter and granddaughters as they deem fit, and the remainder sold and the profits from those sales be divided evenly between my daughter and granddaughters.

Signed, Richard M. Staten

Her nose burned as she blinked back the tears. "He knew."

"He knew."

"How—how did he find me?"

A tall man, with salt and pepper hair and wearing an expensive suit, stepped into the office. Jessie didn't appear at all startled by his entrance. "Who are you?" Paige asked, a nervous twinge to her voice.

"Don Wall, your grandfather's attorney. Five years ago, when Richard Staten was diagnosed with cancer, he retired as the state attorney general and settled back in his beloved hometown to live out the last years of his life. One afternoon, he went golfing with friends and one of the lawyers mentioned a difficult case he was assigned—a twenty-year-old girl arrested for theft. This girl had a history of petty theft as a minor and had spent time at the state juvenile detention center. A Portland firefighter, retired from station number nine, had adopted this girl as an infant. Her name was

Brooklyn McDonald. Richard surmised that this girl was the granddaughter he'd abandoned on their doorstep twenty years before. Calling in some favors, he pulled some strings and kept you out of jail."

That's why the judge had mercy.

"He asked me to keep an eye on you ever since that day. There should be a personal letter in the envelope as well."

Paige's hands shook as she unfolded the piece of paper.

Dear Brooklyn,

Twenty-five years ago, I made the greatest mistake of my life, and I have regretted it every day since. Not only did I give you away, but I lied to my only daughter. Instead of finding you a family, I left you on the steps of Portland's Fire Department station #9.

Five years ago, I found true peace in God's forgiveness, found only through salvation in Jesus Christ. I hope someday, you will find it too, if you haven't already. I also seek your forgiveness. Because of my pride and quest for power, I prevented you from being raised in a loving family, or maybe God intervened, and you were…"

Her eyes misted over as she read the rest. *I wish I could have known you, Grandfather.* "I have found true peace. God has forgiven me."

Tears formed in Jessie's eyes. "Oh, child. How I prayed for that." She pulled Paige into her arms and hugged her. She let go and wiped the moisture from her weathered skin. "There's something else I'd like to show you."

Paige wiped her eyes with her sleeve as Jessie moved to the corner of the office. "I'm giving you the bookstore. You can have a good life here in Whitman if you're willing to take the chance." With a flourish, she raised a white sheet. Underneath was an old-fashioned wooden shingle carved with the words: Paige's Second Chance Books.

Hamilton sulked into the Rustic Cup the morning after the grand reopening. He still hadn't spoken to Paige. He'd seen her for only a moment at the party, and then she'd disappeared. Was she still avoiding him? *Lord, I need the chance to explain. I need her to know how much I care. How can I make things right if I can't even get a moment with her?* His heart was conflicted. *I want her in my life, but as long as she's unsaved, I can't marry her. At least, I can help her accept what I do, and we can be friends. Maybe someday, if she finds you, Lord, we could be more than that.* He went to his usual booth and winced as he took a seat. His wound was healing but still tender. The café was busy as usual, energized with the hum of voices and smell of coffee. He took a deep breath. Jenn had made apple empanadas. He licked his lips. *I'll take one of those and a hot coffee.* He pulled out his cell phone. *I'll ask Paige to join me. Maybe we can finally talk.*

Kylie approached the table, carrying her notepad. His finger hovered over Paige's number. "Morning, Kylie. Have you seen Paige this morning?" She shook her head but didn't speak. She sniffled her nose and her red eyes shimmered with unshed tears. If Kylie was silent, something was terribly wrong. "What's happened?"

Kylie collapsed on the bench and produced a pitiful wail. "She left."

She left? "Who left?"

"Paige."

Paige left? "What do you mean?"

"She's going back to Portland. The bus pulled out of town fifteen minutes ago."

Hamilton jumped to his feet. *Oh, man. That hurt.* He sucked in his breath. *I've got to stop her.*

The bus squealed as the driver hit the brakes. Paige stopped reading and pulled her earbuds out of her ears. She and the other passengers leaned forward. *Why are we stopping?*

A police barricade blocked the road. A patrol car sat in the middle, lights flashing red and blue. Hamilton stood in front of the car. He held a bull horn to his lips. "Paige McDonald. Please exit the bus immediately."

Paige's cheeks warmed as she paraded down the center aisle. The driver opened the folding door and she stepped down onto the blacktop. "Hamilton, what are you doing?" She walked to where he stood.

He lowered the bull horn. "You can't leave."

"Why not?"

"I can't quit being a police officer. There are risks involved, but if we work together, I know we can overcome these challenges and give our fears to God."

Paige stepped close to the officer and pressed her finger to his lips. "Hamilton. I'm not leaving."

"You're not?" He glanced behind her at the bus. "Having to blockade a city bus to catch you had me pretty convinced."

She held up a set of keys from her pocket. "I bought the bookstore. Jessie was going to give it to me, but I insisted I pay for it. I'm the new owner of Paige's Second Chance Books. I also bought Jessie's house. Aunt Hattie and I will live there with her and take care of her until she passes, but I have to go back to Portland and sell our house and pack up our belongings."

Hamilton's mouth hit the ground. "When Kylie said you'd left, I thought she meant forever."

"When I talked with her last night, I was going to leave forever. But something changed my mind." Paige clasped hold of his hands. "I can't leave. I want to be with you."

He cleared his throat and ran his finger through his collar. "My job is still dangerous. That's never going to change."

She met Hamilton's gaze. His heart pleaded for her to understand. And she did. "I know. But I also know that whatever time God gives us on this earth, I want to spend it with you."

His eyes widened. "Did you say, *God*? I thought you

weren't a Christian."

"I wasn't. Until recently. I found peace with God and gave my life to Him."

The relief that washed over him was visible. "I've been praying for that."

A smile spread over her face as she remembered what Jessie had told her that afternoon at her house. *He loves me. And I love him.*

Her smile tugged at his heart and warmed his toes. *Thank you, Lord, that she's put her trust in you. I don't want to live without her.* His eyes dropped to her mouth. So soft and inviting. He leaned forward and brushed his lips against her forehead. She didn't flinch or push him away. "What are you smiling about?"

"Just something Jessie said."

He kissed the end of her nose. "Yeah?"

"She said, you're in love with me."

"Did she?" He leaned back so he could see her face. "What did you say?"

Paige slipped her arms around his neck. "That I'm in love with you."

"You don't say?" He pulled her to his chest and claimed her lips with his own.

She sighed when he released her. "I'd like to see where this"—she motioned between them— "takes us?"

"I'd like that, but I can't guarantee the future…"

"I'm willing to take the risk if you are."

He grinned. "It'll be a real page-turner."

She punched him playfully in the left shoulder. He laughed and gathered her into his arms and kissed her on the lips. Cell phone cameras flashed as the busload of travelers crowded around.

EPILOGUE

"Thanks for calling and letting me know. Love you. Bye." Paige hung up her cell phone and laid it on the bed beside her. She focused on breathing, urging her racing pulse to slow down. Hamilton had called her with the results from the ballistics and DNA tests. The weapon, belonging to Bill Haversly, the bulldog man, matched the slugs from the bookstore shooting. A .22 pistol was found in Jeremiah Bennett's apartment and matched the bullets from the Mario Montory case. Mario had also identified Erik as the priest who'd threatened him in the hospital and Jeremiah, as the man who shot him. Jeremiah confessed to endangering the mayor and to stealing everything at Erik's request, hoping to gain a lesser sentence, but Hamilton expected both to be put away for a long time. Portland police had found ties between Erik Staten and J.R. Electronics. There was no evidence, however, connecting either of them to the mayor's car accident or the stolen city funds. *There's still someone out there trying to ruin my mother.*

None of this, though, was what had raised Paige's blood pressure. *The DNA on the cigarette butts didn't match any of the suspects. The test was inconclusive. What does that mean? Who was watching me?*

The TV news stations had played Erik Staten's court hearing on a loop, and Mayor Phillips was subjected to questions and ridicule. Her brother was head of a notorious Northwestern crime ring. It was still to be seen how this scandal would impact the gubernatorial election. Through it all, Kathleen's secret had remained hidden and no one knew that Paige was her daughter. No one, that is, except for Hamilton, Jessie, and Aunt Hattie.

The doorbell echoed through the house. Soft voices carried upstairs. Paige stood to her feet, lured downstairs by curiosity. "Paigey, someone's here to see you."

Paige drew her eyebrows together. Who would be coming to see her? She'd just gotten off the phone with Hamilton, so it couldn't be him. She thumped down the stairs and into the living room, careful not to knock over any of the stacks of moving boxes.

"Pastor Whitestone. What are you doing here?" *Why is the pastor from Whitman in my house?*

The pastor gave her a weak smile and twisted his fedora in his hands. "I apologize for not calling first, but I was wondering if I could have a word."

That's a long drive for a word. Hopefully, he had other errands in town. "Sure, come in and have a seat. Excuse the mess." Paige grabbed a stack of clothes off the couch and moved it to the dining table, along with books and kitchen utensils. Pastor Whitestone perched on the edge of the couch, his hand resting on a roll of bubble wrap. "Can I get you some coffee or water?"

The preacher waved his hand. "No, thank you. I'm fine." Beads of sweat ran down his sideburns. The skin along his collar looked flushed. His Adam's apple bobbed as he swallowed. His odd behavior puzzled her. She sat in a chair opposite him.

"Are you sure you're OK?"

"You know what, I will take a glass of water." His voice cracked.

Paige glanced at Aunt Hattie, who headed into the kitchen. She returned with a glass of ice water and handed it to the preacher. He gulped it down like a dying man in a desert. "Thank you." He handed it back to Aunt Hattie. Delilah came out from behind the couch and jumped up beside him. She rubbed her head on his sleeve. Pastor Whitestone stroked the long silky fur. "She's beautiful. What's her name?"

"Delilah," Paige answered.

The preacher chuckled and shook the fur from his fingers. "Paige."

"Yes, Pastor Whitestone?"

"Paige."

"Yes?"

"When I was a senior in high school, I fell in love with the smartest and most amazing girl in school. She, too, was a senior, and I felt so honored that she would be my girlfriend. Unfortunately, I let passion override common sense. I'm not proud of what we did, and I've regretted my actions ever since that day. But God, in his mercy, allowed something wonderful to come from our transgression."

Paige tipped her head. "I'm not sure I follow, pastor."

"My name is Ryan. Ryan Whitestone. I'm your father."

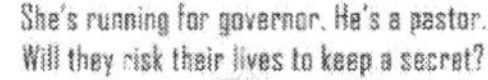

Shadows Over Whitman #2

Forgiven Again

Gina Holder

She's running for governor.
He's a pastor.
Will they risk their lives to keep a secret?

Acknowledgements

As always, a book does not create itself nor is it a one man show. I could not have accomplished this task without the love and support of my friends and family. I want to thank each one for their part in making No Greater Love a success.

First, I want to thank my Lord and Savior Jesus Christ without whom I would have no story to tell. It's because of His great love for me that I desire to share that love with others through story.

Thank you to my husband and daughter. It's meant a lot to me to have you backing my endeavors. Thank you for allowing me to hole myself up at my computer for entire days.

Thank you to my beta readers: Karen, Marta, Vicki, Fayelle, Marilyn, Donna, Amy, and Tabitha. Your input and insight helped make this story what it is today.

Thank you to Rikki for her help with finding the perfect setting for the town of Whitman. Your local knowledge was invaluable as I researched about a state I have never visited.

Thank you to Jeanenne for your suggestion for the coffee shop's name, Rustic Cup.

Thank you to Powell's City of Books for answering my questions.

Thank you to my proofreaders, Caitlin and Sheree. I so appreciate you catching all those little mistakes that I miss. Your hard work helped polish this book to a shine.

Thank you to my husband, Daniel, for all your hard work to make No Greater Love successful. Thank you for the beautiful cover design and your attention to all the little details.